More demonic mon

warfare, and a pain

tour de force in the final volume of *The Coming Evil Trilogy*. It is impossible to put down this taut, supernatural thriller until the last, gut-wrenching page!

—BRUCE HENNIGAN
AUTHOR OF
THE 13th DEMON and *THE 12th DEMON*

Flawed but heroic characters? Check. Memorably evil bad guys? Check. Spiritual lessons tucked into scenes that could live and breathe on a movie screen? Check.

Greg Mitchell has crafted a trilogy that should not be ignored. Not only is it full of unforgettable villains and confrontations, but it reminds us of the importance of knowing God's Word, walking in unity as believers, and identifying sin for what it really is.

Mitchell pulls no punches. *Dark Hour* gives us scene after scene of good and evil in a battle for souls. Whether you're a tired pastor and his wife, a drug addict looking for freedom, or a teenager wanting to know more about God's power, this is a trilogy you need to devour this week.

—ERIC WILSON
NEW YORK TIMES BESTSELLING AUTHOR OF
FIELD OF BLOOD and *2 SECONDS LATE*

DARK HOUR

THE COMING EVIL TRILOGY | BOOK THREE

GREG MITCHELL

Dark Hour

ISBN: 978-0-9876531-4-7

Published by Splashdown Darkwater
An imprint of Splashdown Books, New Zealand
www.splashdownbooks.com/darkwater

Cover Photo:
Lewes Bonfire Night 2007—Burning Town and Hillside Watchers, by Flickr user Dominic Alves
http://www.flickr.com/photos/dominicspics/1901603041

Cover Design by Grace Bridges and Greg Mitchell
With special thanks to Cory Clubb

Visit Greg Mitchell at
www.thecomingevil.com

To Jo Beth and Dani, who remind me daily what's really important.

ACKNOWLEDGEMENTS

It has been an incredible journey that's lasted nearly fifteen years to see *The Coming Evil Trilogy* published in its entirety. Through the support and encouragement of many friends and family along the way, we're finally here to read of the fate that will soon befall our heroes as they face the toughest battle of their lives. Thanks as always to my wife, Meghan, who has devoted nearly as much time, energy, and hard work to this series as I have—serving as my first editor and never being afraid to tell me when something sounds stupid. It's been her honesty and practicality that has kept me grounded in my flights of fancy. At Realms, thanks to Debbie Marrie for seeing something worthwhile in my story and assembling a great team to help bring it to a reality: Alton Gansky, Jack Cavanaugh, Anna Silva, Deborah Moss, Jihan Watkins, Woodley Auguste, Amanda Quain, and all the beta readers who gave me encouragement and some nice endorsements. My eternal gratitude to Grace Bridges at Splashdown Darkwater for seeing me through to the end. Thank you to the fans for making yourself at home in Greensboro, despite the monsters that lurk there. And most of all, thanks to God. With Him, all things are possible.

Prologue

Truth is nowhere to be found,
and whoever shuns evil becomes a prey.
—Isaiah 59:15

All in all, Dras Weldon mused as he finished a bite of instant potatoes, *prison is a whole lot like high school.*

While matriculating in Wexler State Pen—the City's maximum security prison—for the last ten months, Dras couldn't help but make the comparison. Prison had its cliques too. To his left, Dras spotted the black guys in their makeshift congregation, flexing their biceps and sizing each other up, aspiring to be the biggest and baddest. To his right, the rough-looking Mexicans, badmouthing everyone else in Spanish and behaving pretty cocky about it. Somewhere in the middle were the white guys, throwing gang signs all their own, tattoos coloring their shaved heads. Each racial section trying to out-show the "competition".

And, at a secluded table like the Senior Class—the kids everyone wanted to be—sat the lifers. Most importantly Old Nick. Old Nick, a lifer who looked like Santa Claus' evil twin in a prison uniform, lounged, surrounded by other long-term convicts like a pride of lions lazily keeping their watch over their fellow inmates. As Dras observed, no one went to the lifer table. Old Nick and his crew were legends in Wexler, content to rule their makeshift kingdom inside these stone walls. In prison, the food chain went up pretty high and a man had to claw his way from minnow to Great White. Old Nick was a Great White.

Dras was a minnow. Minnows were easy pickings.

"Hey," a gruff voice snapped just over Dras's head, as a very large and scowling Mexican with long, greasy hair draped over broad shoulders interrupted his lunch. The man shadowed over him like a mountain, and Dras, his spoon hovering in front of his mouth, faced the imposing figure with nonchalance.

"Can I help you?" Dras recognized the man. Scuttlebutt was that the guy was Raul "Machete" Rodriguez—a new arrival and close friend to the penal system—who was nicked after a botched convenience store robbery. No doubt he was looking to establish his rep pretty quick, especially with Old Nick taking notice of the scene.

Machete Rodriguez said, "You're in my seat."

Dras looked down to his chair. "Am I? Sorry 'bout that."

Dras kindly stood and gathered his tray, ready to leave. But, Machete grew red in the face and slapped his tray away. Dras frowned at the sight of his instant potatoes sailing across the cafeteria. *Bummer.*

Turning back to his new friend, Dras remained unfazed. Machete sneered down at him. "You disrespecting me, small fry? Trying to make me look like a chump?"

Dras shrugged. "I generally don't try to make people look like chumps until I've known them for awhile."

A few snickers rippled through the surrounding tables and Dras saw that even Old Nick found the exchange amusing. Machete must have spotted it too. Outraged, the ogre seized Dras by the collar and hoisted him to eye level. "You laughing at me?"

Dras brightened when he saw Rhino headed across the cafeteria.

"This guy bothering you, Jesus?"

George "Rhino" Beasley lived up to his namesake. He was a stocky dark-skinned man with drooping jowls and rolls of fat hanging off his thick frame. When he charged, anyone with good sense knew to get out of the way. Rhino huffed up to Dras and Machete, backed by an entourage of equally hungry-eyed predators. "You okay?"

Machete turned around to see the troop of muscles marching his way and nearly gulped. Dras looked over the man's shoulder, indifferent. "Yeah, I'm all right, Rhino." Dras nodded to the floor, where the remains of his lunch lay splattered. "I really had my heart set on those potatoes…but, other than that, I'm fine."

Machete turned back to Dras, his stony expression giving way to a hint of anxiety. Dras raised his eyebrows. "Right?"

Machete nodded, slowly and deliberately. "Yeah…sure."

Rodriguez turned back to the imposing figures behind him, saw Old Nick and the rest of the lifers laughing in hysterics, then gave one last menacing snarl to Dras in a vain attempt to salvage his reputation.

"But this isn't over," he said.

Dras sighed. "I was afraid you'd say something like that."

Machete left, his fists clenched, wincing as he passed the other inmates, humiliated. Dras watched as the man slammed the doors and left the dining area, then released an honest to goodness breath of relief.

Rhino said, "If he gives you more problems, you come to us."

"Will do. Thanks, Rhino."

"Anytime, Jesus." Rhino clapped a sweaty, meaty palm on Dras's back then nodded towards the boys. With a few grunts, the men retreated back to their corners until they were needed again.

When the two were alone, Dras turned to the burly inmate, a bit embarrassed. "I told you to quit calling me that, big guy."

Rhino shook his head, good-natured but defiant. "I see Jesus in you. So, you as close to Jesus as I'm gonna know."

Dras smiled, touched by his friend's respect, before: "Weldon! You causing trouble again?"

He wheeled about as a salt-and-pepper-haired man in a beige uniform, flanked by two more uniformed gorillas twice his size, stomped full force towards him. Heat immediately flushing in his face, Dras scratched the back of his messy blonde mop top. "Uh, hey, Sergeant Winters."

Winters, the leader of the trio, already had his nightstick in hand. "Can't turn my back on you for one second."

Under the cold stare of Winters, Dras shifted unpleasantly, noticing that the rough-and-tumble convicts around him were quickly finding other places to be.

Sgt. Winters had that kind of reputation.

Rhino stepped in between Dras and the commanding authority figure. "He wasn't startin' nuthin', Sarge."

"Shut it, Rhino. I didn't ask you to be a character witness." In an instant, Winters had his nightstick pressed against Dras's chin, lifting his face to size him up. "I say you just earned yourself another night in solitary."

Dras's smirk sank as Rhino protested louder. "He ain't done nuthin'!"

Winters leveled a glower at the husky prisoner, his hardened face the antithesis of compassion. "You looking to spend time in Blackout with him, tough guy?"

Rhino puffed out his chest. "You bet I am!"

"Rhino, no," Dras interrupted, patting his friend on the chest. "It's not worth it. I'll be all right."

"But—"

"Really." Dras nodded, trying to look braver than he felt. "What's one more night, right? I've got this one."

Dras appreciated his friend taking up for him. Rhino was a good man who had a bad day once, coming home from work early to discover his wife in bed with another man. So enraged was he that Rhino strangled the other man to death before realizing that that man was, in fact, his own brother. Broken and wrought with grief at what he had done, Rhino put up no fight as he was arrested and later sentenced to life imprisonment. Despite that one moment of wrath, deep down Rhino was a softhearted man who always watched out for Dras. But, as Dras had learned since his arrest, there were some things he had to do on his own.

Winters' expression was stone as, with a jerk of the chiseled chin, he wordlessly ordered his men to take Dras into custody. The guards escorted him out of the cafeteria while Winters stayed, fixing Rhino in place with a harsh glance that made Dras afraid for the big guy.

Dras heard Rhino still sticking up for him. "You know he ain't done nuthin'. That's Jesus. He always innocent."

Eyeing the bold man, Dras saw as Winters' granite features threatened to crack. Then he stiffened suddenly. "Stay out of it, Rhino," he said and followed Dras.

The buzzers sounded as the security doors parted. His armed chaperones solidly gripped each elbow, keeping Dras to his path. The familiar *click click click* of Sgt. Winters' polished shoes grew louder until the man caught up with him, grouchy as always.

"I'll take him the rest of the way," Winters muttered and the two behemoth guards left to attend to other business. Using his faithful nightstick, Winters prodded the small of Dras's back, herding him down the lonely cement corridor that led to solitary—"Blackout". It wasn't the first time Dras had spent the night in Blackout. And thanks to Winters, who seemed to derive some sick pleasure from punishing "the new kid" at every available opportunity, Dras worried it wouldn't be his last.

"You know I wasn't hurting anybody, Sergeant," Dras defended. "Why are you putting me in Blackout? I mean, what have I ever done?"

Winters' craggy face split into a real smile. "What can I say, Weldon? You must have that kind of face. Just ticks people off."

"Yeah," Dras groaned. "Story of my life."

Winters led Dras to an all-too familiar door and opened it with a *creak*. With a mocking bow, Winters presented, "Your room, sir."

"Where should I check my luggage?" Dras feebly retorted, hoping a little humor would lighten the mood.

"I'll have the bellhop up in a minute. Don't you worry about that."

Dras entered the dark bay of solitary, resigned to his fate. "Guess this is 'good night', then, Sarge."

"Don't let the bed bugs bite," Winters humorlessly responded, shutting and locking the door, sentencing Dras to his solitude, leaving him to reflect for the thousandth time on the events that led him here.

Prison was the last place in the world Dras Weldon ever imagined himself winding up. The closest he ever came to the Big House in his crime-free life was an old Clint Eastwood movie he watched with his dad when he was ten.

Those first couple of months in Wexler, Dras had been isolated, bandages all over his body; jaw wired shut with some horrifying brace. He assumed he looked like some kind of B-movie horror monster—which *in theory* sounded sort of cool to him—and most inmates stayed away from him early on. He was locked up in a cell, mostly lying down, sometimes sitting in silence, healing.

After he started recovering, though, when the bandages came off and Dras's trial started, he was introduced into the wonderful world of prison life, a clumsy, baby-faced boy who had made the—what some might consider *unwise*—decision to stand against a centuries-old evil force looking to steal the soul of his best friend.

Rosalyn. He thought about her every day.

Settling in for the rest of the afternoon, Dras sat down on the cold floor of Blackout, leaning his head against the wall. He wondered how Rosalyn was doing these days, if she'd read his letter, if she'd withstood the Strange Man.

As he often did when Winters stuck him in solitary, Dras reached into his pocket and pulled out the small Bible that once belonged to his brother, Reverend Jeff Weldon. On the night Dras went to his short-lived war with the Strange Man, he'd taken the pocket Bible as a weapon. Upon his prison sentencing, Dras had asked only for that Bible to keep him company in lockdown. Now, by the slim light of the food tray slot in the steel door, Dras cracked open his brother's old Bible, thumbing through its worn pages. Multi-colored notes scribbled on tattered pages served as warm reminders of the spiritual journey Jeff had taken in studying this book. Now they functioned as a map for Dras, guiding him to discover the truths of the old manuscript for himself.

Finding familiar passages, Dras read the Scriptures aloud, taking comfort in the sound of his own voice. In keeping with his normal routine, he knew he would continue to do this until "lights out", when the darkness rolled in. Then he would recite the Scriptures from memory, warding off the terrible loneliness as long as he could before sleep finally overtook him. But, nighttime was still a few hours off. He could still read, could still focus on *something*, anything to keep his mind off the unending quiet of solitary.

Setting aside the Bible verses for the moment, Dras removed a hand-written letter from his brother, tucked between the pages. After unfolding it, Dras held the note to the sliver of light, eyes poring over Jeff's sloppy cursive.

Hey, freak –

Just wanted to give you a little update on things at home. First off, Dad's doing well. I mean, he's not getting better, but he's not getting worse, either, so thank God for small favors, right? Mom's constantly hovering over him, as usual, and she keeps asking if you can get DVDs in prison. She thinks you'd be happier if you had one of your crappy movies to watch.

"She'd be right," Dras glumly muttered.

I keep telling her that they already give you TV privileges, which sounds pretty cushy to me. Why don't they just let you serve your time at home if they're going to feed you and give you free cable? Ah, I'm just kidding. You know that.

Iz and I are doing all right. She's still working at the Laundromat and I'm doing pretty well for myself at the hardware store. I guess all those years working with Dad on roofs finally paid off…or royally screwed me up for life, I can't tell which. But we're making ends meet. Which reminds me, they're almost done building the new church. It won't be like Dad's church, though. I keep hearing talk that it's going to be a Universal Church or something like that. Iz and I are thinking about becoming Catholic and going to Father Joe's church in Russellville, ha ha. He's a pretty good guy, as we've gotten to know him. You know Mom would kill me, though, if I started saying "Hail Mary" and all of that, ha ha.

Anyway, I want to get serious for a minute. Things are getting <u>strange</u> in *town, and you know what I mean. I don't know how much is safe to say, but just know that it's getting harder here. There're not many people left who believe like we do so we've had to start sticking together. We're holding Bible studies, but I can't say where. People are starting to disappear around here and our numbers are growing smaller. They're looking for us, Dras. So far we've stayed ahead of them but we have to get creative. Some folks have already asked Iz and me if we can help them get out of town, but we've got to be really careful. Usually I'd say that I wish you were here, and you know I do, but at the same time, maybe you're safer where you are for the time being, as crazy as that sounds. I believe God's taking care of you in prison. He's got a plan for you yet, little brother. Keep following Him and I'll write you again when I can.*

~Jeff

The letter was dated four months ago, and it was the last. Since that time, no contact from Jeff. No phone calls, no visits, nothing. Mom evaded all his questions in her phone calls, as if afraid someone else would hear her answers.

"What happened, man?" Dras asked the quiet dark surrounding him. "Where'd you go?"

It worried him greatly. Another thing that bothered him was that he *still* had no word on Rosalyn. Jeff seemed to purposefully exclude her from his letters, and whenever Dras asked about her during his phone privileges, Jeff always got real twitchy and would say things like "Ah, you know, Rosalyn," or "She's going through a tough time." Dras didn't blame Rosalyn for not wanting to come see him in prison. Sure, it was painful not to see his best friend—his soul mate—but he could understand it if Rosalyn didn't want her last memory of Dras to be of him in an orange jumper behind bars.

But to go so long without hearing about her, without knowing that she was safe from the Strange Man…it was thousands of times worse than solitary. And now, added to that uncertainty, was his brother's recent silence.

Dras slipped the letter back in the Bible, closed the cover, and shut his eyes, anxious for his friends. *What's going on in Greensboro?*

CHAPTER ONE

"JEFF, GET DOWN!"

At Danny's command, Jeff Weldon dropped to a crouch, a slimy black tentacle narrowly missing his head.

Immediately, Danny Carpenter was by his partner's side, helping him to run. "How did they sneak up on us so fast?" he hollered over the incessant moaning of the slippery obsidian monstrosities surrounding them.

Jeff shook his head, furious that they had gotten the drop on them. "I don't know. We just have to keep moving!"

Normally the two young men—both in the prime of their lives, Jeff noted—would have been able to easily outmaneuver the slumping, slobbering things behind them, but tonight they were held back by the very people they had dared enter Greensboro at night to save.

With wife Tessa, eleven-year-old daughter Nancy, and nine-year-old daughter Michelle in tow, Milton Wilbanks squeaked, "What do we do?"

Jeff didn't know. He hadn't planned on running out of gas halfway out of town, or on fleeing a small horde of Shamblers, the North Woods' late night wanderers.

Danny tugged on Jeff's arm, pointing to an abandoned yellow one-story sporting a FOR SALE sign in its overgrown yard. Jeff, Danny, Milton, and his frightened family were reaching the north edge of Greensboro, getting closer to the dreaded North Woods. Danny pushed forward, full steam ahead like usual, towards the quiet shell of the house, with Jeff keeping back long enough to make sure Milton and his family stayed ahead of the Shamblers. Jeff didn't like the idea of holing up in a house. Especially when said house was in plain sight of the monsters behind them. Shamblers were a little slow and certainly deranged, but they weren't stupid. Jeff could hide these people, but the creatures would come knocking.

For the moment, however, it seemed the best solution. They needed to secure a location, hide out, and call for backup. He just prayed Isabella would arrive in time.

"Well?" Isabella Weldon asked impatiently, biting a dirtied nail.

Hank Berkley leaned against Jeff's old work truck, holding a walkie talkie. He depressed the trigger and spoke into the receiver. "Steak and Potatoes, this is Donut Boy, do you read?"

Despite the quirky code names Jeff and Hank used, Isabella did not smile.

"Steak and Potatoes, this is Donut Boy, come back."

Only dead air. Hank set the radio in the truck and looked squarely at her. "It don't mean nothing. Just that they're out of range."

"I don't like this. They've been gone too long. He found out. Somehow he found out and he was waiting for them."

"Jeff's faced the Strange Man before. He can do it again."

Isabella marched for the driver's side of her husband's truck. "We're going down there."

"Whoa, there, cowboy. Not a good idea. We've lasted this long because we have a system that works. Everyone has a part to play, a post to watch. If we start breaking the rules—"

"Someone's already broken the rules, Hank," Isabella snapped, a bit more fervently than she'd meant to. "Greensboro's not our town anymore. We're not out here having church bake sales. In case you've forgotten, they burnt *down* the church."

"I haven't forgotten," Hank said evenly.

Isabella cooled. *Of course he hasn't. He almost died in that fire.* "I'm sorry," she softly recanted. "But you know what I mean. We're in the middle of a war. And I don't want my husband to be another casualty." She looked away from her old friend, murmuring, "We've lost too many as it is."

She got in the truck and started up the engine. "You coming?"

Hank tipped back the sheriff's cowboy hat he still wore, and whistled. "Lands, yes. This ain't my first rodeo."

Danny slammed into the door, out of breath. He jiggled the knob as Jeff and the Wilbankses caught up.

"Hurry! Hurry!" Tessa Wilbanks cried, huddling her sobbing children closer. The Shamblers were coming.

Jeff shadowed Danny. "Well?"

"Locked. Who knew, huh?"

Jeff growled in frustration, searching the dark horizon. "We need more time," he said. Danny saw the bobbing shapes of the shiny tentacled creatures lurching in the moonlight. Heard their slurping and sloshing and gurgling carrying over the dead wind, the tormented moans getting ever closer.

"I didn't want this!" Milton yelled. "I asked you to help get my family out of town, Jeff. *Away* from danger!"

"I'm trying, all right, Milton?" Jeff barked.

"We have to hide!" Tessa hollered, attempting to shield her daughters' eyes from the sight of the slithering, hissing things in the dark.

"Break the door down!" Milton roared, fear in his voice.

Danny looked to the small man and growled. "Yeah, and leave it wide open so those things can follow us right on inside, huh? Smart thinkin', Milton."

"Stop." Jeff touched Danny on the shoulder. "That's not helping."

Danny rushed to the youngest of Milton's daughters. Little Michelle Wilbanks trembled uncontrollably and had already wet herself, though no one made mention of it. When the car ran out of gas and the monsters landed on the car and reached for her—actually *touched* her—she lost it. She looked red-faced with shame. But Danny took special notice of the girl.

Michelle had her hair pulled back and held together by bobby pins. Danny reached for one of the pins, giving it a good yank, disentangling a few strands of red hair.

"Ouch!" Michelle gasped, but Danny made no apology. He pushed past Jeff and dropped to his knees before the doorknob.

"What are you doing?" Jeff asked.

"Picking the lock."

"You can do that?"

Danny briefly paused in his task and rolled his head to look at Jeff. "Are you kidding me?"

Despite the good man Danny had become in the last seven months, he had spent the previous years dealing drugs, breaking into homes for high-priced DVD players, and being a general menace to society.

Of course he knew how to pick a lock.

"Right." Jeff corrected himself and Danny went back to work.

In no time the lock was sprung and Danny hurried everyone inside the empty and humid house, before closing the door and locking it tight.

"What now?" He looked to Jeff, ready to follow him into any plan he had cooked up. But right now, he wasn't offering any brilliant strategy. "Jeff?" Danny asked again, sounding a smidgen concerned. "What are you thinking?"

Jeff turned to him with a shrug, as if to say, *Your guess is as good as mine*. He wasn't about to say that out loud.

Milton ran up to the ex-reverend and squeezed his arm, sweat beading up underneath his John Deere hat. "You won't let us die out here, will ya, Reverend? On account of what Earl and us tried to do to ya?"

"No, Milton. You're not going to die." He paused and then added, "And don't call me 'Reverend'. I'm not a reverend anymore. Just your friend."

Milton nodded, the soft-spoken words appearing to soothe him.

The older girl, Nancy, wept quietly, "Daddy, I wanna go back home." As Milton started to explain to his daughter that they couldn't, Danny hurried to the window and looked out.

"They're on their way," he reported and Michelle began to whimper again. Tessa immediately embraced her.

"I don't want to be here," the mother said. "I just wanted to be safe."

Danny looked around, frantic. "Maybe there's like a basement or something."

"No, we'd be trapped down there for sure," Jeff said. "Too easy to access and with nothing to barricade the door, a lock wouldn't hold against their strength for long. But, maybe…" Jeff raced into the hallway, madly looking along the ceiling until finally spotting a dangling cord.

"Danny!" Jeff pointed upwards as Danny caught on. He shepherded the terrified Wilbanks family as Jeff pulled the cord and released the drop-down ladder to the attic.

"Everybody up," Jeff commanded.

The girls scrambled up the ladder, but Milton was less enthusiastic. "Up there? We'll be trapped!"

"Got any better ideas?" Danny retaliated.

Jeff eased his hands on the father's bony shoulders. "Look, Milton, it's the only way. We'll be safe up there for a little while. Even if the Shamblers get in—"

"You've given them a *name*?" Milton interjected, terrified.

"If they get in, it'll still take them some time to figure out we're up there."

"They're not very bright," Danny assured.

"We'll be safe up there until help arrives."

Milton bought it and nodded his haggard face. "O-Okay. Okay."

He scurried up. Danny held back a moment and gave Jeff a serious look. "You really think help's coming, right?"

Jeff considered. "Iz hasn't let me down yet."

The ride down the beaten path was a rocky one. Hank held onto his hat with one hand and the dashboard of the truck with the other, as if riding a mechanical bull. Isabella, stone faced and fiery-eyed, kept a steady gaze, piloting the rickety piece of junk down the uneven terrain.

"We could have taken the road!" Hank jittered, feeling his teeth rattle.

"We could have been spotted. Besides," she barreled forward, hitting a dip and nearly sending them airborne, "this is quicker."

"Isabella Weldon, you are one fearless woman."

A deafening silence permeated the musty attic. Jeff's heart rebounded in his chest until it hurt to hold his breath any longer, but held it he did. His mouth tasted chalky and he desperately needed to cough something loose, but he remained perfectly still and silent.

Just outside the house, the sounds of the Shamblers' grunting and snorting rose through the seams in the attic's wooden door like misty apparitions. The sounds were like the calls of the dead that beckoned curious sailors to their watery doom. Hell was down below, and it wanted them all.

Jeff braved a solid look at Danny, and in the process discovered just how tense his muscles were. He craned his neck and found Danny just as terse, just as concentrating. The young man kept a vigilant watch, his eyes focused on the seams in the attic door, watching. Waiting.

Milton was holding up all right, it seemed. He and his family were quiet and attentive and Jeff was glad for it. The last thing they needed was panic. Things were bad enough.

When he heard the sound of breaking glass in the house underneath them, Jeff knew that the creatures were starting to get in. Immediately he felt a cold revulsion in the pit of his soul and the hackles on his neck stood at attention. His skin prickled and he shuddered, stifling the urge to heave—the body's natural reaction to the Shamblers.

Danny's eyes remained eerily open as his mouth slowly

slackened. Jeff watched his friend's horrified expression and could tell that more were coming in. Indeed, he could hear their shuffling.

When the front door broke open with the sound of splintering wood and bending hinges, Michelle clamped her hand over her mouth to conceal a scream and closed her eyes until the tears ran freely.

Danny, on hands and knees looking through the attic door, jerked his head away, as though trying to erase the image of the slick black beasts below. Some of the others back at camp had said they'd heard that someone went literally insane from staring at those things for too long. Jeff didn't know if Danny believed such superstitious nonsense, but the young man didn't seem ready to prove the theory either way. He rubbed his eyes, fighting to escape the horror.

Though Jeff knew he'd regret it, he took up his friend's watch. Carefully, he lowered to his hands and knees and pressed an eye to one of the cracks in the wooden trapdoor.

He gasped.

There were at least ten, if not more of them, in the house. Writhing over each other. Lashing out with awful ebony tentacles. They had no faces to speak of, for what faces their hosts once had were drowned somewhere in that oil. Like mindless fish they flapped against each other, against the walls, scraping their claws on the sheetrock, digging into doors, tearing the house apart from the inside. All reason had left them. All hope had seemingly escaped them. They were only creatures.

But, Jeff knew, they once were men.

They, like Ray McCormick, had once been good, decent people. But, for whatever reasons—reasons they would take with them to their graves—they had been lured out to Greensboro Park Lake, had touched its thick, murky sludge, and had been *transformed.*

The lake, or rather, the evil inside the lake, had made them monsters.

Jeff pitied them, for he knew that he came close to joining their ranks not so long ago. Even as he watched them growling and wailing helplessly below, he remembered his encounter with the lake's sludge. It had tried to consume him, slurping its way up his body, drowning him in cold desperation and filling his head with profane images and words.

"Kill." That's what the goo had told him.

Jeff turned to Milton, who appeared oddly calm, gingerly stroking his girls' hair as they rested on his chest, Tessa lying against his shoulder. Jeff lightened, but his brow creased. Either Milton really was calming down, or he had given up.

Not good.

Jeff looked to heaven and prayed, *Whenever You're ready.*

The faded red Nova was dead right smack in the middle of Highway 65. Isabella turned to Hank as they got out of Jeff's truck. "I knew it."

Hank didn't apologize, only dutifully followed her to investigate the scene. Isabella was thankful for his cooperation.

Extracting—or "redeeming", as they called it—new believers out of Greensboro was a tricky business. The Strange Man's spies were everywhere and took many forms. Crows, frogs, even some cats and dogs had been touched by the evil at Greensboro Park Lake. Now they were like walking surveillance cameras. Other than that there were, of course, the Strange Man's faithful gremlins, which Isabella and Hank had a little experience dealing with. With enemies stacked against them, sneaking a few people out of town was very difficult.

There were seven main routes of transportation that were used to redeem families, all rotated on a regular basis to prevent the Strange Man's forces from figuring out their method. Highway 65 was Route Four. Tonight's route. The Nova sat there with its rear right door open. The headlights illuminated the empty stretch of country road before them, slowly beginning to flicker and dim.

"Battery's dying," Hank said, moving over to the car.

He bent down by the open driver's door and took stock, a reflex from his bygone days as sheriff.

"Key's still in the ignition," he grunted. "Must've left in a hurry."

Isabella, her knees knocking together at the frightening reality that they were standing in open country where any number of enemies could see them, forced herself closer to the Nova. She looked in the backseat and saw three small suitcases, gutted. Clothes lay scattered in the seat and, upon looking on the opposite side of the car, she saw still more clothes strewn across the highway and into the ditch.

The Wilbankses' clothes.

One particular article caught her attention. It was a dress fit for a little girl. Isabella reached down and picked it up off of the hot pavement. Held it before her, examining it, imagining the beautiful girl who would wear it.

The beautiful girl who might be dead and never wear it again.

Outraged, she crumpled the dress and tucked it under her arm. Furiously, she began to pick up the Wilbanks family's clothes, holding as many as she could.

Meanwhile, in the car, Hank studied the broken glass littering the passenger seat where Danny would have been sitting. Took quick measure of the gauges. "Looks like they ran out of gas. Shamblers must have been waiting for them." He shook his head. "No blood, though," he called in relief. "Signs of a struggle, all right, but no blood. That's a *good* thing."

He looked out of the busted-out passenger side window and saw Isabella weeping to herself, picking up clothes on the side of the road. He frowned. "Hey," he muttered, watching as she wiped away a few tears, stuffing more clothes in one of the suitcases.

"They'll need these," she stammered, blinking back tears. "We'll find them and the girls will be upset that they won't have their things. We have to take these with us."

He nodded, not denying the woman an opportunity to feel less helpless. "Okay."

Hurriedly, she packed wrinkled clothes in the suitcases before loading Jeff's truck. Hank gave her space and brought out his radio.

She saw him reaching for it, stopped, and held her breath.

Hank paused, as well, maintaining eye contact with her. "Ready?"

She nodded, frowning.

He depressed the button. "This is Donut Boy. Come in, Steak and Potatoes."

"I rep…t, come …n, Steak …nd Potatoes." The radio strapped to Jeff's belt squawked to life with the static-filled sound of Hank Berkley's voice and immediately he sprang to his feet.

"Steak an… Potatoes, thi… …onut Boy."

"Turn it off!" Milton shouted, his voice a hoarse whisper.

Jeff fumbled with the radio as if it were burning hot, desperate to turn down the volume. Danny rushed to him, ready to help, but Jeff finally clicked the radio quiet just as Hank started up again, "Ste… and Potatoes, d… you read—"

Click. Hank jerked back from the abrupt white noise that emitted over his radio. He looked to Isabella. "It just went dead. What do you think that means?"

Isabella did not respond.

In the deathly silent attic, Jeff froze in place with the others, as the echo of Hank's call faded. At last, Danny braved, "Do you think *they* heard that?" He pointed past his feet.

Jeff stared at his young friend, breathing shallow.

Then, the hissing started.

Sssss…

It began underneath their feet, rising up through the floor.

Sssssss…

The girls scrambled closer to their father, burying their faces in his scrawny chest, covering their ears to shut out the terrible snake-like hissing.

Sssssss!

The hissing turned violent. Intense. And, above all else, closer.

Jeff and Danny stared at each other, transfixed by the unsettling sound as it turned into a rattle. In his mind's eye, Jeff imagined the inky tentacles separating from the Shamblers' backs, standing erect and clattering. It meant they were preparing to strike.

Danny went rigid as the racket intensified, filling the space directly below them. It grew so loud, so uproarious, that he nearly had to shout to be heard.

"Jeff?"

The floor beneath the girls' feet erupted in plaster and wood as a hook-shaped arm jettisoned through the opening and flailed about, seeking prey. Michelle and Nancy screamed, clawing at their petrified father's sweaty work shirt, tearing at him, begging him to do something. Milton cried and shook his head, as if trying to wake from some horrible nightmare. Tessa dumbly reached out, screaming for her children. The squid-like appendage slapped her away, sending her twirling in mid-air across the room, then latched around Nancy's thigh and tugged. She shrieked, ripped away from her parents and pulled towards the Shambler pit below.

"*No!*" Jeff cried.

He and Danny leapt forward, landing hard on their stomachs, reaching for the girl. She grasped aimlessly, screaming in unbridled terror as the monster pulled her towards the pit. Danny fought against her struggles and managed to grab on to her. "*Hold on!*"

Jeff reached to take hold higher up on her frail arm, and in so doing, leaned out over the new hole in their hiding place.

Directly below them, the Shamblers, now agitated, abandoned their zombie-like roam. Slick wet claws adorned their hands, gleaming in the moonlight. Though the goo covered their human faces, the oil managed to form some sort of sick, dripping maw that opened wide and let out a horrible, hungry groan. They were climbing over each other, scraping at the walls, trying to tear down the attic floor.

"Pull!" Danny commanded.

Jeff shook himself from his vision of hell and worked feverishly to rescue the hysterical girl. She squirmed, unable to discern what hand helped her and what hand meant her harm. Jeff and Danny held on, striving to heave her up.

Then another Shambler burst through the floor behind them. This one managed to climb its way into the attic space.

"Things are really bad!" Danny shouted.

A second Shambler grasped on the heels of the previous one, pulling its way up.

They'll use each other for a ladder until they're all up here! Jeff's mind whirled with possibilities as he and Danny fought to hold onto Milton's dangling daughter.

"We have to get down!" Danny yelled over the screams of Nancy and the insane babbling of the monsters in the house.

Jeff didn't like that plan. But he also didn't like the thought of staying in the attic where two Shamblers were clawing towards Milton and Tessa.

"Ah! AAH!" Milton hollered, holding Michelle, trying to keep his wife behind him. He scooted away from the hulking, slurping, gurgling dark things, his eyes so wide they almost popped out, tears spilling down his stubbly cheeks. "Stay away!" he commanded feebly, "*Stay away from us!*"

Jeff looked to Nancy, whose feet poked at the shiny, slime-covered heads beneath. "Nancy!"

She looked to him, attentive, and he praised God for that.

"Climb up!" he ordered, stern and clear.

Somehow, in the jaws of death, the girl found the presence of mind to act. Without wasting another moment, she drew herself up Jeff and Danny's arms. With the three of them working together, it took no time to rescue the young girl. Nancy was through the hole and back into the attic again, crawling safely into Danny's arms. She held onto her rescuer tight, weeping. Danny, himself, was trembling.

Milton, Michelle, and Tessa were pressed to their backs. They pushed across the attic floor, desperate to stay out of the greedy clutches of the hissing things in the attic. Jeff sprang to his feet, gave one last look to Danny—with Nancy in his arms—and ordered, "Get outside. I don't care how. Just get outside."

"What about you?"

Jeff left Danny to his own devices and charged headlong into the two Shamblers reaching for Milton and his family. In some sort of awkward double clothesline maneuver, Jeff tackled the beasts, knocking them to the floor. The thud of the train wreck reverberated through the attic, and the move left the monsters dazed long enough for Jeff to prod Milton. "Go! Go *now*!"

Milton only stared at the creatures, his face pale and his eyes red from crying. It was finally Michelle who pulled at his arm, bringing him back to himself. "Daddy! Let's go!"

Danny, with Nancy riding piggy back, huddled by the hole in the floor. Milton, Tessa, and Michelle joined him. Tessa stumbled and spat out, "What do we do? What do we *do*?"

Jeff rose to his feet and the two Shamblers did likewise. Their hissing intensified as they glared at him with their fathomless obsidian masks. They clicked in some alien tongue, and for the first time Jeff wondered if maybe they could communicate with each other. Maybe they weren't as mindless as everyone believed.

Maybe they can still be saved.

The Shambler on the left lurched forward in a feint, distracting Jeff long enough for the Shambler on the right to roar to the hidden stars and swing an extended, crackling black tentacle. Jeff jumped back, reminded of how fast they really were despite their slow, awkward movements, and pulled away from the strike in time to lose only a strip of his shirt.

The left Shambler rose and brought both muscled arms down with a thunder strike. Jeff rolled out of the way and came up swinging, throwing a knuckled fist into the smooth face of the right creature. Jeff recoiled in sudden grotesque fright as he felt the sludge squish underneath his fist.

His hand was stuck.

The goop on the thing's face latched onto Jeff's fist and pulled him in, sucking and oozing up his arm. *It's got me!* In that moment, he remembered when it had him once before. The things it whispered to him. The things it tried to convince him to do.

He tugged as if caught in an electrical current, putting a muddy boot against the Shambler's chest and pushing. Despite his best efforts, he couldn't suppress a terrified scream as the thing relaxed and the goo reeled Jeff closer. Bonding with him. Devouring him.

"No!" Jeff screamed, his heart pounding hard, feeling the cold emptiness numbing his fingers and moving up to his wrist. "No, please, *God*, no!"

Danny held onto Nancy and looked down into the Shambler pit, gauging their chances of simply jumping down and making a run for it. At the sound of his best friend's cries, Danny turned and saw the strange portrait of Jeff melting into the body of a Shambler.

Danny stood alert. "*Jeff!*"

Jeff swung his free fist, beating at the Shambler's body, screaming in fear.

Danny put Nancy on the attic floor and readied to rush into the fray to rescue his friend.

"Stay here," he absently said to the young girl. Clenching his jaw in rage, Danny set out to—

"Wait!"

Danny, his mind nearly overcome by battle lust, spun to see Milton, eyes gleaming with delighted tears, pointing down into the Shambler pit below. "Look!" he exclaimed. "They're leaving!"

Danny dropped to his knees and peered into the hole. Blinding light bathed the living room beneath them and the Shamblers, squealing like mice caught in traps, were fleeing!

"Day-Lights…" Danny muttered, feeling a broad wonderstruck

smile spread across his face.

"Day-*whats*?" Milton asked, confused.

Danny hurried to the trap door and kicked it down. He set out the ladder and waved for Milton and the girls to hurry. "They're afraid because of the lights! Go! Go! Hurry!"

Milton and his family eagerly left the dark confines of the attic and headed for the light. With them safe at last, Danny turned to Jeff.

Without another thought, he ran straight for Jeff and his Shambler twin, wrapped his tattooed arms around them both, and lunged…right for the second hole in the attic.

The threesome fell through a cloud of wood and spackling dust, careening into the house like an asteroid. Under the brilliant barrage of the Day-Lights, the Shambler—and all of his sticky goo with him—shrieked and clamored in a fit before leaving the house in one gorilla-like leap.

And, just like that, Jeff was whole again.

Jeff lay on his back, the bright UVs of the Day-Lights filling the house around him, and stared up at the black hole that led to the attic. He could still see the remaining Shambler watching him from the black. Too afraid to jump down in the glaring lights to attack, but still watching him.

Jeff shivered in his soul, realizing how close he came to being one of their kind. For the second time.

Danny stood over him, covered in so much dust and plaster that he was nearly completely white and Jeff figured he looked the same. The young man cracked a cavalier grin. "You okay, Boss?"

He held out a hand and Jeff took it. Danny helped him to his feet, Jeff's knees wobbling and threatening to give. After their close call, he forced himself to relax.

"Next time," Jeff began, coughing up a little spackling dust, "Remind me to check the gas tank before we leave."

Danny laughed and slapped his friend on the back, sending a

plume of white everywhere. "You bet."

"Jeff?"

Jeff heard her outside, calling his name, sounding like she had been through the scare of her life.

Isabella.

Immediately, he shot Danny a dark warning look. "Don't tell her how close—"

Before he could finish, Isabella stumbled through one of the impromptu entryways the Shamblers had made in the walls, her face drawn. Jeff remained fixed on Danny until the younger man nodded, silently agreeing to spare Isabella the grisly details of their night. Then, Jeff let out a long sigh and turned to his wife.

Isabella crashed into his arms, checking his face and arms and chest, gasping at the sight of his ripped shirt.

"Did they—? Are you—?"

He smiled, exhausted. "I'm fine."

She held him to her again, squeezing him tight. "I was…I thought that…"

She broke down. Burying her face in her husband's shoulder, Isabella sobbed.

Jeff looked up and saw Danny blushing, looking out of place. The young man finally left the remains of the house to go check on Milton and his family, giving Jeff and Isabella a chance to be alone and cry together.

It's over. For awhile, anyway…

CHAPTER TWO

HANK BERKLEY DROVE the truck back to their home deep in the North Woods, the dull roar of tire on gravel grating his nerves. The truck had an old tape deck, but the only cassettes within reach were Danny's heavy metal music. Hank once had a Merle Haggard in the collection, but the truck ate it. Danny got a good laugh out of that, saying the truck had better taste than Hank.

Presently, Danny, Jeff, and Isabella sat in the bed of the truck while Milton and Tessa—with a daughter on each lap, despite the law—were with Hank in the cab. The Wilbankses hadn't said much after their rescue, too petrified, no doubt, so Hank tried his best to keep the mood light, lest they get any ideas about moving back to Greensboro.

Hank finished explaining the purpose of the Day-Lights to Milton, "Shamblers are 'fraid of bright lights. That's why they stay away from town and stick close to the woods out here. Not so many lights, see? Who knows why or what goes through their minds, but they run from it like a cat from water. So we…er…*acquired* these big yoo-vee lights above us, fastened them to the top of the truck. A girl back at the camp did some wiring work for us and put in this here switch," he fondled it for effect, "and we've got 'Day-Lights'. We don't like to use 'em often seeing as how it kind of alerts the whole world to where we're at but, in a jam, it sure comes in handy."

Milton only nodded, blank-faced.

Hank saw the fear in the man's eyes and leaned in kindly. "We don't want you thinking that we're new to this sort of thing. You and your family will be real safe where we're going. We just had a rough night. That's all."

"I-If you say so."

Jeff and Isabella held each other underneath a blanket in the truck bed. Danny sat across from them, calm after their run-in with the Shamblers, still eyeing the shadows in the thick of the woods while Hank drove back to camp. Jeff kissed Isabella on her forehead for the upteenth time since the rescue, just to reassure her that they were safe and everything was all right. It reassured him, as well. They had a scare back at that house, and for a moment there, Jeff wasn't so sure he would be able to give his wife a kiss or hold her ever again. But Isabella had come through for him.

Danny had come through for him too. After kissing Isabella, Jeff looked to Danny, watching the hardened young man squint against the wind, keeping vigil on the darkness.

"We did a good thing tonight, Danny. Milton's family's gonna be safe."

Danny nodded. "Yeah. I know."

Isabella snuggled a bit closer to Jeff, relaxing in his embrace. "Your sons are safe too," she added.

Danny grinned, sad. "Yeah, I know that too."

"Have you tried contacting Tabitha in Watcher's Grove?" she asked.

Shaking his head, he managed, "Nah. We're too busy saving the world, right? Besides, I don't want to get them mixed up in any of this."

"When it's all over," Jeff said, but did not finish. He didn't need to.

"Right," Danny smiled wanly across the distance of the truck bed. "When it's all over."

Behind them, Jeff watched the large hill disappearing in the distance. His father used to call this place "God's Cliff". These days, Jeff just called it "home."

The truck bounded down the gravel road, traveling the rest of the way to their hidden destination: his father's old church. The original Good Church of the Faithful—the church his father and Leonard Fergus built so long ago—still stood today, far away from the reaches of the Strange Man in Greensboro. What once was an abandoned church, left to rot in the elements, had been converted into a haven. The all-too-familiar muffled hum of the nighttime gas-powered generator perked Jeff's ears.

"I hate it when Sarah runs that thing," Isabella hissed, the genny rattling from the church's basement. "I'm always afraid they'll hear us."

It wasn't entirely safe, she was right about that. In the day, everybody at camp kept a watch out for danger, but at night—when the Shamblers emerged and most people were asleep—they relied on Sarah's computerized security protocols. *Better a little noise than being blind in the dark*, Jeff thought to tell his wife. She worried too much, which he found ironic. In the past, he was the one prone to anxiety. But that was before the world fell apart. Now, with everything in chaos, Jeff actually found it easier to stay clear-headed, but Isabella…

He noticed that she seemed a lot more anxious these days. It concerned him.

The truck bucked up the rocky slope leading to the old church. Two men with rifles approached as Hank pulled over, and one of the men came to the bed.

"We were starting to wonder," the man told Jeff. He was short, with a mustache and scruffy five o'clock shadow, and a Raiders ball cap pulled down over his eyes. He frowned, holding his rifle as Jeff, Isabella, and Danny climbed down.

"We ran into some complications, Carter," he told the Raiders fan. "But we're all right."

"Told ya you should've had more men with you," Carter Ross grumbled.

Danny took what was left of the Wilbankses' belongings out of the bed. "We had it covered. 'Sides, more guys would have just slowed us down."

Carter grumbled something else before returning to the church.

Hank hopped out of the cab and moved to the passenger side to help Michelle and Nancy to their feet. Tessa was next, nervous at the sight of so many guns. Finally Milton, still trembling like a kindergartener on his first day of "big school," shakily left the truck. The scared man looked at the old, decrepit church and gave Jeff a very concerned look. "Is this *it*?"

He smiled. "Doesn't look like much, I know. But it's only until the transport can get here and take you and the girls to Russellville."

"H-How long will that take?"

"The last transport came and went last week, so you'll have two or three weeks with us before they're able to come and get you."

"Can't they come sooner?"

Jeff shook his head. "Sorry, Milton. Father Joe is putting his parish in Russellville at great risk as it is. They've been really nice to help us, but it's not safe for them to come too often. But, don't worry. You and the girls will be just fine until they get here."

Milton gulped. "That's what you said about getting us out of town."

Isabella sidled up to her husband, defensive. "That wasn't Jeff's fault. You're fine now. The Shamblers won't come out this far."

"How can you be so sure?"

Isabella pointed to the steeple of the old church where a man was positioned, surrounded by three mounted Day-Lights.

"We've got Day *and* Night Guards. There's someone up there at all times," Isabella informed him. "Any sign of a Shambler and he flips the switch."

Danny, carrying luggage to the camp, laughed. "Yep. Lights the place up like Christmas and gives the Shamblers the heebie jeebies."

Jeff patted Milton's shoulder. "You're safe now, Milton. Relax."

Milton shook his head, but relaxation didn't seem to be setting in. Instead, he hurried to his daughters by his wife's side, warning, "Don't get too far from Daddy," and nearly tripped on Hank's heels all the way to the church doors.

Jeff and Isabella hung back. "How bad was it tonight?" she asked, now that she and her husband were alone. "I've wanted to ask you the whole ride over, but I knew that, with Danny around, you would just gang up and start acting like boys and talk about how it was no big deal for big bad monster hunters like you."

Jeff smirked. Isabella didn't. "I want to know the truth."

"It was a close call, Iz. Too close. There's more of them than we thought."

Isabella sighed. "How?"

"I don't know. Ray…me…the lake fed on our fears. It called to us. It's like a trap."

"And you think the lake trapped all those people?"

Jeff shrugged, his mind burdened by memories of what the lake had tried to do to him. They spent so much time running from the monsters, they barely had a moment's peace to guess at what they were or what they wanted.

"I hit one of them tonight," he finally confessed. "It…the slime grabbed me. Tried to pull me in."

Isabella listened patiently, her eyes widening in horror. "Jeff…"

"Danny pulled me away and, by that time, you had arrived with the cavalry. But…I was really scared. We're going to have to get a meeting together and warn the others. If Shamblers can infect people just by *touching* them, then we need to be prepared."

She took a step past him, running her fingers through her tangled hair. She hadn't been able to wash it in a week—hadn't been able to bathe in a week—and Jeff knew her declining personal hygiene really bothered her. It was just another reminder that their old life was only a memory now.

"How long can we keep this up?" She looked to the starless sky.

Jeff hung his head and wrapped an arm around her waist. "As long as we need to."

"It's getting harder. Things get worse every day and we've been real lucky to have avoided as much trouble as we have."

"It wasn't luck, Isabella. God's with us."

Isabella stiffened and muttered, "We'd better get inside. It's not safe out here at night."

Jeff pursed his lips as Isabella retreated to the church. Now alone in the darkness, he turned to heaven. He couldn't see Him, but Jeff knew that God was somewhere up there, putting together a plan to deliver them all.

Can't wait to see it. He frowned, then joined his wife.

CHAPTER THREE

DRAS DREAMT OF dancing salt and pepper shakers in Blackout when he woke with a start. Shivering from head to foot, he looked around his darkened cell with only the strip of faint light shining in through the food slot. All was quiet in solitary, but it was suddenly very cold in his cell—colder than it had ever been before—and as he watched his breath leaving his body, Dras remembered the last time he had felt this cold.

"Oh, no…" he whispered in the dark. *Not him…not again…not here.*

He gripped the wall, too petrified to move, his fingers numbly searching for his Bible. *Is he here?* He forced himself to remain calm, clutching his Bible for strength. The Strange Man had beaten him before. But things were different now. *I'm different.*

Then he heard it.

Scratching.

He leaned forward slowly.

Scratching.

His heart picked up as he anticipated what was coming.

Scratching again, followed by a grating, scraping sound. A strange green mist poured in through the food slot, filling his cell. Dras heard whispering and giggling and he knew…*Gremlins.*

His thoughts flashed back to his chase down Greensboro's Main Street, with those awful twitching things behind him. He remembered their devastation, their insatiable hunger. How they toyed with him. What they did to Deputy Dane Adams.

Clicking of heels on tile drew Dras's attention outside.

He crawled to his cell door, green mist pooling around his wrists, and pressed his face to the slot. Peering into the hallway, he saw a dark shape marching towards him, nearly in slow motion, green mist parting before his shiny black shoes. He walked, determined and purposeful.

Dras backed away, knowing that the shape was coming for him. It seemed that the Strange Man was finally going to make good on his promise and tie up loose ends.

The shape approached the cell, blocking the light from the slot.

"Dras Weldon," the figure spoke from the other side of the steel door.

"Uh…yeah?"

There was a loud snap of rent metal, and the door to Blackout pried open, bathing Dras in newfound light. Before him stood a tall man, clad in a black turtleneck and dark trench coat. He extended a strong hand to Dras and said, "We need to get you out of here."

"Who are you?"

The figure stepped closer and his face seemed to softly glow. Dras mused in an odd moment of humor, *He kind of looks like a young Robert Redford.* However, despite the man's clean-cut looks and very friendly blue eyes, his face failed to answer Dras's immediate question.

"I'm a friend," Robert Redford Guy answered.

A shrill cacophony of cackling gremlins echoed down the hall and Dras jumped to his feet. Without warning, the ground shook and the hallway walls split.

"What was *that*?"

Urgent, the man turned to leave. "We need to hurry. They're already here."

Dras followed his rescuer into the hallway. "Where are we going?"

Redford hurried down the hall at a brisk pace, Dras fumbling to keep up. Cell Block 8 slowly came alive as prisoners still in captivity, seeing one of their own making an envied getaway, banged on their doors, shouting. Like animals in a zoo, the prisoners hollered for Dras, some begging for him to rescue them, some cursing him for leaving them behind. Dras tried to drown out the roar of murderous men all wanting a piece of him. He felt the cool around his ankles and saw the green mist rolling along the floor as if an intellect within the fog searched for something.

It's searching for me, Dras knew. He also knew that somewhere behind him, somewhere in the labyrinth of steel and concrete, were the gremlins he had grown to fear.

Another thunderous roar shook the walls, stone dust crumbling from the ceiling and powdering Dras's head. Overhanging lights blacked out and swung loose, nearly smacking Dras in their descent. He ducked and fought to hold his balance.

"What's going on?" he shouted over the racket, terrified to see that the locks on some of the cells had come undone, allowing their dangerous prisoners a chance at freedom.

"They're coming for you!" the man in the coat hollered over his shoulder. "And they're really, *really* mad."

"Where are we go—?" Redford shushed him and pushed him down a darker corridor as two guards hurried by in riot gear, entering the lion's den to fight back the wild escapees. Sirens sounded all around, disorienting Dras. Redford stood with his back to the wall, one finger held to his lips as the guards passed. He turned to Dras and nodded, then emerged into the corridor, moving ahead, scanning every new hallway before entering. Dras took one look back at the escalating riot, watching prisoners and guards clashing in war, spotting Machete among the recently released, fighting for his ill-deserved liberty. Dras chased after Redford, following as best he could, though the man in the coat was not slowing down for anything. The clamor of the inmates fell away as they distanced themselves from the chaos. Even the green mist was starting to dissipate and Dras really thought they were coming out of the woods.

"Do you know where you're going?" he asked Redford.

Again, the man in the coat did not respond. Only moved, keeping a lookout. Dras wanted to trust this guy. There was definitely something *otherworldly* to him and Dras knew otherworldly. He had been in the presence of the Strange Man. Redford didn't exude any of the general creepiness of the Strange

Man, but he definitely wasn't quite human.

Dras couldn't go any farther without some explanation. He stopped. "Wait."

Redford soldiered on a couple more steps before realizing Dras was no longer in tow. His eyes lit with disbelief, and he swiveled to face his younger counterpart. "What are you doing?"

"I want to know what's going on."

"We don't have time. We have to keep moving."

He knew Redford was right. With the guards mobilized, it was only a matter of time before he would be recaptured and he didn't want to think about what kind of field day Winters would have *then.* In fact, as he stopped only now to think about it, Dras realized that there were security cameras covering every inch of the prison. More to the point, there was a blinking camera aimed at him right now.

They see me, it dawned on him. *Why aren't they coming for me?*

Then he looked to Redford. "Can't they see us?"

Redford clenched his jaw, looking quite flustered. "You've more things to worry about than guards."

"You mean the gremlins."

"They're everywhere. All around. Moving through the walls, destroying everything in their path. Looking for *you* right now."

"But…why?"

"Because you know the truth."

Dras chuckled nervously. "I thought the truth was supposed to set me free."

Redford frowned and raised an eyebrow. "Well, we're *trying* to if you'd cooperate."

Without explaining any further, Redford turned and continued down the hall. This time Dras followed. Redford tapped his ear and spoke to thin air. "Watchtower One, how are we doing?"

Sitting in a van, surrounded by three monitors and surveillance equipment, a skinny man appearing to be pushing forty with long, oily blonde hair, thick glasses, an old flannel overshirt and a faded black "God Is Nifty" T-shirt, spoke into a headset. "So far so good." The slacker hacker surveyed the monitors. One monitor held the image of the slacker's partner and Dras hurrying down the hallway. The other two were of the upcoming hallways, devoid of life—both natural and *super*natural. "This one's really gone to pot. The place is a madhouse."

"Couldn't be helped," the forlorn voice crackled over the radio, filling the crowded van-space. "How do we look?"

"I got nothing ahead of you."

"Which way to the yard?"

The hacker frowned. "Uh…"

"Reid."

"I'm looking, I'm looking," he moaned, pulling out a phone book's width of spreadsheets. Humming anxiously, Reid unfolded the sheets, making a mess, looking everywhere through his schematics. "Uh…I think right."

"You *think*?"

"Well…Hey, I can't help it that these blueprints were made in the fifties, all right? I'm just going by what I know here."

While Reid busied himself with his blueprints, a large Mexican entered one of the monitors—in the hallways right ahead of Dras. Catching sight of the man headed for their charge, Reid dropped the spreadsheets and—

"Tell the kid to get down!" Redford's earpiece squawked so loud Dras heard it, feedback ringing. Redford looked ready to shout a warning, but a beefy arm shot out of the corridor, clotheslining Dras, sending him backwards. He landed square on the hard ground, his Bible sliding across the floor. Machete Rodriguez stepped out of the hallway, glowering down at his fallen prey. Dras coughed air back into his lungs, massaging his windpipe, as he looked up to see Machete's crooked, grinning mug.

"You think you can walk right on out of here?"

Dras rolled onto his knees, trying to stand, but Machete sent a swift kick to his stomach. Dras flew over, bright flashes of pain coursing through his body.

Machete towered over him. "Not so tough without your bodyguards, are you, small fry?"

He reared back his leg and swung but Dras countered, grabbing the foot and giving it a good twist. Machete wobbled off balance and Dras, still holding the foot, stood up and leaned into the giant, pushing him backwards. The shocked expression on the man's face made Dras smile in pride. *No, ladies, these muscles aren't just for show. Papa's got a brand new bag.*

Infuriated, Machete picked himself up and charged, roaring. Dras sidestepped, hooked arms with Machete and spun. The man rolled over Dras's back and fell to the floor again. Dras stood, out of breath. Hoping to settle the conflict before it went on any longer, he reached out a helpful hand.

"Look, can we just call it a 'truce'? I'm kinda in the middle of something and—"

Machete slapped the hand away, choosing to rise on his own. "It ain't ever gonna be over, you hear me? It don't matter if you get out of here, kid, I will hunt you down. I won't stop until you're *dead*."

Dras trembled in terror. Machete grinned. "Yeah, you like that?"

But it wasn't Machete he feared.

"Uh…" he barely made out before Machete paled, hearing it too.

Scratching. Clicking. Giggling.

Slowly, his snide grin melting into a dawning realization, Machete turned and—

"Dras, run!" came Redford's voice from behind, leaving the younger man to wonder why his rescuer hadn't stepped in while he was getting the stuffing kicked out of him.

Machete faced the hallway beyond as the halogen bulbs flickered, one by one, darkness swallowing the corridor. With each fading light, Dras made out some unnamable mass spinning toward them, like a tornado of teeth and glimmering sharp claws and piercing twinkling eyes until finally the things in the darkness emerged. The beasts filled the halls, their tiny, charred bodies pressed to all sides. Dras heard the whirring of their sharp teeth, like chainsaw blades, and felt his soul wither within him. The devils washed over Machete Rodriguez like a tidal wave.

He was instantly devoured.

As the things spilled over Machete's remains, whirling and twirling his way, Dras yanked the Bible off the ground and ran. He pushed through the front doors, the courtyard alarms blaring, guards shouting and firing at him. The gremlin horde expanded behind him, nearing the height of a two-story building.

"Watchtower One!" Redford hollered over the deafening roar of the demonic disaster catching up to them. "Watchtower One, repeat! We are rolling to the extraction point! Where are you?"

God, Dras prayed, *help me. Don't let me die. Please, not yet. I've got to find Rosalyn.*

"*Reid?*" Redford shouted shrilly.

Dras tried not to look back. He had made that mistake in the past. No, he needed to keep focused ahead. Unfortunately for him, however, up ahead there was only the chain link fence that stood between him and freedom. He skidded to a halt at the dead end, sweating profusely. Unable to put it off any longer, he turned to face the demonic forces storming his way.

"Uh..." he called out to Redford, who seemed to be preoccupied with something. "They're—uh—they're getting closer."

Face twisted in frustration, Redford concentrated his intense blue eyes on the chain link fence. With all of his might and will, he lifted a single hand, held it palm out to the fence, and to Dras's surprise, the chain link began to *undo* itself. Once intertwined, the links began to unweave, straightening and bending forward, creating a perfect little hole for one terrified kid from Greensboro to fit through.

Through gritted teeth, Redford barely turned to Dras and managed a grunt. "Go."

Dras did not hesitate. He passed through the hole, then turned to thank his rescuer, but saw the gremlins closing in on them. He waited for Redford to come through. Instead, the mystery man continued his immense concentration, this time willing the fence to close, trapping Redford on the other side with the gremlins.

Dras gripped the newly tightening coils of the chain link. "Wait! What are you doing?"

Redford breathed heavily once his strenuous task was done, and leveled darkly at him through the fence. "You have much to do, Dras. I was sent to get you out safely, and that's what I've done."

Dras made to protest, but didn't have the chance. The roar of an old engine sounded close by and a cloud of dust dissipated to reveal an old beat up van. The driver's side door popped open and a gangly ex-hippie hurried to slide the side hatch.

Redford grimaced. "For pity's sake, where *were* you, Reid?"

Reid blushed. "Just trying to make an entrance."

Redford, still clutching the fence for support, nodded weakly towards Dras, who could only stare at the approaching gremlins in stunned silence. "Get him out of here," he panted.

"Wait! Slow down. Where are you taking me?"

Reid looked to Redford, as if checking to see if it were okay to divulge the info. Redford nodded and Reid looked to Dras. "Back to Greensboro, kid. That's where it all started. That's where it's all gotta end."

"But—"

"*Go*," Redford ordered and Reid ushered Dras inside the van.

Dras reached out to Redford, seeing his rescuer falter as the gremlins slowed in their approach and stacked into a black tower of grinding teeth and glinting razors, savoring a gruesome kill to come. "Wait! You have to come with us!"

Reid didn't bother to look to his partner. Only to Dras. "Come on, kid. Chrysti can handle himself."

"Chrysti..." Dras repeated the name. *Chrysti saved me and I'll never have the chance to thank him.*

"Go!" Chrysti—not Redford—shouted and Dras slid the door closed. Reid rushed to the driver's side, cranked the engine, and floored it. The van spewed dirt upon takeoff, vaulting over the deserted fields, bouncing and lurching with every bump in the hard ground.

Chrysti watched the van disappear into the darkness beyond and smiled. *Praise Jesus. The kid's safe. Humanity has a chance.* His spirits lifted, he turned to look the gibbering, twitching creatures right in the eyes. The monsters reared back, gathering all of their might, buzzing and clamoring so loud that the ground trembled. The things built a solid wall of malice all around the lone figure and swelled with hatred and rage.

It was time for the attack.

"*In the Name of Jesus, I command you to depart!*"

The blurring mass of monstrosities whirled and nipped and scratched at Chrysti as they moved over him, but he stood his ground. They tore at his clothes, cut all over his face, but he would not be moved.

Not while I still have authority over these children.

Their oppressive numbers finally forced him to one knee, but he did not give up. He raised a single hand, as he had done to the fence, and mustered all of the power God had imbued within him and concentrated it into a shout.

"*Depart!*"

The gremlins trilled, still tearing at him, biting at him, gnawing at him, trying to devour him, trying to destroy him. Blood drained from his nostrils, but he would not falter. Finally, he released one final howl, "*Christ commands you to depart!*"

There was a loud thunderclap, a supernatural sonic boom, and Chrysti was thrown clear off his feet and clanged against the chain link fence he had previously undone and remade. The gremlins shrieked, and in one unnatural, unified movement, clasped their tiny clawed hands to their ears and fled. The tornado dispersed as the gremlins retreated to the four winds, taking their green mist with them, and all was finally silent.

Dras huddled in the back of the speeding van, bracing himself on the equipment as it rocked loosely back and forth. He sat in silence, thinking of Chrysti and what he had done for him. *And for what? What's so special about me? There's gotta be a mistake. I'm not worth all of this.*

He looked to the front seat where Reid fought to keep control of the van on the rocky landscape. Dras wanted to say something to him. The guy had just lost a partner to save his life. It seemed that some sort of condolences were in order. But he couldn't find the words.

A thud overhead startled him.

He looked to Reid to see if he had noticed too. He hadn't. There was another thud, and this time Dras's heart raced.

"They're here…" he whispered.

Another thud and the side door creaked.

"They're trying to get in…"

A jerk, a jiggle, and *swoosh!* The side door opened up on the night air and—

Chrysti eased himself inside.

Reid craned his neck to get a look at his partner as he closed the door behind him. "What kept you?"

Chrysti smirked, his grim face covered in dirt and blood, and turned to Dras. "You okay?"

Dras laughed. Reid turned around, taking his eyes off the road to get a better look at his partner. "You look terrible."

Chrysti waved over his face with the same hand that had undone the fence. At once his face was completely healed, all signs of a bloody battle totally washed away and a faint blue glimmer highlighting his chiseled features.

"You're angels, aren't you?" Dras asked, spellbound by the act.

Reid chuckled. "What tipped you off?"

Chrysti took a seat next to Dras. He called out to Reid, "Get us to the safehouse. We'll contact the General from there with a report."

Reid saluted in the rearview mirror and kept on driving.

"Your name is 'Chrysti'?" Dras asked.

Chrysti looked to Reid, as if a bit annoyed with his partner. "Chrysostom or, when I'm down here, Christopher," he corrected. "*Reid* just calls me Chrysti."

Dras had so many questions. But the one he felt summed it up best was, "What's going on?"

Chrysti—or *Christopher*, as he seemed to prefer—replied, "We have a lot to talk about. For now, just rest. You're going to need all you can get." More ominously, the angel added, "It begins now."

CHAPTER FOUR

HANK CALLED THE Town Hall meeting to order. "Okay, folks. We're about to get started if everyone wants to get settled in."

Jeff made it a practice to hold these refresher courses: a crash course in spiritual warfare to the "newbies" and a chance to fine tune the "soldiers" who stayed behind. Now he had the Wilbanks family to think about. He was almost for certain that, when Father Joe made his rounds to extract all those at the Haven desiring relocation, Milton would be the first one to scuttle on the bus, but, if things went bad—as they had last night during his evacuation—then Milton needed to be prepared for the worst.

That morning Jeff organized the Town Hall meeting inside the rustic old church. He always felt it was better to talk of the Enemy when the sun was shining. Somehow it made the work less futile and gave the most tenderhearted of his new congregation the strength to believe that they actually had a shot of making a difference. Sometimes, even Jeff needed to be reminded of that.

The congregation kept their Bibles close, as Jeff often gave them specific verses to use in a pinch. Most of the Bibles in town had been burned back when the community declared they were no longer bound to the "old way of things". A few Bibles had been saved from the book burning, however, becoming rare treasures. Before, Bibles had been so common in Greensboro. Each household below the sleeping eye of God's Cliff had at least two Bibles to claim, collecting dust somewhere. But now, when they needed God's Word the most, it was the hardest thing to find.

Jeff stood at the pulpit, getting a look at the crowd below. Milton's wasn't the only new face he saw. There was Ed Mathers and Jeremy Breckim and Lisa Simcox.

We are *making a difference*, Jeff reminded himself.

Isabella, Hank, and Danny stood behind him. The four of them had become the sort of leading body at the Haven, primarily because they knew the most about what was going on. Jeff wanted them to be regarded as equals in seniority, but as he took the stage to address the crowd and saw all the hungry, smudged, scared faces looking back at him, he realized that these people were still looking to *him* to lead. He and he alone. As if he were the only one who had access to God.

Am I helping them, or standing in their way?

"Because we have some new people," he began, "I'll cover the basics. This is what we know."

Isabella moved to an overhead projector that had been donated to the cause a month ago. She flipped on the machine, casting the square light on the wall, and slid a transparency over the light. Everyone in the room suddenly bore witness to the gruesome visage of the Strange Man—

As drawn by a five-year-old.

What every Havenite considered to be the vilest creature not already in hell was now reduced to a charming little scribble monster with larger than life fangs that resembled the front teeth of a rabbit.

Jeff pointed to the picture. "This is the Strange Man."

There were a couple of snickers from the audience. Amused, Jeff turned to the little girl sitting on the floor in front with a wink. "You can thank Millie Walker for the pictures."

Millie beamed with pride and her mother, Rebecca, patted an encouraging hand on her shoulder as Franklin Whitaker, always seated by Rebecca these days, whispered her job well done.

"He's the demon behind the trouble in Greensboro. He also has a human form and he's taken the name John Graves when dealing with the public."

With everyone watching, Isabella swapped out the Strange Man's picture with one depicting a small army of little green men with nasty looking claws. This time, Isabella narrated, "He is helped by these pint-sized guys. They are nothing but teeth and claws, and, believe me, they will eat through *anything* that gets in their way. We've come to learn that the best defense against them is quoting Scripture. *If* you ever come across them—and let's hope that doesn't happen—hold your ground and recite the verses you've been learning. Above all, trust in God. Faith is like hydrochloric acid to these guys."

Jeff took over, "What we know for sure is that, two years ago, after the highway moved, the Strange Man approached the town leadership, promising prosperity. For awhile it seemed he provided, but the deal came with a price: This 'Committee' was to protect him as he went about putting things into motion that would lead to what he refers to as, 'The Dark Hour'."

Isabella finished, grimly. "We believe that time is here now."

None of this was news to most of the people in the Haven, but still, speaking about such things usually caused them to grow very wide-eyed and unnaturally quiet. It was obvious to Jeff that most of the people didn't want these matters discussed, even though the monsters were lurking on their very doorstep. In fact, when Jeff and Isabella were alone together—which was very rare in a small church packed with sleeping bags, cots, and a mess of cooking supplies—they both worried that if all they did out in the Haven were hide from the horrible things going on in Greensboro—singing their songs, saying their prayers, and having their Bible studies—that would be perfectly acceptable to the Havenites. Sure, living conditions were harsh, cleanliness was an endangered species, food was hard to come by, but it could all be managed eventually.

As long as they didn't have to deal with the *monsters.*

But that's exactly what we have to do if we want to reach the people in Greensboro. Jeff forged ahead, "Things have already started changing in town. It started with Greensboro Park Lake. The Strange Man... *changed* it somehow and now, anyone who gets near it gets covered in this black sludge. If the goo touches you, it takes you over. It tells you to do awful things, and it drives you to do even worse." Jeff looked the crowd squarely, realizing the seriousness of what he was saying all too well. "When that happens, you become a creature that we call a 'Shambler'. Over the last seven months, the Shambler population has grown considerably. We haven't discovered the reason for that, but it's a fact we need to be mindful of. Because of their fear of lights, the Shamblers stick to the shadows of the North Woods…which makes us neighbors. Thankfully, Sarah's Day-Lights have kept them away so far."

"There's something else," Isabella cut in, louder. "We've just discovered that this disease can be spread. It can be passed on to whoever touches a Shambler."

A fresh wave of gasps and cries from the audience. Jeff calmed them down, waving his hands. "Now, don't panic. This only reinforces what we've already told you. Do not engage a Shambler—or any of these creatures, for that matter. *Stay away* from them. I know some of them were your friends, your family, but they're not now. They're not the people you knew."

Jeff wanted to further encourage them by telling them that the people who became Shamblers were, in fact, dead, and not present at all in the monsters, but he didn't know that for sure. When *he* was almost taken over, he still had presence of mind. It was hard to think, but he was still in there, underneath the goo. Hank Berkley had even told him about chasing Ray McCormick, the first known case of a Shambler, and recounted to him the events of the mysterious Special Agent Christopher Perdu—who Hank believed to be an angel in disguise—and how Perdu had literally exorcised Ray of the black substance. Hank said that, in Ray's last moments on Earth, he was wholly sane and wholly himself. Jeff feared that the friends and family lost to the black slime were still alive and trapped in some kind of hell underneath that mountain of venomous mud, but he didn't want to say any of that to the people. Not yet.

"They're not your family," he reiterated. "Not anymore."

"How do we stop the Shamblers?" came a frightened, if not agitated, voice from the front row.

"I don't know. Light scares them off, like we said, but beyond that, we don't have any idea what they really are or what they want."

The crowd, all having lost people to the madness at Greensboro Park Lake, grew reverently silent. Feeling the need to remind them that what they were experiencing was not the worst of it, but rather the beginning, Jeff placed another transparency on the projector. This one was only a great black blob adorned in tentacles with a single white question mark within its body. "The Strange Man told me, himself, that he is merely a prophet. A servant of a greater beast. Those of us who had the dreams a few months back remember this thing by another name."

Jeff remembered those horrible images of a town gone mad, men turning to monsters, death coming to all. Danny had had the dreams, too.

"The Coming Evil," a few in the crowd—others who had suffered the nightmares—muttered.

Jeff nodded, encouraging them to say the name of the thing. It was the only way they would conquer their fear of it to fight. "That's right."

Gus Reynolds, an older man who had been with the Haven Resistance since the beginning four months ago, finally stood and raised a hand. "But what is it? Have you figured that out yet?"

As if free to talk, a few of the others nodded and murmured their confusion also. All eyes turned to Jeff.

"We still don't know."

A couple moans. A grumble. Isabella looked to Jeff, anxious, and he spoke louder to be heard, "But his arrival will coincide with the climax of the Dark Hour. What that climax is…well, I don't know that, either."

"Then what *do* you know?"

Startled by the anger in the gruff voice, Jeff turned and saw the man in the Raiders ball cap. He frowned. *Carter.*

Some of the people faced Carter, and Jeff saw desperation in their eyes. *They want someone to lead them. Anyone. Just as long as it's somebody else. Just as long as they don't have to think for themselves. When are we going to learn?*

Carter stood up among the others and walked closer to the podium. "We keep having these meetings and going over the same old stuff, but you haven't told us anything *useful*. I mean, we've been at this for months now and we've barely made a dent in this thing! The whole town has been totally taken! We've got Shamblers in the woods. We've got gremlins making the rounds looking for us. We've been cut off from all our friends and families back in town—if they ever caught us, you know what they'd do to us!"

"They'd kill us!" shouted a frightened voice.

"That's right they'd kill us!" Carter encouraged him. "And without hesitation, too, because they think *we're* the evil ones."

Jeff remained standing, unsure of how to handle the situation. Carter was, in a lot of ways, like a certain local loudmouth by the name of Earl Canton. Jeff had tried to match Earl shout for shout before and that road eventually led him to dangling in the back of Earl's pickup truck with a noose around his neck.

Not an experience he fancied living through again.

Jeff wasn't prepared to shoot down Carter's opinion, partly because he respected it. Carter was a man of action, a man who was ready and willing to do whatever it took to demolish the Enemy. Except for sitting around and waiting on God. *That*, Carter didn't like so much.

The man softened a bit, sincerity showing through. "Jeff, I believe what you're saying. I think we all do. We've staked our lives on it, but we need some definite answers now. How are we going to fight these monsters?"

Truthfully, Jeff didn't know what they were going to do. Isabella, seeing him falter at the question, immediately stepped in. "We pray."

Carter and a few others groaned. Persistent, Jeff said, "God has not forgotten us. He *will* deliver us. I don't know how but we've got to stay in His Will. He will show us the way. In the meantime, we keep on keeping on. We lay low during the dark, try and get the Word out during the day. *That's* our mission."

Carter turned back to the four leaders on the stage, face

flustered. "I was a deputy for ten years. There are enough firearms in the locker at the station to equip a small army! We could use those weapons and—"

Clenched fists and jaw taut, Isabella nearly pushed Jeff out of the way to directly address Carter. "And *what?*" she shouted, causing Jeff to stop and take notice.

She's really mad this time, he thought to himself. Hearing complaints from the people was nothing new. Finding brave folks to journey out at night for extractions or even for posting some Scripture on telephone poles was a great chore. *No one* wanted to go out. They just wanted to hide in the Haven and help by being "moral support". It was frustrating, yeah, but Isabella seemed to be taking it all the more personal lately. *Is she okay?*

"You haven't seen these things, Carter! You don't know what they can do! I've fired a shotgun point blank on them and they barely limped afterwards." She spun to Hank, pointing at her friend. "Hank and I nearly *died* and guns didn't help!"

Carter cooled. "I understand, but we need an offensive. We need to fight this thing head on."

"I tried," Jeff told him, thinking back on his test in the caverns below The Rave Scene and how his rage almost cost him everything. "It's not the way. This is too big. We don't know how big yet. We have to wait."

"We have to fight!" Carter countered, his whiskers blustering.

"What do you think we're doing?" Isabella shouted as Jeff and Hank shared a worried look for their girl.

Carter shouted right back, getting closer to the stage, the frightened eyes of the crowd moving from Isabella to Carter like a tennis match. "Sitting on our thumbs having Sunday School is not how you win a war!"

Off to the side, seeing Isabella rearing up, Danny muttered out of the corner of his mouth, "She's gonna blow…"

Finally, Hank stepped between the two warring factions. "All right, that's enough, Carter. Let's just cool down."

As if being scolded by his father, the man pleaded his case, "I'm just saying, Sheriff…"

"You've said enough," Hank grumbled. "And don't call me 'Sheriff'. We ain't sheriffs, no more. We ain't doctors, or pastors, rich people or poor. We're all just regular folk trying to get by. Now, we up here have heard what you've been saying, Carter. Heck, the four of us have gone round the bin about it a time or two, ourselves. But that's not what any of this is about."

Now, all eyes were on Hank and Jeff found himself eager to hear what his soft-spoken friend had to say.

"This is about who's in charge. And that ain't you, Carter, and that ain't us up here. It's Him up there," Hank said, pointing to the sky, giving Millie a little giggle. "He's the one calling the shots around here. When He says we move, we move. When He says we wait, we wait. When He doesn't say anything at all, we pray and don't go runnin' off half-cocked."

Frustrated, but receding, Carter put his hands on his hips and shook his head at the ground.

Hank said, "If you don't like that—any of you, now—then I suggest the next time Father Joe comes through, you be on the next bus outta town, because we've got enough to worry about *out there*, we don't need trouble *in here*. Understood?"

No one said anything, but everyone understood.

Hank gave his head a good nod, settling the case, and looked to Jeff, sternly. "I say we have some breakfast."

Jeff couldn't agree more.

Canned peaches and oatmeal were on the breakfast menu at the Haven. Sully Thompson who owned the local grocery store, though not a believer in Christ, hated the thought of his neighbors living out in the sticks, shunned from civilized society. He was generously "clumsy" with his stock, often leaving food in places where certain people could happen to stumble across them. Thanks to his last misplacement of goods, they had a hearty supply of canned food to last them a couple weeks if they all ate sparingly.

Danny Carpenter shoved a spoonful of slop into his mouth, swallowing hard. He hated oatmeal, but it was either choke it down or go hungry. While he struggled with another bite, he heard a slight throat-clearing and popped one eye open to see Sarah Browning meekly standing before him, her plate in hand. Sarah was their resident tech and nerd-of-all-things-computer, with a head-full of dark curly hair and round glasses. She wasn't unattractive, per se. Just mousy.

"You…uh…mind if I sit down?"

Danny looked around, confused, then shrugged, indifferently. "I don't own the table."

Sarah blushed and took a seat across from him. He shut his eyes and worked through the oatmeal. Sarah watched him and snickered, then took a bite, as well.

"What are you laughing at?" he asked, bordering on embarrassed.

"I've just never seen anyone eat oatmeal like that," she said.

"Yeah, well, if we get out of this, I'm never eating oatmeal again. Stuff tastes like wet cardboard. Makes you realize you shouldn't take things for granted."

"Really?" Her green eyes widened.

"Sure," he shrugged, stabbing his slop with his spoon. "Life's short, you know? You only get one go-around, so it might as well mean something."

"I agree. I think that we need to cherish the people in our lives while we have them."

Danny paused, his spoon hovering in front of his mouth. She was doing it again. Batting her eyes, wanting to *talk* all the time. But no matter how hard she tried, Sarah could never be Tabitha.

Thinking of his kids, now, Danny was no longer hungry. He laid his spoon back in the bowl and got up, before taking off. "See ya, Sarah."

He caught her in a frown, as she softly muttered, "See ya."

Isabella scrubbed furiously by the little stream that lay about a hundred yards away from the Haven and all prying eyes. Luckily, this path of water made no contact with the supernaturally polluted contents of Greensboro Park Lake. It was clean and devoid of the ability to turn people into slime-encrusted mindless zombies. Once a week, some of the women from the camp would go down to wash their clothes in the cool, refreshing water.

Isabella went alone today. She needed time away from those people. Just the thought of them made her scrub harder. Washing clothes was a lot more difficult without soap, and a lot less satisfying, as well, but Isabella enjoyed the task. Hard work reminded her of better times on her father's farm, working with her brothers. Things seemed to be much simpler when she was washing or cooking or cleaning the horses. Nothing to think about. Nothing to worry over. Just the work. *Just do the work, Iz.*

A branch snapped behind her and she wheeled about in an instant, raising high the smooth large stone she had been using to grind out the crustier messes on her clothes. Jeff held his hands in surrender. "Whoa, you got me."

She huffed and went back to scrubbing. "You know I hate it when you do that."

His grin still lingered as he stepped close to her on the bank of the stream. Isabella continued to clean.

"You shouldn't be out here alone."

Wincing as she looked up to the sun, she drawled, "It's broad daylight. Shamblers are long gone for now."

"But there's other things, you know."

"Believe me, I know."

And he knew she did. He'd told her repeatedly how he hated himself for not being with her and Hank when they were tearing through town, a horde of demons on them. It haunted him. That night haunted her too.

"Are you okay?" he asked the Million Dollar Question.

"Why? Have you been talking to Hank?"

"Didn't need to." Jeff shrugged, a bit defensive. "I'd like to think I can still tell when my wife's upset."

"Honestly?" she asked, looking at him, to make sure he was okay with the truth.

He nodded. "Shoot."

"I'm sick of them," she said, bluntly, and Jeff blinked.

"Oh."

Isabella kept her voice down, throwing suspicious looks back up the path that led to the Haven, and let it all out. "All they do is complain. They argue and they fuss…you'd think we *kidnapped* them from Greensboro, or something. They *chose* to come out here. We didn't twist their arm. Don't they remember how bad it is in town?" She stopped and answered her own question, sardonically, "No, of course they don't, because they won't step foot *in* town again. Forget all the others still back there. *We're* all safe, right? That's all that matters. All those other suckers? Too bad for them."

"Iz…" She huffed once more and scrubbed with her rock, rendering the cloth nearly threadbare. "I know you're frustrated," Jeff said, calmly. "I am too. But we can't give up. It takes time."

"It's coming. Can't you feel it? They want a war, Jeff. But one *they* don't have to fight in. Let someone else die for their freedom, right? Like me? Like you or Danny or Hank? Just so long as it's over and they can go back to their normal lives."

When Jeff didn't immediately respond, she continued, her voice wavering with emotion. "I get tired too, you know? Sometimes, I wish it were all over. I'm sick of this place. Father Joe has been so kind to us, Jeff, and I see him pull in every month, taking a few more with him and…I wanna go sometimes. I wanna take you, me, Hank—heck, even Danny—and just get out of here while we still can."

"But we can't do that."

Scrubbing, still. Softer, though. Her eyes trailed from the clothes and to the sparkling stream. "I know," she said, thinking she might cry. Jeff reached out for her, and took her in his arms. She didn't protest. Still clutching the stone and garment, she rested her head on his chest and was not ashamed to whimper, just a little.

"I just want to go home," she said, trembling.

"I didn't think you liked the brownstone so much." Jeff tried to lighten the mood.

"No, Jeff," she said, not kidding. "I mean 'home'. Back when we were on Grover's Pond. That was our home. That was when we were happy."

"Hey," he said firmly, but gentle. He pulled back to look at her directly. "*We're* home. No matter where we are. It's you and me."

She hesitated, wanting to say something, but not ready yet, and lay on his chest again. "Tell me again," she sighed.

Jeff stroked her hair, and she looked at the clouds overhead. It looked so pretty up there. So peaceful. And, for a moment, she almost forgot what their world had become.

"What's that?" he asked.

"Tell me why we're out here. I mean, I *know.* I remember. But, when you say it, I believe in you all over again and I'm not afraid."

He kissed the top of her head, and recited, "We're out here to help people. We're out here, not to hide, but to provide a safe place for those who want to follow the Lord. We're here to do our part to spread the message in a world that doesn't want to hear about God ever again. We're here because we haven't given up on the people back there. We're here because we prayed about it and we both felt that this is exactly what God wanted us to do. We're here because we remember the good times and we believe it's worth fighting for."

"Yeah?" She smiled, loving him so much.

"Yeah."

CHAPTER FIVE

DRAS STARED OUT the van window into the bleached farmlands streaking past. The sun nearly blinded him and he squinted against the light, feeling pensive. In the front sat Reid behind the wheel and Christopher at his side.

I'm riding in a van with two angels who just busted me out of prison to save the world.

At any other time in his life, Dras might have found the situation funny, but today, all he could think about was Rosalyn.

His mysterious rescuers had taken good care of him, giving him a change of clothes and granting his request for a Beefy Burger at a turn-off on the highway between the City and Greensboro—though Reid insisted he not touch any of the equipment in the back with his greasy fingers. Yet, both angels were keeping mum on the specifics of the so-called "Dark Hour" and the fate of his family. In his heart, he believed Jeff and Isabella were okay—they knew what they were up against and were prepared. *But Rosalyn...* It worried him that, when he thought of her, he only felt a gnawing uncertainty in his stomach.

Please, God, let her be okay.

He turned to his guardians, wanting to think of something else for awhile. "So, what am I supposed to be doing?"

Reid talked over his shoulder. "Kick back and enjoy the ride, sport. We'll be in town before you know it."

Dras groaned, aggravated, and leaned against the console in the back of the van decorated with Reid's hi-tech monitoring equipment. Christopher turned around, his eyes kind. "I'm sure this is hard for you, but you've got to trust us."

"How am I supposed to stop the Strange Man?"

"You'll know when the time comes," Christopher told him.

"Don't you have any cool angel weapons?"

"Yeah." Reid considered then returned his eyes to the road. "But only cool angels can use them."

Christopher grinned at his friend. "Trust us, Dras. If you saw the things we saw, it'd…*damage* you. We're hardwired for combat, able to sustain horrors you couldn't even begin to fathom, let alone describe. But you humans are designed for compassion."

"Yay, us." Dras slumped. "So I just gotta rely on my karate-action love, then. Greeeaat."

Reid chuckled, but Christopher swiveled in his seat, leaning closer, the hint of excitement and alien marvel in his eye. "You don't understand. Just like you can't grasp the mind of God and all that He really has planned for you, angels can't come *close* to comprehending your capacity to love. We only know love as a word. As loyalty and service to our King. But you know love in so many ways. Friendship, mercy, charity, grace, forgiveness…these are all characteristics that you share with the Lord that we will never have."

Dras saw the longing in Christopher's eyes and felt a little bad for the angel. "You mean…you don't feel love?"

"Not like you do. We feel appreciation. We feel happy when we please God. We feel camaraderie and kinship. But, no. We don't feel love."

"Then why do you help us?"

"We minister to you so that you might find the strength to do what we can't. We can't love for you. We can't show mercy or forgiveness. We can only encourage *you* to do those things."

Dras considered that for a moment. "So," he started, finding himself growing a bit fearful to know. "What's heaven like, anyway?"

Reid shared a sidelong glance with his partner. Christopher seemed to reminisce. "Earth's a lot different than where we come from. In the heavenlies, we're never removed from the presence of God. He's our light and our strength. But down here…Down here, things are gray. Muddled. The Light is so much harder to see."

Dras sat upright, facing the angel, feeling an incredible loss in his own heart.

"Sin abounds down here. It's a disease that permeates all of God's creation and even angels aren't immune to it. But, unlike humans, we don't have souls for saving. We are simply vessels to be filled. If we follow God, we are filled with His Presence. But to break that fellowship…it's broken forever. Where I come from, angels *fear* Earth. We're quick to come here when God sends us but we always know that some of us won't come back. The temptation here is so strong, and, this far from God, we have to be so careful. One sin can corrupt us, Dras, and we'd be exiled from our King forever."

Dras's eyes widened. "You sin once and you're out of heaven? Dude, I sin at least five times *a day*."

Reid sniggered and Christopher chuckled. "You have to understand. We don't have the Holy Spirit as you do. When you repent and return to God, He fills your hearts with His Spirit and you are restored, forever considered righteous in the eyes of God because of what Christ did for you on Golgotha. No matter what sin you commit, God's love for you never changes. With His Spirit at your disposal, you never have to doubt, never question. You never have to face anything alone. We're made differently. Our role to play is different than yours. Here on Earth, we feel cold—separated from our God and fearful that the sin Adam brought into this world will claim us too. I don't know if you can imagine how terrible a feeling that is."

"…I had no idea."

Christopher grinned quickly, as if suddenly embarrassed that he had revealed too much. "We have our ways of keeping our fellowship with God while we're on Earth, though."

"How's that?"

"*You* Believers. Your faith encourages us. You have the Holy Spirit within you—the very breath of God is inside you."

Reid jumped in, "Believe it or not, being around you makes us feel a little closer to home."

"We've been watching Greensboro for a long, long time," Christopher said. "We're just ready to get back home, Dras, where we can eat with our kindred in the House of the Lord again." A frown escaped the angel as though he thought of better days and better places.

Dras nodded. "But you can't, can you?"

"Not yet. Not until the job is done."

"Have you ever thought about what it'd be like to be human? You know, to, like, love and be loved and all of that?"

Christopher and Reid exchanged a dark look. Dras stared at the two of them, startled by their sudden change of expression. "What? What did I say?"

The angel's jaw tensed. "No. I've never wanted that for myself. Sure, once or twice, I've wondered what it would be like to feel and experience God's love as you do, but…"

Reid cut in, "Not all of us feel the same way, unfortunately."

"What do you mean?"

"Your friend, the Strange Man, for one," Reid said.

Dras nearly laughed. "You mean the Strange Man wanted to know what it was like to be in *love*?"

Christopher wasn't laughing. His expression was pained and foreboding. "It's why he fell, Dras."

Dras thought his heart might stop. *That thing that came after me…He became like that because he wanted to love?*

"We're here," Reid cut into his thoughts. Dras glimpsed the familiar sights of Main Street; of Smokey's Bar and Grill, Don's Barber Shop, and the old movie theater that now seemed to be open for business again. He was *back*. He was home.

Christopher took a deep breath. "This is it."

Nausea seized Dras's stomach. He at once felt nothing but doubt and self-consciousness. All the Scriptures he had memorized in prison were nowhere to be found as he stood on the precipice of a brand new world. They were in Greensboro now, ready for him to do…well, whatever it was he was supposed to do. He felt like he used to feel at the public pool when Rosalyn stood behind him on the diving board, telling him to hurry and jump off. *I don't wanna jump. I want to stay in the van with the angels where it's safe. I'm not a hero*, he thought, his heart pumping furiously at the thought of the unknown waiting for him on the other side of the van. *Choose someone else, God. Please.*

Christopher must have seen the fear in Dras's eyes, for he crawled into the back of the van to take the stool in front of the console across from him.

"Listen closely. His plan is almost complete now and the Dark Hour is close."

"I don't know about this. I'm not ready. I mean, I don't even know what a Dark Hour *is*. How am I supposed to stop one?"

Reid cast a worried look in the rearview mirror. "Better spill it, Chrysti. I think the kid's about to pop."

"We aren't allowed to tell you much, but we can tell you that the Strange Man is trying to bring about a return to the pagan age before Christ's birth. He's trying to bring back the Ancient Ones."

"Ancient Ones…? I don't understand. What does that mean?"

Reid shook his head in frustration and Dras felt very small and ignorant. "Ancient Ones." Dras tried to piece the information together in his mind. "You mean like Old Testament? Human sacrifices, wild orgies, pagan gods—"

Reid guffawed. "*Gods*," he snorted. "They wish."

Before Dras had a chance to probe further, Christopher captured his attention. "What's important is that you understand what is at risk and how vital your part is."

"Yeah, that's the part I'm not so crazy about. I mean, really, what can *I* do? I already tried to fight him before and I failed spectacularly."

Christopher put his hardened hands over Dras's. "What happened is exactly what God had planned to happen. You were *meant* to be broken and locked away in that cell. Everything has worked together for your good—and for theirs."

"It was training, kid," Reid chimed in.

Christopher leaned in closer and lowered his voice. The angel's whisper was full of power and promise as he fixed on Dras's eyes. "Why do you think Winters put you in Blackout all the time?"

"Primarily because he hated me."

"He was one of ours," Reid called. "A human who was 'on the level'."

Dras blinked. "Wait. What?"

"We had him keep an eye out for you. Keep you as safe as possible, to give you time alone with God to work out some things. To prepare you, Dras. For this moment."

Dras thought of Winters. "You mean he was a *good* guy?" *Who'd've thought?*

"You've grown into the man you were always meant to be and now it's time to come out of hiding and show *them* what you were meant to be too. The Strange Man is already afraid. He sent that army at Wexler to stop you from coming back. He's close now to achieving his goal. Very soon the Dark Hour will be here and he can't have you returning to mess things up. But that's *exactly* what you're going to do. It's what you were *meant* to do."

Dras sucked in a deep breath, awed by the conviction in Christopher's face.

His stomach didn't hurt as much now. But he still felt like he was hovering over the deep end of the pool.

"You're about to enter a war zone, Dras. Purifying agents like light, salt, and fire will be your tools. But those are only deterrents. Faith will be your shield and the Scriptures will be your sword. Just keep doing what you've been doing all this time," Christopher encouraged him. "Trust your King. He will give you the answers in due time. He will protect you. But whatever you do, it is *imperative* that you not be afraid. Do you understand me? Whatever fear you have, forget it. Shove it aside. Your work is too important and there's no time for it."

Dras nodded, unable to find the words to answer this important call.

"Do you understand?" Christopher leveled with him, the blue light in his eyes nearly consuming him, the holy fire within the angel building. "Fear not, for Christ has overcome the world. Remember that."

"I'll try."

"*No*," Christopher barked, causing Dras to jump. "Don't try. Just do."

"O-okay. Got it, Master Yoda."

Dras felt inertia's forward pull as the van slowed, and the peace he felt a moment ago was instantly diminished.

"This is it," Reid pronounced.

"Wait," Dras began, but Christopher cut him off.

"We have to go now. There are things left for us to do before we see you again."

Christopher reached for the handle on the sliding door, ready to expose Dras to a world he had not seen since going to prison.

"Wait! I'm not ready!"

"Yes, you are," Christopher said in all confidence. "God will lead you where you need to go. Think back to your Scriptures, Dras. Don't forget what you've learned. *Think*. Isaiah thirty twenty-one. What is it?"

"I don't remember, I—"

"That's fear talking. You know it, Dras. You've learned it. What is it?"

"Uh…" Dras struggled to think through his panic and saw the words in his mind's eye. …"Whether you turn to the right or to the left, your ears will hear a voice behind you saying, 'This is the way; walk in it.'"

Christopher swelled proudly. Much more calmly, the angel tested again, "And John ten twenty-seven?"

This came more quickly to Dras's mind and he repeated the scripture almost automatically. "My sheep listen to my voice; I know them, and they follow me."

Reid finished the promise of Christ, "I give them eternal life, and they shall never perish; no one can snatch them out of my hand."

Dras, his breath slowing, felt the words leave his mouth before he realized he was thinking them, "My Father, who has given them to me, is greater than all, no one can snatch them out of my Father's hand. I and the Father are one."

Christopher clapped his hands once in subdued excitement. "*Exactly*."

Dras's heart beat faster as confidence bloomed within.

"You have the Word in you, Dras. That's your weapon against the Strange Man. Trust in it and the authority of Christ and you'll be okay. No matter what happens."

"Your Heavenly Father is the King, man. You're the Boss's kid, get it? Time to go throw your weight around."

Dras nodded, calming.

"Better get a move on too," Reid reminded.

Dras looked to the closed door and Christopher's hand on the handle.

"Oh, and before you go," Reid piped up and Dras really wished he wouldn't go on. He was just beginning to feel a bit better about things. "This isn't the Greensboro you left ten months ago, sport. It's become a den of monsters and a haven for the wicked. In the shadowed places of the world the superstitious refer to it as 'The Place Where Satan Lives'."

Christopher winked. "So brace yourself."

Dras groaned. "Thanks a lot. I probably could have gone all day without hearing that."

Christopher smirked then flung the door open.

Brilliant daylight bombarded Dras and he raised his hands to defend himself from the onslaught. By the door, Christopher said his good-byes. "May the grace of our Lord Jesus Christ keep you."

Reid leaned over the seat and gave a thumbs-up. "Watch your back, tiger."

"Yeah. Thanks."

And with that, Dras stepped out into the light. Into Greensboro.

Here we go.

Dras took one step onto the streets of Greensboro and stared in amazement at the picturesque display of Americana that unfolded before his eyes. It wasn't the small town he had left behind, it was now almost a theme park, a carefully manufactured Hollywood-style small town. To his bewilderment, he heard the sounds of *Mr. Sandman* wafting through the air from speakers mounted on nearly every building. Warm, spicy fragrances of freshly cooked food danced under his nose. All the old storefronts were restored and sporting all sorts of merchandise that reminded Dras of what Greensboro must have been like back in its heyday. There was a leather store filled with boots and belts, a quaint little ice cream shoppe, a handmade dulcimer store, and a tourist station directing out-of-towners to the beautiful sights of Greensboro Park.

And the people! There were people *everywhere.* Couples holding hands, dog walkers, kids running around, teenagers huddled up in excited groups on the corner. Dras didn't even know this many people *lived* in Greensboro.

Before the highway moved, Greensboro was a nice place to live, but the sight before Dras was far above any nostalgic images of the past. The place looked brand new. The East Side, that derelict part of town that had become a hunting ground for drug dealers and thieves, now sparkled with new life. Everyone seemed happy and genuinely content with everyone else. An alien observer, Dras just stood there on the sidewalk, marveling at Greensboro's dazzling appearance.

Is this really the town that's so close to being devoured into the belly of hell?

His eyes drinking in the sights, Dras absently stumbled around the Town Square where he'd fled the gremlins some months back, his enchantment only broken when a teenage girl thrust a blue flyer in his face out of nowhere. "Do your part!" she sang, and Dras saw that there were other pretty girls with her, all handing out blue flyers to everyone who walked by.

"What?"

"Celebration Day!" she laughed. "Change is coming, but it all starts with you! Come to the Center. Check it out and don't forget to do your part!"

"Uh, sure." Stuffing the flyer in his pocket, his mind continued to swirl. He tried to convince himself that he had fallen into some portal to the past or an alternate dimension or something. Everything was so oddly perfect and wonderful. Soon, all thoughts of angels and Dark Hours and Rosalyn—and even his brother and why he hadn't contacted him in four months—instantly left him and only one thought remained.

He wanted to go home. He wanted to see his parents.

And he wanted to know what had happened here.

Dras was stunned to see that the white picket fences and white picket people continued well on into the neighborhood where his parents lived. He had always thought Greensboro was a charming place before, but it was like Disney World now.

Despite the shiny new look, however, there was something trembling within him that told him it was all very, very wrong. His general unease turned to paranoia when he glimpsed the Widow Cromwell—his parents' neighbor across the street—out in her yard, and he ducked behind a hedgerow, strangely afraid of the familiar woman. Peering over the bush, he watched as she mindlessly watered one patch of grass, distracted. Stranger still, she kept a finger to her ear and talked to air.

Okay, that's new.

Dras wondered what that was all about, but now was not the time to investigate. He was an escaped convict and had much to do before the deputies with the shotguns came to get him.

It settled like a heavy weight in his gut. He was only here on borrowed time. Now he wanted to see Rosalyn more than ever. If he only had a few hours before he was taken again, he wanted to spend them with her. But right now, he had to see his parents.

With the Widow Cromwell nodding with her finger pressed to her ear, staring off into space as if listening to some inner voice, Dras crept to his parents' back porch. He opened the screen door and the door beyond it, relieved to find it still unlocked.

Maybe some things never changed.

He carefully closed the door as he entered the empty kitchen. He wanted to call out to his parents and run up to his old room and rummage through the fridge and everything else that he had been denied for ten months. However, he was unsure what would await him. He hadn't heard from Jeff or his parents in a long time.

Was his dad even still alive?

They would have told me if something had happened to him, Dras tried to assure himself. But what if they had been prevented from contacting him by the Strange Man, somehow? What if his father was dead? What if he never got the chance to say good-bye?

Tears built in his eyes and Dras crossed the kitchen, eager to cling to something recognizable, some shred of his old life that seemed so long ago and far away. Passing by the pictures on the wall, Dras was struck by images of his past. In a heartbeat he was faced with his entire life, seeing all of his school pictures and the older ones when Jeff was little and Dras was only a baby.

He missed his brother.

There were all the family portraits that Dras found silly and pointless at the time of the taking, but now, he wanted to take just one more. Just one more with Jeff and his mom and his dad, alive and well. The four of them smiling and Jeff worried about his hair and what any potential dates might think and mom gazing at the proofs and commenting on how Dras looked so grown-up in this one or that. He wanted his family back. He wanted *himself* back. Staring into the pictures, he caught a reflection of his face. His eyes were still blue and soft, but his face was different. It was edged, partly because of the steel plates from the re-constructive surgery. Partly because he had lost the baby fat and slimmed down on the prison yard.

Prison. Dras Weldon in prison. What a strange, funny thing to say.

In Wexler, he had focused so intently on surviving, he didn't know who he was anymore. Surely he wasn't the doe-eyed kid who made a joke out of everything. He had grown up.

Am I a man now?

He didn't know. But when he looked at these pictures of a

family he had left behind, Dras realized that it didn't matter right now. The mission didn't matter. The Dark Hour didn't matter.

He was home. *That* was what mattered.

"Dras?"

His mother's voice startled him from his self reflection. She stood in the doorway to the other room, her body trembling. She was crying and Dras wondered how long she had been there, awed at the sight of her lost son come home.

"Mom," he breathed, startled by the sound of his own voice and how it cracked. "Hey."

Louise wailed and enveloped her son in her arms, clinging to him and weeping, her tears staining the shoulder of his shirt, seeping into his neck. He hugged her back, comforting her, realizing how much worry he had put her through.

Holding his mother, feeling how fragile she was in his strong arms and wondering how she had ever found the strength to raise him, Dras looked up and felt his knees grow weak.

Jack Weldon waited for him.

Tears sparkled in the corners of the old man's eyes. Dras had never seen his dad cry.

Most people in Greensboro had a mythic image of Jack Weldon as some super-man of God. Indeed, Jack Weldon's shadow spread far and wide in their community and Dras had spent many years trying to escape it, to make a name for himself apart from his father.

But now…he only wanted to be in the shadow again, where it was safe.

"Dad," he wept.

Louise parted from her son, giving him a chance to be alone with his father. Dras approached his dad, shaking. Seeing his dad here, alive…there was so much he wanted to say to him. So much he wanted to ask him about life and manhood and fishing and old black and white westerns and all the things his dad loved but Dras had never taken the time to share with him. Dras was born later in the old man's life. For almost as long as he could remember, Jack had been too tired to play ball with him or teach him to drive or tell him how to treat a girl. He had missed so much with his dad but now wondered if he could have that all back.

Once the Dark Hour is stopped, I'll have more time, he reminded himself, hearing Christopher in his head.

Yes, he couldn't lose himself in this. He couldn't grow comfortable again.

Things to do. The job's got to get done.

Nevertheless, he walked to his dad and wrapped his arms around him. He was home.

Let the world wait a few more minutes.

"Mom, really, that's enough."

Dras leaned back from the table as Louise swiftly descended, snatching away the empty plates with the remains of the fried chicken, mashed potatoes, sweet peas, and corn on the cob she had made for her newly-returned son.

"Are you sure?" she asked with a whine, her brow crinkled. "I've got an apple pie in the freezer that I could cook for you. I know how you like—"

"*Mom*," Dras chuckled. "It's okay, really. I'm full."

"Okay," she sighed. "Well you let me know if you change your mind."

He nodded and she eagerly cleared her plate and Jack's, stacking them together and carrying them to the sink. She was nearly floating, looking so happy doing something so *normal.* So far they had managed to cook and eat an entire dinner together without talking about the obvious fact that Dras was not in Wexler where he was supposed to be. Instead, they talked about old memories and stories, careful to avoid the present lest they ruin the moment, though Jack barely divulged in the dinner talk. He waited quietly as Louise talked about so and so and that time they did that thing that everyone found so funny. But Dras knew that the ugly truth had to be faced. It was wonderful eating a normal meal with his family, carrying on in mundane conversation, but it was time for business.

Jack rested with his elbows on the table, hands clasped around the better part of a roll that he was still chewing on. The wrinkles around his bright blue eyes gave him an almost magical appearance, like an old wizard in a fairy tale. He had always been a man of few words, but his eyes spoke well.

Right now they were looking straight at Dras. Not condemning or accusing, though Dras had seen that look a good deal growing up. No, now they almost regarded the youngest son as an equal. A man.

It was that confiding look that gave him the courage to begin.

"We have a lot to talk about."

Jack nodded, finishing off a bite. "I suppose we do."

Louise ran water in the sink, as if doing dishes would help her avoid this conversation.

"You in trouble?" Jack asked.

"Yeah. Quite a bit, actually."

Jack pursed his lips in thought, his soft eyes full of a cunning intelligence Dras had never noticed before. "This have something to do with the Strange Man?"

Louise nearly dropped a plate in the sink, but recovered, muttering a soft prayer.

Dras was nearly speechless. "You mean, you know who he is?"

"Oh, yeah. We know all about *him*."

"Well…How much do you know?"

Jack leaned in his chair, failing to hide a grimace, reminding Dras, once again, that his father was a dying man. "He's a demon, by all rights," he replied matter-of-factly. "Your brother isn't convinced he isn't the devil himself, but I don't suppose it matters."

Dras had once thought the same. Talk of the demon nearly overwhelmed him, bringing to mind his horrible encounter last time. Yet, strangely, he had more peace with talking about the devil than the Norman Rockwell painting outside gave him. "So what's up with the town? And your neighbors? The Widow Cromwell across the street seems awfully fond of watering that one patch of grass."

Louise laughed desperately. "She waters her yard *a lot*."

"When it's not her," Jack added, "it's Mr. Bradshaw next door trimming his hedges, even in the dead of winter. And when it's not *him*, it's that bouncy brunette number down the street walking her dog up and down the road."

Dras turned to his father. "They're spies."

"The new mayor's got them thinking they're doing their civic duty, keeping an eye on any potential 'religious terrorists' who might disrupt the status quo."

Dras leaned in, energetic. "Then we need to get to the mayor. We have to convince him that he's working for the Strange Man."

"Oh, Dras," Louise said, sadly, as if he had just fallen off his bike and scraped his knee. "The Strange Man *is* the new mayor."

"Oh."

"Only, he goes by 'John Graves'. Nobody remembered voting for him, though everyone swears they did," Jack said. "It's like some sort of spell and the people don't think about it too much. When he took over, he cleaned the town up, good as new; *better* than new. Men had jobs again, crime rate dropped to near zero, and families are happy. Spring came early and the shine never dulled."

"There's only one rule," Louise said. "They just installed a new curfew at dusk. Never go out after curfew."

"Why not?"

Jack shot him a hard look. "Just don't."

Dras nodded. "Got it."

The kitchen fell quiet for a moment as he let the information sink in. It was a lot to digest, but Christopher and Reid had already given him the crash course in Dark Hour 101, so his father's words were pedestrian compared to ancient dark pagan gods rising to rule the world. Still, he knew it was all connected. It was one giant mess and he was freed from prison to come and help fix it.

He realized how important his job was, and how *crazy* God must be to have chosen him to do it.

But I trust you, God.

War was on the horizon and Dras knew that if anyone would be there, fighting at his side, it would be the ole watchdog. He needed to find him.

"Dad, I need to know. Where's Jeff?"

CHAPTER SIX

HANK LOOKED OUT on the Havenites quietly enjoying their evening. Guards were posted on the perimeter and on the roof, and everyone looked relaxed.

But we're not safe, he reflected. *Not even a little bit.*

"Something on your mind, Hank?" Jeff asked upon approach.

Hank, despite his size, felt very small. "Are we just kidding ourselves out here, thinking that we're doing anyone a bit of good?"

"I think we really are doing good. A lot of people have come through those doors, and with Father Joe's help, we've gotten them to safety."

"But is anywhere really safe? We don't know anything about the Dark Hour, and if the Strange Man wins, what's happened here in Greensboro will light up like wildfire across the state, the country, who knows, maybe even the whole world will be like this."

Jeff joined Hank in surveying the frightened people huddling together inside the crusty four walls of the old church near God's Cliff. "I wish I knew what to tell you, Hank. I wish I could tell you that things were going to work out all right but…I honestly don't know if they really will or not. I *hope* they will and I know God is powerful enough to make it happen…but I don't know if the people will let Him."

"Yeah. That's what I was afraid you'd say."

"I wish Carter were right, you know? We could just load up our guns, hop in the trucks, and raze Greensboro. If I thought that would work, I'd almost consider it, I really would. But God's got a plan. I can just *feel* it, Hank. I know things look dark, but there's something there, something that's going to be our salvation, I just don't know what it is yet. But I'm praying. Isabella's praying. We have to wait for it to happen."

Hank knew that Jeff sincerely believed that. After a lifetime of trying to control his fate, the boy seemed finally able to let go and trust God to do God's business. For his part, Hank too, believed that God was still at work in His people.

But Doris and Becky were miserable hiding out in the woods, and right now, knowing God was in charge did little to comfort the old ex-sheriff.

Hank thought to tell Jeff what was going on with his wife and daughter but the boy had so much else to worry about, he didn't want to bother him with it.

The Havenites' children huddled around Isabella on the floor as she sat in a chair, trying to pay adequate attention to each of them. They fidgeted constantly, all talking to her at once, some standing to be noticed above the other children before Isabella reminded them to sit back down. It was a chaotic, noisy ordeal, but finally, through determination and perspiration, Isabella managed to get them to be still and quiet for a brief twenty seconds.

"Okay, whose turn is it tonight?"

Immediately the children raised their hands and Isabella realized she should've known better than to pose the question. On one of their trips through town, Danny and Hank discovered a slightly trampled children's picture Bible and brought it back with them to camp. The original plan was to leave the book intact, but the overzealous children fought over it until Jeff deemed it best to let each child have a story of his own. To make the most of the situation, Isabella and Jeff decided to have daily "story time", giving the children an opportunity to ask what their particular pictures were about. They had gone through many rotations in story time, but the children all eagerly anticipated hearing about the same old heroes from the Bible and all that they had accomplished with the help of God.

Finally, Timmy Whitaker, a rare generous child, stood up. "It's Chase's turn," he admitted with a sullen expression, obviously disappointed that it wasn't *his* turn instead.

"You know, I think that's right. It *is* Chase's turn."

"Aaawww," came the collective moan from the children as, defeated, they sat cross-legged on the floor. Little Chase, face red from the attention, stood and handed Isabella his picture with both eyes firmly shut. Isabella snickered at his cuteness.

"Thank you, Chase."

The boy quickly retreated and joined the others. Isabella turned the picture over to find a cartoon drawing of a scrawny man with long curly hair swimming away from a giant fish.

"Looks like it's Jonah and the big fish today."

Applause from the children, some of them whispering to others about what a great story this was and how it really was their favorite. Isabella could've sworn that they said that about every story.

"Okay," Isabella took a deep breath, rubbing her hands together and bracing herself, "story of Jonah. Here we go."

All the kids ground into spot, getting nice and cozy, anticipation building in their little faces.

"There was a man named Jonah who lived a long, long time ago. And one day God told Jonah that he wanted him to go to a town called Nineveh and give them a warning. You see, Nineveh was a very bad place—"

"Like Greensboro?" one little girl held up a hand, her eyes wide.

Isabella's heart broke.

"Much worse," she finally said, with a wink for levity. "Nineveh was such a bad place that God was going to punish all the people there."

"Why?"

"Because they were all very, very mean and did a lot of nasty things and God didn't like it," Isabella explained. "But God still loved the mean people and—"

"Why?"

"Because God loves everybody," Isabella quickly answered, hoping to finish her thought. "He wanted Jonah to go and warn the people that if they continued to be bad, they would be punished, but if they stopped doing bad things and started listening to God and being good, then God would forgive them and not punish them. Do any of you remember the scripture we've been reading this week?"

Every hand shot up, and Isabella wondered how many really remembered. She decided to try her luck and picked a boy sitting beside Chase. "Okay, Dustin, what is it? It's first John one-nine, do you remember it?"

Dustin looked to the ceiling, thinking about it, then as he began to pick his nose, he drawled out, "Um…If we…ummm…"

"Confess," Isabella softy urged.

"Yeah, um, confess our sins…he is fateful and just to fagive us our sins and perify us from all un…un…"

"Unrighteousness," she finished.

Dustin nodded, blankly, and Isabella smiled. *Close enough.*

"Now, what does that mean?"

Still picking his nose, Dustin shrugged. "I dunno."

"Does anyone remember what that means?"

Millie was the only one who raised her hand this time and Isabella wasn't surprised. There was something special about the kindergartener, a maturity beyond her years. It was why she was Isabella's favorite student.

"Okay, Millie, what does it mean?"

She stood, all-business. "It means that if we are sorry for doing bad things and ask Mr. God to help us to be good instead, then He won't be mad anymore."

"That's right," Isabella encouraged as Millie sat. "God loves all of us and when we do bad things, it makes Him cry. He doesn't like to see how much we hurt each other. So, sometimes, He has to punish us so we won't do it anymore, but God hates to punish us. That's why he wanted Jonah to tell the people that they needed to stop being bad, but Jonah didn't want to go."

"Why didn't he want to go to Ninny-vuh?"

"Was he afraid?"

"Eh…a little, I guess. Like I said, Nineveh was a bad place, but Jonah really didn't want to go because he didn't *like* the people in Nineveh. He thought that they *deserved* to be punished and he didn't want to help them. He knew that if he went and the people listened to him and told God they were sorry, then, like Millie said, God wouldn't be mad anymore and he wouldn't hurt Nineveh. So Jonah decided that he would try and run away and hide from God so that God wouldn't make him go."

"That's when he went on the ship!"

"That's right. He got on a ship that went out to sea but God knew where he was hiding so God made this huge storm," Isabella swirled her arms wide, capturing imaginations, "and the boat was rocking back and forth and the crew of the ship knew that all of this was happening because God was mad at Jonah. So they threw Jonah overboard and into the water!"

"Ooooh."

"And when he fell in the water, this big fish came and swallowed him up!"

The kids started wiggling, recognizing this as their favorite part—the *exciting* part.

"Jonah stayed alive in the fish's stomach for three days! While Jonah was in there, he realized that he was being bad like the people in Nineveh because he didn't want to do the right thing and help people. He knew that he was being punished and he told God that he was sorry. He told God that he would go to Nineveh and warn the people so that they could be saved. And, immediately, the fish spit Jonah out and he was covered in slime and all kinds of gross things!"

"Ewww!" the kids squealed, looking to each other with scrunched up faces and stuck-out tongues. Isabella laughed.

"But Jonah learned his lesson. He went to Nineveh and told them that God was very mad at them, but that He still loved them, and if they said they were sorry and stopped being bad, God would forgive them."

The kids started cheering and clapping, getting the attention of most of the adults spread throughout the church. Isabella had to speak louder to be heard by her young students as she said, "Now the lesson of the story is that God loves everyone and we should too. No matter how bad they are, people still need our help."

"Even Shamblers?"

Instantly, the whole church fell silent. All warmth left Isabella's face as she looked to the little girl who had posed the difficult question.

Chelsea Ross. Carter's daughter.

Isabella realized that the adults were looking at her now too. Even Jeff and Hank had stopped to watch her reaction. Off to the side, waiting expectantly with arms crossed, stood Carter, himself.

"Well," Isabella began, knowing the truth in her heart but wondering how well it would go over. "Yes, Chelsea. Even Shamblers."

"But my daddy said Shamblers are monsters," Chelsea retorted automatically.

Isabella looked up and saw Carter, face like ice.

"The devil and his demons are the only *real* monsters, Chelsea. The Shamblers were people once…and they could be again. They just need our help."

"You don't know that," Carter said from across the room, startling everyone.

Isabella met his accusing stare head on. "We can hope, Carter."

Danny watched the confrontation and felt the tension in the room. He stood by the security monitors with Sarah, keeping a lookout on the setting sun through the video feed, hoping for something to distract him from the uncomfortable situation. Jeff stepped between Isabella and Carter. "We don't know enough about the Shamblers to make any kind of judgment call but we *can* hope that there's a way to save them. If we work together, maybe we can figure it out."

Isabella walked off, upset. Carter let out a "hmph" and said, "Come on, Chelsea." The little girl left the group and rejoined her father and Danny watched as Jeff followed after Isabella.

What's with her anyway? Danny wondered. She seemed touchy lately and Isabella was usually made of steel.

"Wow," Sarah muttered beside him, turning back to the monitors as everyone else within the Haven's walls tried to look busy and less nosy. "Talk about cabin fever."

Danny stared at the boring security monitors. "I don't think we'll be able to keep this up much longer."

Sarah awkwardly brushed a handful of dark hair behind her ear. "I heard a lot more people are going to be going with Father Joe this trip. A lot of people just want out of here."

"Do you?" Danny asked without looking at her.

"What? *Me* leave? Ha, I wish! This place would fall apart without me. Let's face it, handsome, you couldn't run this system even if I left you the manual."

He shrugged, distant. "Whatever."

Sarah waited for Danny to laugh or to pick up on the fact that she had called him "handsome" but he did neither of those things. "Unless," she began, her smile fading, "You think this place won't be around much longer. Well?"

Danny finally turned to her, confused. "Well, what?"

"Is that a possibility? Do you think we'll just close up the doors and leave town?"

He chuckled, grim. "You obviously don't know Jeff."

Sarah frowned. No, she didn't. Not really. She didn't really know any of them very well.

Though she was trying *desperately* to get to know one Danny Carpenter.

"Still, though," she said, "I think people are going to have to decide for themselves why they stay out here, you know? I think a lot of people just wanted to stay until the town fixed itself so that they could move back home, but I don't think that's going to be happening. Any time soon, at least. We could be out here for a year, or longer, for all we know."

"No," Danny breathed. "We won't. Good or bad, this is going to end real soon." His jaw tensing, he finished, "I can feel it."

He is so dark, Sarah marveled. *So cocky and arrogant when Jeff is around, but alone…he's so vulnerable. So scared.*

Sarah wanted to say something along the lines of "I'll take care of you" or "I'll stay with you" or something equally heartfelt and sentimental, but there was no time.

She saw a shadow pass by the camera.

"Whoa," she gasped. "Did you see that?"

"See what?" Danny grumbled.

She pointed at the monitor and, at just that moment, the same shadow moved across a different screen. "There."

"Could just be a guard."

She shook her locks, her heart picking up, and cycled through a few different views, noting three guards walking the edges of the grounds, minding their own business.

"No," Sarah said. "That's something else."

"Sun just went down." Danny looked to her. "Shambler?"

"We haven't had one this close in a month."

"Let's keep it that way."

He nodded to her, giving her a silent order, as he left to get Jeff. Sarah swallowed hard and, after seeing the shape pass out of sight again, hit the alarm.

WHIIIRRR!

At the sound of the siren, Jeff and Isabella emerged from one of the classrooms, meeting Danny.

"We have a problem," he reported.

"Everybody in the back!" Hank yelled.

The schoolchildren shrieked and Sarah watched as Isabella hurried them all into a group. Parents rushed in a panic to collect their children like little hens.

"Stay together," Isabella hollered to the kids, sounding calm under duress.

But everyone knew what the siren meant. *Shamblers.* Sarah

waited by the monitors, shaking. Tears were shed and people exclaimed in fright as the alarm blared. Jeff and Danny returned to Sarah at the security station, leaning over the keyboard, closely observing the monitors. Danny yanked the microphone. "Yo, Red One! Where you at?"

"How many?" Jeff muttered to Sarah.

She kept her voice even, trying to stay cool. "Just one, I think."

A hefty man with a rifle stepped into view of the out-of-date black and white security camera, his face pale, even in the grayscale. "We don't see anything."

Jeff cut his eyes to Danny. "Day-Lights."

Danny switched frequencies. "Hey, you guys up there awake? Hit the lights already!"

The hum of the engine roaring to life thundered above and the monitors immediately lit up in bright white. The hefty man hurried off, shouting something to another guard off-camera. Sarah continued to shuffle through the camera views, trying to spot the intruder.

People raced to their pre-designated lookouts and safety holes. Isabella and a few parents hustled the children to a back room adjacent to a makeshift infirmary. Isabella threw open the door and scooted the weeping kids inside. The parents too, most of them women, looked beside themselves with anxiety. But Isabella knew there was still one person she could count on.

"Millie," she commanded. "Pray."

Millie, the only child not crying, nodded solemnly as Isabella gave her a reaffirming nod. "All right," the girl said with authority. "Pray after me." Without waiting for the others to get in line, she shut her eyes tight. "Dear Mr. God…"

"Dear Mr. God," the other children began, and soon the parents joined in.

Leaving them on their own, Isabella pushed her way through the crowd, finding her husband. "How bad is it?"

Jeff bit at his thumbnail. “Sarah thinks only one. We can’t find it, though.”

Behind him, Danny shouted more orders to the men on the grounds via the mic, but took a moment to offer Jeff a frustrated shrug.

Jeff tensed. “Maybe the Day-Lights scared it off.”

Danny replied, “Or maybe he has friends and they’re planning something.”

“They’re getting bolder,” Isabella said.

Carter marched for the group, cocking a shotgun with might. “Because we’re nearing the end and they can feel it. Why can’t you?”

Jeff remained focused on the screens, grinding his teeth.

“Permission to open fire on the intruder, *sir*,” Carter said, then turned to Isabella, hateful, “Or do you want me to just preach to it? Maybe give it a big hug?”

Isabella ignored the man, forcing herself to study the monitors too, lest she lose her temper. Jeff faced down Carter. “Line up at the door. If they get in, do what you can.”

Carter hurried off, shouting to his men, already standing by with guns and hopeful faces. “All right, boys! Line up! This is not a drill. It may take every round you’ve got, but don’t stop until that thing ain’t moving. Those gremlins might be bulletproof, but a Shambler ain’t! They’re tough, but we’ve hurt ’em before!”

The men hurried to form a line of defense as the last of the Havenites found their hiding places. Isabella mumbled to Jeff, “You sure that was smart?”

He didn’t respond.

“There! There!” Sarah jumped, gesturing at the security panel. “I saw it again! There’s just one!”

“Day-Lights, shine on the second quadrant!” Danny barked into the mic.

The yard illuminated just as the shadow passed again, stealing around a corner, followed by three heavyset men, trying to keep up.

“They’ll get him,” Jeff said shakily as he and Isabella watched

Carter's line. The men eyed the door with bated breath, sweat trickling down their foreheads, trigger fingers flexing.

"Steady," Carter muttered to his men.

He's finally got some action, Isabella grimaced. She turned back to the monitors. *God help us.*

Hank returned, out of breath. "That's the last of it. Everyone's tucked away. We've got a clear path to the woods, if it comes to that. We can make a run for it."

"Let's hope it doesn't come to that," Jeff said tersely. "I'd rather not take our chances in the North Woods, especially at night."

"What do you want me to do now?" Hank asked.

"He's on the other side!" Danny shouted over the radio, flustered. "Where *are* you guys? Come on!"

"You want to send more men out there?" Hank again.

"Too dangerous. We wait."

Suddenly a gunshot outside split the quiet of the church and everyone jumped. Carter leaned into his weapon, locking it tight against his shoulder. "All right, boys. Here we go."

Jeff turned to Isabella, fear and doubt in his eyes. She knew what he was thinking. *Have I done the right thing bringing all these people out here? Or are we all going to die?*

Isabella wondered that same thing every day.

She took his hand and a deep breath.

Sarah jolted again, as if a mouse just ran across her foot. "He's still out there! They didn't hit him!"

Danny rolled his eyes and threw down the radio. "That's it," he snapped. "I'm going out there."

"No," Jeff ordered.

There was a sudden knock at the front door. Everyone froze.

Knock.

A thick, heavy beating.

Knock.

Pounding.

KNOCK. KNOCK.

"Jeff—" Isabella whispered.

Carter laughed, nearly giddy with anticipation. "Get ready," he said, getting a better grip on his shotgun. The other men did the same.

Banging on the door, then a soft, slow, agonizing *creeeeaaak.*

Isabella held her hand to her mouth to conceal a gasp. *They're coming through.*

Then Dras Weldon appeared in the doorway.

Carter took quick aim, locking and loading, and Jeff must have realized the truth of the situation in a split second. He ran for the frontline, screaming, "No! *Wait!*"

But it was too late. Carter pulled the trigger.

CHAPTER SEVEN

ALL AT ONCE, the worst moment in Jeff's life replayed in his mind's eye. He saw his brother horrendously beaten by Deputy Ryan Stevenson and the corrupt deputies on the Committee's payroll. Jeff watched, helplessly pinned to the floor by police, as his brother's hair was pulled loose and his face was kicked in and his teeth were knocked out and his skull was literally broken. Jeff had screamed, horrible, tortured screams that he would never have thought could emerge from a man, let alone himself. But they had.

And they did again.

"*Stop!*" he cried.

Dras was back, and the front line was opening fire.

"*STOP!*" Jeff screamed at the top of his lungs as the rifles went off, splintering wood, sending fragments and dust everywhere. Unable to be heard over the report of the guns, Jeff broke through the ranks of gung-ho hunters, jerking the shotgun out of Carter's hand. "Stop it! That's enough!"

"What are you doing?" Carter barked as his men lowered their weapons, their faces aglow with bloodthirst.

Jeff pushed past Carter and hurried towards the front door.

"Dras? *Dras!*"

The Havenites rustled from their hiding places, returning to the sanctuary to see if the "Shambler" was dead as Jeff edged closer to the door, fearing what he would find outside.

Before he could reach the entrance, a white T-shirt wrapped around a broken stick waved slowly in front of the open doorway, followed closely by a pair of bright baby blue eyes.

"I give up," Dras squeaked from outside.

A grin split Jeff's tear-soaked face as Dras, shirtless and

otherwise unscathed, stepped into view. At last, the outside guards came huffing and puffing behind him.

"It's okay," Jeff explained, watching a look of disappointment cross their faces as they had missed all the excitement.

Dras carefully walked into the church, taken aback by all of the eyeballs in dirty faces gawking at him. As if realizing his partial nudity, he threw his shirt on and found Jeff's face in the crowd.

"Did I come through the right door?" he asked sheepishly, still looking at all the strangers in the room.

Jeff laughed, stepping closer to his long-lost brother. "We thought you were someone else."

"Wow," he chuckled. "I feel sorry for that guy."

"Dras…"

"Hey, big brother."

The two men edged into each other, Jeff hardly able to believe this moment was really happening. He threw his arms around Dras, releasing a hearty laugh and sob all at the same time. Isabella cried and rushed to the brothers. She swallowed Dras in a hug, holding him close. The three Weldons laughed and cried and touched faces and patted arms and anything else they could to feel close to each other again.

Danny, meanwhile, frowned and leaned aside to Hank. "Is that—?"

"Yep," Hank said.

Danny slumped.

Jeff gave Dras another firm hug before forcing himself away, feeling the curious stares of the Havenites. Dras surveyed the crowd. His casual observation soon turned to intent examination, a smile on his face growing wider and wider.

"Where is she?" he asked.

Jeff froze. He knew who he meant. Isabella turned to Jeff, her face flushed.

"Uh..." Jeff began, but didn't have the heart to continue.

Dras pushed past his brother. "Rosalyn?" he called, laughing. "Hey? Where are you?"

"Dras," Jeff stopped him.

His laugh wavered. Dras turned to his brother, his nose wrinkling, and forced a chuckle. "Where's Rosalyn? Where is she?"

Jeff took a deep breath. "We need to talk."

The last of the setting sun's fading light shimmered on the MYERS grave as twilight fell. Alone in a spot of tall grass on the edge of an unkempt cemetery in Trysdale, the headstone had not seen many visitors. It rested quietly, facing the east, waiting for the Lord to come and take the buried away in His coming.

That is, if the Lord would claim the buried as His own.

Rosalyn had to admit she didn't know if the Lord would return for her dad. Kneeling before her father's tombstone, she brushed her fingers against his name—JOHN PAUL MYERS—wiping away the grit and dirt that had settled there over the years. Rosalyn Myers' father committed suicide when she was twelve. Seven months ago she finally learned why. Her mother had been unfaithful in marriage, and Paul couldn't handle the betrayal. Death seemed the only way to escape the pain.

If the movies were to be believed, anyone who committed suicide was sent straight to hell, no questions asked. But Jack Weldon—she almost smiled at the thought of him—Jack Weldon had told her differently. He read the Scriptures of the Lord's promise to keep and forgive His own. She supposed there was a chance that her father was somewhere in heaven, finally away from that which drove him to death. But she didn't know if her dad even believed in God in the first place.

She couldn't answer for him. Only for herself.

If only you could see me now, she thought to her dead father.

And what a sight Rosalyn had become. She had lost ten pounds, and her lovely curves, along with her youthful glow, were gone.

These days the mirror showed how sickly she looked, the dark makeup she wore only bringing out the paleness in her skin. She'd colored her long, kinky locks variations of blues and reds, hiding their natural auburn shade. Tight leather clothes clung to her gaunt frame.

I look more like him every day, she knew. No, not her father. Not Paul. Her *new* "father". Her lover. Her provider. Her everything. The Strange Man.

She had given up everything for him. Her friends, her family, her job at Larrezo's, any hope of returning to college and finishing what she had started. It was all gone. She took one bite of the fruit he offered her seven months ago and Rosalyn Myers—the girl who used to laugh and dance and sing and goof around—was dead. Drowned in that black goop. In her wake was a new Rosalyn. Sleek and scary, she followed behind the Strange Man, answering to his every whim, no matter the cost.

Even now, his brand was visible on the small of her back, just above the waistband of her low-rider leather pants. The mark of the sun, the same one the Committee wore. She was his property, never to wander or stray. *Forever his.*

Grimly, she pulled her hand away from the cold stone of her father's grave and spoke aloud to him, hoping that, if his spirit were in heaven, God allowed long distance calls from time to time. "Hey, Dad. It's me. I know I haven't been by to see you in awhile. A lot's been going on and I just haven't…been able to." Rosalyn fidgeted with her thin fingers, absently chipping away at the black fingernail polish, wondering if her father would have yelled at her for wearing such trashy makeup. "I wish you were still here. I guess I…I wish I knew why you did it, you know? Why you killed yourself…what was it? I mean, I know about Mom, but…What made you get the gun? Why did you take it that far? Because…" she put her hands down and looked around at the trees waving at her with their full, green leaves. The sky was a deepening dark blue and, this far away from Greensboro Park Lake, she could still hear a few naïve birds singing. The world was still alive and she didn't know how it could be after all that had happened.

Looking back to the stone, she forbade herself to shed a tear. "…things are really bad here, Dad. I've done…I'm not who I used to be and I don't know what to do to fix it and I'm starting to think that maybe—"

Maybe what? Maybe Dad wasn't so wrong?

The blare of the car horn startled her. A sleek black limousine parked on the outskirts of the burial ground, and a very familiar driver stepped out to open the back door.

The gentleman driver kindly proclaimed over the grassy gulf, "Mr. Simms would like a word with you."

Rosalyn frowned. She turned back to the grave, softer. "I'd better go, Dad." Her smile faded. "I'll see you soon."

Elderly Mr. Simms waited patiently in the back of the limousine as Rosalyn trudged through the tall weeds of the Trysdale Community Cemetery. The dark girl gave a nod to the driver and entered the car, flopping down on the plush leather seat and planting her dirty Army boots adjacent to Mr. Simms.

"Let me guess. *He* sent you?" she growled.

Mr. Simms smiled coyly as the driver sat behind the wheel and began the trek back into haunted Greensboro.

"Mr. Graves has been worried about you. You've been gone all morning."

Rosalyn snickered at the dapper old man. "*Me*, gone? What about you and Gibson? Hadn't heard from you in a couple days. Where were you guys anyway?"

"Last time I checked, the Committee did not answer to 'the girlfriend'."

Rosalyn leaned back in her seat, relaxing. She didn't really care where Simms and Gibson had gone. *Let them run their top-secret errands. I've got my own crap to deal with.*

"Your friends were quite busy last night," Simms began.

Rosalyn stared out the window at the passing countryside. "They're not my friends. Not anymore."

"We've had some reports that they managed to infect another

family with their propaganda and escaped from town right beneath our noses."

Unable to resist, Rosalyn grinned warmly. "Jeff never knows when to quit."

"Nevertheless," Simms replied curtly, "his crusade is useless. The Ancient One is returning as we speak. The world is about to fall into darkness and there will be nothing that the former Reverend can do about it."

Rosalyn watched the trees blurring by the side window of the limousine—watched them become progressively thinner and frailer—as they made their way into Greensboro. In her stomach she felt a sick pull, the same uncomfortable sensation she experienced every time she re-entered the city limits. She was bound here. She had sold her soul to leave this stupid town and now she was more entrenched here than ever before. She was now part of the disease. Part of the Evil.

Rosalyn shivered, rubbing the goosebumps on her arm. As they entered Greensboro proper, slowly rolling down its Main Street, Rosalyn looked into the passing faces of the cold, soulless people who populated the business district, shutting down for the curfew. Their eyes were utterly empty, and worse yet, none of them seemed to notice as they shopped and carried on.

Maybe they're the lucky ones. She bit her lip. "They have no idea, do they?"

Simms followed her gaze and remained indifferent, as if they were only dumb cattle and not worthy of his compassion. "They don't know because they choose not to."

"Maybe they didn't have the chance."

But what's your excuse, Rosalyn? You had the chance and you screwed up anyway.

Simms sighed, like the conversation was already more than those beyond the glass of the limousine deserved. "The Christians' God has given them plenty of chances. They like stumbling in the dark. As long as they remain ignorant, they can live however their wicked hearts desire and not accept any responsibility." Then, with a cruel grin, he craned to leer at her. "Isn't that why *you* choose not to believe?"

Rosalyn could feel his hateful eyes on her and turned to meet his glare head on. "I believe in God." She looked back out at the hell her home had become. "I just don't like Him."

The all-too familiar storefronts of Greensboro's East Side District passed across the window until the limousine slowed to a halt in front of The Rave Scene. Rosalyn looked at the building, disturbed. It had been her sanctuary just a few months earlier. A place where she and…

They used to come here together. Laugh and dance and party. But that was then. Grim, Rosalyn opened the car door and stepped out. Pausing briefly, she turned to the old man behind her. "You comin'?"

Simms said, "I believe I have other matters to attend to. *Committee* matters. Tell Mr. Graves I will make a full report."

Rosalyn shrugged. "Yeah. Whatever."

Simms watched the girl march to the front door of The Rave Scene and vanish inside. At this hour of the evening, the place would be gearing up for another night of debauchery, as the lost children would come out to pay homage to their dark god of pleasure, here, where the curfew held no power.

As Rosalyn disappeared inside the club, Simms nodded darkly to the driver. The driver returned the sentiment and pulled away from the curb as Simms grabbed a cell phone and dialed. "It's me. Yes, I'm alone…Alert the others. We must meet."

Rosalyn climbed the stairs to the Man's private office inside the dance club, dreading the visit already. At the top of the stairs, standing guard outside the office door, stood Deputy Roy Miller. She didn't know many of the deputies very well, but Miller was one of Stevenson's go-to guys. He mostly kept to himself, but the other men seemed to fall in behind him. Miller briefly glanced her way, then purposefully turned to look at the club below. Rosalyn felt a pang of shame, as even the bad guys didn't want anything to do with her. But Miller was odd like that, following orders, but with a decidedly morose set to his jaw.

He doesn't want this. He's just trying to stay on the Man's good side.

Aren't we all.

For now, she stowed her regrets and put on her best sinister grin, just like Big Daddy wanted. She left Miller behind, pushed open the door, and entered the office. Behind the immaculate mahogany desk a leather seat creaked as its occupant stood to his full stature. He dressed in an expensive suit, with his designer silk shirt carelessly untucked and hanging down past his coat. His collar was pulled up, giving him an air of rebelliousness. On his fingers sparkled rings of various shapes, sizes, and colors, all radiant and exuding his wealth. Around his neck hung a single pendant, in the shape of a sun—just like her brand—resting on his tanned chest. With curly dark hair and deep-set eyes, the man was beautiful and alluring in every way. He smiled boyishly, twinkling with mischief, brightening at the sight of the woman entering his office.

"Ah, there's my girl!" The Strange Man held out his arms. "Come give Daddy a kiss!"

Next to the Strange Man, she spotted a large brute with steely eyes, dark hair and beard, and a crescent-shaped scar under his left eye that Jeff gave him some months back. Seeing Rosalyn, the towering giant grimaced and set his large hands on his hips.

"Hey, Stevenson," Rosalyn made a point to address the man and sound as venomous as possible.

"That's '*Sheriff* Stevenson', to you, girlie."

Rosalyn ignored him, hopping into the Strange Man's arms, wrapping her legs around his waist, and pulling him in for a full, wet kiss.

It disgusted her.

When at last the kiss ended, the two lovers parted and the Strange Man grinned, satisfied. "Now that's the kind of sugar Papa likes."

"Miss me, Big Daddy?" she cooed, sliding down him and onto her own two feet.

He placed a melodramatic hand to his chest and closed his eyes, as if reciting poetry. "Ne'er did a moment pass that I thought not of your sweet face."

"Gimme a break," Stevenson huffed under his breath.

Rosalyn moved around the desk and flopped down in the Strange Man's chair, leaning back comfortably, and resting her Army boots on his desk. "So," she began, folding her hands in her lap, "what's up?"

The Strange Man raised a reprimanding finger and shook it politely. "Ah, ah, sweetie. You know we don't put our muddy boots on Daddy's desk."

The comfortable moment broken, Rosalyn frowned. She removed her feet and sat straighter. The Strange Man nodded approval and went back to business. "The good sheriff was just telling me the latest effort of Reverend Weldon to convert the masses."

Rosalyn's smile flickered, but held. "Yeah?"

Stevenson spoke up, hoping to win a gold star or something. "We think they've moved out of town and are hiding somewhere in the North Woods, which—"

"Which just gives us miles and miles of uncharted backroads," Rosalyn interrupted, grinning sarcastically. "Good job, Stevenson. I can see why they made you sheriff. With brains like that, I'm surprised you haven't found them already."

The sheriff clenched his fists. "Keep it up. One day I'm gonna shut that smart mouth for good."

"Now, now, children," the Strange Man chuckled, then held a hand to his cheek to fake-whisper an aside to Stevenson. "A pistol, isn't she?"

Rosalyn cocked her eyebrows at the sheriff, daring him to make a move against her. Knowing that it was a lost cause, Stevenson finally gave in and asked, "Sir? What should I do?"

"Nothing," the Strange Man said. "We'll send my new pet monster."

Stevenson glowered. "I don't trust that freak. He's too unpredictable. Last time you let him out, it took us days to catch him again."

"So?"

"He made it as far as Highway 65. That's where the old road hits the new highway. Your little *pet* is trying to get out of town. If that happens, we'll never be able to get him back."

The Strange Man waved off the notion and moved to sit on his desk. Rosalyn leaned forward and he stroked her hair like a kitten's. "I wouldn't worry about that. By this time next week we'll have a whole town full of those things, and then we'll be deemed worthy and my Master will return to the Earth and—"

"And we'll live happily ever after," Rosalyn finished with a smile.

The Strange Man looked down to her, his sneer broadening. "That's my girl."

Suddenly, a single gremlin emerged from the shadows of the swanky office and skittered across the floor, scurrying up the Strange Man's arm to whisper something in his attentive ear. After the gremlin finished its secretive report, it scuttled back into the darkness.

The Strange Man darkened, all previous mirth wiped from his face. His eyes grew thoughtful and he was very, very quiet.

Not something he was prone to being.

"What is it?" Rosalyn ventured. "What did it want?"

The Strange Man sucked in a deep, dramatic breath, as if breaking the news to his two lieutenants would be heartbreaking. "The Committee has turned against me, it seems. They're planning a meeting. Tonight."

"Why?" Stevenson asked, feigning concern for his master, yet Rosalyn knew he was secretly hoping that the old geezers were close to their goal. Stevenson had his eye on running the show.

The Strange Man turned to the sheriff. "They've been plotting against me. I've known for awhile now. They've been holding little clandestine meetings, discussing how they might...*do away* with me. Can you believe it? Is that really all they think of me? That I'm just some kind of pest that can be exterminated? They have no idea." He slumped, turning away. "None of you do."

Rosalyn edged closer. "What are you going to do?"

He didn't face her. "They have outlived their usefulness to me. They must be disciplined for this action."

Stevenson jutted his chin. "I'll handle it, sir."

"No," the monster croaked, and Stevenson balked, as if slapped in the face.

"What?"

"Rosalyn will deal with them."

She stared back numbly. "W-What?"

"But—" Stevenson made to interject, but Rosalyn stood, cutting him off and facing the Strange Man.

"But I've never...Busting a few noses is one thing. I'm your girl, there, but I don't know if I can—"

The Strange Man pouted, as if coddling a small child. He reached for her with his immaculate hands, cupping her face and stroking the blue strands of hair away from her eyes. "Ooh...I know it's asking a lot, princess. But I don't trust Stevenson to do the job and not negotiate with them instead."

Stevenson's face flushed, his secret motives revealed, and he pleaded, "I'd *never* do that."

The Strange Man turned to face him, eyes glowing. "Remove yourself from my sight before I remove your wagging, lying tongue."

Stevenson made no protest. He just left.

The Strange Man waited for the unwanted company to empty out of the room before he turned back to petting his prized possession.

"I don't want to do this," Rosalyn said, trying not to cry.

"I know, I know," he sang to her. "But we've talked about this. How are you going to be able to truly take your place at my side if you're not willing to do what's asked of you?"

Why did I ever listen to you? she asked herself, blinking back tears of rage. *What did you ever say to me that sounded so good that I'd turn my back on everyone I ever loved?*

"We have enough to worry about with Jeff Weldon trying to ruin our plans," the Man encouraged in a relaxed tone she'd never heard him use with Stevenson. It was all a trick, she knew. Just a lie to make her feel special, like she mattered to him. "We can't have conflict from within, dear. The work is too important and the Dark Hour requires many things of us. It's *so close*, don't you understand? And I promise you," he kissed her forehead delicately, then pulled back so she could meet his soulless eyes, "before long, there will be no more need for sacrifices. When my Master comes, all will be taken care of and you'll be *free*."

I'll never be free of you.

Hanging her head, trying to steel her resolve, she muttered, "Okay."

"Okay? Wonderful!"

She moved past him, heading for the door, wondering how she was ever going to find the strength to kill a man. No, not just one. *The entire Committee*. She wanted to throw up. *Am I really doing this? Am I really going to take a life?* Reaching for the doorknob, she felt her eyes stinging, but was yanked from her thoughts when the Strange Man called, "Oh, Rosalyn?"

She wiped the few escaping tears from her cheek and turned back to face him. "Yeah?"

"Bring me back some ice cream on your way home, will you? Rocky Road, though. None of that fruity stuff like last time, okay?"

Straining, she forced a grin. "Okay."

"Excellent. Make me proud, princess."

"I always do, Big Daddy."

CHAPTER EIGHT

HUDDLED AROUND A lonely oil drum underneath the 12th Street Overpass, Mr. Gibson, Mr. Simms, and Mr. Nigel waited in silence. All their planning came down to tonight. Ever since the Strange Man murdered their leader, Mayor Richard Hayden, before their very eyes, Jarvis Gibson knew that their lives and allegiance meant nothing to the monster. They were only cogs in his master plan and none of them were safe.

The light of the fire danced across the grim faces of the old men looking into the flame, casting writhing shadows behind them on the overpass walls. The mood was solemn and Gibson reasoned each man was considering the works of his hands, wondering if he had done enough. Wondering if their plan would work and the Strange Man would finally die.

The sound of a small puddle splashing behind them surprised Gibson, and he and the others swiveled to see one of their own.

"Jacobson," Gibson exclaimed harshly. "You nearly gave us our final fright."

Newt Jacobson emerged from the shadow, just as stone-faced and resolved as each of his kin.

Tom Simms stepped forward. "Do you have it?"

Jacobson reached within his coat and pulled out a wrapped package. He held it out to Mr. Simms with a dark, pained expression, as if glad to be rid of the thing. "Of course."

Simms took the package and hurriedly unwrapped it, revealing a book. He looked at the thing in his hands with a scrutinizing stare, before glancing to Jacobson. "And?"

Jacobson rubbed his eyes and moved closer to the fire, no doubt to find some solace from Greensboro's unnaturally cold winds. "I've read it all afternoon and evening and have come to nothing."

Gibson stepped in, now, very confused by the book in Simms' hand. "I don't understand. What is this?"

Simms looked to Jacobson, then to Nigel, and Gibson realized that he alone was perplexed. "What have you been hiding from me?"

Jacobson answered tiredly. "Nothing of much importance, as it turns out."

Simms explained, "This is a diary, Jarvis. Ray McCormick's diary. Caroline found it after Ray's unfortunate death." Simms handed the diary to Gibson, who took it eagerly and began flipping through it.

"She was startled by what she found within its latter pages."

Gibson quickly thumbed towards the end of the diary and, indeed, was stunned himself. There were horrible pictures; charcoal scribblings of monsters along with the muddled and confused babblings of a madman. Words were repeated over and over, written in a circle, spiraling down. Creatures and demons, mouths dripping with gore, and eyes—too many to count—blinking back at the reader without sympathy but possessing great intelligence, even for a crude drawing.

Gibson quickly closed the book, unable to bear any more. Now he knew why Jacobson looked so sallow.

Simms continued, "We know that, in his last days, Ray was consumed by the 'virus' that was introduced into Greensboro Park Lake. We had hoped that by reading his writings, we might better understand his ailment and maybe even discover a cure." Simms inhaled. "We've all lost many to this…disease. *Too* many."

Gibson turned to Jacobson, hopeful. "Well, Jacobson? Did you find anything?"

The man only shook his head.

Gibson flailed, agitated. "*This* was your plan? You said that you had found something, but…*this*? Why wasn't I told?"

"It was a hollow hope, Jarvis," Mr. Nigel snarled. "Let it go."

Gibson fumed, storming up to him. "I will not! Don't you understand what I hold here? First person account of the terrible darkness that has shadowed our people! There must be something here, buried underneath the babbling, that is of value. I'm sure of it!"

"I told you," Jacobson reported, "There's nothing there but the ravings of a lunatic. It's gibberish. He was out of his mind, writing about nonsensical nightmares."

"What about Caroline?" Gibson's voice broke. "We could ask her. Surely she could better elaborate on her husband's condition."

"Caroline will be of no use to us now." Jacobson shot Simms a guilty look. Gibson saw the blood dotting the rag that covered the book and finally understood.

He backed away from his old friends as if they were a pack of hungry jackals.

"My God…" he breathed, aghast. "My God, what have we done to ourselves?"

"What we had to, to survive," Simms informed without emotion.

"No." Gibson shook his head, his heart breaking for Caroline McCormick. He had grown up with her. Attended church with her. Before he became Superintendent, he had been the principal of the elementary school and Caroline's daughter, little Lindsey McCormick, always brought him her mother's fresh baked cookies just before Christmas.

And now the woman was dead. The entire McCormick family was.

"No," he said again, fueled by righteous anger. "We could have sought another way. We could have—"

"Careful, Jarvis," Nigel warned, displeased.

Jacobson drawled in exhaustion, "We've already tried to remove the Strange Man by force."

"We could have gone to Jeff!"

The three Committee members turned on Gibson, enraged. "How dare you speak that name out here in the night!" Simms became uncharacteristically alive, throwing surreptitious glances over his shoulder.

"You know where they are." Gibson pointed at him. "We all know. We always have! We've only kept the secret to ourselves in case it proved to be useful. And now it *has*!"

Simms raced towards the thin man, raising a trembling fist, preparing to strike. Gibson stood his ground, unafraid of the attack and believing he deserved it for all that he had been party to. Yet, it was Jacobson who held back the older man. "No, Tom. We can't turn on each other now. We have to stay united. It's all we have left."

Simms cooled. Gibson's shoulders relaxed, though he still fumed. Nigel, meanwhile, stood by the fire, always the sort who preferred not to get involved in anyone's personal affairs.

Looking like the tired old man he really was, Simms turned from Gibson and lumbered back to the oil drum fire. Jacobson's gaze remained on Gibson for a moment, seeing that the would-be insurrectionist still held the diary in his shaky hands. "As for the book," Jacobson addressed the gathered, though locked eyes with Gibson, "it's useless and unnecessary. We will find another way and we have no need to involve…*other persons* who shall now and forevermore remain nameless. Agreed?"

Simms stared unblinking into the flame. "Agreed."

Nigel huffed and hugged his arms together, rubbing them by the fire. "Of course, I agree. I don't know why we have to have such squabbling anyway."

Jacobson turned back to Gibson, who remained silent. Jacobson nodded, relieved. "I take that as a 'yes', then. Maybe now we can let the topic sleep."

There was a horrible clatter as a nearby trashcan careened across the pavement. The four men turned in their places and Gibson's eyes widened in dark realization as he saw—

"A gremlin!"

One of the Strange Man's wicked little spies cackled as it hurried into the darkness.

"Catch him!" Simms cried, animated once more, breaking into a run. "If he reports back to his master—!"

But he didn't have to finish the statement. Everyone knew what would happen.

The four ran after the beast, huffing as the gleeful little monster bounded off walls and trashcans.

"Hurry!"

They followed the gremlin under the overpass and watched as it disappeared behind a stone pillar.

"There!"

They rounded the corner to catch their impish prey, but instead found the gremlin perched on the shoulder of a dark figure.

Rosalyn Myers stepped into the light, backed by the twitching, snickering shadows, and smiled.

"Evening, fellas."

CHAPTER NINE

"NO," DRAS SAID again, staring at his hands, unable to believe the terrible truth.

He and Jeff sat alone in a corner of the Haven, the others giving him space to deal with his grief.

"She's not Rosalyn anymore," Jeff said, voice nearly a whisper. "She's one of them now."

"I don't believe that. I have to see her. To talk to her. She'll listen to me."

Dras stood, wiping his tears away with the back of his hand, but Jeff blocked his path. "No way. It's dangerous going back to Greensboro—for you, most of all."

"I don't care!" Dras shouted, then realized he had disrupted the quiet church. He relaxed. "Sorry…"

"It's okay." Jeff looked away and Dras considered how hard this was for his brother. Rosalyn was a sister to both of them.

No, Dras understood. *She's more than that to me. She…* "She can't be evil. All of this…I did all of this for her. I can't believe that everything I went through was for nothing."

Jeff put a hand on his brother's shoulder. "It wasn't for nothing. You said it yourself, right? The angels recruited you to help. We can fix this now. You're the break we've been waiting for."

But if Rosalyn is lost, none of that matters. "I'm going to see her. Tonight. There's no time to waste. I'm not asking you to come, just give me the keys to the truck and I'll take it from here."

Jeff looked ready to protest, then stiffened. "I'm not letting you out of my sight."

"Jeff—"

"If you're going, I am too. We do this together from now on."

Dras softened, feeling braver already, though he spotted Jeff's friend Danny to the side, looking on, a bit dejected. Danny stepped up, hands in his pockets. "I guess that means I'm coming too."

The gremlins were sloppy in their dirty work, and Rosalyn had the blood stains to prove it. As it turned out, blood didn't wash out of clothes easily.

Nor out of the conscience.

Rosalyn scrubbed her shirt, desperate to remove the blood of the four men she had murdered tonight. She had already taken a scalding hot shower and cleaned every nook in her apartment—dusting under every knick-knack, vacuuming each room, even going so far as to utilize the hose and nozzle, crawling around on her hands and knees to reach every crack, trying to make things right. Pulling back her oily hair into a ponytail, she had stayed on all fours—like a beast—cleaning her kitchen tile. Washing and waxing, polishing and scraping until her grim reflection sparkled back at her.

Yet, it was not enough. She still felt covered in filth.

Now, three failed washer cycles later, murky, sudsy water filled her kitchen sink as she worked furiously to remove the brown stains that refused to dissipate.

Barbecue sauce, she lied to herself, working feverishly. *That's all this is. Dras spilt barbecue sauce on me again. Just like he did that time in seventh grade when I was making eyes at Neil West.*

"I don't know why you wanna hang around me all the time anyway," Dras had said. *"We're in junior high now. You could have a whole bunch of new friends."*

But Rosalyn had faced him and waited until his eyes met hers. *"Maybe I like the friend I got."*

"Why's that?" he had asked.

"You make me laugh," Rosalyn said aloud, still washing the blood off her clothes.

"What's that?"

She huffed and spun to see the Strange Man hovering in her apartment, clicking his enflamed fingers, making an insect-like noise.

"Did I interrupt something?" he asked casually.

Only an old memory.

The monster floated through the air. Long gone were his beautiful features. In their place remained only the horrible chalky white visage that had been the last thing Lindsey McCormick—among many others—saw before she died. Tight leather strips and iron chains wrapped around his crooked, skeletal frame.

He doesn't even bother trying to hide what he is anymore. Honeymoon's over, I guess.

She returned to her washing, unable to get clean.

"So," the Strange Man began, "How'd it go tonight?"

Rosalyn didn't look up from her chore. "Fine."

"Did they give you any trouble?"

"Jacobson pulled a gun but…it was the last mistake he'll ever make."

"That's my girl," he grinned his green toothy smile. "And howabout the kids? Did they listen to Mommy?"

The Man often referred to the gremlins as "the kids". *Our kids.* "Yeah," she answered curtly. *They listened just fine when I sicced them on the Committee like rabid dogs.* Somewhere inside, Rosalyn tried to tell herself that she didn't really kill anyone. That she was still innocent; that it had been the *gremlins'* doing.

But they only did it because I told them to. They listen to me, now. Just like they do him. *I'm becoming just like him.*

"Is Stevenson handling cleanup?" she asked, unable to bear further reflection.

"You betcha," the monster said, so chipper, as though they were not discussing the disposal of four dead bodies. "Cleanup is the only thing our fair sheriff is any good at. Which is why I keep him around."

Why do you keep me *around?* she thought, though did not voice it. Did not ever voice it.

Rosalyn gave up trying to clean. With an aggravated splash she slopped the ruined shirt into the dirty water and grabbed a towel, drying her hands. Leaning against the counter now, she sighed.

"Never mind them, dear," he motioned toward the sink. "We'll go on a shopping trip tomorrow and I'll buy you a whole new wardrobe, what do you say?"

"I say 'yay'," she answered in a flat tone.

Leaving her clothes to drown, Rosalyn passed the Strange Man's hanging, bent body, moving to a small bundle she had sitting in a chair. She lifted the package and unwrapped it before the devil's eyes.

"By the way. I found this on them."

The Strange Man raised a curious eyebrow and held out his talons and she slid a tattered, blood-stained book into his grasp, careful not to touch his skin. He flipped the book over in his hands, thumbing through it with very little interest until—

His eyes widened, the light buried deep within flaring for just a moment.

What was that? Rosalyn nearly jumped at the display. *Is he…scared?*

It sent excited shivers all up and down her back.

"What is it?" she said.

The Strange Man, however, seemed lost in the scribbling and babbling nonsense, his mind silently decoding the gibberish. Perhaps finding something threatening therein. At once, he slammed the book closed and tucked it under his arm.

"Nothing," he said sharply. "Trash. I'll burn it."

Rosalyn held out her hand, now very desperate to have one last look at the seemingly unimportant book. *Could I use it to get out of this deal?*

Is there really a chance for me after all?

"Here." She tried very hard not to sound anxious. "I'll do it. I know how you feel about fire."

The Strange Man considered her long and hard, weighing the choice. Rosalyn remained fixed, her palm out before him, secretly pleading with him to give her the book. She had absently flipped through it when she first brought it home, but it seemed filled with nonsense. Just a bunch of strange words thrown together with no pattern or meaning. *Maybe I missed something.*

Much to her surprise, he slowly withdrew the book and handed it back, scrutinizing her as he did so. "I don't see what harm it could do," he said, though obviously he was deeply considering the harm it could do.

Rosalyn took the book, and, just to make sure he didn't have any second thoughts about giving it to her, she didn't even glance at it. Instead, she tossed it across the counter with a loud *slap*.

"I'll get it later," she forced herself to sound nonchalant as she moved past the Strange Man, eager to put distance between herself and the book for the time being. She crashed down on the couch and placed her feet on the coffee table. In his office, he would have chastised her for this carelessness. *But it's my place; I can do it if I want to. Let him try and stop me.*

The Strange Man made a *tsk* noise at the sight of her boots on the newly-polished oak table, but let the objection pass. "Get dressed. We're headed to the club."

"I don't really feel dancing if it's all the same to you."

The Strange Man noticed her sudden withdrawal. "What's wrong with you?" he asked bluntly, all dramatic flare aside.

Finally honesty. No grand gestures, no waving of hands and big talk. Just a real question.

"Are you upset about tonight?" he asked, his eyes searching her.

She nodded, ashamed.

He hovered before her, pacing back and forth in the air, studying her, as if trying to pry loose the thoughts she hid from him. His eyes wide and unblinking, he addressed her, "I know it troubles you. You don't see things like I do. You don't understand the bigger picture."

"The Dark Hour?" Rosalyn looked at his awful face.

"It's a time of change for the world, Rosalyn. Humanity has been held back by the dogmatic Church and you've lost sight of your true purpose on this earth."

"And that would be…?" she pushed further, wondering how

long he would let her.

"To *live*," he said, as if that were obvious. "You are here to enjoy every pleasure, to experience everything, both the good and the bad, the holy and the profane. You are here to take part in the human experience in all of its fullness, without some hoity toity system telling you 'this is right' or 'this is wrong'."

"But, if that's how some people choose to—" Rosalyn considered her words, "experience the human condition, shouldn't they be allowed to?" He glowered at her, but she continued, "I mean, I get it that you want to free people, allow them to make their own decisions, but what if they *choose* to follow God? Shouldn't they have the freedom to?"

"But that's never enough for them!" he snapped at her, pressing his nose to hers in an instant, so fast that she gasped. "Do you think they are content to hide in their homes and pray to their God? *Oh!* If only it were that simple! But no! They have to parade it in front of the rest of us, trying to convert everyone!"

"Calm down, Big Daddy" she stuttered, shocked and frightened by his sudden anger. "I didn't mean—"

"Tell me something, *sweetheart*," his voice oozed with venom. "Think about what kind of world we'd live in if the Christians had their way. We'd all be walking around like zombies, all choice stripped from us, just bowing down to their God, doing whatever He wanted. Is that the kind of world you want to live in? Is it?"

"*No*," she said, standing.

He flung his tapered talons to and fro, eyes glowing as he raged. "I don't believe you people! I come here trying to help you! Trying to give you what you want and you throw it back in my face!" At the peak of his fury, the Strange Man grabbed the vase on the stand beside the couch and violently slung it across the room, smashing it to pieces. Rosalyn shrieked.

"Stop," she quietly pleaded, "Please. I'm sorry. I didn't mean to—"

"Oh, you never *mean* to. You just pose your questions and make your debates and you think you have such a grasp of the world around you, but you have no idea. You can't even begin to understand the places *in between*, the unknowable depths of eternity, the *mind-shattering* realizations that wait just beyond your rather limited peripheral understanding of space and time. What are you, huh? You *people*! You're just dust! Dirt thrown together and given breath and yet you think you are owed *explanations*? You think you deserve to be in charge?"

He zoomed towards her, slapped her hard across the face, then gripped her by the back of her hair, pulling her face to his green-oozing smile. The smell of rotting flesh stung her nostrils as spittle formed at the edges of his mouth and he cackled. She winced, blood trickling from her nose, gasping for breath. "I'm sorry…Please…I'm sorry…"

Face still frozen in a gruesome sadistic mask, the Strange Man finally settled and slowly melted from the girl, his pale features resuming a haunted tranquility and the glow in his eyes dimming.

Rosalyn collapsed to the floor, crying, and he stared through her. "I pity your frailty. Maybe I was wrong about you." He looked caught and confused, and Rosalyn held her breath, unable to anticipate his next move. "You're not ready. But you will be. Very soon…you will be. Now," he commanded. "Get dressed. I'll be waiting for you."

Without another word, he disappeared into shadow.

But the book on the kitchen counter remained.

CHAPTER TEN

ROSALYN DANCED AMID the flashing lights of The Rave Scene. As she twirled, tousling her hair in a devil-may-care display, she was surrounded by a throng of worthy suitors, all good-looking men, dressed for the evening, sporting bright white smiles and expensive clothes. But she wasn't impressed.

It amused her that so many men fought to be near her. She had always attracted a healthy amount of attention back in the old days at The Rave Scene, but now she was a celebrity. The men all vied for her attention and she spared a little for each, throwing her arms around their thick necks, whipping her long, kinky, multi-colored locks in their faces, enticing them, *teasing* them. She made eyes at them—her dark doe eyes always full of passion and fire, however manufactured for the moment—and pouted her lips and smiled and laughed, stealing the show. It seemed everyone wanted to come get a better look at her—

Always hoping that they would get a better look at *him* in the process.

From the private door upstairs, the Strange Man exited his office, all smiles in his handsome mask, as droves of leather-clad Goth kids flocked to him with outstretched hands, hoping to touch him, to be close to him. He obliged them, shaking hands and smiling at all the girls, acting just like a rock star.

Rosalyn stared at her man as he descended the stairs, wading through the multitudes of adoring fans, finding herself infatuated with him all over again. Even as she danced with the other men, she remembered how much the Man had set her soul on fire with just one look not so long ago. He had seen her—chosen her—out of the flock, and she had felt so special. Since then, he had asked her to do things, terrible things, but now, when she saw him again, with all the young girls throwing themselves at him, she disregarded those sacrifices. It was worth it to be with him, wasn't it?

It was worth it to be special? *Right?*

He chose me, she reminded herself, watching him wink at the girls—some prettier than she—and cupped their chins or gave them a slight kiss on the cheek. *He doesn't want them, right? He still wants me, doesn't he? I didn't give everything up for nothing, did I?*

Feeling a strange sense of jealousy overcome her, her heart hardened and she spun to face the nearest boy-toy. She threw herself on him suddenly, dancing seductively. The man chuckled in bewilderment, enjoying the sudden attention, and Rosalyn grabbed his neck, forcing him to lock his gaze with hers.

As Rosalyn had hoped, her carousing did not escape the Strange Man's notice.

Stopping in the middle of his fans, he shoved aside an eager partygoer and pushed his way through the crowd. Despite the fact that he was disguised in his smooth skin and beautiful dark hair, the evil within him was barely contained and the edges of his eyes glowed with hellfire.

Rosalyn kept grinding on her new boy, daring him to kiss her, but as the dance continued, he looked scared and tried to push her away. Rosalyn knew her real suitor must be approaching.

"Come on," she whispered to her partner. "Just kiss me."

"Uh-uh, that's okay. I think I should go."

He fled just as the Strange Man reached Rosalyn. Without facing him, Rosalyn smiled a Cheshire grin, similar to the Strange Man's own. *He still wants me.*

"What are you doing?" he said.

She turned on him, out of breath from dancing so zealously, and smiled, affecting a mad glint in her eye. *Let's see how* you *like the games.* "Jealous?"

With a flick of his wrist, his fingers instantly clutched her throat and jerked her towards him, his eyes full of malice, taking Rosalyn's breath away. She stared at him, fearful, not expecting him to react so harshly in public.

He strangled her for a moment, as the rest of the club looked the other way.

"Don't ever tempt me," he hissed.

Rosalyn tried to laugh. "Come on, Big Daddy, I was just teasing."

"Tell me you love me," he demanded with a sense of desperation in his rage-filled voice.

"I love you, baby," she said, quivering. "Y-You know that."

Still clutching her throat—her very life—in his hand, he forced her into a passionate kiss, nearly swallowing her, devouring her with lust. For her part, Rosalyn did not resist, but kissed him just as passionately, trying to, once again, remind herself why she loved him. Why she stayed. A moment later, the Strange Man pulled away, almost tossing her aside. She stood taller, all smiles again, and cooed, "You know I love it when you play rough."

He smiled, once again, but still seemed shaken. "I know, baby. I know."

Now that the situation was defused, Rosalyn motioned for her man with a finger. "Come here. Let me give you something."

He chuckled, as if feeling silly he had lost his temper over such a foolish game, and allowed her to lead him deeper onto the dance floor. There he stood motionless, watching her like a wolf while she danced around him, rubbing her curves on him, whispering in his ear, kissing his neck.

I love him, she lied to herself. *I love him and that's why I stay. He took care of me when there was no one else. He took me in when no one would.*

She danced for him, all for him, giving into all her animalistic impulses, letting all the other girls who stared on in jealousy know that the Man was hers and they could never have him. No, he wouldn't be taken from her.

Not like my dad. Not like Dras.

With her back to his chest, she wrapped her arms backwards around his neck, sliding up and down him, rocking her head slowly side to side, letting her hair fall where it would, always tempting him, wanting him to be proud of her. Wanting him to want her.

But then she looked up and her world fell apart.

Across the club, someone else stood like a grim statue, watching her too, with tears in his eyes. She froze. Dropping her arms from around the Man, her heart stopped in her chest.

Dras?

Without a word, Dras disappeared into the crowd, walking away. Rosalyn began to cry, shamed by her behavior, her decisions, everything. She left the Strange Man behind, stupefied.

"Where are you going?" the devil called after her.

But she only barely heard him. She was running now, shoving her way through the crowd despite jeers and protests, not caring about any of these people. They were sheep! Stupid kids who were taken in by the devil, just like her. She hated them now and never wanted to see them again. She never wanted to see *him* again—the Strange Man, the supposed man of her dreams.

She only wanted to see Dras.

"No..." she whimpered, feeling tears splash down her face, as she swam upstream in the sea of dancing people, trying to find the only person who really understood her, the one man she really loved.

How much did he see? Did he see me dancing with those other guys? Did he see me fighting with the Strange Man?

Did he see me kiss him?

Her heart broke and she hated herself.

Rosalyn burst through the back door of the club into the empty night. The street was deserted. No one waited for her.

"Dras?" she called. "Dras!"

She ran to the side of the building, down the alley, looking into the darkness. "Dras! *Dras?*"

She was alone. *All alone.*

"Dras, please..." she whimpered. "I'm sorry..."

But he did not answer her. *He's gone.*

At last she gathered herself and marched back to the door, disappointed beyond all words, and entered her old world once again.

As the door slammed shut, Dras exhaled from his hiding place at the other corner of the building, slid down the wall, and cried.

GOD IS DEAD—NIETZSCHE.

Many in Greensboro shared the sentiment these days, and one person in particular apparently believed it so much, Danny noted, that he decided to spray paint the quote in the alleyway down a block from The Rave Scene.

Jeff shook his head with a frown before bringing out his very own can of spray paint. He jiggled it, rattling the metal ball against the inside, then popped off the cap and went to work.

Danny leaned on the back of the pick-up truck, observing the two men they had brought with them on this mission to Greensboro. Being in town after dark did not sit well with Danny, especially being so close to The Rave Scene. That was asking for trouble. Nonetheless, Dras needed to see what had become of his friend and Jeff was willing to risk quite a bit, apparently, to give his brother peace of mind. And if Jeff was coming out here, putting his life on the line, then Danny was going to be here too.

But did we have to bring these *guys?*

Standing erect with rifles ready waited two of the guards from the Haven. *Some backup*, Danny surmised. It wasn't like bullets would do a whole lotta good if the Strange Man or his merry band of gremlins showed up. But, these men were clearly new at devil smashing. Their eyes were round with suspicion and they started at every moving shadow, every noise in the distance. *We'll be lucky if they don't shoot each other.*

Stepping next to Jeff, Danny threw a nod over his shoulder at the rookies. "Newbies. Still thinking guns are gonna matter when hell comes."

"They're scared," Jeff said, spray painting on the brick, beside the other graffiti. "It's understandable. Are you armed?"

Danny nodded and reached into his coat, pulling out a pocket Bible tucked in his belt as if it were a 9mm. "Heck, yeah."

Jeff paused to glance at the Bible, which Danny displayed like a fine weapon.

"Managed to grab this baby before it went up in smoke with the rest of the Bibles on the bonfire," he said.

Jeff went back to his work. "Been reading it?"

"Every day." He nodded proudly.

"Doing anything for you?"

"Shyeah," Danny grumbled. "It's helped me to see that people have always been stupid when it comes to what's really going on in this world."

"Not stupid, Danny," Jeff corrected as he finished his task and stood to admire the work. "Just blind."

Danny moved closer to Jeff so that, by the moonlight, he could see the art as well. Now the sign read:

NIETZSCHE IS DEAD—GOD.

"Not bad," Danny remarked.

"Every little bit helps," Jeff sighed, tossing the paint can into a nearby trash bin. "I figure if we keep posting Scripture and leaving little reminders like this all over town—someone's bound to take notice, and it might be enough to lead them to Christ."

Danny shrugged and pulled out a pack of cigarettes, beating the bottom with a *shmack*, bringing a fresh one to the surface. He popped it in his mouth and retrieved his trusty Zippo to light it.

Jeff smirked. "You really should quit those things."

Danny took a long drag and pulled the cigarette from his lips. He held in the smoke for a moment, then blew it out serenely. "Look, preacher, I've given up drinking, drugs, pornos, fornication, and swearing for the sake of the kingdom of God." Danny took another puff and smiled. "Let me keep the smokes."

Jeff grinned. "Fair enough."

The two men chuckled and it felt right. When Dras walked in a few hours earlier, Jeff had made such a big deal about it. Danny had never seen Jeff that happy and, well, not to sound like a girl or anything, but he was a little worried that the Boss wouldn't need him so much now. Jeff had talked a lot about Dras in the beginning and Danny didn't blame him. The kid got a bum deal and everything, but Danny was the Number Two next to Isabella and, in a way, he needed that. He needed to be needed in the fight. *But if Dras is here and Jeff is going to be palling around with him all the time…where does that leave me?*

Maybe Carter was the way to go. Maybe Dras could stay at the Haven with Jeff and the two of them could take care of everybody with Isabella and Hank. After all, there was enough to worry about with feeding everybody and taking care of the sick and keeping Shamblers off the lawn. Maybe that's what *they* needed to do and maybe Danny needed to join Carter's crew and be the militant arm of the Haven. Take the war to the Strange Man's door to end this thing a whole lot quicker.

Maybe then I could see Tabitha again.

He wondered where she was now. He figured still with her mother in Watcher's Grove, but he wasn't sure. Danny hadn't heard anything from her since sending her away on that bus seven months ago.

Seven long months.

The boys are probably crawling around by now…

He was ready for the war to be over and, though he hated to say it, maybe Carter was on to something.

Yet the thought of going behind Jeff's back bothered him more than he wanted to say. He cared a lot about what the preacher thought and he wanted his blessing if he *did* choose to side with Carter. Danny had given the whole idea a lot of consideration—not much else to do at the Haven, after all—and he decided that, while he and Jeff were in good spirits, he would try out the theory to gauge his reaction.

"We should call ourselves something," Danny said.

"What?"

"Something catchy," he said, looking to the starless sky. "Something that can spread and start us a rep. Something that will get the Strange Man and his guys shaking with fear. What do you think about 'The Devil Smashers'?"

"The *what*?" Jeff raised his eyebrows.

Danny faced him, rummaging in his pockets, cigarette clenched in his teeth. "Nah, man, I'm serious. Look, look." He pulled out a folded sheet of notebook paper and opened it for Jeff to see. Drawn on the paper in pencil was the image of a squashed cartoon devil wincing in pain with his pointy tail jutting out in alarm as a large mallet mashed on his head.

"Devil Smashers," Danny repeated, as if the drawing said it all. "We can make up T-shirts and cards and when we leave our little notes behind in town, we can sign it 'The Devil Smashers'. I think it would really help with our image of being rogue monster hunters."

Jeff laughed it off—not the reaction Danny was going for, unfortunately. He slumped and slipped the picture back in his pocket. "Just a thought."

Dras emerged from the shadows, face red and puffy, dried tears on his cheeks. Immediately, the two newbies whirled about, pointing their guns. Danny rolled his eyes at them. "Easy, fellas."

Jeff approached his brother and saw the sadness in him. It was heartbreaking. He was suddenly reminded of when Dras was four and Jack—back when he was still able to do things—decided to take the family to Disney World for summer vacation. It had been a great time and Dras had been so happy. Mom had let him pick out a balloon all his own and he chose Dumbo, his favorite character. He had clutched that balloon like it was his best friend in the world and stared at it, delighted by the way it shimmered in the sun. Yet, when it was time to go home and Louise helped Dras into the car, he had let the balloon go by accident and cried hysterically as it flew into the sky, disappearing from his life. Dras had cried for three days over that balloon.

Now, he looked like he'd lost another balloon.

"How'd it go?" he asked. Dras's silence worried him. "Did you see her?"

"Yeah," Dras mumbled.

Jeff sighed and rubbed his neck, wishing he had the right words to comfort his brother. "Ready to go home, now?"

Dras nodded and sulked to the truck. Jeff motioned for Danny, who called to the men with them, "All right, load up."

The men all too eagerly jumped into the back of the truck, ready to be away from the cursed town.

Dras looked out the passenger window as the truck left town, headed for the old highway.

Rosalyn.

She had looked so thin, so sick. She had worn a smile but, even across a crowded room, Dras could tell that it wasn't genuine. She wasn't happy.

Or is she?

Was Dras just hoping that she was miserable without him? Was she, in truth, happier than she had ever been, despite her appearance? Maybe she liked who she was, what she had done. Maybe she loved the Strange Man.

Maybe…

He hung his head, realizing he had failed. Ten months ago, he had elected to stay behind in Greensboro when the Strange Man had threatened him to leave. He knew it could have cost him his life, but being with Rosalyn—sharing with her the truth—had been too important. He gave himself up to warn her about the devil…

But, now, she was *kissing* him. Holding him. Dancing with him.

No, Dras recognized with a churning stomach, *dancing* on *him*. Rosalyn had always been a sensual dancer, but this was sick. It was cheap and tawdry and it angered him that she had been reduced to that. She was special. She was—she was *Rosalyn*. She deserved better. She was his soul mate and the fact that she was with that monster—

He didn't want to dwell on it anymore, though he knew the image of them together would haunt him for a very long time.

"I want to apologize," Jeff said over the roar of the old truck's engine.

Dras stared out the window at the black sky beyond. "Why?"

Jeff took a deep breath, confessing, "After your trial, I…got dark for awhile. Did some things I'm not proud of. Pushed everyone away." Dras turned, now, to see his brother clenching his jaw. "I should've been there for Rosalyn, but I wasn't. I'm sorry."

"She made her decision," Dras said coldly, hoping to soothe his brother's guilt, as well as his own. "I know you tried to talk to her. We all tried. But she had to choose on her own and she did." He finished with a weak smile and turned back to the window. "She chose him."

Rosalyn entered her darkened apartment, finding that she had left the blinds open, allowing the eerie moonlight to cast her living room in blue-white stripes. She let out a long, defeated sigh, discarding her keys on the end table nearest the door and moving for the lamp.

He's back. He's really, really back. After all this time, after everything she'd been through without him, after all she'd tried not to feel…Dras was back. And he'd seen her. *With him.*

Her heart felt empty at the thought. What did Dras think of her now? Would he try to see her again? Would he ever come back again? Or was it over? Did she just lose her soul mate for the second time?

She started to cry in the darkness of her room, unable to stop herself any longer. Dras was all she had wanted. Just having him back around, having him in her life, that's all that made sense to her. She had made so many stupid choices because she thought he was never returning but he had! Now those same decisions would be the thing to drive him away once again and leave her alone.

I'm not alone, though, she thought sourly. *Never alone in the dark.*

"What happened to you tonight?" his voice called from the blackness.

Rosalyn set her jaw, her sobs catching in her throat. She wiped at her eyes, trying to lessen the redness in her face, streak away her fresh tears before—

Click.

The lamp came on, revealing the Strange Man—in all his demonic poise—seated casually in the chair. She instinctively turned from him, hiding her face, though knew it was pointless. He already knew. He always did.

"Nothing," she lied, not so effectively.

The Strange Man stood, hovering, and zoomed around her. That Cheshire grin grotesquely painted on his face, he spoke through crooked green teeth, "I've just heard some rather upsetting news. Sheriff Stevenson heard on the radio that Dras Weldon somehow—miraculously—escaped from Wexler State Penitentiary last night."

Rosalyn remained quiet.

"He was there tonight, wasn't he?"

"I don't know what you're talking about," she muttered, still smudging her tears.

Violently, the Strange Man grabbed her by the hair and jerked her to face him.

"Liar! You went to him! You would leave me!"

"No!" she screamed back, angry and afraid. "I didn't talk to him! He was gone! He saw us, and he left! I don't know where he went!"

The Strange Man, seeing the truth in her eyes, chuckled and lowered her back to the ground, letting her hair loose. "He saw us?"

Rosalyn felt sick. "Yes."

The devil cocked his head from side to side, studying her. "Good. Then he knows that he's lost. You are mine. Forevermore."

Rosalyn wanted to die. Though, she knew that for her crimes, she would go straight to hell and even then, the Strange Man would be waiting for her. Yes, she was his. *Forevermore.*

The Strange Man turned from the girl, staring at the ceiling. "Still," he called out, conversationally, "His return only means one thing."

"What?" she asked, defeated.

"They are drawing plans against me, of course. They mean to stop the Dark Hour; to stop my Master from coming. They want to bring the fight to me. To *us*, my dear."

Rosalyn, realizing that he wasn't leaving any time soon, slipped off her shoes and went about the business of settling in for the night. She saw as the Strange Man hungrily watched her with desire, thrilled by the way she moved. Even the way she regarded him with contempt turned him on.

"Will you stand with me?" he asked her, darkly. "When they come to war, will you fight by my side?"

"You know I will," she said, not looking at him. "I always do."

"Even if it means killing that boy?"

Rosalyn couldn't answer. Thankfully, the Strange Man did not press the issue any further.

"Did you destroy that book like I asked?" he asked suddenly.

Rosalyn nodded with a sigh, collapsing on the couch, stretching out, wishing he'd just leave already. "Of course."

"Good," he said shortly, not realizing she had lied to him. "Good, we don't need any distractions. It's time we moved up our schedule. If they're making plans, they must feel like they have some sort of advantage. We'll take away that advantage. Crush the very hope from their souls. Contact our preacher tomorrow. Tell him the ceremony will continue as planned."

Rosalyn rose up, concerned. "Are you sure? You don't think maybe we should postpone it in light of everything?"

"Of course not, my love. Big Daddy's got it all planned out. Just leave it to me."

She rolled her eyes and laid her head back on the couch. "Whatever. You're the boss."

He gripped her chin and forced her to face him. "Kiss me," he commanded.

Rosalyn faltered but reached up and kissed him for a moment, until he grabbed her cheeks and jerked her lips from his. "*No*," he growled, incensed. His eyes glimmered with hate, simmering just below the surface. "Kiss me like you *mean* it."

Rosalyn thought back to the last time she'd kissed someone and meant it. It had been Dras, in his kitchen, before this nightmare began. They'd shared a kiss that meant more to her than any sort of pleasure the Strange Man would offer. Just one, simple kiss that could have led to the love of a lifetime. She'd never get that love back. *Not after what I've done.*

Looking to the demon, his demanding glower, Rosalyn feared that this was as close to love as she was going to get. Eyes stinging with humiliated tears, she kissed the Strange Man, full of passion, hate, and loathing. Now, when they parted, he looked absolutely exhilarated. A calm crooked grin marred his handsome features. "Much better."

CHAPTER ELEVEN

DANNY RODE IN the rear of the pickup with the rookies on the way back to the Haven. He rarely rode in the back—and certainly not without Jeff. Usually he sat at his side in the cab, where he felt he belonged.

Dras was currently occupying *that* seat, however.

The cold air chilled him and tossed his already unkempt hair. Danny squinted against the wind to peer into the back window of the cab. He knew that Dras was having a hard time, on account of his girlfriend being a psychotic devil-worshipper and all, so he decided to be the bigger man when Jeff asked him to ride in the back. Jeff needed a little time with his brother. It was understandable.

But it was still cold in the back of the truck. Cold and lonely.

Ah, well, at least I've got the newbies, he thought sarcastically, turning to gaze upon the two—

No, not two. Just one.

"Where's Brian?" Danny shouted over the rushing wind.

The remaining rook swiveled in panic and, upon realizing his partner was missing, turned back to Danny, white as a ghost.

"Where'd he go?" Danny demanded. "He was right here!"

"I don't know, man!" the newbie screamed. "I don't—"

Swoosh!

A giant blur swooped down fast, snatching the man in sharp-looking taloned fingers and, in a heartbeat, returned to the night sky, its prey in tow. Danny stared up, up, up, as the thing disappeared, the rookie's screams disappearing with him.

"Dras," Jeff began again after a long moment's silence settled in the cab. "I know that seeing Rosalyn was hard on you, but you have to let her go."

Dras turned to reply, but Danny was at the rear window, banging with both fists, his eyes wide with fright.

"Pull over!" he screamed, muffled through the glass. "Pull *over*!"

Jeff pressed the brakes and the truck crawled to a halt. He and Dras hurried out of the cab while Danny hopped out of the bed, looking up, watching.

"What is it?" Jeff asked. Then, noticing they were short two members, he asked, "Where's Josh and Brian?"

Danny pushed past him, gesturing furiously. "They're gone! Something flew by and just took them!"

Dras wrinkled his brow, the hair on the back of his neck rising. "Flew by?"

Danny paced, scrambling to light a cigarette. "It had *wings*, man!" Trembling, he struggled to steady the cigarette before his lighter's flame.

"Okay, okay, just calm down," Jeff advised.

"I ain't ridin in the back no more!" Danny yelled.

Dras looked past the two and saw a figure hovering against the moonlit night sky.

"Uh…guys…"

Jeff and Danny spun and saw it.

Flapping giant, leathery wings to keep itself supported in the air, was a muscular, man-like monstrosity, draped in a long, patchwork coat with a hood pulled over its head. What flesh could be seen under its coat was scaly and black, glistening in the light as if covered in oil, like a Shambler. However, unlike a Shambler, it had a face, and what a hideous face it was. Protruding out of the hood was an angular profile with an unnaturally large mouth filled with rows and rows of jagged needles. Its pale and yellow eyes had such a malicious intelligence within them that Dras shivered. Tearing the coat sleeves, long, curved blades that looked made of bone and covered in gore jutted from the Creature's elbows.

The Creature hung suspended in the air, its wings flapping powerfully, studying the three humans below with an arrogant, hungry smile.

Dras leaned into Jeff to whisper, "What is it?"

He shook his head slowly. "It's new to me."

Danny took a long drag off his cigarette and dashed it to the ground, blowing smoke. "Let's just go, man!"

The Creature let out a terrible howl and, with a flap of its wings, dove for the small truck and its frightened passengers.

"Get back in the truck!" Jeff yelled, and everyone scrambled inside, Jeff taking the wheel, Danny squeezing into the middle, and Dras pressed against the edge. Jeff cranked the engine and gunned it hard, switching into gear with a grind, and shot out across the abandoned country highway.

Dras and Danny watched out the back window as the flying Creature sped after them, effortlessly flying faster and faster, the terrible, knowing grin never leaving its black lips.

"Go faster!" Danny screamed.

"I'm flooring it!" Jeff hollered.

As Dras stared through the glass, the Creature gained ground, the bone-like protrusions on its elbows looking ever more real and painful and Dras imagined what it would feel like to be impaled by them.

A feeling he figured Josh and Brian had already experienced firsthand.

"It's right behind us!" Danny again.

"I'm trying! I'm trying!"

The Creature shot at them like a rocket, and it was only a matter of time before—

"It's gonna get us!" Danny yelled.

"Shut up and let me drive!"

The truck rocked to the side, and the entire passenger window was filled with the sight of the flying Creature, its pale yellow eyes and crooked fangs glimmering at the men in sheer, devilish delight.

Danny let out a curse as the Creature careened into the side of the truck, knocking it off balance. Jeff worked to swerve the truck back onto the road, fighting to keep the vehicle on all four wheels as another metal-crunching impact shattered the passenger side window, showering Dras's face with glass.

"Jeff!" Dras yelled, though he had no real idea why. He didn't know what Jeff could do to stop the Creature, but he just wanted someone to help. Someone to save him. He thought of Rosalyn, and knew he would never ever see her again.

The Creature roared, though it sounded more like a squeal—like a pig and a lion in a wrestling match—and reached into the cab of the truck with violent, wild, prying claws. Danny reached over Dras and hit at the beast to keep those bone-blades back. The Creature laughed a deep chuckle, as it grabbed onto Dras's shirt.

"*Jeff!*" he screamed, reaching for his brother.

Jeff, too, stretched for Dras, desperately trying to touch him. But the Creature shouldered the frame of the truck and nearly sent them toppling over. Jeff retracted his hand in an instant to avoid rolling the truck. Danny beat uselessly at the Creature's arm as Dras writhed.

The monster, however, did not budge.

"Don't let him get me!" Dras shrieked.

"Don't let him go!" Jeff raged at Danny.

"*I'm trying!*" Danny yelled, pulling with all his might on Dras's body.

With one, brutal yank, Dras was ripped out of Danny's grasp and through the gaping hole of the passenger side window. He ascended into the air in the Creature's taloned grip within the blink of an eye.

Danny froze and stared at his empty hands that, only a second ago, had held onto Dras, and now held nothing but defeat.

Jeff swerved the truck into a fishtail, slamming on the brakes, and jumped out, running after the fading image of his little brother being dragged across the inky sky.

"Dras! *Draaaas!*" his voice cracked.

Dras's cries of fear and agony soon faded in the night.

Soaring over the treetops of the North Woods, Dras struggled in the clutches of the flying Creature. The thing's claws dug deep into his shoulders, piercing shirt and skin, sending droplets of blood running down his body, raining onto the woods below. Dras had moved beyond screaming; the uppermost part of his torso was cold with anguish. Now there was only the knowledge that this thing was leading him to his demise and he had to get out of its death-grip.

The Creature pounded its wings against the air, beating at the wind, propelling them forward, wearing a blank, expressionless face. Dras continued to fight, clutching the monster's tattered cloak, pulling, twisting, trying to deter the Creature from its course, but the monster flew on, indifferent.

Upon closer inspection, Dras spotted a jersey the beast wore—a football jersey with Greensboro High's colors. And the number…it was familiar and evoked a sense of fear separate from the terror he felt towards the beast already.

Fear gave way to understanding. *Wait a minute…*"Is that *you*?" he asked, seeing features he recognized underneath the black skin. Curiosity overriding alarm, Dras reached out to touch the face. "Is it—?"

The Creature snapped and jerked out of Dras's reach, and the claws sunk deeper into his shoulders, bringing him back to attention. Dras grunted and clenched his teeth, hammering his fists against the dark, oily, muscular chest of the man-beast with the pale eyes.

"Stop!" he yelled against the roaring gales, realizing the futility of his plea. The Creature did not seem to hear him. It only stared ahead and flew.

Dras peered at the rushing treeline below him, knowing that he could survive the fall if he could only break free. *Where are we going?*

The Creature suddenly dropped in altitude, jerking its taloned hands deeper into Dras's body and causing him to yelp with fresh misery. They were plotted on a course and Dras had no intention of staying on the flight until it reached its destination.

His feet dangled, brushing against the highest branches on the trees. Mustering his courage, he recalled Christopher's words:

"Whatever you do, it is imperative that you do not be afraid. Do you understand me? Whatever fear you have, forget it. Shove it aside. Your work is too important and there's no time for it."

"Be ye not afraid," he muttered a fraction of a Bible verse, and the Creature's grip loosened. Dras's eyes shot wide open in surprise, and the beast too, appeared startled by the potent effect of the old words.

The Creature flexed once more, trying to take hold of Dras again, but he resisted. With one shoulder free, he wrapped his newly liberated arm around the Creature's neck and pulled down.

Hard.

The Creature, knocked off course, snorted in frustration as Dras wriggled his other arm free of the sharpened nails that held him. It rolled in the air, its momentum carrying it further, while Dras held onto its neck, dangling wildly. With its bare, clawed feet the Creature scrambled to scrape Dras's clinging frame off of it, while the young man kicked and squirmed, doing whatever he could to slow the beast.

Roaring in rage, the monster shook Dras loose. He tumbled, crashing into branches and leaves and hollering all the way down. Dras plummeted through the forest, snapping wood, tearing his clothes and flesh, and landing hard on the dried, dead leaves, his breath knocked out of him.

Gasping for life, Dras rolled over, his back and legs tingling. Immediately, he looked up and saw the silhouette of the flying Creature circling overhead like a giant vulture, furiously looking for him. Dras picked himself up and ran. His entire body hurt but he pushed through the pain.

Wet-faced and determined, Dras tightened his jaw and stood on shaky legs, hobbling through the brush, the moonlight above smothered by the overhanging branches of the large, twisted trees.

"Please, God…" Dras whispered, his eyelids growing heavy, as he felt faint. Up ahead he spotted a road and he stepped onto it. "I need You, God…Help…"

Headlights blinded him. Then hit him.

Dras was lifted off his feet and rolled against the windshield before flying, end over end, landing on the pavement. His face stung and he thought he might be bleeding, but he was alive. Groaning, he propped up on his knees and spotted the car. It had stopped, its brake lights still on. Just sitting there, like it was waiting for him.

Dras frowned, spitting up blood. "Okay, God. Not what I really had in mind, but it'll do. Thanks."

His legs wobbly, he stumbled for the car. "Hey. Sorry about your car."

The car did not move. Dras's heart picked up, anxious. He eased for the door, holding his side where he feared he'd broken a rib. After that fateful night at The Rave Scene ten months ago, he intimately knew what that felt like. "Hey…you okay?"

Keeping his distance, Dras peered into the driver's side window and saw an older man, pale and sweaty. He had deep lacerations on his chest, blood *everywhere*. This guy was in worse condition than Dras was, but he couldn't have suffered that damage from hitting Dras with the car.

The man lolled his head to the side, seeing Dras. Softly he chuckled. "It *would* be you."

"What happened?" Dras asked, forgetting his own pain. "What can I do to help?"

The man scooted across into the passenger seat. "You can drive. You can take me to him."

"Who?"

"Your brother."

CHAPTER TWELVE

CARTER HOPPED INTO the bed of Jeff's truck with the other men, brandishing his rifle; a revolver tucked in his belt. "All right," he bellowed, "You know the score." The other men listened closely as they slapped clips into their guns, cocked hammers, entered bullets into their chambers. Carter took his seat with them, still shouting. "We got a flyer. That means marksmen in the middle. Rifles only. Handguns, we take sides, knock the fight outta this thing if it gets too close, understand?"

"What about the Day-Lights?" Ed Mathers asked. He exuded more confidence than any of them, and Carter respected that. He needed brave men to do what needed done.

"Not yet. Don't wanna scare the freak off. No, we want him nice and close so we can get a good look at him. Find out what we're up against. And when we do, we'll blast it out of our sky."

Jeff marched toward Carter, his heart burning with rage. Taking giant strides across the grounds, he moved on a mission, only mildly aware that the Havenites stood gaping. Isabella, too, remained off to the side, her eyes full of worry.

"Don't forget," Jeff boomed, as a very quiet and sulking Danny trailed behind, "This is a rescue mission first. We find the Creature and follow it. Find out where it took Dras. After we get my brother back," he nodded to Carter, "it's all yours."

Carter grinned. "We won't disappoint."

"Good. I'm counting on it." Jeff jerked his chin toward Danny. "Let's go."

Danny nodded sullenly and took his place in the cab. Jeff

moved around to the driver's door, but Isabella pulled him to face her. "Jeff, don't do this."

Her brown eyes were hurt and fearful. She had looked at him that way a lot seven months ago when he became a one-man wrecking crew, nearly losing his soul to anger, tearing at the Committee's conspiracy. "I have to, Iz. I won't lose him again."

"But there has to be another way," she pleaded. "We don't even know what took him. Was it a Shambler?"

"I-I don't know. It had wings. It flew."

"*Flew*?"

"Hey," Hank called, jogging up to the team, out of breath. "I hear Carter's getting ready to go hunting."

"That's right, Hank."

"You gonna stop him?"

"No. I'm the one who told him to do it."

"What? When did we decide this?" Hank looked to Isabella for an explanation, but she only held up her hands and walked away, shaking her head.

"*We* didn't," Jeff proclaimed without apology.

Hank crossed his meaty arms. "Is that how this works now? You stomp around like the Terminator, barking orders, and we all just fall in line?"

Jeff had a few choice words on his tongue, but somewhere inside, he knew he'd have to take them all back. Still resolved, he forced himself to slow down, to be as diplomatic as possible. "Things are changing out there, Hank. Getting worse. The Shamblers have evolved. They can fly now. They got Dras and—"

Hank rubbed his tired eyes. "We're out of our league here, Reverend."

"Stop calling me that! I'm not your Reverend! I'm not your leader! I'm just me, Hank, and right now my brother is out there and I'm going to do whatever I have to do to get him back."

"This is suicide, you know?"

"Fine, Hank. *You* be the leader. I'm out."

Jeff climbed in the truck and took one last look at Isabella. She held back, chewing her lip nervously. Hank moved to stand behind her, like her stoic guardian, simmering with anger.

They were his best friends. And he was abandoning them.

What am I doing? I did this once before. I pushed them all away and it didn't help. When will I learn?

Isabella and Hank continued to watch, and Jeff was suddenly not sure what to do. Carter banged on the side of the truck to get his attention. "Hey, we going or what?"

Jeff turned to them. All the men in the truck, clutching their guns. To the side, their weeping women and children trying to savor what might be their final glimpses of them.

I'm going to get every one of them killed.

He felt heat in the pit of his stomach and recognized the Holy Spirit trying to guide him. He couldn't go. *This is suicide. Hank is right.* But he didn't know how to break it to Carter. He—

A car horn interrupted his thoughts.

Headlights illuminated the small band of monster hunters and everyone looked to see an old Volvo lumber toward the church. The car parked and Dras climbed out, hurrying to the passenger side.

"Hey! Miss me?"

Jeff's heart warmed and he let out a sigh of relief. "Dras—"

"I ran into this guy," Dras explained, opening the other door. "Well, he actually ran into *me*, but he needs help."

Dras struggled to remove a bleeding man from the car and a rush of fear and rage flooded Jeff's veins.

"Dras, get away from him!"

He looked caught. "What? What did I do?"

Carter and the others aimed their guns at the man in Dras's arms as the boy froze.

"That's Jarvis Gibson," Jeff told him.

CHAPTER THIRTEEN

HANK BERKLEY TOOK one of the few genuine glasses they had, filled it with water, and hurried towards the classroom where their new "guest" rested.

Jarvis Gibson: Founding member of the Committee.

Hank had not faced the Committee since resigning as sheriff a few months back. They had had a big blow-up and Hank had given them all a piece of his mind. At the time he had been fueled by the fact he had survived death in the fire that consumed the Good Church of the Faithful and was still glowing with his new decision to follow Christ. Everything was fresh and exciting and ole Hank Berkley felt like he could take on hell with a water pistol.

But now…Now he just wanted this business with the Committee to be over. They held sway in town and were in league with the Strange Man.

And I just don't trust them.

He was about to turn the knob to enter the classroom when he felt a familiar hand on his arm. Quite startled, he came face to face with the expectant countenance of his wife, Doris.

Hank and Doris had been college sweethearts. Hank had been on the football team and Doris had been his faithful supporter, following him to all the Away games, cheering louder than the cheerleaders on the field. They were always together, sharing everything in life.

That was then, though.

Urgent and conspiratorial, Doris pressed him. "Well? What does he want?"

Hank groaned. "I don't know yet, Doris. We haven't had the chance to talk to him. Give the man a break. He's hurt real bad and he just wants a glass of water."

"Do you think he's going to make us an offer?" she asked, eyes pleading.

"What offer?"

"Maybe they want to make peace. Maybe they want to let us come back."

Hank hung his head, feeling the pressure of his wife's discomfort. "Doris," he began, patiently, "We've been through this. It wouldn't matter even if he *were* here to invite us back into town. We can't go. It's not safe."

Doris tugged on his thick arm, selfishness in her eyes, leaving him to wonder what had happened to the young girl he had married.

"It doesn't have to be that way, does it?" she asked, breathless. "We're only in danger if we openly talk about God and Jesus. No one's saying we can't believe it, we just can't talk about it to anyone, that's all."

Hank jerked away from her, hurt. "I won't," he said firmly. "I won't live like that. Not after everything Jesus has done for me, I won't...*disown* Him like that."

Doris huffed, as if dealing with a difficult child. "Becky and I are miserable here, Hank."

"I know that, dear."

"And—" she shuffled her feet, avoiding his gaze, "I don't really see why...well, why *we* have to stay."

"What do you mean?"

"We both respect your beliefs. I understand you went through a very upsetting experience and you feel like you need to believe in God to make sense of it all."

"Wait a minute." He towered over her, feeling babied. "You talk like you don't believe I saw the things I saw."

"All these monsters you all are going on about...where are they? I mean," she almost laughed right in his face after everything he'd seen and done, "I've never actually seen any of these things you've described."

Hank grew dark. "Pray to God it stays that way."

Doris momentarily retracted. "Okay. You say you saw something, then I believe you."

Though he knew she was lying.

"Still that doesn't change the fact that Becky and I don't really believe like you do, so I don't see why we have to stay out here."

Hank's heart broke. "You don't believe in God?"

Doris did not reply. Hank felt empty inside.

She leaned in, changing the subject, "When the Campbells were here the other day bringing supplies, they talked about all that's going on back in town. It doesn't sound that bad, Hank. As long as we don't draw attention to ourselves—if we can just play along—then we'll be safe. No one will bother us and we can move back into our old house and buy new clothes and eat real food. Things will be just like they used to be."

"I'd be living a lie."

Doris looked away, though oddly didn't appear hurt, ashamed, or upset by anything she was saying.

She just wants out, Hank realized. *Does she love me anymore?*

She faced him, her eyes devoid of all that he had ever loved in her. "I would think you would want Becky and me to be happy."

He nodded absently, knowing it was what she wanted him to do.

"Well…I think we would be happier back in Greensboro."

"But—"

"I understand if you want to stay here," she quickly stammered.

Too quickly. She doesn't even want me to go with her.

"But for our sakes, I think that—"

"Just go," he said quietly, not able to look at her. "But not back to Greensboro. Stay with your sister. Give us a little more time to sort this out."

Doris's eyes livened and she stared at him, as if finally freed of her imprisonment. "We can leave? Really? Just like that?"

Thirty years of marriage. Yeah, Doris. Just like that.

Jarvis Gibson was dying. Jeff, along with Danny, Isabella, and Sarah stayed by his side as he lay on a cot in the private room designated as the infirmary. There was nothing could be done for his wounds, and Gibson refused to be taken to a hospital, knowing it'd mean death anyway. Jeff still harbored a lot of anger against the Committee, but seeing Gibson fading before his eyes was still difficult.

Dras was wounded too, and Lolly Delarosa sewed up a slash on his head. Lolly was not a doctor, but she was a good seamstress and had the steadiest hand they could find.

Hank entered, brandishing a glass of water and a depressed set in his face. Jeff immediately noticed. Hank seemed to be carrying a weight these days. He would have to check on him as soon as he got the time.

"Here you go," Hank said gruffly, holding out the water.

Jeff took the glass and waited for Isabella to prop up Gibson before giving him a drink. The pale man gulped it down hungrily, then leaned back with a moan.

Danny crossed his arms. "I don't know why we're being so nice to one of the old fogies who started the whole Dark Hour in the first place."

"Not now, Danny," Isabella scolded and Danny paced.

When the pain in Gibson's face seemed to subside for the moment, Jeff took a seat at the man's bedside and leaned in. "All right, Jarvis," he began. "What happened?"

"It was the girl…" he wheezed.

Isabella shot Jeff a worried look and he purposefully dodged it.

"Rosalyn?" he asked, just to be clear, wanting to look at his brother, to gauge his reaction. But he didn't.

Gibson nodded slightly. "She had those blasted imps with her. They obey *her* now too. She…sent them after us."

"How did you get away?" Isabella asked.

Gibson reddened. "Th-they carried me off into the shadows to I-I prayed. I wept and I begged God to let me live."

"And they just let you go?" Danny huffed. "Just like that? I don't buy it."

"Believe what you want," Gibson fixed him with a bitter stare. "God did His part in letting me live long enough to get here, so I'm doing my part by warning you."

"Why did Rosalyn come after you?" Dras asked from the back, his voice heavy.

"He sent her for us."

"Why?" Danny snapped.

"We…we tried, Jeff," Gibson looked to the man, pleading. "We tried to stop it."

"And where are your friends?" Danny asked with a condescending smirk that Jeff didn't appreciate.

Gibson looked to the arrogant young man, gravely serious. "They're dead. All of them. Butchered tonight…I alone managed to get away." With a trembling hand that felt like ice, he touched Jeff's arm. "We-we *found* something. I only learned of it tonight, right before…I hope that it will prove useful in the right hands."

"What is it?" Isabella asked.

Gibson paused, weighing his words as if what he was about to tell was the last secret the Committee had left. "It's Ray McCormick's diary. He wrote in it during his final days when he was…*ill.* I wasn't able to study it. I don't know if it can help or not…the girl took it. You've got to get it. You've got to try, Jeff…There isn't much time now. The Dark Hour is in two days."

The man coughed, a wet hacking that repulsed Jeff, but stoked his pity. "Easy, Jarvis."

"Don't die on us, yet," Danny said, crudely. "We've got more questions."

"Danny," Jeff interjected, but Gibson shushed him.

"It's all right. There's no reason to keep secrets any longer."

"What's the deal with the bat-dude?" Danny asked, ignoring Jeff's call for propriety.

The color left Gibson's face and he calmed, saddened. "Oh. *Him.*"

"It's TJ Walker," Dras said, startling Jeff. As one, the room turned on him, looking just as surprised as Jeff felt. "Isn't it?"

Eyes fell on Gibson and Jeff waited anxiously for his reply.

"Yes," he revealed.

"How did you know?" Isabella asked Dras.

He smirked. "Trust me. I know what it feels like when TJ Walker is about to punch my face in."

Sarah spoke up, "But how is that possible? I thought he was dead."

Hank shook his head. "We never found a body…"

Gibson clarified. "Mr. Graves had him hid for a…gestation period."

"What does TJ have to do with this?" Dras said.

"The Strange Man discovered him first, years ago. TJ was never the same after his football injury. I used to counsel the boy in school…he felt like he didn't belong anymore. He used to spend his nights drinking at the Old Greenesboro ruins. I would discover later that the Strange Man approached him there. Preyed on his insecurities. Gave him a place at the monster's side."

"Poor TJ," Dras said, and when Jeff eyed him, he blushed and defended. "Hey, it's not like I'm his number one fan, but…he didn't deserve that."

"TJ was the one who made first contact with Mayor Hayden," Gibson said. "With all of us. He arranged the Committee on Graves' orders and set up our initial meetings in the North Woods with his master."

Hank pounded a wall, angry. "Why didn't you ever tell me this?"

"Would it have changed anything?'

"Maybe! TJ was just a screwed-up kid. We could have talked him down. Stopped this thing before it ever started!"

"It's too late for that, Hank," Isabella reflected, distraught.

Gibson looked past Jeff to Dras. "We never wanted any of this to happen. You've got to believe us. Please, Dras…please forgive me…"

Jeff faced his brother, expectant. Lolly finished stitching the gash on his temple, and the boy nodded, looking to Jeff like a young Jack Weldon. "I do, Mr. Gibson. We're cool."

Gibson smiled at that. "Thank you…" he muttered, and breathed his last.

The room grew quiet, except for Danny. "Wait! What's the Dark Hour? How do we stop it?"

"Danny," Jeff said, as Hank glumly closed Gibson's eyes. "It's over. He's gone."

Danny swore and kicked over a nearby chair. Jeff shared the sentiment, but tried to keep his cool for the team's sake.

Isabella draped a sheet over Gibson's still form, and Jeff struggled to process the new information. The Dark Hour was the day after tomorrow. *It's not enough time.*

We can't win.

Hank sighed. "So, what does this mean? Shamblers have wings now?"

"It's gotta go back to the lake," Jeff stood, stretching his legs. "That goo out there…it's like pure, concentrated sin. The Strange Man changed it and now it's like a receiver for all the evil in town. The lake stores all that hate and redirects it onto whoever comes in contact with it." He paused, remembering all too well.

Sarah scooted her chair in closer. "So, these Shamblers…that's what sin did to those people."

"Sin has always turned men into monsters," Hank replied gruffly. "I guess now we're just seeing on the outside what was inside."

"But there's something else," Jeff interrupted. "Ray…he was a righteous man. He may have fallen from his faith there at the end, but I know he truly wanted to do the right thing."

"I think the same could be said for most of them folks out there, baying at the moon," Hank said quietly.

"Wait," Dras edged for the group. "Most? Or *all*?"

Jeff eyed him and Dras explained, "Let's face it, TJ has never been a 'righteous man'. Maybe that's why he's different than the others."

Isabella chewed on her lip. "What if the Shamblers we've seen in the past were, like, Type A? Godly people who haven't been mutated, just *covered* in the goo. The sin hasn't taken hold of them. It torments them, battling to do its will, but they're not completely changed. It's like what happened to Jeff. Somewhere inside, they are still themselves, fighting to be free."

"And Type B?" Sarah asked. "Like TJ?"

"Without God in his heart to protect him from the sin, the goo takes hold and *changes* him from the inside out. It's not a shell surrounding him like the Type As, but it's what he's become through and through. Wholly wicked. A monster."

"Man, can you imagine a whole town of those things?" Danny sniggered.

The room grew silent.

Jeff felt his throat grow dry. "Maybe that's what the Strange Man is planning. He's got enough followers in town…Maybe, when his Master comes, *everybody* will turn into those things."

"Just like the dreams," Danny gasped, then gnashed his teeth. "Man, I didn't even think of that."

Isabella blanched. "What are we going to do?"

Sarah looked from face to face, worried. "But Gibson said it's happening in two days, right? How are we going to stop it in time?"

Danny turned to Jeff, frustrated. "Face it, Jeff, we need to rethink our tactics. Maybe Carter's onto something—"

Isabella rolled her eyes. "Oh, come on, Danny. Not you too."

"We gotta try something."

"We can't storm the town like soldiers!" Isabella contested. "Do you know how many people would die?"

Hank spoke softly, "But it might call for that, Iz. I don't want it to happen any more than anyone else does, but we have to be prepared to make that kind of a sacrifice to stop this."

Isabella folded her arms.

"I can talk to Rosalyn," Dras offered. "Get Ray's diary. Maybe there's something—"

"Forget your girlfriend, dude," Danny spat. "She's gonna be first in line to get her monster makeover."

Dras jumped forward, defensive. "You don't know her!"

Jeff held him off. "Stop it. Both of you."

Hank moved in to intervene. "All right, all right, we're all on the same side here. Let's just cool off a minute. This is exactly what the Strange Man wants, so let's not give it to him."

Jeff heaved a great sigh. "The town won't even see this coming. They're so in love with Graves right now, they'll probably think it's a party."

Dras went rigid. "Or…a celebration?" He shoved his hands into his jeans pocket, digging until he retrieved a crumpled blue flyer. He stared at the folded mess, his mind working, then opened it. Read it.

"Dras? What is it?" Isabella asked.

He held up the flyer for Jeff to see. "Something big."

CHAPTER FOURTEEN

THE FOLLOWING SUNNY afternoon, Danny and Hank, with rifles on the ground nearby, dug into the earth, deep within the North Woods.

They had to bury Jarvis Gibson.

Enemy or no, Hank had said, Gibson was still a man, and ought to be paid his last respects.

Jeff, Isabella, and Dras were across town on a recon mission, trying to get the goods on this "Celebration Day" thing. It was dangerous, Danny knew. With night coming soon, it'd be *suicidal.*

Why couldn't I have gone?

But Danny understood all too well why. *Dras.* He liked Dras all right. The guy seemed like a decent dude and he'd had a rough go of things. He'd made it through a stint in Wexler with his humanity intact, so the guy was deserving of respect.

Still, it was hard being left on the sidelines after occupying a frontline position for so long. Danny and Jeff had been an indomitable team, taking on Shamblers and redeeming folks from Greensboro, fighting monsters and taking names. After Tabitha left…well, it was all Danny had now. It was who he was.

A Devil Smasher.

Only, not today. No, today he was a grave digger and a baby-sitter, left behind with the other B-Listers like Hank and Sarah, watching over the 'Nites, making sure no one hurt themselves while Jeff and Isabella were gone. It was an important job, he supposed, but it felt awfully degrading.

There were plenty of men at the Haven who could have performed burial detail today, but Hank confided in Danny the ex-sheriff *needed* to do some grunt work. Work out some issues. He invited Danny along—the first time someone had done so since

Dras arrived—and he had jumped at the chance. So, they left Sarah back at the camp to watch over the others. It was a big job to place on the untried girl's shoulders, but Danny supposed Carter was there to keep things in check.

The two men pushed their shovels into the hard-packed dirt, standing in the hole they made. Gibson's body was wrapped in a sheet beside them, giving Danny the creeps. He worked faster.

Hank struggled against the chore. The old man was heavyset and tired and hadn't worked like this in awhile, Danny figured. But the man was trying and Danny had a newfound respect for the big guy. Despite his eager heart, Hank finally slowed to a stop, straightening his back and panting hard, gripping his chest.

"Whoa, boy," he coughed, and Danny stopped shoveling, breathing hard himself.

"What? What's wrong? You okay?"

"Just need a sec. Gotta catch…my second wind."

Danny nodded, taking a breather, trying hard not to look at Gibson's body.

Am I gonna end up like that? What if we can't stop this, he suddenly feared. *Maybe I'm wasting my time here. Maybe I should be spending these last few moments before the world ends with Tabitha. With my boys.*

He felt sick to his stomach and he jabbed at the dirt with his shovel once more.

Finally breathing normally again, Hank huffed, "All right. I think I'm good for a little while longer. Let's take it slow, though, okay?"

Danny cracked a grin. "Anything you say, old man." He let go a chuckle as the two continued digging. Both men kept their eyes on the job, but the mood was decidedly lighter.

"You think it was smart leaving Sarah in charge?" Hank snickered.

"She can take care of herself."

"She sure has her eye on you," he said, slyly, giving his young counterpart a wink.

Danny looked at him once, blushed, then turned away, gloomy. "Not you, too."

Hank stopped, suddenly surprised. "Yeah? Who else has been telling you so?"

Danny counted off, "Uh, just about every grandma we got back at HQ."

Hank snorted and continued shoveling. "Well, grandmas are like that."

"I ain't got time for stuff like that."

"Says who?"

"Says me. This is war, Hank. No time for love in war."

"What about after war?"

"*Is* there an 'after war'?"

Hank worked, then paused just a bit, his face frowning. "Don't know. Hope so."

"Besides, I'm still countin' on skipping town after we avert the apocalypse and seeing Tabitha and my babies. That's what it's about for me. Sarah's just a school girl. She don't know what she wants."

Hank sighed, forlornly. "Trust me, kid. When they get older, they still don't know what they want."

Now it was Danny's turn to slow. He watched his friend cutting the dirt, pensive. "What's with you?"

Hank plunged the shovel into the ground and leaned on the handle, letting loose a long exhalation. At length, he heavily turned to face Danny. "Doris is leaving me. She's taking Becky with her."

"*What?*"

"Don't tell the others, okay? I haven't even told Jeff. I-I don't think I can bear to right now."

Danny let his handle collapse to the ground and moved closer to his friend, as if he could literally help shoulder his burden. "Why's she leaving?"

"She wants to go back to town."

"*Now?* We're right in the middle of this!"

"I know. I know it's the worst possible time but…I guess that's when these kinds of things happen, right? I don't know. I've never had my wife leave me before."

"Hank…"

"She's leaving with Father Joe, next bus out. I got her convinced to stay with her sister. With imminent doom coming and all, maybe…maybe it's for the best. Maybe after we stop this, it'll be okay for her to come back. If she even really wants to…"

Danny watched Hank, closely. "You really think we can do it? You really think we can fix this mess? Save the world?"

Hank shrugged with a wearied, haggard smile. "Dunno. Gotta try, though, right?"

Danny grinned with a nod. "Can't fault you there."

The two men finished burying Gibson without another word.

The Good Church of the Faithful burned to the ground months ago thanks to Earl Canton and a deluded mob. What the town erected from its ashes was something strange, alien, and altogether unholy.

It was the Family Worship Center.

"The Center", as it was known to the people of Greensboro, boasted of the best that modern day religion had to offer. It was fast, easy, accessible, and didn't require commitment, responsibility, or sacrifice. The services provided were of "universal" spirituality and faith. Every god, creed, doctrine, and religious teaching was accepted as part of the Center's program, save for one.

Jesus Christ, Jeff thought glumly. No, *that* name wasn't allowed, nor were those who called upon it. "Evangelical Christians" were the enemy of rational thought and decent, thinking human beings, after all.

Standing there, on the steps leading to the place where his church had been, Jeff's soul filled with anguish.

"This is the church?" Dras asked in disbelief. "What happened?"

"It's what people wanted," Jeff said. "State-of-the-art sound system. Twenty-four hour entertainment. Even a gift shop on the third story where you can buy ten dollar idols."

Isabella stepped up, the last of their trio, her voice like ice, "And best of all, no Jesus. They found Him too offensive so they asked Him to leave. Nice place, huh?"

Outside the Center, a construction crew labored, hefting large plasma screens and fixing them to the front of the edifice. Whatever Celebration Day was, it seemed that the whole town needed to see it.

"Gives me the creeps," Dras said quietly.

Jeff pulled out the blue paper from his back pocket. "The flyers all point back to this place." Then, Jeff looked up, eyeing the door and imagining the man he knew he would find behind it: Will Baxter. His assistant pastor turned Committee stooge.

"I'm staying out here." Isabella stepped away from the building.

"I don't know if that's safe. We're running enough of a risk showing up in town in broad daylight. We need to stick together."

"The sun's out. The gremlins aren't going to come out and do anything right here in front of God and everybody. I may get some funny looks—"

"Or a visit from a certain sheriff," Jeff argued.

"What's he going to do? Arrest me?"

"You know he could do a whole lot worse than that."

"But I won't be doing anything. Just sitting here not saying 'Jesus'. Besides, if I see Will Baxter again, I'm liable to wring his scrawny neck."

"Okay." Jeff nodded to his wife. "Honk if there's trouble."

Feeling uneasy, but determined to do this, Jeff led Dras up the stone steps to the Center. On the frame of the building, carved into the stone, was a sigil—the same sun-shaped design that the Committee members branded to their arms.

The same sigil Jeff saw in his dreams. *On the church in the burning town…*

Inside, the Center was even more immaculate. Everywhere were high-backed plush leather chairs, red carpet, marble pillars, multi-colored display lights focused on rare and valuable works of art depicting every religion. And that was just the lobby.

"Sheesh," Dras muttered, taking a look at the whole thing.

"How could Greensboro afford this?"

Jeff went rigid as an attractive young couple passed, giving the Weldon brothers—and their unwashed clothes—a disapproving glare.

"Good question," he muttered, as the couple turned away.

Dras moved down the hall, but something caught Jeff's attention before he could join his brother. It was a large poster, depicting a husband and wife running through flowery country fields with their laughing three little children linked between them like a human chain of joy. In fancy, cursive writing above this picture of familial wonderment were the words: DO YOUR PART ON CELEBRATION DAY! SHARE IN THE BLESSING!

"Hey." Jeff turned to his brother. "Check this out."

Following his gaze, Dras eyed the banner. "Celebration Day. What does it mean, anyway?" he asked. "'Do your part'?"

Jeff glowered at the promotional photo in the lower left hand corner of the banner. It depicted a sickeningly familiar well-dressed man. Underneath his picture was printed: SPECIAL GUEST SPEAKER—MAYOR JOHN GRAVES.

Jeff growled. "Let's ask."

Reverend Will Baxter was a busy man. Celebration Day was tomorrow and there was still so much to do. He tapped the microphone on the pulpit at the stage, leaning in. "Can you hear me all right?"

A man in the sound booth gave him the thumbs-up. Men on scaffolding adjusted the spotlights this way and that. Others hung more banners, in the same theme as the family-friendly poster outside. Still more wired the stage for the band that was supposed to come in and lead the congregation of many faiths in worship.

Not for the first time today, Will looked through the glass-domed ceiling above him. It was another beautiful day in Greensboro and the sun nearly blinded him from where he stood at the podium. There was something unsettling about having the heavens opened up just above him where, day after day, he preached lies from the blasphemous pulpit.

His paranoia and guilt multiplied exponentially when he looked back down and saw—

"Jeff?" Will's voice squeaked.

Jeff and Dras Weldon entered the meeting hall, as the older brother muttered to the younger, "Let me handle this."

Moving ahead, he approached the altar as Will stepped down, wiping his sweaty palms on his expensive suit. He adjusted his glasses, trembling. "Uh…what are you doing here? It's—uh—good to see you."

"Drop the act, Will," Jeff said without emotion. "You know why we're here."

From behind him, a stone-faced Dras held out the blue flyer. Jeff intoned, "The Dark Hour."

Will looked around at the technicians continuing in their work and wondered if any of them would save him. "Uh…"

Jeff took the flyer from his brother and dangled it in front of the young prophet's face, calling his attention. "Is *this* the Dark Hour? Celebration Day?"

Will fumbled with his hands, looking to the exits on either side of him, hoping that the Strange Man would come and defend him, speak for him, think for him.

"Uh…"

Jeff stepped closer. Will tried not to shake in the man's presence. Jeff had been his friend once, his pastor. He had taken him under his wing, had him over for dinner, tried to be a mentor to him…but now…*I betrayed him. I betrayed them all.*

"*Will.*"

"It's a private matter between…those involved. When it's time, it'll be broadcast for everyone, but until then—as their pastor, I can't break that confidence—"

"What is it?" Jeff demanded. "What does it mean by 'Do your part'?"

Will faltered at the knees, nearly buckling. "Jeff, you know I can't tell you anything you don't already know. You're…well, you're the enemy, sir. You can't just walk in here and expect me to give you information. It doesn't work like that."

Jeff leaned over, his jaw tensing. "We can change the rules, if you'd like."

"You can threaten me all you want but, as much as I fear you, I fear *him* more."

Dras said, "You know you're working for the devil, right?"

Will balked, ready to defend himself, but his shoulders sagged and he confessed, "The devil can be very convincing."

"Will…please," Jeff urged. "We're trying to save you. We were friends once and I know you…or at least I used to. Whatever this Dark Hour is, I know that a lot of people are going to die. Can you really live with that?"

Will just stared at his shiny shoes.

Jeff pleaded. "Now—*please*—what is Celebration Day?"

Will continued to look at the tips of his toes. "It's an offering."

"Offering what?"

The false prophet lashed out with his arms, defensive. "This town is thriving! No one wants for a job, everybody has plenty of food, and gas prices are down to an all-time low. We're doing better for ourselves than we ever did—even when the highway was still here!"

Tears formed behind his bottle-rimmed glasses, as Will quieted, his heart twisting in guilt and pain.

"What is it?" Jeff asked evenly. "What are you offering, Will?"

"It's what the people *want!*" he yelled in a broken voice. "It's a sacrifice, I know, but it's the only way to ensure our future!"

"*Will!*" Jeff commanded. "What are you offering?"

Sobbing, Will shook his head and looked Jeff square in the eye. "You know, sir…you've seen the ads."

Jeff looked down at the blue flyer in his hand, then up to see another banner stretched across the theater. A banner depicting a young mother holding her newborn baby out before her with a bright smile and a cartoon word balloon attached declaring: I'M

DOING MY PART. HOW ABOUT YOU?

"Dear God…" Jeff gasped.

"It's the babies, sir," Will whispered, sitting in a nearby chair. "It's always been the babies."

"You're going to sacrifice babies?" Dras gasped as Will remained seated, his face in his hands.

The young preacher looked up, dismayed. Whether because he felt guilty for what he was sanctioning or because he had given in and told them the truth, Dras wasn't for sure.

"It's what's required of us to remain prosperous."

"The people won't let this happen," Jeff said.

Will stood. "The people voted for this, Jeff! They want this! You've been away too long, you've lost touch with what this town wants. Greensboro was divided because of your God, but he…"

"The Strange Man," Jeff interrupted. "Say his name."

Will slumped. "The Strange Man. He-he united us under his."

"His god is a lie."

"Does that matter?" Will asked weakly. "The people believe in it. Isn't that enough?"

Dras shook his head. "You can believe a lie completely, but it's still a lie."

"The same might be said of *your* faith," spoke a sing-song voice from behind them.

Dras's blood ran cold. For all the world, he didn't want to turn around. Didn't want to see. Will cowered in place, hiding his face from his master, as Dras and Jeff turned to face their worst fears realized.

The Strange Man stood before them.

He was concealed in beauty and light, thankfully refraining from loosing his true monstrous visage on them. Dras didn't know if he could stand to see that face again.

Moving gracefully down the aisle, he approached the Weldon brothers as old friends. "Hello, boys."

Will remained behind Jeff, using him as a shield. "They wanted to know about Celebration Day. I didn't say anything!"

The Strange Man looked to the weakling and waved his hand. "Leave."

Will Baxter left without a word, scrambling to get far, far away.

Dras watched the preacher go, suddenly realizing that the workers had gone too. There was no one else in the sanctuary. No one but he, his brother, and the devil.

The Strange Man raised his arms in the air, as if stretching for the first time this morning, and let out a good, long, relaxing breath, before finally reclining in one of the chairs. "Have a seat."

"Drop dead," Jeff said.

"Jeff…" Dras whispered, his heart shuddering in his chest. He was suddenly reminded of a trip to the zoo when he was a kid. He had visited the tiger's cage and remembered seeing the big cat pacing back and forth, back and forth, studying the humans watching him. Dras remembered thinking that, were it not for the bars, that tiger could have killed them all, just like on the Discovery Channel.

It was *that* feeling gripping Dras now. The Strange Man was a caged tiger, but where were his bars? Was he holding back his power on purpose?

Or is God holding him in place?

Either way, Dras was grateful, but he didn't want to provoke the animal. He just wanted to leave before feeding time.

"Come on, Jeff," he muttered, "Let's go. We shouldn't be here."

But Jeff showed no sign of moving, his fists clenched in righteous fury.

"I was wondering when you two would show up," the Strange Man said, picking an inconsequential piece of lint off his suit. "I must ask, where's Isabella?"

"Leave her out of this," Jeff said.

"I sure do like her, Jeff," the Strange Man winked. "She's a powerful girl. A lot of spunk, that one. You'd do best to hang on to her as long as you can. After all, we never know how long we'll have the people we love in our lives."

Jeff started for the monster, but Dras held him back. "Whoa, killer."

The Strange Man chuckled, and his eyes sparkled with delight as he turned his attention to the younger Weldon brother. "And looky here. Dras Weldon, all grown up and out of the slammer. My, it feels like it's been an age, boy."

Dras half-smiled, sheepishly. "Yeah. You're looking good, there."

The Strange Man lightened, amused. "Yes? You like the suit? I tell you, Rosalyn sure does. Can't keep her off of me when I wear it."

Dras's heart sank.

"She picked it out for me, in fact. She's got better taste than I do, let's face it. But, I guess you'd know that better than anyone, wouldn't you, boy?"

Dras couldn't look at him anymore.

A honk outside. *The truck.*

Jeff's eyes widened in alarm. "Isabella," he said, and started for the door.

Dras followed, eager to be away from here, and the Strange Man remained relaxed, spread out with his feet propped on the chair in front of him. Craning his head, he laughed at them.

"See you tomorrow, boys! It's gonna be a blast!"

Outside, Isabella sat in the truck, the windows rolled up, as a small mob of angry people clamored around her. When Jeff emerged from the Center, he saw her face—her eyes. She was terrified.

"Move! Let me through!" he hollered, hurrying down the steps, pushing his way to his wife.

"Go home!" the voices shouted, turning their aggression toward Jeff. "Go spread your hate somewhere else!"

"This is bad," Dras muttered, keeping up with him.

A man in the crowd shouted, "You wanna tell me I'm going to

hell for not believing in your God? Why don't you tell me to my face?"

Jeff ground his teeth, but kept his head low, opening the driver's door. "You okay?" he asked his wife.

She was in tears. "They just showed up all of a sudden. I tried to talk to them, but—"

"It's all right. Scoot over, I'll drive."

"Hey!" the persistent man screamed, picking up a rock. "I'm talking to you!"

He threw the rock like a baseball, hitting Isabella in the head. She yelped in pain, fresh blood trickling from the open wound, and slumped over. Dras rushed to her side. "Isabella!"

Jeff, though, only saw red.

He let go of his wife, his blood boiling, and spun to face Isabella's attacker, growling with rage. The man smiled and put up his fists, ready for a fight. "Yeah, come on, preacher man. Show me what you got."

Jeff balled his fists and stormed after the man, who suddenly shrank back. Jeff's shoulder reared up, readying for the punch…but he hesitated. Suddenly, a face across the street, away from the crowd caught his attention. A face he had not seen in a very long time. It was a man he had hurt once in anger.

Earl Canton watched Jeff very closely, to see what the preacher would do.

A hush blanketed the crowd, and Jeff let his hands fall to his sides, returning to Isabella without further incident. The crowd seemed to come to their senses and stood by in silence. He examined the small cut on Isabella's head. "Okay?"

She met his eyes, pained but all right.

"Come on," Jeff said to Dras, keeping a lookout for any more attacks. "We need to go before Stevenson shows up."

Dras held back, even as the crowd began to disperse. "I can't."

Jeff sighed. "You want to see her. Don't you?"

"You know I have to."

"How are you going to get back to the camp?"

"Don't worry," Dras smiled a familiar goofy grin. "God will get me back. I'm the hero around here, remember? Destined to stop the Dark Hour and be all cool."

Jeff considered, then lowered his gaze. "You'd better be right about that, little brother."

Dras's smile widened and he nodded to Isabella. "Get her out of here."

Isabella warned him, "Be careful."

Dras winked, then ran into the shadows. Jeff started up his truck and drove away. But in the rearview mirror, he glimpsed Earl Canton lingering a moment longer, watching the departing truck with a thoughtful frown.

CHAPTER FIFTEEN

ROSALYN SAT ON her couch as darkness fell, quietly thumbing through the pages of Ray McCormick's diary. The first entry was written the day Lindsey was born. In his own words, Ray said that he had never felt more important than when he first looked down at his little girl.

Rosalyn wondered if her own dad had felt the same.

Ray went on to explain that he wanted to keep a diary of Lindsey's life and present it to her on her wedding day so that her husband could read it and see the heart of the man who had loved Lindsey first.

Rosalyn grinned at the sentiment. Ray was always so sweet, so tenderhearted. She had known him briefly when Dras dated Lindsey. At the time, Dras was very keen on being friends with Lindsey's friends—most of whom Rosalyn utterly hated—and he dragged his best friend along to many pool parties and family barbecues. Dras wanted so badly for Rosalyn and Lindsey to get along, but they never really hit it off. Looking back, Rosalyn didn't know if it was Lindsey she didn't like, or the fact that she was dating Dras.

Although she was miserable at every single one of those parties, Rosalyn thought fondly now of Ray, always behind the grill in an apron and Ray Ban sunglasses, cheerfully serving his daughter and her friends and telling the best jokes, even if they were kind of lame.

Even then, through Rosalyn's angsty haze, she had recognized that he was a good man and a good father.

And now he's dead. Lindsey too.

Her smile faded and she turned another page.

Most of the diary consisted of simple entries, dedicated to the ups and downs of raising a little girl. Some of them were very personal and, even though the McCormick family was all dead and gone, Rosalyn still felt a bit embarrassed for invading their cherished memories.

Soon, though, her walk-through of Lindsey's life in Ray's words led her to the pages that made this book so valuable. The pages that had cost the lives of Caroline McCormick and the members of the Committee. Rosalyn carefully read the last fully coherent entry:

Date—I can't remember the date. What day is it? Is it still summer? No—no, I saw the leaves changing.

I thought of you today, Lindsey. I think of you every day. I went to the Sheriff to see if anything had been done to find you but Hank fears the worst. They've all given up on you—even your Mom, she thinks that I'm fooling myself—but I still wait by the door, listening for your footsteps. I'm never more than a few feet from a phone, waiting for you to call. This town's already buried an empty coffin, but I won't accept that. I know you're still out there and I'll keep writing in this diary so that you'll know that I never gave up on you. Never.

The phone is ringing—I have to go. It might be the man I've been talking to. He says he might know where you are. I have to go—

Rosalyn turned the page in rapt attention.

Things started to get weird in the diary after that entry. Ray's loving words were replaced by strange drawings and symbols. At first they were only doodles at the corners of the page, but as the diary progressed, so did the scribbles, in intensity and morbidity. Before long, whole pages were devoted to the bizarre configurations. One symbol, in particular, Rosalyn painfully recognized.

It was branded on her lower back. The symbol of the sun. *His* symbol. She still didn't really know what it meant, but the Man was fond of it.

Rosalyn sifted through the diary, coming across more bizarre sketches of impossible slimy creatures with tentacles and hair and eyes. They looked a lot like the black goo-guys wandering around the North Woods. They also looked like that terrible flying beast that TJ had become.

She knew that the same thing was going to happen to her as what happened to TJ. She could already feel the change beginning. Her bones ached and she was always so cold. *And the voices...*Most days she could ignore them, but they were still there. Whispering to her. Tempting her.

Rosalyn remembered that fateful day she tasted the Strange Man's fruit. The day that damned her. *If only I could go back. If only things had been different.*

She somberly closed Ray McCormick's diary.

It didn't make any sense to her. Just strings of letters that didn't have a pattern. For a second, she thought to give the book to Annie and give her little sister explicit instructions to get it to Jeff. However, that just would have put her family in danger and she'd done enough of that already.

Just as well. I don't know what good this gibberish could do.

Standing now, Rosalyn moved to the window and her thoughts turned to Dras. She'd thought of little else since seeing him last night. *What is he doing? Where is he? Is he thinking of me?*

"Oh, Dras..." she moaned, trying hard not to cry. She could really use him now.

Would he have her? After the way he had seen her last...would he still love her just the same?

A lump formed in her throat and she wanted to break down, but couldn't. The Strange Man had already called a meeting of the Legion of Doom and she needed to get going. They had a ceremony to prepare for, after all. All these months of planning were coming to a head tomorrow, and after that...

The Change.

She would be different after tomorrow. Like TJ and then...well, then she wouldn't hurt anymore. She wouldn't think of the people she'd betrayed to be by the devil's side. It would all be gone, and there would only be the darkness.

It was a cold comfort. But, right now, it was all the comfort she had.

Jeff told Isabella about the babies. She'd cried, shouted, and wished death upon the entire town. After that, the two of them prayed, wept together, and decided they'd return to the Haven and figure out their next step. In the meantime, she needed to catch her breath. To have a moment that wasn't about death and horror.

They decided to go back home.

The house on Grover's Pond sat cold and empty. With their truck parked at the end of the gravel drive, Jeff and Isabella walked toward the shadowed structure, hand in hand. During their engagement, they had pinched and saved for almost a year, going so far as to postpone their wedding, all in the hopes of buying this house, their dream house, and it *had* been a dream.

But the dream had ended.

"It looks so sad," she said softly as they stepped onto the porch, the wood beneath her creaking.

Jeff cupped his eyes against the window, peering inside. "Wow…"

Isabella brushed against the house, eager to touch it, to feel its familiar roughness, hoping to connect to that old life that had made this place so special.

"I think they painted the living room," Jeff grumbled.

She turned to him and smiled, realizing that maybe *he* was the magic about this place. Them, here, together.

She rubbed his back. "Hey."

He stood straight and sighed, taking a great big look at the house. Isabella placed her hands on his shoulders and turned him to face her. "*Hey.*"

He tried to return her warm expression but failed. "Hey."

"It's like you said. You're my home. You know that, don't you?"

Shrugging, he whined. "Yeah. I know. But the house was nice too."

It was, Isabella admitted. This was their first home. Where they used to snuggle, and play, and fight. Where Isabella burned dinner on their first anniversary and cried all night, thinking she had failed as a wife and Jeff held her and stroked her hair. This was where they dreamed big and thought about children. This was supposed to have been the yard where their children would play. The halls where their children would run. This was their future.

But now…

Jeff exhaled again, unable to express how much he felt. But Isabella knew. She felt the same.

"You wanna sit in the swing?" She raised a playful eyebrow. "Old times' sake?"

He squeezed her hand and let her lead the way. Thankfully the Houstons—the house's most recent owners before they vacated Greensboro and all its newfound weirdness—had left behind the porch swing, its rusty chain squeaking against the hooks in the overhang. It was a rickety old swing, here long before Jeff and Isabella had moved in, and it had been the couple's favorite part of the house. The two of them sat on the uncomfortable, peeling boards and rocked back and forth, listening to the whistling wind and watching the gentle ripples of Grover's Pond.

They were quiet for a long moment and Isabella remembered better times when every summer evening was spent out here, watching the water, talking about anything, or sometimes not talking at all, but just sitting. Holding. Loving.

"Feels the same." She looked out over the moonlit pond, breathing in the nostalgia.

"We shouldn't stay long."

"I know. Just a little bit longer."

She knew he wanted to stay too. Back at the Haven, they hardly had any time to be alone. Their lives were not their own anymore. They belonged to Danny, to Hank, to Sarah, and to everyone else who looked to them for guidance and protection. For a place that was called "the Haven" it sure seemed like a prison sometimes.

But this place…this was just for Jeff and Isabella.

She wished they could run inside to their old room, jump in

their cozy bed, and make love. They had taken those intimate moments for granted before, but now she missed them so much. She never realized before how much they needed to be together, to hold each other, to kiss, to feel…It had been weeks since they were that close and it was beginning to feel like they were on separate planets.

Yet, here, on the swing, with Grover's Pond before her, Isabella finally felt like they were re-establishing the lines of communication. That's why they needed to come out here tonight. Their marriage was headed for disaster a few months ago, but they had worked hard to mend it. They had invested too much in each other to give up now.

Jeff held out an arm and she slid underneath it, burying her face in his chest, snuggling close. He squeezed Isabella tighter, and she took comfort in his familiar body.

"They won't take you," he said.

Isabella kept her head to his shoulder. "What do you mean?"

"They've taken everything away from us. But they won't take you."

"No." She grinned. "I'm right here."

At last, Jeff said, "We'd better get headed back. I left Danny in charge. He's probably fit to be tied, by now."

"Just one more minute," she whispered. "Give me one more minute with you and I can die happy."

Die happy.

Something scary and final in her heart told Isabella that very soon they were going to start losing the people they cared about.

And it was going to be anything but happy.

After returning from Gibson's fresh grave, Danny needed a smoke.

In an abandoned church out in the middle of the sticks, holed up with two hundred other hungry, tired, and smelly people, being alone was a rare commodity. For Danny, a loner by nature, it was especially precious to find some quiet place to gather his thoughts and just take a breather from all the drama and chaos that living "off the grid" created.

Behind the church, Danny lit his cigarette and leaned against the faded red Nova that they retrieved following the close call with the Wilbanks family. He took a long, slow drag off his cigarette, holding the smoke in ecstasy, then blew it out, along with all of his worries. Finally, he had a chance to be by himself.

"Hey."

Danny looked up, half-heartedly, and took another puff on his cigarette. *Carter.*

"You mind?" Carter asked.

He exhaled and shrugged. "Suit yourself."

"Thanks." Carter lit a cigarette of his own.

The two men smoked in silence for a few beats, and Danny grew increasingly anxious. For one, Carter Ross used to be a deputy and had actually arrested Danny a time or two back in the day. Secondly, Carter was a staunch detractor of Jeff's and, being that he was Jeff's right-hand man—*or at least I was before Dràs showed up*—the two seemed fated to be at odds.

"So…uh…" Carter began. Danny tensed, taking another deliberate drag off his cigarette. "What's going on?"

"What do you mean?" he played dumb.

"Jeff went into town. Is he onto something?"

"We don't know yet, Carter. Maybe."

Carter turned to the younger man, his impatience flaring. "Aw, come on, Danny. You're the guy's Number Two. What's the word? What are we going to do?"

Danny reddened. He didn't know what bothered him more—Carter grilling him with questions, or the fact that he had no answers.

"We keep doing what we do," Danny replied in a hollow tone, echoing Jeff's mantra.

"Man, that's not going to cut it and you know it." Carter stepped closer, his voice a low hush and his eyes intense under his Raiders cap. "Look, I appreciate what Jeff wants to do. Really, I get it. He's responsible for all these folks and that puts a lot more pressure on him. But, if you ask me, it's causing him to get too careful. I don't think he's ready to take the risks that need to be taken to solve this."

Danny tried not to listen. Carter didn't know Jeff. Jeff was a good man. He only wanted to do what was right. Carter just seemed to want to shoot his gun off.

"Why don't you take it up at the next Church Meeting," Danny suggested, walking away.

But Carter pulled him back. "We need to do something, Danny. Listen..." He looked over his shoulder. "Some of the boys and I have been talking about...starting up a little group. Totally Black Ops. Jeff wouldn't even have to know about it. We've already got some guns and we've got a friend of mine back at the sheriff's station who could get us some more. We'd be loaded for bear and organized and we could take out the Strange Man, once and for all."

Danny laughed at the absurdity of such a notion, but Carter cut him off. "Join up with us, man. You're smart on your feet and good with a gun. Let Jeff worry about the people here. We can take care of the Strange Man ourselves."

"Better men than you have tried, Carter. You know bullets won't hurt the Man."

Carter lit up. "I know, I know. That's just it. We're going to play this smart. We've got some men who are going to back us up as Prayers. And we've got one guy, you know, Ed Mathers? He's just going to be reading the Bible. Scripture is like demon-repellent, right? That's what Isabella said."

Danny snorted...though he secretly thought this plan was making a little bit of sense.

"We've got to do *something*. Even Jeff and Isabella have been saying it. The Dark Hour is tomorrow, and the Strange Man's Master is gonna be riding into town. When he hits, no one's going to be safe. You think we can hide out here forever?"

Danny didn't say anything.

"Okay, here's the deal," Carter began his final plea. "This little group of ours is going to be meeting in thirty minutes at the Old Greenesboro ruins."

"That's a little too close to Shamblers for me."

"It'll be all right. Like I said, we'll have a couple men praying around the circle to mask us from any unwanted *supernatural* attention."

Danny wrinkled his face. "You really think that'll work?"

"It has been."

"You mean…you've met before?"

"For a month or so. We've got some really good ideas and we could use you. You know more about this than Jeff gives you credit for."

Danny slumped, sticking his hands in his pockets. He didn't want to hear any more. He already felt like he was betraying Jeff just by listening to this insanity and he wanted to be gone.

"See ya, Carter."

"Think about it, will you?"

Danny didn't say so…but he would.

Jeff, whatever you're waiting for, I hope it happens soon.

CHAPTER SIXTEEN

THERE WAS NOTHING left at the Old Greenesboro ruins but the charred stone foundations of a long lost colony, and an old wooden sign close to the ground that simply read "Old Greenesboro". A place of a mythic past, of prairie settlers, big dreams, and hard times, it was the birthplace of Greensboro.

Torches lit the darkened faces of men standing in the high grass next to the sign. When Danny pushed through the thick of the North Woods to enter the clearing, he heard the mumbling of men praying at three corners around the perimeter. What they were saying, he couldn't tell, but they were chanting, low and melodic.

Never had praying given him the creeps before.

Carter was at the forefront of the group and spotted the young man entering their midst. As he did, the others turned in their spots, a look of fright flashing over their faces, which quickly gave way to relief.

"Started the party without me, huh?" Danny chuckled, anxious to break the tension.

"Danny." Carter grinned, looking touched. "Glad you could make it."

He shrugged and stuck his hands in his pockets. "Well, I thought I'd come out and see what the big fuss was."

Looking around, Danny saw that Carter had an army of ten men strong. He recognized all the faces. There was Milton Wilbanks, shaking like a leaf, Ed Mathers by Carter's side with a weathered Bible in his hands, a grizzled farmer by the name of Burt Simmons and his sixteen-year-old boy, Andrew, both sporting rifles and determined looks. Others too, Danny noticed, like Jake Tucker, a burly twenty-six-year-old ex-college football player, a pistol strapped to his right thigh, and Gus Reynolds, the short, plump man in a floppy straw hat and a tackle vest lined with bandoliers of shotgun ammunition.

Carter waded through the group, approaching Danny with an air of camaraderie and trust. "You're just in time."

"Hey, I ain't signed up for nothing yet. I'm just out here to make sure you guys don't get yourselves killed."

Carter gave the boy his space, but still looked relieved to have him at the meeting. "Whatever you need this to be. Just know that we're doing this, with or without your approval."

"Jeff's on his way back," Danny said, hoping that that might stay Carter's hand long enough for everyone to think this through before they did something really stupid.

Carter hardened. "We're not waitin'. Tonight's our night. Our man on the inside's already told us that the Strange Man will be at the club tonight, at a party. He's already living up his victory for tomorrow; he won't see us coming."

"Who's this guy on the inside you keep talking about? Where is he?"

As if on cue, Danny heard the low rumble of an engine as a pair of headlights elucidated the clearing. The men raised their guns and took aim, but Carter smiled wide. "Easy, guys. Here he is now."

Like a lumbering beast, a shiny black Humvee grumbled, inching its way to the group. Danny held his hand to shield his eyes from the light, trying to get a good look at the driver as he stepped out of the side and approached the ragtag band of monster hunters.

"Hey, fellas."

Danny's stomach lurched. It was Sheriff Ryan Stevenson.

Immediately, all men lowered their weapons just when Danny was thinking they should start firing, and Carter approached the man with a hearty laugh and handshake.

"What's *he* doing out here?" Danny snapped.

Stevenson craned his neck to see Danny. His mirthful sneer was replaced by a low snarl. The sheriff turned to Carter. "I said come alone. You bringing the whole God Squad out here?"

Carter waved his hands. "Wait, wait. He's good. He's with us, now."

Stevenson cooled, but obviously didn't approve of the new addition.

"You got what we asked for?"

Stevenson hesitated, still considering Danny. "Yeah, I got it." Complaining under his breath, the sheriff disappeared behind the Humvee, digging around in the back. Carter explained to Danny, "Ryan's got connections. We've got body armor, flash-bangs, gas grenades—"

"And lots and lots of these," Stevenson beamed with pride, coming into view holding two .45 SMG automatic rifles by the barrels.

He tossed one each to Jake Tucker and Gus Reynolds, and both men received them like boys on Christmas morning. Eyeing their new gear, the two whistled and talked excitedly. Carter glowed at their joy, and Danny recognized how much the man's team meant to him.

Stevenson returned to the Humvee, grabbing two armloads of bulletproof vests and handing them out. Danny noticed Andrew, only a kid, quietly strapping on his flak jacket, fear in his eyes. The kid kept a straight face in front of his father, but Danny could tell he was scared witless.

"Listen up," Carter announced as the Praying Men huddled closer, fastening on their own jackets and equipping themselves with pistols and automatics. "This town was built so that Christians could worship freely and we're gonna make sure it stays that way." He paused, looking each man in the eye. "I won't lie to you, some of us ain't gonna make it back tonight. So I hope you've made peace with God and your family. If you wanna turn back, that's okay. But if you're ready to fight to win this town back, then it's time we made our stand."

The men raised their guns in the air, hollering, rallying their strength, their gusto. It seemed only Stevenson was untouched by Carter's speech. The sheriff, instead, leaned on the Humvee and bit his nails, bored. Carter's words moved Danny, as well, and he was half-tempted to jump right in, slap on a jacket and a gun and join them, but he forced himself to stop. To think.

"Wait a minute."

The pep rally broke for a moment as all eyes, even Stevenson, sought out Danny. "Look, I know what you guys are trying to do. I've wanted to do this too, but this ain't the way. We gotta stop. We gotta talk this out. Plan this through."

"We've already made a plan, Carpenter," Ed Mathers spoke up, impatient. "Stevenson's got us a window to make our move."

Stevenson waved and winked from his position. Danny fumed.

"You can't trust Stevenson. He's been hunting us for months! The guy's a creep and the only dude he's looking out for is himself."

"*Hey,*" Stevenson mildly protested.

Danny paced the crowd, looking to each of them. "I bet the only reason he's doing this is so he can hand you over to the Man and win some brownie points."

Stevenson chuckled. "Kid's got a point."

Carter sighed, gave Stevenson a warning look, and faced Danny. "Stevenson's a good cop. I trust him with my life."

"That's exactly what you're doing." Surveying the group, Danny continued, "Listen, man, Jeff's not deaf, okay? And he ain't stupid, neither. The guy knows about this demon stuff; we should listen to him. You really think you're gonna hurt the bogeyman with *guns*?"

The men grew agitated, though they did not lose their resolve. All except for Milton, who seemed perpetually nervous. He looked this way and that, as if trying to find his solace in the eyes of his buddies.

Carter saw the effect Danny was having on his men and stepped forward. "He's right. We need an edge, it's true. But we've got one. One that I *know* will work."

Danny waited, ready to hear what this secret weapon was and why it hadn't been brought to Jeff's attention before. Even Stevenson inclined his head, looking eager to be in on the secret.

Carter shared a concerned glance with Ed Mathers and the man laid his Bible on a nearby stump, then reached into his coat pocket. What he pulled out was a plastic soda bottle filled with a thick, viscous, black oil that glistened in the moonlight.

"Is that…?" Gus asked breathlessly.

Carter nodded. "It's that gunk from the lake. We got some of it. Caught it as it was trying to leave the body of one of the Man's possessed crows I shot down a couple days ago. The goop's *alive*."

Danny's blood turned cold.

"What do you plan on doing with it?" Burt snorted.

Stevenson stood straighter, his jaw tightening.

"I say we use it," Carter announced. "Time to fight fire with fire. This is the stuff that gives the Shamblers super strength. I say we take a little bit of that for ourselves and give it back to the Strange Man in spades."

Milton raised a trembling hand, "Won't that turn *us* into Shamblers too?"

"No," Ed assured them. "Not if we take just a little. Just enough to give us a boost."

"This is insane!" Danny exclaimed, and young Andrew inched closer. "Listen to yourselves! You gonna take a hit off that thing just to go fight this guy! That's pure *sin*, Carter! Do you know what you're doin'? You could be damnin' the whole lot of ya!"

Carter stared at Danny with haunted eyes. "Better a few be damned than the whole town."

Danny moved swiftly to the older man. Carter was a pain in the butt most of the time, it was true. But Danny had also grown to respect the man, if not for his actions, for his convictions. "That ain't for you to take on yourself, Carter. Man, didn't Jesus die to free us from this stuff? If you do this, if *all* of you do this, you'll be throwing that back in His face. You can't do that, man. It ain't right."

"Ain't nothing right anymore," Burt barked. "I say we do it. Whatever needs to be done."

"I-I don't really want to," Andrew stuttered in the gigantic presence of his father.

Burt stared him down. "Boy, you'll do it."

"But Danny's got a point, Dad. There's got to be another way. I don't think God would want us to do it like this."

Gus came to the young man's defense. "You don't have to do it, Andrew. We'd all understand." Pausing, the short man turned to the others. "Wouldn't we, fellas?"

Understanding nods all around.

Burt, though, looked ashamed, and that was the look Andrew cared about the most.

"Don't do it, kid," Danny urged.

Andrew bit his lip and stared up at his father with cold, dead eyes. "No. I wanna do it. We're all in this together."

Burt placed a firm hand on his son's shoulder, his face as stone, and turned to the group. "Let's get on with it then. We're wasting moonlight."

The group gathered around Ed as he twisted the cap off the bottle.

Carter faced Danny. "What's it gonna be, Danny?"

Danny watched helplessly as Ed poured a sliver of black oil into Andrew's hand and the boy lifted the squirming dark worm to his ear and let it fall. He twitched and jerked, coughing hard and deep. His father slapped him on the back. "You all right, boy?"

Andrew took a deep breath, a little blood trickling from his ear, then nodded. "Yeah, Dad. I'm okay."

Burt smiled, and was next in line to take a hit of the Shambler-strain earwig. Danny felt sick to his soul. This was wrong. It was a *perversion.* Good intentions or no, this wasn't the way to save Greensboro.

"I'm out," he told Carter, turning his back on the group and walking into the treeline.

Danny stomped through the woods, sucking on the butt of another cigarette. It was his last one, and he would have to find a way to get more in town on their next visit.

Yeah, right. There won't be a next time. Come tomorrow, all this will be over.

His head filled with confusion. His would-be Devil Smashers turned out to be suicidal rednecks with guns, his best friend Jeff had pretty much rendered him invisible since Dras showed up, the Strange Man's Boss was coming fast with no real chance of stopping It, and, above all, he just wanted to see Tabitha.

I miss my boys, God.

He'd been gone from camp for awhile, now, and he knew that Sarah would be by the door, looking hopefully into the North Woods, waiting for him to return. By now, Hank was probably worried about him too. But Jeff and Iz would be back soon enough.

They won't even miss me.

With a beleaguered sigh, he ground the end of his cigarette on the heel of his boot and tossed it aside. His shoulders sagging, he pressed on, back to camp.

But he didn't make it very far.

In the distance, he heard singing. A chorus of voices, drifting through the trees.

"What…?"

Changing directions, Danny pushed deeper into the unknown of the North Woods. Headed towards the lake.

He slowed as he neared the soft singing. Peering through the foliage, he saw a most unusual sight: The esteemed Reverend Will Baxter and a small congregation of couples holding infants stood together around the withered grass outlining Greensboro Park Lake. Most of them seemed to be crying, holding each other close, holding their babies closer, while Will led them in song, conducting the makeshift choir with delicate hands that, Danny figured, had never seen a hard day's work. He didn't recognize the tune as any church song *he* ever heard.

Will trailed off at the end of the odd melody, letting his hands drift to his side. His expression calm but empathetic, he gently addressed the crowd as Danny crouched low, careful not to be seen.

"I'm glad you all came out here. I was afraid it might be harder for you, but I hope that this will make your decision easier. You are prepared to make a great sacrifice for your community and I wanted to show you that you made the right decision."

Danny's brow furrowed. Will motioned to his right for a new man with a long, dark braided beard, and pock-marked face. He couldn't identify the bearded man, but felt that his presence here was *wrong*, somehow. The man solemnly approached, carrying a jar with a frog inside. Will took the jar and unscrewed the top, before reaching down with his dainty fingers. He jumped slightly when the frog *ribbited* at his touch.

What a wuss.

Will tried to look the picture of professionalism, to keep a brave face before the frightened few. Taking the rambunctious amphibian by its extended leg, Will lifted the creature from the jar and held it out for all to see.

"Mr. Graves has told us," he proclaimed, as though he were preaching, "that what we give to the lake…"

Awkwardly, as if eager to be rid of it, Will tossed the tiny creature into the opaque sludge. The crowd gasped as a leathery, membranous string whipped out from the black surface, encircled the frog, and jerked it down under the muck, in the blink of an eye.

Danny gagged.

Will too, looked a bit squeamish and reddened. All eyes remained fixed on the lake, hushed faces staring gravely, while the children in the arms of their parents began to cry. Mothers rocked their babies, trying to appease them, but even the children must have known that there was something terribly wrong.

The lake was unmoving, its slick top reflecting the moonlight above. Danny wondered what everyone was waiting on and if it would ever happen. He knew that he was already pushing his luck being out so late. He needed to get back to camp and warn the others…but warn them of what? *Crazed congregations offering frogs to the lake?*

Then it hit him. His stomach churned. He realized with dread that every single couple gathered held an infant, clinging to the child as if for dear life. Suddenly, every tiny crying baby below seemed to call out just to him, as if they were begging and pleading to be rescued.

No way…

There was a belch from the lake and the people backed away, murmuring in shock, as the frog emerged from the water. Silent and calm, the frog mechanically hopped with an unnatural slowness.

Will gestured as if to say "Ta-da" and faced the crowd with an accomplished beam. "Now, as I was saying. What we give to the lake…the lake gives back to us."

The frog sat perfectly still, staring at the audience, its eyes dark and hollow.

The crowd whispered to each other and held their children close, kissing the tops of their heads and weeping.

"So you see," Will comforted, "your children will return to you, perfectly safe."

They're going to feed those kids to the lake!

He thought of his sons. His sweet kids, who only wanted to laugh and play with their toys and hold his finger. Just kids, little babies just like those up ahead, and these godless heathens were gonna kill them?

Not on my watch.

Danny's soul raged within him, and he stood, ready to charge the masses, to beat them all to bloody pulps for being willing to kill the one thing he treasured most in this world. *You're outnumbered*, he told himself firmly, though a part of him didn't care. He'd die fighting these butchers just for the pure satisfaction.

But that wasn't smart. *Think this through. Get help*. He rotated on his heel, ready to head back to camp, ready to tell the others, ready to stop the massacre, when—

He came face to face with the barrel of Stevenson's gun.

Sneering, the sheriff cocked the weapon. "Looks like my lucky night."

Chapter Seventeen

LARRY KICKED OPEN the side door of The Rave Scene and hefted a giant garbage bag into the alley. It was his fifth bag and his heart thudded with exertion. Despite his tiresome errand, Larry was thankful for the rare moment of quiet to be away from the booming cacophony of the dance club. Things were especially wild tonight, and it made Larry nervous.

They can feel it comin'. Celebration Day.

Larry didn't spend many hours in the company of rational adults in his role as bartender at The Rave Scene, therefore his knowledge of the "Great Day" was rather limited. Even on his off-hours, Larry preferred shutting himself in his house—and shutting the world *out.* He didn't know what was going to happen tomorrow and, more to the point, he didn't want to know. *None of my business*, Larry tried to convince himself. He was just a bartender. He didn't want to get mixed up in whatever dark, appalling thing was growing within this old town and its people. *Just leave me alone.*

However, when the gloved hand clamped over his mouth, Larry knew he no longer had any choice in the matter. A second man, in a skull-faced balaclava, entered the startled bartender's vision, placing a gloved finger to his covered mouth.

"Not a word," the masked man said in a muffle. "We don't want to hurt you. We just came for Graves."

Larry's eyes searched the nine other men, all in similar masks, with bulletproof vests, helmets, gloved hands, and guns.

Lots of guns.

"Do you understand?" the leader asked, and Larry nodded.

The men in masks hurried through the side door, entering The Rave Scene through its kitchen. The tall man holding the bartender in place released his grip of Larry's mouth, hoisted his automatic to firing position, and fell in line with the others, disappearing into the club. The skull-faced leader watched his team enter the building and turned back to Larry, his voice sympathetic.

"You'd better go home for the night, Larry."

As Larry tried to picture the face that belonged to that familiar voice, the leader rushed into the building. Now alone in the alleyway, Larry stood speechless for a moment until finally deciding that this would be a good night to leave town and take his sister on that cruise she'd always wanted to go on.

"Run! Go! Keep moving!"

The ravers flew like frightened pigeons, screaming and shoving as Carter let off a quick burst of gunfire from his SMG into the ceiling. Panicked, the clubgoers scrambled for the exits and the dance hall cleared, revealing Carter's Commandos.

Months of dreaming, planning, and preparing. It all came down to this moment. Yet, somehow, Carter didn't feel the satisfaction he thought he would. There was only a sick sensation in his chest. A cold numbness that pulsated there, whispering doubt and confusion in his mind.

It's just the gunk, he told himself. *You knew it would do this. It's just trying to trick you. Don't let it use you. You use* it.

A battalion of bouncers swarmed the group but Burt, Andrew, and Jake were quick to intercept them, slinging their guns behind their backs and drawing police ASP batons. Swinging the rods of iron, the three bruisers managed to ward off the unwanted interference.

Ed Mathers took control of the DJ's booth, killed the music, and began reading Psalms 16, broadcasting his voice over the bombastic sound system. The words of the Holy Scriptures rebounded off the walls with power and authority:

"'Keep me safe, O God, for in you I take refuge. I said to the Lord, "You are my Lord; apart from you I have no good thing." As for the saints who are in the land, they are the glorious ones in whom is all my delight. The sorrows of those will increase who run after other gods. I will not pour out their libations of blood or take their names on my lips.'"

Carter watched as Ed, visibly shaking but staying firm, read the Scripture methodically and with great confidence. But even over Ed's amplified voice, Carter heard terrible shrieking. Startled, he raised his weapon and spun around, a wilting Milton at his side, and witnessed the very shadows surrounding them quaking with fear.

But, no…it wasn't the shadows. It was those things *in* the shadows. The gremlins.

Ever since Isabella cracked their secret—that they were repelled by Scripture—the beasts rarely were sent to attack. They had simply lost their power over their Christian foes.

"Keep reading, Eddie," Carter muttered, his finger close to the trigger, ready for anything.

"'Lord, you have assigned me my portion and my cup; you have made my lot secure. The boundary lines have fallen for me in pleasant places; surely I have a delightful inheritance. I will praise the Lord, who counsels me; even at night my heart instructs me. I have set the Lord always before me. Because he is at my right hand, I will not be shaken. Therefore my heart is glad and my tongue rejoices; my body also will rest secure, because you will not abandon me to the grave, nor will you let your Holy One see decay. You have made known to me the path of life; you will fill me with joy in your presence, with eternal pleasures at your right hand.'"

With the dance hall all but cleared, Carter surveyed the situation. The Praying Men were hidden safely in their corners, huddled and praying earnestly by now. Ed only took his eyes off the Bible for seconds at a time to make sure the gremlins lurking in the shadows stayed at bay. He read on, moving to the next Psalm and the next as his thunderous voice filled the building.

The bouncers had been subdued and Burt backed away, catching his breath. Considerably younger and less winded, Andrew and Jake drooped their shoulders, the battle done. All three converged on Gus, Carter, and Milton in the center of the room.

Gus shouted over the shrill cries of the gremlins, "It's working!"

Maybe it is *working*, Carter allowed himself the luxury to believe. But still…there had been no sign of *him*, yet. Carter spotted a door marked PRIVATE on the level above them.

Narrowing his eyes, he turned to his men and barked, "Milton! You, Andrew, and Burt cover us. Gus and Jake, with me! We're taking this fight straight to the devil!"

Gus and Jake hefted their SMGs, following Carter as he hurried for the stairs. Ed continued reading. The gremlins screamed and howled in pain, held back by the barrier of God's Holy Word as Carter, Gus, and Jake ascended the spiraling metal staircase to the Man's office. As they neared the second floor, Jake threw his hands to his ears, the deafening pitch of the gremlins' tortured wails finally too much for him.

"Agh!" he cried, stumbling to his knees.

Carter looked back and Gus shouted, "I'll get him!"

Gus hurried to the young man, as Carter turned his attention to the office door.

This is it, he steadied himself. "Hurry!"

Gus helped Jake hobble along until the boy was able to shut out the din around them. Carter took a brief second to huddle, their moment finally arriving. "He's through that door! We get in, we start shooting, and we don't let up until he's down!"

Jake winced in pain and shouted back, "What if that doesn't work?"

Carter hesitated, that cold inside him whispering, *"You'll never make it out of here alive."*

"Then we burn the place down around him. When God appeared to His people in the past, He came as fire, right? Way I see it, fire's the demons' weakness. Why do you think hell is full of it? It *binds* them. They like the cold."

Without realizing it, Carter gripped his icy chest and muttered again, "Yeah…they like the cold. Fire purifies. These guys don't want to be purified."

Jake bit his lip, but Gus nodded. "Then let's hurry."

Carter took the lead, his rifle out and ready to fire as he, Gus, and Jake cleared the threshold of the Man's office.

"Light him up!"

RATA TATA TATA TATATATA

They lit the office in sporadic gunfire as Carter leaned on his SMG, keeping the gun steady. Beside him, Gus and Jake emptied an entire clip each, determined to kill the monster. Yet, as their guns ran dry, Carter held out a staying hand and looked on in horror.

The Strange Man was gone.

"Where is he?" Jake asked dumbly.

Carter pushed past the young man, angered at the turn of events, and clasped the railing overlooking the dance hall below. He gripped his radio and barked, "He's not here! Do you see him? We need a visual, *now*!"

Carter heard a scream echo from the DJ booth. The Scriptures were silenced.

Anxious and alert, recognizing that the shadows around them—pregnant with wicked monstrosities—were now unhindered and simply silently biding their time before an attack, he carefully reached for his walkie talkie.

"Ed?" he tested. "Ed, come back."

No reply. He peered over the edge of the railing. The DJ booth was empty. Beside him, Gus and Jake stared on expectantly.

Carter flushed with anger. He was losing control of the situation and he knew it. Worse, he knew he had never *been* in control. This had all been a terrible, terrible mistake. He had just wanted to help. To save his town. His family.

"You're all going to die," the chilly doubt within him sang.

"No," Carter mumbled.

Gus asked, "What?"

Carter ignored him. Instead, he jerked his radio to his lips. "Fall back! Everybody fall back! It's an ambush!"

Before anyone had a chance to move, the shadows exploded with movement as the legions of gremlins leapt from their hiding places in the unseen realm.

"*Run!*" Carter screamed at Gus and Jake, already following his own command.

Gus shouted something inaudible over the delighted shrieks of the tiny devils, and hurried alongside Carter, headed for the stairs. Jake, however, stood his ground, too terrified to move. He raised his gun and fired off a consistent stream of bullets. They were armor piercing rounds, lethal to a man, but totally useless against Evil itself.

The gremlins overwhelmed him and Jake was gone.

Carter and Gus toppled down the stairs, hurrying away from the hive of feeding beasts hot on their heels. When they reached the dance floor, things were not much better.

Already hidden in the shadows for concealment, the Praying Men had been the first to go. At the sight of the gremlins, their faith must have left them and their automated prayers became useless.

Ed was nowhere to be found, his discarded Bible left lonely on the floor where he'd stood. Carter wanted to grieve for his friend, but quickly pushed that aside. To think right now would cost him his life. He had to react. He could mourn later. *If I live that long.*

Burt and Andrew Simmons set their matching jaws in resolve. They sprayed the unending gremlin multitudes with hot lead, even after Carter shouted, "No! We can't stop them! Run! RUN!"

"No!" Burt yelled over his shoulder, concentrating hard on pushing bullets through the gremlins' bodies, sending purple glittery goop everywhere. "Take the others! Head for the door! My boy and I will cover you!"

Carter nodded, his heart breaking at the Simmons' men's sacrifice, and gripped Gus by the arm, determined to save at least one man from this nightmare.

"Milton!" Carter yelled, spotting the cowering man standing limp, stunned by the maelstrom of malevolence swirling about him. "Milton! Come on!"

Milton remained frozen, his back to Carter. "I-I'm too scared…It's telling me I can't get out. It's telling me there's no hope."

That blasted gunk, Carter cursed himself. *How could I have been so stupid?* He motioned for Gus to hurry on before rushing for Milton. Grabbing his arms and spinning him around, he said, "Milton, you gotta fight—"

But Milton's eyes were solid black.

Slack-jawed and drooling, the thing that had been Milton Wilbanks stuttered, "It says I gotta give in. It says the only way I'll be saved is if I surrender."

"Milton…" Carter wanted to cry. "Think of your girls…"

"I gotta give in, Carter. It's got me…"

In a brilliant blast of force, Milton threw up his hands and, at once, his clothes tore off him, revealing nothing but a writhing, slick, obsidian mass.

Carter backed away, aghast. Milton had become a Shambler, right before his very eyes.

"No…"

The newborn Shambler reared back and loosed a rattling roar that sent Carter to his knees, clutching his ringing ears. Andrew caught sight of the beast and hollered, "Dad!"

Burt was reloading when he turned to see what had stolen his boy's attention away from the gremlins. At the sight of the Shambler, his face went pale.

"Milton—"

Then the gremlins seized the elder Simmons and yanked him away.

Seeing his father dragged into the shadows—to his death—Andrew reached for him, weeping. "Dad!"

Carter felt sick. *God, what have I done?*

A gang of demons broke from the bunch and swarmed the young Simmons boy, but Carter saw it a moment sooner. He leapt forward, past the spindly swinging arms of the Shambler that had been Milton, and tackled the crying boy to the ground.

"No," the boy wailed, his face red and soaked with tears. "No, I gotta help my Dad, I gotta see my Dad!"

Tears stung Carter's eyes and he wanted to die. "He's gone, boy. He's gone. We have to go."

Andrew struggled, prepared to share in his father's fate, but Carter dragged him to his feet, pulling him towards the kitchen. The gremlins swooped down, laughing and squealing, slashing with their claws and biting with their teeth. Carter did his best to bat them away and fired a few rounds into their incomprehensible mass, hoping to buy time.

Luckily, Gus emerged from the kitchen, keeping low under the diving evil beasts. Carter passed Andrew into the old man's arms. "Take him! *Go, go, go!*"

Gus and Andrew disappeared into the kitchen. Carter saw them leaving The Rave Scene, into the quiet night outside. *Thank God. Someone made it.*

Before he could join them, however, a bony white hand caught the side of his face and sent him sliding across the expanse of the ruined dance hall toward the DJ booth.

The gremlins, still whispering and snickering, parted as their lord—now exposed in his true demonic countenance—floated in their midst, untouched.

Carter scrambled to get to his feet, to face his end standing like a man, but discovered that one of his ankles was sprained. The Strange Man hovered to him, in no hurry. The gremlin hordes silently watched, relishing their master's work.

"My, my, my," the Strange Man cooed. "This has been quite the night for you."

Moaning like an unthinking zombie, the Milton-Shambler dragged its long, slippery tentacles behind it as it joined the Strange Man's side. As if it were a darling child, the demon caressed the smooth, obsidian head of his new Shambler pet.

"Hello there, my friend. Come to see Daddy work?"

Carter managed to support himself on the booth and stood. In defiance, he ripped off his helmet and mask, revealing himself to the demon.

The Strange Man considered the man before him. "I suspected

the preacher's people would mount an offensive, but *this*? Was this all that you had? Has living like animals in the woods, resting in your Lord's protection, His Spirit and His Word at your immediate and constant disposal, taught you *nothing*? You come at me with guns? You take hate into your heart and hope to stand up to me in your unrighteousness?"

Carter grimaced under the pain of his ankle, but remained standing.

The Strange Man laughed. "You really have no idea, do you? No. Of course you don't. If you 'Christians' had an inkling of what it means to be in the Will of God, things like me wouldn't even be here. I guess I should say 'lucky for me' then, yes?"

Edging closer, the bogle-king of Greensboro lolled his head from side to side, studying Carter's trembling frame.

"Just come on with it," Carter braved. "Do your worst."

"Oh, I will. But, please, allow me the simple pleasures in life. It's this dissecting part that I do so enjoy in a kill." Tapping his chin thoughtfully, the Strange Man said, "It's you humans. You fascinate me. I've been among you for thousands of years and you never cease to surprise me. At once you are so faithful, so bold and righteous, brave and heroic. Yet, in the very next moment, you can become so cowardly and wicked. Then, in the *next* moment, you switch back. And yet, in all of this," he pointed to the ceiling with a roll of his eyes, "He will always take you back. Will always give you that second chance if you ask Him for it. Boggles the mind, doesn't it? Why He would accept the tears and repentance of nothing more than walking, talking clods of dirt, is beyond me. For *my* kind…there is no turning back. We make one mistake and," a snap of the fingers, "that's that. We're done. Our fate is sealed." Snarling now, the Strange Man's glowing eyes dimmed. "Does that seem fair to you?"

Carter's mind raced, desperate to find some way to protect himself. Then, he saw Ed's Bible not three feet from where he was standing.

"I could kill you," the Strange Man continued. "I've had

millennia to experiment on your species, to find the most gruesome forms of torture…I could torture you for days, my friend. Weeks, if I choose. Would you like that? I'd be glad to share my suffering with you."

Carter ignored the verbose beast, focusing on that Bible and how he might get to it. *God, please…*

"But perhaps, I should let your own sin consume you."

Carter surprised himself with a sudden scream, his body going taut, the cold slithering in his chest contracting around his heart as the voices in his head became a dissonance of accusation: *"Sinner! You've failed, Christian! You've turned your back on your faith! There is no hope for you! You've forgotten your Father and He has forgotten you!"*

"No…" Carter grunted, twisting in pain.

"You're useless! Your team is dead because of you! Because of your recklessness!"

"No, please…"

The Strange Man grinned cruelly. "Doesn't feel good, does it? Being tormented by your mistakes, haunted by your sin." Bending down to press his crooked nose to Carter's sweaty cheek, he breathed foully, "Try living with it forever."

Carter buckled under the weight of his faults and stared in horror as thick, viscous, black goo seeped out of the pores on his arm, slowly consuming him. "No," he sobbed. "It's all my fault…God…I'm so sorry…I should've waited on you…should've listened…Jesus forgive my pride…"

The Strange Man stood straighter, his eyes burning bright. "No," he growled. "No, you can't do that. You can't ask for forgiveness! I won't let you!"

The black goo oozed out of Carter's body, exorcised, and slithered away from the renewed fellowship of the Holy Spirit within him, when the Strange Man pulled back and brought his taloned hand down *hard.* The left side of Carter's face opened up in three bloody strips and he yelped in excruciating pain.

However, the blow had thrown him right beside the Bible.

At once, Carter grabbed it and thrust it forward. Immediately the gremlins in the room shrieked and scurried for cover in the shadows and the Strange Man floated back a few inches.

"Run, then," the ancient demon droned. "Come tomorrow, it won't matter. My Master will finally arrive and you'll all be dead."

The Strange Man's eyes smoldered with hatred as he watched the crusader. "I *will* get my revenge."

Clutching the Bible tight, Carter backed away from the monster and his minions, edged closer to the front door, and limped out into the night.

CHAPTER EIGHTEEN

"MOM, YOU HAVE to listen to me," Rosalyn pleaded from the other side of the screen door at her mother's house in Trysdale.

Meredith Myers shook her head sadly, as if to say anything at all would be too much. She began to shut the door, to shut her daughter out forever, when Rosalyn stopped her.

"Mom, *wait.*"

"Rosalyn," she began, and Rosalyn realized how long it had been since she'd heard her mother's voice. Months, in fact.

Seven months ago, things had actually started to heal between Rosalyn and her mother, until the Strange Man revealed that Meredith's infidelity had driven Rosalyn's father to suicide. Filled with hate and betrayal, Rosalyn chose to taste the Strange Man's weird fruit. She hadn't spoken to her mother since, but tonight, she had something to say.

Retreating into the living room, Meredith shooed, "Whatever you're involved in, I don't want any part of it."

Rosalyn entered the house. "Mom, please. This is important. You have to take Annie and you have to leave."

"What's going on?" fourteen-year-old Annie asked as she trotted down the steps. Then, upon seeing her big sister, her eyes widened in excitement. "Roz!"

"Rosalyn, please just leave," Meredith said, her face twisted in grief.

"Listen to me! You have to leave Greensboro. It's not safe here anymore."

Meredith took a seat, busying herself so that she wouldn't have to face her wayward child. Annie, however, approached Rosalyn, her brow lined. "What's going on?"

"It's the Strange Man. Whatever he has planned…it all happens tomorrow. It's—it's going to be bad. I want you and Mom to get out of here—"

"What about *you*?" Annie asked, worried, and Rosalyn smiled warmly.

"I can't," she said. "I've got to try something first." She turned to her mother. "I gotta try to make things right."

Meredith looked to her daughter, her expression cautious.

Rosalyn's heart broke as she realized how much she'd put her family through. Kneeling before her mother, she clasped the woman's hands. "I know I'm not the daughter you wanted."

"Rosalyn…"

"No, I'm not. But I'm going to try to be."

Meredith touched Rosalyn's face, her own a mixture of pride and pain.

Rosalyn said, "But you have to take Annie and leave. I can't do what I've got to do if I'm worried about you."

"Where would we go?" Meredith fretted.

Rosalyn stood, still holding her mother's hand, and faced her sister. "Go to Jeff. He's somewhere in the North Woods. If I had to guess, he's probably at that old cliff where his dad used to take us when we were kids. Jeff's a fairly predictable guy."

Annie turned beet red. "I know. I've…been going out there for a couple months now. Helping out."

"Annie!" Meredith objected, leading Rosalyn to believe this was news to her mother.

"They're not bad people, Mom," Annie defended. "They're not doing anything wrong. I'm one of them now. I believe like they do."

Rosalyn wanted to chastise her sister for throwing in her lot with a lost cause, but the conviction with which Annie made her declaration filled her with pride. Annie really was a better person than she had any hope of being.

"I want you to take this." Rosalyn reached into her black denim jacket and pulled out a parcel wrapped in newspaper. "It's Ray

McCormick's diary. Most of it's just crazy talk, but it might be able to help. If I don't…if something goes wrong…Well…Jeff should be able to figure something out." She managed a bittersweet smile, thinking of a big brother she once had. "He's pretty good at that."

Annie took the package and stared at it, tears building in her eyes. Unable to control herself, she threw her skinny arms around her sister.

"I love you, brat." Rosalyn sniffed.

Annie held on tight. "I love you."

"Say a prayer, or whatever," Rosalyn quipped. "Couldn't hurt, right?"

"Right."

"Take care of Mom."

Rosalyn stroked her sister's hair, as she had done for a lifetime, knowing that this might be the last time. When she parted, Rosalyn joined Meredith. The woman's eyes were red with tears, but she remained seated, looking the other way.

"Mom…" she started.

Meredith did not say anything. Perhaps there was too much to say.

Rosalyn accepted her silence. "I love you, Mom."

She gave her sister a brief kiss and left the Myers house behind.

When Rosalyn entered The Rave Scene twenty minutes later, she was astonished to find the place ransacked and empty of its usual patrons. A few bruised bouncers sullenly turned over tables, setting them in their upright positions. The Strange Man, in his demonic form, remained floating in the middle of the room, surveying the damage and conversing with two other security men.

"What happened here?" Rosalyn strode across the floor.

The Strange Man regarded her with a slight snarl and waved to the men beside him, mumbling something. Dismissed, they marched toward the kitchen. Rosalyn felt nervous and wondered if the look was somehow connected to her visit to her mother.

Does he know? Was he watching?

For the time being, she decided to play innocent. "What happened, Big Daddy?"

The Strange Man gestured to the room, as if presenting a brand new car to his lady love, and said, "We had company tonight, darling. Dinner guests…*with guns.*"

"Who…?"

"Seems the Christians thought a change in leadership was in order. They thought to dethrone me." A slight chuckle escaped his black lips.

Immediately, Rosalyn's heart fluttered and she looked around, trying to spot survivors…or the remains of the dead. Sensing her worry, the Strange Man hissed through his front fangs, "Don't worry. Your *boyfriend* was not with them."

"He's not…What did you do?"

"I defended myself, obviously. What choice did I have?"

Rosalyn's heart felt heavy in her chest. *So much death…*

The Strange Man paced in the air casually, dragging the tips of his buckled shoes behind him. "To be truthful, I feel a bit relieved now. I had expected the Christians to try something but…I admit I was worried it would be a little more…effective. Really, if this is all they have, then tomorrow will go off without a hitch."

Just keep thinking that. Rosalyn glared at the back of his bald head.

"Still," he mused, "begs the question where they got all those guns."

The front doors banged open and Sheriff Ryan Stevenson entered The Rave Scene, Danny Carpenter struggling in his vice-like grip. The Strange Man grinned and proclaimed, "I suppose now I'll get my answer."

Stevenson hustled along, his prisoner in tow. Danny was handcuffed, his face adorned with fresh welts and bruises.

"Let go of me!" he hollered, twisting but unable to break free.

"Caught us a big one," Stevenson laughed. He tossed Danny before the Man's gaunt frame, then looked around. The worn and injured bouncers carried on reassembling the place, some sweeping, some picking up broken bottles.

"Wha…? Looks like a tornado hit this place."

On the floor, Danny pushed himself up with his elbows and looked into the true face of the Strange Man.

"No…" he whispered, spellbound.

The bogeyman considered him with a curious leer. "Hello, Danny."

The young man fell backwards and kicked away. Stevenson stepped in, his stocky legs barring escape. "Not so fast, junior."

The Strange Man slithered forward, his dark, cold shadow falling over Danny.

"No…no, stay back…"

Rosalyn held her ground. She knew Danny by reputation as one of Jeff's closest confidants, though she'd never met the guy personally. For Jeff's sake, she wanted to help him, but knew she couldn't show her hand. *Not yet.* Instead, she bit her lip and waited to see what the Strange Man would do.

The bogeyman paused upon reaching Danny and looked to the sheriff. "You brought me a present, Stevenson. How nice."

Stevenson shifted his weight uncomfortably. "Uh…heh, heh. Yeah. Caught him snooping around the lake, watching the preacher and them parents out there getting ready for tomorrow."

The Strange Man nodded his head as Stevenson relayed his story, as if buying every word of it, though his wide, staring eyes, and toothy sneer told Rosalyn differently. "And what were *you* doing out there, Sheriff Stevenson?"

"Me? Uh…"

"Perhaps selling guns to our enemies."

"I…" Stevenson pulled at his collar.

"Or perhaps you were just *giving* them away, yes? Hoping they would have more guts than you and do your dirty work by removing me so that you could be in charge? Am I getting close?"

Stevenson grew red in the face, sweating.

The Strange Man winked. "Ah, Sheriff. Always plotting."

With a fatherly air, the devil draped his leather-bound arm

across Stevenson's shoulder and hugged him close. The brute stared straight ahead, too petrified to move. He looked to Rosalyn, as if hoping that she would help him, save him.

But Rosalyn would not help him. He was on his own.

Speechless, Stevenson trembled, the keys on his belt jangling.

The Strange Man sighed loudly. "I suppose you brought this boy back as a peace offering in case your plans fell through. Well, as you can see," he gave the room a broad sweep, "they have. But, I admire your thinking, Sheriff, and that's why I'm not going to kill you."

Rosalyn halted. Stevenson too. "You're…not?"

The Strange Man cocked his head to the side, as if giving it a second thought, then said, "Nah. If I didn't have you trying to stab me in the back, life would just get boring."

Rosalyn shook her head in disapproval. *There he goes again with his games.*

"No," the Strange Man continued, sneering at Stevenson, "When my Master comes, he will most assuredly want to meet *you.*"

The sheriff beamed, the idea of mingling with an ancient pagan god probably filling his heart with pride, but the Strange Man moved on with business, now circling Danny. "Let's have a look at this one, shall we?" Clutching the young man's chin, he lifted Danny's face to get a better look at him. "Well, well, well. If it isn't Robin. And where is your Batman, Boy Wonder?"

"Go to hell!" Danny shouted, rearing up on his knees to stiffen, and pulled his chin away from the Strange Man's dead fingers.

The Strange Man barked a laugh. "Already been there, boy. Not planning on going back anytime soon."

The gruesome specter gave Stevenson a nod and the sheriff hefted Danny to his feet to face the bogle-king. The Strange Man zoomed close and the air chilled around them. Rosalyn's breath became visible. Danny's too. He started to shiver, his eyes filling with dread.

"Where are your friends?" the Strange Man asked smoothly.

Danny didn't respond, only shut his eyes tight.

Tracing his talon along the edge of Danny's rough face, the monster pouted, "Oh, Daniel…I can see how tired you are. Always fighting, always living like vermin, running from shadows, trying to survive on so little."

Danny shivered, visibly concentrating, trying to keep in control.

"Sounds to me like you're no better off than when you were living on the streets."

"But I know the truth now," Danny sputtered back, his voice full of rage and fear.

"Does the truth keep you warm at night? Does the truth feed your stomach?"

Danny slumped. Rosalyn watched as his eyelids grew heavy and he swooned. Her heart thundered and she wanted to help him. The Strange Man was toying with him—preparing for the kill. She couldn't just watch a good man murdered right in front of her. *But you have to. You've got to buy Annie time to get to Jeff with the diary. Jeff never gives up. He'll stop this.*

"You're tired of fighting," the Strange Man said. "It's okay. I am too. We keep warring back and forth over who's right and who's wrong. People die and it seems like we're not getting anywhere. I'm offering you a way out of the war, Danny. What is it you want the most? Money? Fame? Power?" He paused, waiting for him to respond, then grinned. "No…I don't think so. You're too noble for that. I think *this* is what you really want."

Reaching out, the Strange Man pressed his thumb to Danny's forehead. In a brilliant flash, Danny opened his eyes and saw Tabitha, her hair full and vibrant, her eyes sparkling and lively. He'd never seen her so beautiful before. Then he saw himself entering the picture, embracing her and looking down with a laugh at his twin sons toddling at his feet. Overjoyed, Danny scooped them up, kissed their fat cheeks, and held them in his arms, finally a father.

In The Rave Scene, Danny wept.

The Strange Man retracted the visions and stared at the sobbing young man. Rosalyn's stomach soured.

"Tabitha..." Danny weakly called.

"She's beautiful, isn't she? I check up on her now and again," the demon began casually, circling Danny. "You know she's cleaned up her act. She's even holding down a steady job. And your boys! They're walking now! Learning to talk! You should see them."

Danny shut his eyes, "Stop..."

"I've seen them, Danny," the Strange Man whispered. "Just last night, I visited your boys as they slept. I tucked them in, kissed their sweet little heads. I even brought back a gift for their daddy."

Danny whimpered, watching as the Strange Man pulled a lock of curly golden hair from within the folds of his twisted clothing, like magic. "I took this from their precious heads. Just for you."

Danny pressed his face to the ground, weeping. Rosalyn felt fresh tears sting her eyes and bit her tongue to hold in her emotion.

"They need you, Danny!" The Strange Man dropped the golden hair to the floor. "They need their dad! Isn't that what you want? Look at what your God has gotten you into! You forsook your family for Him and what has He given you in return?"

Danny hung his head, sobbing.

The Strange Man flicked his wrist and an envelope appeared in his hand. He dangled it in front of Danny's slack face. "Look, boy. Look here."

He raised his swollen eyes. "What...what is that?"

"Tabitha's new address, a bus ticket, and a hundred thousand dollars just for kicks and giggles. You can go to your family, Danny. You can have the life you want. All you have to do is..."

"No," Danny whimpered.

Bowing in close again, the Strange Man hissed, "Tell me where your friends are. That's all. Just tell me where they're hiding and I promise no one will have to know you said a word."

Rosalyn inched forward. *Annie's on her way...No, Danny. Please don't tell him. She needs more time.*

But poor Danny could stand it no longer. His teeth chattering, cold breath leaving him, he muttered, "The old church…where Jeff's father used to preach…just past God's Cliff."

Rosalyn caught her breath. *Oh no…*

The Strange Man clapped his hands in glee. "There. See? All better. Thank you, Daniel. You made the right choice."

Stevenson released Danny and the shattered man fell to the floor. "Can I see my family now?"

"Of course," the Strange Man replied immediately, dropping the envelope in Danny's lap.

Danny gripped the money and stared at it long and hard.

Rosalyn hated him for selling out Jeff and the others. *Annie*…But when Danny looked up and his tired, defeated eyes met hers, she felt nothing but pity for him. He had betrayed those closest to him. *Just like you did, Roz,* she scolded herself.

The young man shut his eyes, crying anew. He picked himself up and ran out the door. Stevenson leered and slowly drew his pistol, taking careful aim at the man's back. He pulled back the hammer just as Danny reached the front door and—

"No," the Strange Man ordered, quiet.

Stevenson lowered his gun and Danny safely left The Rave Scene behind. Turning to the Man in surprise, the sheriff asked, "You're just going to let him go?"

"We have what we need. Besides, death is too short. I'd rather he live with the guilt of what he's done for many, *many* more years."

Rosalyn slowly approached the Strange Man, trembling and trying to hide it. "What are you going to do?" Her mind raced with the possible fate of her family and friends.

The Strange Man regarded her with a sidelong glance as the bouncers emerged from the kitchen, dragging a terrible lumbering behemoth in chains. The thing snarled and tugged and lashed out at its captors, but the chains held and the men pulled the raving beast before its dark lord.

Rosalyn turned and beheld the winged Creature.

The Strange Man approached his favorite pet, its leathery wings bound in cords, twitching to be free. The grotesque bat-like beast snorted and sniffed, its eyes milky and blind, disorientated by its new surroundings. It gnashed and raved, and even the men holding the Creature cowered, despite the chains. Rosalyn kept her distance as well, backing from the monster's crooked elbow blades. The Creature was irrepressible and she'd had to wrestle it a time or two to keep it in line. She knew its unparalleled strength, firsthand.

Jeff doesn't stand a chance…

The Strange Man cooed, easing into the monster and stroking its twisted, feral face. "Awww…" he sang, as the animal bit at the air, its only urge to kill. "There, there, TJ. You're okay, yes you are."

Rosalyn felt revulsion at the sight of the thing. She knew that it was TJ. Or, at least, it used to be, before the goo mutated him into that thing. A very unsettling fact, since the same fate awaited *her* tomorrow.

The Strange Man called it his "gift" and had imparted it to TJ, first, then to Rosalyn, citing that they were his favorite children. Sheriff Stevenson had begged and pleaded for the gift, wanting that power for himself, but the Strange Man had refused.

He doesn't trust him with that kind of power, Rosalyn knew. *But he trusts me.*

I'll use that trust to kill him, she swore.

The TJ Creature growled as the Strange Man stroked its oily black head. "Shhhh…" the demon father soothed. "It's all right, now. I know it's no fun being cooped up in that gloomy cave below, but now…" his lips parted in a twisted, greenish grin, "now, you get to play again."

The monster snorted its pleasure and the Strange Man chuckled. "You like that, don't you? Yes, it's time to play, TJ." He looked purposefully to Rosalyn, as if detecting her treasonous thoughts, and his eyes glowed with delight. "Time to play indeed."

CHAPTER NINETEEN

HANDS IN HIS pockets, leaning against the door frame to the small classroom that had been their room—their home—for months, Hank Berkley watched the love of his life prepare to leave him.

Doris didn't even look at him as she packed, stuffing clothes into the bag they brought out here in the beginning. Their teenage daughter Becky had already packed, and now sat in the main hall, filing her nails, passing the time. She seemed bored, and whenever Hank tried to talk to her, to strike up any conversation to hold onto his last precious moments with his daughter, she shrugged indifferently.

"Father Joe will be here at sunup," Hank offered to Doris's back.

Father Joe's early arrival was public knowledge; Jeff had already told them all as much, but Hank was desperate to gauge his wife's feelings.

"I don't want to leave with Father Joe," Doris replied in a huff, still packing.

"We talked about this. You're better off going to Russellville with Father Joe and staying there for a week or so before you can go to your sister's in Minnesota."

"I want to go *home*, Hank. To *my* home."

"I know, but I thought you understood that going back to Greensboro ain't safe for you *or* for Becky."

Doris zipped the bag shut. "I won't run away from this bogeyman of yours. Greensboro isn't like it used to be. People have put aside their differences and they're all willing to live together in peace. You are all so paranoid. You've been hanging around Jeff Weldon too long, if you ask me. You never used to talk about religion before you got mixed up with him and that crazy family of his."

"Don't you talk about them like that!" Hank hollered, thinking of his friends and the sacrifices they had made for his family.

"See how you rush to defend them? We're your family, Hank. What about what we want?"

"This isn't about us," Hank growled, barely able to believe that she was saying these things to him. "This is about helping those families out there. Land's sake, Doris, it isn't always about you!"

"Wrong, Hank. It's *never* about me. First it's about your job, now it's about your faith. But it's always about you and what you want."

Hank hesitated, struck. Was she right? Was he being selfish by staying? *What should I do, Lord? Leave with my family or stay out here?*

Please tell me.

"Doris—"

Franklin Whitaker poked his head into their room. "Hank," he said, wild and out of breath. "We've got visitors."

Hank opened the entrance door to see Annie and Meredith Myers, wrapped in coats and holding two duffel bags between them, looking lost, scared, and cold. "Come on in," he ushered them inside the old church, and barked to the gawkers, "Get them some blankets."

The two auburn-haired women entered, shivering. "Tarnation, Annie," Hank addressed the younger girl first, more familiar with her. Aside from surviving their little adventure in the burning church seven months ago, Annie had visited the Haven frequently, attending their makeshift services and wanting to know more about the faith. Annie was a friend, and right now he could tell she was in trouble.

Seeing Meredith, however, was quite a surprise.

"Meredith..." he hesitated. "Didn't expect to see you out here."

Annie answered, "Rosalyn asked us to come."

Franklin, who now stood nearby with Rebecca Walker, shot

Hank a worried look and asked the girl, "Your sister knows we're out here?"

"It's okay. She's trying to help us," Annie quickly clarified.

Hank turned to Franklin. "Better check."

Franklin grabbed his rifle from his console station and hurried outside with two other men, giving Rebecca a "don't worry" look. The two of them were real close lately, and Hank wondered if Franklin was ever going to make his move and start a romance with Rebecca. She certainly seemed interested. *Someone might as well find some happiness in the middle of all of this.* It couldn't have happened to two better people.

Annie watched Franklin go, confused. "What's he doing, Hank?"

He held the girl's shoulders and looked her square in her brown eyes. "Are you sure we can trust Rosalyn, Anne? You sure you weren't followed?"

"Of course I'm sure. She's my *sister.*"

Just then, young Millie Walker entered the room. "Annie!" She rushed to give her favorite baby-sitter a hard hug. Annie squeezed the girl, but kept an angry glare fixed on the ex-sheriff. Meredith, meanwhile, kept to herself and presented the church a disgusted once over.

"So…this is…*it*?"

Hank, still feeling the weight of Annie's silent accusations, gruffly replied, "It's home. At least, for now."

Franklin returned, much calmer than before, and shook his head. "Looks clear, as far as I can tell."

Hank relaxed. "Good. Lock 'er up for the night."

Franklin left as Hank took his handkerchief from his back pocket. He wiped his brow before looking to Annie. "I'm sorry, girl. We just can't be too sure these days. The Dark Hour is tomorrow and—"

"I know," Annie said boldly, Millie still clutching her leg "That's why Rosalyn wanted us to come. She wanted me to give you this."

Reaching into her coat, she withdrew a small package wrapped in a cloth. "Hope this helps."

"Come to argue?" Jay Evans mumbled, biting into a grilled cheese sandwich at the kitchen table, which seemed too big for a man living alone.

Isabella hung back in the doorway, her eyes downcast as she addressed her aged father. "No."

Jay dropped his sandwich and adjusted the dingy, weathered cap he'd worn for years. "You been good?"

She nodded, touched by his concern and sensing his discomfort. "As good as can be expected, given the circumstances."

The bald-headed man nodded. "Jeff with you?"

"He's out front."

"Wanted to miss the fireworks, huh?"

Isabella and her dad had a distant relationship, despite the fact they lived close by. Jay liked his solitude, out in the country near Trysdale. He also harbored a lot of guilt and bitterness from years of living without Isabella's mother. It was hard to talk to him. She'd hardly spoken to him in months, but tomorrow was…well, Isabella didn't know what tomorrow would bring. Following their trip to Grover's Pond, she knew she had to set one last piece of her life in order before she faced the Strange Man and whatever hell he was bringing.

Trying to get through to her dad, though, seemed nearly as insurmountable a task as fighting back the forces of hell.

"Dad…" Isabella began, her heart thumping. "Greensboro's not safe anymore—"

"Hasn't been safe for a long time."

She shuffled. "But it's getting worse. We know that the Dark Hour is tomorrow and I wanted to come by and tell you that you should probably leave."

"Where would I go?" Jay asked, picking up his grilled cheese again.

"You've got four sons all over the country," she half-grinned. "I'm sure you can find a place."

"This is my home."

"Dad—"

"*No*," he said firmly and finally. "I ain't leaving the farm just because things are getting rough. We don't run. I taught you that."

Isabella looked to her feet, feeling like a little girl again in his presence. "Yeah, you did." She bit her lip. "But you also taught me not to turn my back on the people I care about."

Now her father stood, nearly knocking over his plate in the process. "You were the one who left last time, Izzy, don't you forget that."

Suddenly old feelings of hurt and betrayal rushed to the surface as Isabella stood toe to toe with her father. "Because I can't *talk* to you! You never listen."

"I listen fine." Jay sat back down and picked at his grilled cheese sandwich, avoiding the conversation. Isabella pulled up a chair too, and sat beside her father, placing her hand on his gnarled one. Jay still believed in hand plowing his tomato garden and had the leathered hands to prove it. He was a simple man who took pride in a hard day's work. She'd always admired that in him, but he could be *too* simple sometimes.

"Then why don't you do something, Dad? You could help me and Jeff stop this. You could—"

"Folks want this town to go to hell, what do I care?" He stood, gathering his plate. "Let them shake hands with the devil, doesn't bother me. I just want to be left alone."

Isabella nearly slammed her hands on the table. "How can you be so callous?"

"Who am I to tell people what to believe?" He swore and said, "I ain't even sure what *I* believe. Is this guy a devil? I don't know. You say he is. John Graves is evil, but that don't make him supernatural, Izzy. That just makes him a politician."

"This is so typical. You never want to talk about God. You—"

He waved her off. "Ah, this ain't got nothing to do with God."

"It has everything to do with Him."

"You don't think I believe in God," he accused her, insulted.

"All the time I was growing up, you never once mentioned God other than praying over Thanksgiving dinner or saying 'Hope the Good Lord lets it rain'," she accentuated the last part with the best grumpy impersonation of her father she could muster.

"I read my Psalms," Jay defended, turning away.

"That's not enough! You can't sit on the fence anymore, Dad. Tomorrow the Strange Man is going to do something terrible and we've got to warn people."

"I don't want no part in it. I told you, I just want everyone to leave me alone." He braced himself on the counter, his whole body trembling with rage or sadness, Isabella wasn't sure which.

Frowning, she spoke to the back of his balding head, "Then that's what you'll get, Dad. You'll stay out here all alone for the rest of your life, just like you've always wanted."

He didn't respond and Isabella found it impossible to hold back. "She's *gone*. Mom's gone. Hiding in here isn't going to bring her back."

Surprisingly, he quickly responded, "Neither will going out there."

"No," Isabella admitted. "But it'll save you losing what you have left."

Unable to stand arguing with the stubborn man any longer, Isabella turned and left the farmhouse behind.

CHAPTER TWENTY

PRISSY MEREDITH MYERS sat in the main hall of the church with her arms and legs crossed, looking to Hank like she thought she had better places to be. Rebecca Walker sat nearby with Millie on her lap and tried to make small talk with the manicured woman. He watched the awkward conversation from the doorway to a classroom they'd designated the "War Room" until he was certain that Meredith was all right for the time being. Then he quietly closed the door and turned to face the meeting already in progress.

Sarah sat at the table, immersed in Ray's diary. Annie leaned on her elbows, reading over Sarah's shoulder. The two girls were going on about something, pointing out recurring symbols and pictures, leaving Hank feeling absolutely out of his depth. He wanted to be back with Doris, to revisit her decision to return to town, but he knew it was of no use. His family had moved on. They didn't need or want him anymore and he had to start trying to let them go. Besides, the very edge the team needed to fight the Strange Man was now in their possession. Maybe now they could start making some sense of their enemy.

If only Jeff was here, he sighed. *Or Danny. Or Carter, for that matter.*

It seemed all leadership was missing and the Haven was operating on a very under-prepared skeleton crew. *I hope they hurry back.*

"Well?" Hank grumbled, moving to the strange book that rested on the table and the two bright young women studying it.

"Read some," Sarah offered.

Hank glanced at the diary, squinting at the gibberish in the last entries. "Ezrka... blahnim...rod, alih... nimrodbalpa, ielmnim...rodpup...anuo..." Finally he gave up, rubbing his eyes.

"I don't get it. Looks like chicken scratch to me."

Sarah flatly said, "Nimrod."

Hank recoiled. "*Hey*."

"No," Annie giggled. "Not you. *Nimrod*. It's the name of a guy."

Hank cooled, "Oh," and slumped down in the chair, his thoughts still drifting to Doris. "So who's Nimrod?"

Annie turned to Sarah, but she was back to burying her nose in the book, skimming over words and phrases with her index finger. Annie rested her chin in her palm and explained, "Nimrod used to be, like, this *major* bad king who founded the city of Babylon, which is, like, you know, birthplace of wickedness by Bible standards. You know about the Tower of Babel?"

Hank raised an eyebrow, finding the famous Sunday School Bible story vaguely familiar. "Yeah, everybody wanted to build a tower to climb up to God and ask Him who gave Him the right to be in charge, right?"

Annie nodded. "Something like that. That was Nimrod's doing."

"How do you know all of this?"

The girl shrugged. "I like history."

Hank moved on, "So what's this Nimrod guy got to do with what's going on in Greensboro?"

Annie frowned, devoid of answers.

Sarah chimed in, now, her face still scrunched up, studying the text before her, "There's an entry here, right in the middle of all the weirdness." She spun the book around so that Hank could get a better look. Hoping that he would understand this time—lest he look like a moron again—he concentrated. Immediately, violent dark marks, as if from a black crayon, assaulted his vision. The writing and drawing were so aggressive that the paper was wrinkled and nearly torn in strips.

"See here? Look," Sarah sounded out the words, trailing with her finger, "Hukanimrodbolo, Jkilonimrodmpah—"

"Yeah, I get it," Hank waved her off, the hairs on the back of his neck standing at attention as she read. "Might not be a good idea just spouting that stuff off, Sarah. How do we know it's not some Satanic spell or curse or something?"

Sarah paused and gave him a look, as if trying to determine if he was serious. She smiled, at ease, and held in a chuckle, "No, Hank, look closer. At the center of all these words, there's *this* word."

Hank swallowed hard and gave the diary another look. Sarah carefully pointed out each individual letter, until he spelled it all in his head. "N-I-M…Nimrod."

Sarah nodded enthusiastically, the thrill of the intellectual hunt stimulating. "Exactly."

"What kind of language has 'Nimrod' in every word?"

"None," Annie said, re-entering the conversation. "Well…none that I know of."

"I don't think it *is* a language," Sarah elaborated. "It really *is* just gibberish."

"But Nimrod," Hank blinked tiredly. "That has to mean something, right?"

"It's at the center of everything here." Sarah pulled the book to her chest and flipped through the pages again, recreationally. "Ray makes mention of the Coming Evil and the Ancient One and the Great Change, but he mentions Nimrod more than anything, if only in code."

"Why code it?" Hank asked with growing interest, the old cop in him waking up from his slumber. "Who's he hiding that information from? Us?"

Sarah bit at the tip of her thumb, looking over a page filled with make-believe words that all held NIMROD. "I don't know…it almost seems…subconscious."

Annie slid into her seat, taking a gander at the script. "Like, he didn't know he was writing it?"

"Yeah. Maybe it *is* a code…but maybe it was to confuse *him*."

"You mean Ray?" Hank sighed. "This isn't making any sense."

"Think about it," Sarah corrected, her eyes lighting up. "He was only a Type A Shambler, right? Meaning that, somewhere inside of him, the Holy Spirit was still present. That's why the sin couldn't take root and corrupt Ray from the inside."

"Right, right."

"Ray's mind might have been tormented by the goo, but the Holy Spirit was still active and…*maybe*," she paused, grinning wider, "Maybe this was God's way of speaking through Ray."

"Speaking to us?"

Sarah nodded to Annie. "He wanted us to know that it was Nimrod."

"Okay," Hank began slowly. "Let's say that's true and, for what it's worth, that's the best theory we've got to play with…So, let's say it's true. That the Holy Ghost was trapped inside of ole Ray and this was His way of communicating to us to let us know we were up against Nimrod. Who's Nimrod? What are we dealing with, here? Some old Babylonian ruler who died thousands of years ago?"

Sarah snickered, "Hey, *my* brilliance is spent."

Hank turned to Annie. "Howabout you? History help us out?"

Annie twisted her mouth. "Well, history says that after Nimrod's death, his wife…Queen Semiramis, I think, claimed that Nimrod had become the sun god Baal and then—after she conceived a child through adultery—she even bragged that the child was Nimrod supernaturally reincarnated. Sort of like the virgin birth. Of course it was all null, but the Babylonians, and even Israel when they fell away, worshipped Baal and believed that one day he would return to the Earth. In fact, Baal is the predominant enemy of God's people in the Old Testament, before anyone ever mentioned anything about Satan or Beelzebub."

Annie glanced from Sarah to Hank, uncertain. "Does that help?"

Sarah's face went white and she flipped to one of the many pages that bore the Strange Man's sigil. She flattened the page and held up the book for both Annie and Hank to see.

"Look familiar?" she asked.

Of course it did to Hank. He saw it every time he rolled back the sleeve on his shirt. It was the sigil etched in his flesh and his conscience.

"A sun," Sarah said when no one else did. "As in sun god. *Baal*."

Hank looked Sarah dead in the eye, those hairs on his neck tingling again. "So…is that it then? The Ancient One. The Coming Evil…is it Baal? Is he coming *back*?"

Franklin Whitaker hurried into the War Room. "Hey, Sarah? We got a camera down out here."

Sarah, Annie, and Hank all stared at Franklin, reverentially fearful.

He started and frowned. "What?"

Franklin sat at the security console as Hank and his huge gut leaned over him, propped up by meaty arms. Pretty Rebecca Walker, who was with Franklin when the monitor went blank, waited off to the side.

Progressing through the monitors from right to left, Hank saw Sarah outside, a flashlight in one hand and her small toolkit in her other, making her way for the non-responsive camera. Hank watched her closely as she moved out of one screen and into the next, passing by the posted cameras surrounding the Haven's perimeter.

I don't like this. Hank grimaced. Things were tense enough around here, what with Jeff and the others gone—*where the Sam Hill are they?*—but his anxiety was multiplied by the sudden realization that the Strange Man's Master could actually be an ancient pagan god looking to reclaim the Earth that expunged him so long ago. On top of everything else, one of their main security cameras simply blinked dark?

No, Hank did not like this at all. Danger was all around, it was tangible in the air, just as it had been when he and Special Angel Christopher Perdu walked into that dark train car to confront the mutated Ray McCormick. *If only Perdu were here now.*

He grabbed the walkie talkie on the counter and depressed the button. "Anything?"

Through the grainy black and white feed, Sarah lifted her radio and her frustrated voice echoed back, covered in static. "Hold on a sec, will ya?"

Hank nodded, not that she could see it, and breathed out of his nose, steady. *Something's not right.* He was about to recall Sarah from her repair mission. *Gotta circle the wagons. Trouble's coming.* However, as he raised the walkie, ready to order Sarah back inside, she disappeared from sight.

Franklin leaned forward. "Whoa. Where did she go?"

Hank barked into the radio, "Sarah?"

The monitors were empty. Nothing but the darkness creeping in at the edges of the forest. *Out to get us*, he couldn't help but think. *They've finally come to get us.*

As his heart quickened and he made to shout the Browning girl's name once more, Sarah's gleaming eyes, made larger by her glasses, poked into view on the monitor nearest the black one. She looked perturbed, but otherwise unharmed.

"Hank, it looks like the line just came undone," she said. Hank breathed in relief.

"Can you fix it?"

Sarah guffawed proudly. "'Can I fix it'? I can fix anything. It'll be back up in a jiff."

Pushing her glasses up on her nose, Sarah rummaged through her tiny toolkit, fumbling with the flashlight to aid in her search. Mumbling to herself, she was too busy to notice the black shape emerging from the dark woods behind her.

Hank's heart faltered. "Sarah!"

Sarah dropped her toolkit and whipped around with a gasp, shining her flashlight into the face of a dark winged creature in a tattered hooded coat. A shriek later she was swept from the camera view in a blur of motion. Her terrified cries echoed throughout the sanctuary, fading in the distance until they could be heard no longer.

"Sarah!" Hank hollered into the radio, knowing in his heart he'd just lost his friend forever. He instantly thought of Doris and Becky, of their safety, but he had the whole Haven to worry about. Changing frequencies on his walkie talkie, he roared to the guardsman standing watch, manning the Day-Lights on the church roof.

"Night Guard, what do you see? What is it? What happened?"

Only static.

"Come back, Night Guard. Red One, Red Two—report!"

There was no report from the grounds, either. Just Hank Berkley shouting on the radio, every face in the Haven focused intently on him, waiting for him to save them.

They've taken out all our guards. We're defenseless.

The door to the War Room opened and Annie exited, the diary in her hand, her finger holding her place as if she were only pausing in reading a good book. "Why did it get so quiet all of a sudden?"

The flapping of powerful wings on the night air outside answered her.

No one moved. No one said a word.

The wings beat hard against the air, growing louder as the thing—the TJ Creature, Hank knew—drew closer to its prey: a churchful of frightened people. Hank waited, absently hoping that the slow and steady *whoosh-whoosh* would pass, that the Creature would overlook them or show mercy. But the sound grew steadily louder. The thing wasn't going to go away. It was coming right for them.

Move, you old man! Hank commanded his petrified legs. "Take cover!"

The Creature exploded through the stained glass oval above the church door with a horrible crash, sending rainbow-colored shards over the screaming congregation. The TJ Creature tore off its tattered coat, revealing hairy, black, oily and altogether bat-like features. The man-devil swooped in, its wings stretching to scrape the edge of the girding. The beast roared as the Havenites scrambled beneath it, seeking shelter. Rebecca collected Millie and Timmy as Franklin shielded them, and Hank was only dimly aware that the monster that sought their death was Rebecca's son. Jeff had decided not to tell Rebecca just yet, but now Hank wondered if they'd ever have the chance before TJ killed them all. Looking back,

Hank couldn't decide if it were for the better or not.

Franklin pushed Rebecca and the kids away, holding his ground. "Go. Take Tim. I'll stay."

Rebecca hesitated, but Hank watched her oblige through building tears. Hank moved to Franklin, his face hot and his mind racing. Scripture was the only weapon that worked against demons, but this thing wasn't a demon. It was a *Shambler*, albeit one unlike anything they'd ever encountered. Somewhere in there was a man and maybe it could die like a man too. Deciding in a split second, Hank shouted, "Gather some others. Get guns. Shoot that thing down!"

Franklin waved down two men who had already shooed their women and children in the direction of the fleeing herd. "Guns!" was all he said. It was all he *had* to say.

Annie fought against the tide of confusion, clutching Ray's diary to her breast and searching for Meredith Myers in the pandemonium. "Mom! *Mom!*"

Rifles were quickly distributed and the riflemen filled the church with thunderous gunshots, exciting the crowd all the more into screams. Hank joined the fray, hurrying to his room to plunder from beneath the mattress the Colt revolver his grandfather had given to him on the day he graduated from the police academy. He grabbed the gun and pouch of loose ammo beside it and hurried to load the six-shooter as he entered the main hall, tying the strings of the pouch around his thick wrist. Slapping the cylinder shut, ready for action, he caught sight of his wife and daughter, their bags in hand, huddled together and running out the front door.

Neither spared him a second look.

He smiled wanly. *At least they're safe.*

Shutting out all thoughts of his family, all thoughts of his life before this moment, Hank focused on one thing. *Defend the Haven.*

Grim-faced and determined, he hauled himself to the front line with the other men. "Bring him down, boys! Bring him *down*!"

Invigorated, the men opened fire, shooting at the winged beast circling the rafters as it screeched and snarled at the shooters below.

Franklin took quick but careful aim and fired, blinking as the spent cartridges from his rifle bounced into his hardened, but handsome face.

With one arm braced on the other, Hank let another loud *pop* fly from his Colt, a bullet whizzing into the TJ Creature's shoulder. The monster howled in rage and gnashed its teeth. All the time Hank watched out of the corner of his eye, until the last of the Havenites made it to open air.

"Keep firing!" he shouted over the blasts. He knew they had to draw the Creature's attention. *Gotta give them folks more time to get away.*

The beast clawed at the air, swatting the bullets as if they were flies, screeching hellishly. Finally having enough, the TJ Creature flicked its forearm, a jagged shard of bone jutting out from its elbow, and made its first swoop at the attacking gunmen.

Hank's eyes widened in horror. "Down!"

Throwing his weight to the floor, Hank rolled with an overworked grunt to see if others had done the same. Franklin had—*and still firing, God bless the boy*—as well as most others. But the Creature did not go unsatisfied. A man named Wesley Faulk failed to escape and was cut in two at the hip with one swipe of the Creature's massive elbow-blade. Hank pounded the floor with a beefy fist and hefted himself to a stand, firing once at the retreating monster before reaching into the ammo pouch, fumbling for more bullets to reload his grandfather's revolver.

Franklin knelt with the others, alternately firing and reloading as the Creature circled and came down again. Hank saw the bat-man diving for him and he balked, the opened gun in his hand slipping and spilling bullets to the floor. He had no time to get them, to reload at all, and froze as TJ Walker's transformed face came closer and closer still. Ready to die—to see God, Jesus, and Christopher Perdu—Hank closed his eyes and braced for contact.

With a grunt, he toppled over sideways, landing hard on his discarded bullets, and looked to see that Franklin had pushed him out of the way and was now standing in the path of the rampaging monster. Teeth gritted, Franklin sidestepped the winged thing and swung hard with his rifle, smacking the back of the monster's head with the stock. Knocked off-balance in mid-air, the TJ Creature went reeling, head low, into the security console. Sparks blew out of the wrecked hardware as the table careened forward, the Creature scrambling in the mess to right itself.

Franklin bent low and gripped Hank's arm. "Move, move!"

Hank braced himself as the other men fell back towards the front door, taking the opportunity to reload. Franklin kept his eye on the Creature as it flailed, trying to stand, rendering the computers to rubble. The monitors and towers, all operational, sputtered and coughed up smoke and flames. At last the Creature lifted the table and angrily tossed it aside, then rose to its full stature.

"Lord Almighty," Hank breathed.

Franklin tugged wildly at the ex-sheriff's arm. "Come on! *Hurry!*"

A couple gunshots popped from behind them as the gunmen at the door laid down cover. Hank stumbled backwards on weak legs and used every bit of Franklin's support to keep moving. Franklin draped Hank's arm over his shoulder and hurried along, letting his rifle drop to the ground in the process. At the door, the men fired without ceasing, but in their efforts to avoid hitting their friends, their shots flew wide and were largely ineffective.

Hank threw a terrified look behind as the muscular beast marched for them, its wings contracting, its elbow-blades extending. The fire from the computers was catching on, spreading to the church itself, swallowing up the wall behind the monster in flames—but the thing kept coming, a bat out of hell.

The thing's shimmering black face cracked, revealing long, yellow, curved teeth. It was grinning.

"No—" Hank muttered, Franklin hurrying him along, but they were too slow and the Creature's elbow-blade sliced Franklin's back. In an instant, the color drained from Franklin's face, and he grew limp and slumped over, sliding off Hank and collapsing as his warm blood splashed to the floor.

Hank released a pitiful moan before tripping over his own clumsy feet and looking straight up into the malicious eyes of the TJ Creature. The men at the door shouted in rage, firing directly at the exposed chest of the beast, but the monster did not flinch. Beyond pain, beyond death, it towered over Hank, grinning as it lifted its blade, glistening with the blood of brave Franklin Whitaker.

Crack!

The TJ Creature's head jerked hard to the right at an odd angle that would have broken the neck of an ordinary man, and the monster squealed in surprise, listing sideways.

Standing with a metal pipe in his hand, his chest heaving and his hair matted with sweat, glowered Danny Carpenter.

Hank started at the sight of the young man, his savior. The boy's face was painted in tears, twisted in a mask of pain and anguish. The sorrowful look broke Hank's heart and he didn't even know why.

"Danny?"

The boy pointed to the door, crying, "Go!"

"But—"

Danny shouted again as the Creature took two strong hands and straightened its neck. "*Go!*"

His strength renewed, Hank dragged Franklin. Two more men from the door hurried to help him haul their friend out of the burning church.

Danny watched them retreat before staring down the beast, tightening his grip on the steel pipe. The TJ Creature circled him, a pleased grin on its face, flexing its muscles and long, powerful fingers.

"I won't let you do this," Danny said, his bottom lip quivering with guilt. Rage.

The fire quickly spread up the side of the building and the heat proved blistering. The Creature pulled its arms upward, forearms out, jagged bone-blades ready to impale, and lunged forward.

Danny slid aside with a fright, the fight starting faster than he had anticipated, and held up the rod to block the attack. The pipe in his hands held, and Danny used the leverage to throw the Creature off-balance once again. The distraction was only momentary as the beast quickly backhanded Danny, sending him flying and landing on his back. With a cough, Danny rolled to his side and reached for the pipe he had lost in the fall.

The Creature reached him first and stomped a scaly, taloned foot on the blunt weapon. Twisting on the ground, Danny swung with his leg and caught the Creature behind the knee. The man-devil scooted sideways, giving Danny just enough room to pry the rod free and stand, bracing his pipe for another attack. Before the monster had a chance to turn around, Danny brought the beam up high with both hands and slammed it down with a cry of pure adrenaline.

The TJ Creature buckled under the attack but turned its head to peer at Danny with an arrogant sneer. Enraged, Danny raised the metal pipe once more, but in a flash, the Creature's leathery wings snapped open. With a thunderous *whoosh*, he tackled Danny and carried him off the ground, through the south wall.

Both combatants burst through the side of the church, spitting flaming wooden planks in all directions, landing hard on the grassy lawn outside. Danny squirmed in the monster's grip, dropping his weapon to the ground and beating furiously with his fists on the thing's back.

"I won't let you do this!" he screamed, punching the beast's slick, rubbery hide. Danny knew his feeble attempts to overpower the monster were just that, but he had to do something. Beyond the TJ Creature, Danny saw the flames from the church, dancing to touch the twinkling stars, as all that they had worked for literally went up in smoke. He had caused this. Now they were all doomed.

"No!" Danny shouted, hitting the Creature, wrestling with it, wrestling with himself and his own sins. He had only wanted to see Tabitha. To see his boys and hold them and smell their baby smell and kiss their soft, fuzzy heads. He had wanted that so bad. But he was never going to get that. He knew that now. It wasn't his part to play. It wasn't what the Lord had prepared him to do.

I'm a Devil Smasher.

Danny delivered a hard punch to the Creature's jaw and heard something break loose.

Good! Take that! He hit again. Again.

The Creature roared in frustration, working to pin Danny's arms to the ground or to get those wicked blades close enough to kill, but Danny moved too fast. He'd scrapped enough in his short life to know how to do it well. He might die tonight, but he wasn't going down without a fight.

The Creature blocked as many punches as he could before finally growling and thrusting his skull forward, smacking Danny's forehead and sending a brilliant flash of red across his eyes. He moaned, putting a hand to his head, feeling something sticky and warm. As he opened his bleary eyes, he saw that the beast was already standing.

Had already picked up Danny's discarded steel pipe.

Was already bringing it down. "Tab—"

Thwump.

Danny shivered then went still. His body felt numb but he managed just enough strength to lift his head. He saw the pipe jutting out of his stomach, pinning him to the earth like an insect in a kid's collection.

The TJ Creature examined its handiwork, then twitched to attention at the shrill screams of frightened Havenites somewhere in the North Woods. Sneering once more, it flapped its wings and shot off into the dark, eager to claim more prey.

Danny rested his head back on the soft dirt and thought of Tabitha. Of his boys. What they would be one day. What they would think of him…

CHAPTER TWENTY-ONE

CLOUDS OF DUST billowed behind the old pickup as Jeff turned down the gravel road that led to the Haven. Creedence Clearwater Revival's "Bad Moon Rising"—one of Danny's cassette tapes—played in the tapedeck as Jeff absently tapped at the steering wheel and Isabella stared at the passing forest, lost in thought. It had been an eventful night. Both had visited their parents, warned them of the dangers to come, and said good-bye to their old house on Grover's Pond. Tomorrow, life was going to change forever—either for good or ill—and they both felt it. The realization was overwhelming and neither one spoke the entire trip back.

The silence was broken when Jeff saw the flames in the distance.

"Wha…?" he leaned forward, gaping.

Isabella stiffened. "Oh no. *Oh no.*"

Jeff floored the gas pedal.

Hank and a 'Nite named Kurt Daughtry held Franklin Whitaker on the ground. He was still alive, but shivering. "Hang on, boy," Hank said, dour and covered in his brave friend's blood.

"You're gonna be okay, man," Kurt eagerly declared, keeping eye contact with the trembling Franklin.

Hank knew better, though. Franklin was losing a lot of blood and going into shock. He'd be dead within the hour if they didn't get him to a hospital. Only, what hospital would take them? According to the populace at large, they were hate-mongering religious zealots preaching a doomsday message, and no self-respecting doctor in town would even see them.

Even if they could make it through the armada of gremlins who wanted to rend them flesh from bone.

The other men who defended the Haven were now fighting against the fire that had already pulled down the gentle giant, once Jack Weldon's church. The old king on God's Cliff was dead but the men were able to contain the fire with water from the stream and the coats from their backs, preventing it from spreading to the surrounding North Woods.

At once headlights blinded them all. Hank heard the familiar and welcome grumble of Jeff's truck. For a second, he felt a flash of unbridled anger towards the Weldons. *Where were you*, he wanted to demand. But when he saw Jeff and Isabella, their eyes shocked, running towards them, he was reminded of his love for them.

"Hank?" Isabella cried, rushing to her friend, nearly stumbling over Franklin's outstretched legs. "What…?"

He shook his head. "We were hit. It was TJ."

Jeff stood speechless, running his hand through his hair, nearly hyperventilating. There was so much devastation, Hank knew. The church was gone, now Jeff's second church to be burnt to the ground.

"Where is everybody?" he blurted.

"They ran off into the woods," Hank said. "Jeff," he slowed deliberately. "We lost Sarah."

Isabella held her hand to her mouth. "*What?*"

Jeff's eyes squinted back tears. He searched the small group, suddenly and desperately. "Where's—?"

"Danny's gone too," Hank said, his voice cracking.

Jeff let out a simple cry and slumped to the ground beside Isabella. She leaned on her husband, crying hysterically.

With the fire under control, their home reduced to nothing more than a bonfire, the men hurried to Hank, faces covered in ash and clothes reeking of smoke. "All set," one of them reported. "What do we do?"

Jeff looked up to answer, but realized the men were asking

Hank.

Hank saw the uncomfortable expression in his young friend's eyes, as though Jeff felt he was no longer fit to lead, and he understood it. But there was no time to discuss it now. "Franklin needs a hospital. *Now.* Kurt, here, says he saw the Creature shoot off into the woods, after our folks. We stayed behind to deal with the fire, to keep it from eating up the whole countryside. Jeff...They could all be dead. We have no way of knowing."

Jeff stood, marching for the truck. Isabella, her face puffy with tears, cried, "Where are you going?"

"I'm going to get them. I've got to save them."

Isabella scrambled to her feet and nearly pounced on him, pulling at his arm. "*No!* It's too late!"

Jeff looked past her to Hank. "How long ago?"

Hank pursed his lips. "Ten minutes."

"Then there's still time."

"Jeff," Hank called in a stern voice, still cradling Franklin in his arms. "That thing did this to the church in under ninety *seconds.* Ten minutes is plenty of time to kill every man, woman, and child we had here."

Jeff shoved past Isabella, his voice a shriek, "*Don't say that!* We can save them!"

"No!" Hank bellowed, his jowls shaking, blood rising. "We *could've* saved them. If we'd all been here together, you, me, Danny, Carter, we could have saved them."

"Carter—" Jeff hesitated. "Where's Carter?"

"Gone," Hank replied. "He wasn't here during the attack, either. Must be the thing to do."

Jeff cursed and banged his fist on the hood of the truck. Hank felt like doing the same. It was all falling apart. They had built a life out here, had things under control...but it was all folly. They weren't in control of what was going on in Greensboro any more than they were in control of the sun rising and setting. This was a supernatural war that had been raging since the dawn of time and would continue to rage until Christ returned to make things right once and for all.

We're just a tiny blip in the grand scheme of things, Hank knew.

Suddenly, Jeff looked very small and hopeless. They were all going to die. For all Hank knew, he, Isabella, Jeff, and the men there with them were the only ones left at all. If that were so, how would they ever stop the Dark Hour? How would they ever make the world right again?

It's useless.

Jeff hung his head, bracing himself on the truck. Isabella stroked his arm, her lip quivering. "What do we do?" she asked him.

"I'm not the leader," he said softly. Nearly whimpering.

Yet, as he looked to his left and saw Franklin Whitaker, clinging to life, Jeff's expression hardened. "Hank," he said with authority, moving to help Kurt get Franklin to his feet. "Take the Nova. I filled it up yesterday. Take Kurt and get Franklin to the hospital."

"They won't let them in," Isabella reminded him.

"They'd better," Jeff said, his eyes aflame. "Or there'll be hell to pay."

Hank nodded and hefted Franklin, aiming for the back where the old Nova slept. The men remaining turned to Jeff, eager to be busy. "What do *we* do?"

Jeff paused. "Pray."

They looked to one another, hesitant at first, but eventually took hands and began to pray.

Hank smiled. *Maybe we got a little more fight in us after all.*

He and Kurt hurried for the Nova with their friend.

Determined, Jeff headed for the truck, Isabella hot on his heels.

"We're going after the others," he said, his mind made up. *Please, God, don't let me be too late.*

Isabella didn't bother to argue. She hopped into the passenger seat, her fingers roving over the console that operated the Day-Lights fastened to the top of the cab, ready to use them at a moment's notice. The Nova croaked and squealed until it finally sputtered to life and drove away. Jeff swung open the driver's side door to the old truck, but stopped when he heard, "…Jeff? That you, Boss…?"

Leaning out of the truck, Jeff worriedly scanned the yard of the smoldering church.

"Danny?"

Leaving the door hanging open, Jeff dashed across the yard, his arms wide, as if preparing to dive into a haystack to find a precious needle. "Danny! Danny, where are you?"

"Down here…"

The boy sounded bored, distant, and Jeff felt an uncontrollable chuckle. Hope swelled in him. Hank said that Danny was dead, but he'd been mistaken. Danny was all right!

But when he saw Danny…

"Oh." His throat tightened.

Danny lay spread-eagle on the lawn, a steel pole grotesquely standing erect, as if it had grown out of his abdomen. "Danny," he whispered, and slowly moved to his friend, kneeling beside him.

Blood running from his nose and mouth, Danny barely turned his head to smile. "Hey, Boss…"

Jeff verbalized without thinking, "Danny…there's a big pole sticking out of your stomach."

"S'okay…I don't feel it anymore…"

Jeff's eyes watered and he stroked his friend's dirty hair, brushing loose strands from his face. "I'm sorry," he said at length, those words incapable of expressing how he really felt.

"No," Danny said. "It's *my* fault…" He hesitated, then began to weep, "I'm so sorry, Jeff. I was supposed to protect them but I told the Strange Man where we were…"

Jeff's chest heaved. "What?"

"He told me…" Danny cried, his body shaking, letting go his one last confession. "Ah, man, Jeff, he told me I'd see my babies again…I wanted to believe him…we been fighting so hard, so long…I just wanted to see them one more time…"

Jeff caressed his friend's brow, his love for him overcoming any sense of betrayal he might have felt. "It's okay, Danny."

"I couldn't let him do it, Jeff…I had to try and stop him…I tried my best…"

"Yeah, you did, Danny. You did real good."

"Is Sarah okay? Did she make it out?"

"Yeah, Danny," Jeff lied. "She's safe with the others."

"Good," he smiled, relieved, another stream of blood escaping through his teeth. "She always kind of got on my nerves, but she was a good lady. I'd like to have known her a little better. I should've taken more time…"

Jeff felt the wetness of Danny's spilt blood soaking through his jeans as it leaked out onto the ground. *It's almost done now.*

"It's okay, Danny. Just try and relax, okay?"

"Jeff…?" he asked quietly.

"Yeah?"

"Will Jesus still forgive me? Even though I slipped up?"

Jeff laughed through his tears. "Jesus will forgive you, Danny. He already has. He already did before you ever did a thing."

"Good," the other man sobbed, "'Cause I gotta see Tabitha and my boys one day…I promised them…I don't wanna miss them in heaven."

"You won't."

"I'm so sorry…I really screwed up…"

"Shhh."

Danny was growing paler by the second, the blood from his grievous wound flowing like a river. He looked to Jeff, his eyes glassy and blank. "Wait…" he said. "I can't go yet. Not yet. One more second, God!"

"Danny—"

"No, listen…" Danny choked and spit up blood. "I saw that phony preacher at the lake tonight…with a lot of people from town…they were talking…getting ready for tomorrow…"

Tomorrow Jeff suddenly remembered the Dark Hour was still looming over them. He didn't honestly know how he'd handle it without Danny there, wisecracking beside him before the gates of hell. *God, what are we going to do?*

"I know what it is they're doing tomorrow, Jeff…it's the *babies*…they're going to feed the babies to the lake…a sacrifice…one, great big…"

He grew silent, struggling for words, and Jeff shushed him. "Okay. Okay."

"I really…" Danny's eyes lolled from side to side, as if he were drowsy. "I really wish I had a…had a brother like you, man…"

"You do, Danny," Jeff wept, leaning over to kiss Danny's head. "You do."

"Yeah," Danny smiled at the thought. "I guess I do…"

And that was it. Danny was gone.

Jeff felt Isabella's hand on his shoulder. He hadn't even realized she was standing there. By now, her tears were depleted and her face was stained with the quiet understanding that Death walked among them tonight.

"I'm sorry," she whispered.

Jeff nodded, his heart somehow relieved. He'd just lost his best friend. At the same time, he knew that Danny was with the Lord now. After a lifetime of running, getting into trouble, hurting those who loved him, after being redeemed and giving up what mattered most to him to fight in a war that seemed impossible to win…he could finally rest now.

He deserves it.

The corner of a folded sheet of paper poked out of Danny's bloodied jacket and Jeff reached for it, already realizing what it was. Sure enough, as he unfolded the paper, he saw the cartoon that Danny had shown him last night.

Devil Smashers.

Jeff took a deep, stabilizing breath, and stood, still looking at the peaceful face of Danny Carpenter. His respects paid, he turned to Isabella, calm and resolved.

"Come on. It's time to save the others."

Somewhere in the distance another voice screamed for the last time. With Ray McCormick's diary, Annie lay on her back underneath a bramble with her mother. Meredith Myers had always hated the outdoors, preferring cocktail parties to camping, and swatted an insect—real or imagined—off her shoulder.

"Is it gone?" Meredith hissed.

"*Shhh*," Annie chided, looking through the tangled twigs into the starless night beyond.

Things were quiet again. It was a pattern that Annie had quickly picked up on. The man-devil would come, snatch up another hapless victim, and be gone for a few moments' time. Whether the thing was taking the poor soul to its nest, or was just waiting up in the trees, eager to see which ignorant human would be the first to poke out into the clearing, Annie wasn't sure. But it was time to see.

"Come on," she said to her mother, rolling to her stomach and sliding along the foliage.

"Annie," Meredith whined.

Annie shimmied along, careful to stay close to the bottom of the small cliff she had tripped down on her mad dash into the North Woods. When the Creature made its first dive attack, they had all scattered, hiding wherever they could. After the beast left that first time, some thought the coast was clear.

They paid for that mistake with their lives.

The Creature had inhuman patience, sitting and waiting for someone to move. Still, Annie couldn't sit by idle. The others were close; she heard their whimpering and shushed tones. She just had to get to them. Together they were stronger. They could figure this out.

Maybe even kill that freak once and for all.

If Rosalyn were here, she'd know what to do. The sad fact remained, however, that Rosalyn was not here.

Besides, Annie had fought monsters before. *You're not just the kid sister anymore. Suck it up. Save the others.*

Defiance welled inside the young girl and she pushed on harder, her mother huffing and puffing behind, flopping helplessly in the dead leaves like a beached fish.

She rolled her eyes. "Come on, Mother."

Up ahead, Annie made out a familiar voice placating a whimpering child.

"I want my Dad," the boy sobbed as Rebecca Walker held him close. Through her own weeping, the woman tried to soothe him.

"Shhh, Timmy. It's going to be okay."

Annie saw Rebecca, Millie, and Timmy Whitaker huddled together in the shade of a twisted oak, the moonlight barely catching their features.

"*Ms. Walker.*"

Rebecca caught her breath and went rigid, not daring to speak into the darkness.

"It's me," Annie whispered. "Anne."

"*Anne?*"

Immediately, Rebecca made to rush out into the open, but Annie shouted as quietly as possible, "No! Stay low. Don't let him see you."

Rebecca froze with the two small children and pulled them to the ground.

"Mommy?" Millie asked. "What's going on?"

"It's a game," Annie whispered back, remembering the games she used to play with Millie when she baby-sat her. "Wriggle like worms. Try to get to me."

Chuckling, Millie got into the spirit and crawled on her belly, muddying her little clothes, but Timmy hesitated. "I want my Dad," he moaned.

Annie didn't know what had happened to Franklin Whitaker, but she knew she couldn't let on. "Come on, Timmy. Millie's going to beat you."

Timmy frowned, still unsure, but being a boy and all, he determined not to be outdone by a girl, especially one two years his junior. Staying on his tummy, he kicked and pushed with his feet like a little Army man, working hard to catch up to Millie. Rebecca followed behind the children, looking fearful. She looked up a couple times, probably to see if the bat-man was circling them, but she pushed on, focusing on Annie, who was coaxing the children forward, inch by inch.

"Come on, you guys," she encouraged with a smile. "You've almost made it."

Millie giggled in anticipation while Timmy seemed to be concentrating too hard on victory to be reminded of the loss of his father.

"When did you get to be so grown up?" Meredith said. Annie regarded her mother and saw great pride in her eyes.

She grinned, then looked back to the kids. "Almost, you guys…"

Millie was the first to reach Annie, with Timmy in a close second. She scooped both little ones up, a hen gathering her chicks. "Good job."

Rebecca joined them, her breathing starting to slow, but her eyes large and alert. "What do we do now?"

There was a honk from the dark woods to their left and Annie brightened. "You hear that?"

The honk sounded again, followed by the sputter of a truck engine. Headlights pierced the darkness, sifting through the thick forestation. Annie rose to her knees, peering over the knoll.

"Annie…" Meredith warned.

Annie saw an old truck bouncing along the rough terrain, headed their way. Other Havenites peered out of their hidey-holes like prairie dogs checking the coast for predators. The honks grew more persistent and she could make out Jeff's voice calling into the night. "Hey! *Hello?*"

She spun to her mother and Rebecca. "It's Jeff!"

Standing to her feet, she crawled over the small ledge with her mother, Rebecca, and the kids behind her, as the surviving church members converged on the approaching vehicle. Isabella immediately stepped out of the truck.

"Is everyone okay?" she asked breathlessly.

Annie's bunch joined the congregation, the weeping of newly

widowed spouses and parentless children permeating the still night. "Is it gone?" she asked when no one else did.

Isabella quickly scanned the skies, but Jeff said, "Hurry, while there's time. Pile the kids into the back, as many as you can fit. We have to find somewhere safe to hide."

"Where?" Annie asked, a bit annoyed that everyone seemed to be cycling through the same lines of logic, with no solid solutions.

Isabella locked eyes with her husband through the windshield and spoke low, as if only he could hear her. "Dad's."

"You sure?"

"It's closest and the Strange Man won't think to look there."

"Everyone in the truck. Hurry."

Rebecca hoisted Millie into the truck bed. Chelsea Ross—Carter's daughter—was lifted in by her mother, sniffling, "Where's my Daddy? Why isn't he here?"

Isabella moved fast, grabbing children in her arms and loading them in the truck like bags of sand. Parents kissed and hugged their children, assuring them that it was going to be all right and that they would be reunited soon. Jeff told the adults, "We'll go ahead and take the kids to safety. You all start heading that way. It's the old Evans farm out on County 216. As soon as your kids are safe, we'll meet you halfway and give you an escort."

There were nods of agreement and tearful good-byes, and Annie hoped this was a good idea. Suddenly, the moon flickered off above her head, and she looked up. Saw outstretched leathery wings, flapping against the stars.

The Creature had returned.

Absently, she turned to the church people helping their children into the back of the truck, oblivious that they were vulnerable to another attack. She wanted to warn them, but her terrified voice would not thaw. She only stuttered, gradually catching the attention of the congregation. One by one the crowd turned to her, until, from his place in the cab, Jeff looked through the busted passenger side window to see the scared girl. As the mob quieted, the *fwoop fwoop* of powerful, portentous wings could be heard.

"Everybody duck!" Jeff screamed as the Creature broke through the treetops and zoomed over the heads of the shouting mass. Circling back into the sky, arching up, then down again. Isabella screamed, "Take the children!"

"Get in!"

"There's no time," she shouted, leaping away from the truck and covering her head as the elbow blades of the Creature grazed the top of Jeff's truck, nearly taking her head with them.

"Iz!"

"*Go!*"

Jeff cranked the engine, slamming the steering wheel furiously, and pressed his foot to the gas pedal. The truck lurched forward, bucking and tipping on the rocky earth, as the children with him reached out for their parents, screaming and crying.

Looking in his rearview mirror, Jeff watched as the TJ Creature took another pass, scooping up one of the weeping mothers in its arm and whisking her away to certain death. Isabella was still back there…

What have I done?

He was so afraid. *Everyone* was so afraid.

"Afraid…" he said the word aloud, as if it were alien and worth dissecting.

The TJ Creature was unlike any Shambler they had ever encountered. But he *was* a Shambler. *Maybe*…It was worth a shot.

Jeff slammed on the brakes, wheeling the truck around, careful to swerve around a prominent evergreen. Reaching up with his free hand to the back window, he slid open the Plexiglas. "Millie!"

Millie pushed her face past the other screaming children in the truck bed, mildly curious. "Yeah?"

"Crawl in here."

She did as she was told, landing next to Jeff's lap. He had an idea.

"See that switch?"

Pantomiming wildly, he aimed at the Day-Light toggle. Millie nodded to him. "Yeah."

"When I tell you, flip it. Got it?"

"Got it."

Jeff ground his teeth. "Hold on, Iz…"

One of the older men was taken, warbling as the TJ Creature carried him off into the tops of the trees, where his screams ended in a wet gargle. The crowd below fell to pandemonium, crashing into each other, running every which way. Isabella stood in the maelstrom, trying to herd the terrified people.

"Stay calm!" Isabella shouted, but she was not heard above the screaming.

Her mind struggled to keep clear. She'd combated devils before. She could *do* this. *But this is different. This isn't a demon—just a man, corrupted by the power of hell.* Fear climbed on her back, weighing her down, and she felt like giving in.

It was at this precise moment that the Creature stopped, mid-flight, and looked directly at her. Like it had seen her, all of a sudden. Sneering, the winged Shambler dove straight for her, but Isabella ground her teeth. *No. I won't be afraid.* She held her ground, reining in her fears, centering her spirit. She was about to pray, to quote Scripture—*something*—when the beast halted, just above her head. He looked around, as if confused. Isabella held her breath, the thing hovering just feet from her, but it was like he didn't see her. Another scream from a scared Havenite stole the Creature's attention and it zipped off, for other prey.

Isabella stood there, marveling. *It only sees us when we're afraid.*

Annie, ahead of her, hollered, "Everyone stay together! Wait!" She was promptly knocked over by a rampaging woman. Above there was a screech and a *shwoosh* of wings as the Creature began its descent once more. Isabella watched the Creature sweep right over Annie, as if it didn't even see her, and pluck at lanky fifteen-year-old Douglas Scott, who fought and clawed to remain with his parents.

"Don't!" she shouted, grabbing onto the arm of a couple racing past her. "Wait! If you're not afraid it can't hurt you!"

Annie hoisted herself up, her mother helping her to her feet.

"Don't be afraid!"

Meredith balked. "*Are you crazy?*"

Isabella shouted, exuberant, "It can't see us if we're not afraid!"

"How do you expect people *not* to be afraid!"

A honk of the horn signaled that Jeff's truck had re-entered the fray. Isabella glimpsed Millie in the cab with her husband and heard Jeff shout, "Now, Millie!"

The toddler thumbed the switch, suffusing the forest in bright UV spotlights. The people calmed for a moment, the famed Day-Lights at work, believing their salvation had finally arrived. The Creature squawked, showered in the incandescent glow, staggering mid-air, and released its grip on the Scott boy, who crashed to the ground and was immediately recovered by his weeping parents.

"Yeah!" Jeff exclaimed, pumping his fist in the air at the sight of the monster shielding itself with its wings.

The people rallied together, gasping in awe at the retreating creature. Jeff pulled up and left the truck to join Isabella as parents hastened to unload their children, covering them in tearful kisses of relief. Before the celebrations could truly begin, however, the TJ Creature barked and snorted, and the gargoyle began to arc back to them, passing through the light, unaffected.

"I don't understand," Jeff said, awed.

When the people's shouts returned, Isabella held her ground, confident. "No, it's okay!" she told her husband. "It wasn't the lights that scared it off! It just didn't see us anymore because we stopped being afraid! Don't be afraid. It sees us because of our fear! If we're not afraid, it'll be blind."

But no one seemed to be listening. Parents clung to their children, bracing for the worst, but Annie turned to Isabella, desperate. "It's hopeless."

"No!" Jeff shouted to be heard. He looked lost and confused, then sharply focused on Isabella and sang, "*This is the day…*"

She halted, blinked once, then hollered, "What?"

Without explaining, Jeff broke out into glorious song: "*This is the day…*"

"What are you doing?"

He didn't respond, only continued to sing, "*That the Lord has made, that the Lord has made…*" He skittered across the lawn, carrying on with his musical number, and more than one person paused to look at him as if he'd lost his mind. Jeff Weldon couldn't carry a tune in a bucket with both hands, as anyone who'd ever sat near him in church could attest. Now, dividing his attention between singing and the plummeting creature above, he concentrated on catching everyone's attention.

"*We will rejoice,*" he bellowed off cue, "*We will rejoice…*"

Gaping now, the people seemed all but oblivious to the bat-man approaching fast.

But Isabella was catching on.

"*And be glad in it,*" she finished the song, drawing mortified stares.

Jeff laughed. "Yeah, that's it. Sing! *Sing!*"

He started the chorus, and this time, Isabella joined him, their voices bold and loud.

"*This is the day that the Lord has made! We will rejoice and be glad in it!*"

The children slowly began to snicker, their fears evaporating.

Annie jumped in, "*This is the day, this is the day, that the—Lord—has—made.*"

The Creature *shwished* by, rustling their hair, but harming no one, generating an "Oh!" from the crowd.

Jeff laughed excitedly. "It's okay to sing! It's okay to laugh! Come on!"

Isabella and Annie continued to sing, clapping their hands in time to the rhythm, laughing at the fools they were making of themselves. Millie and the other children joined in, miming the adults' movements, singing the song, drawing more than a few smiles from the grown-ups. "That's right!" Jeff encouraged, racing through the crowd, taking a moment to pat shoulders, hug necks. "Laugh! Sing!"

One by one, others caught on and joined in "This is the Day" as Jeff leapt onto the hood of his truck and shouted, "The Lord is our Shepherd, we shall *not* want! He makes us to lie down in green pastures! He leads us beside still waters! He restores our soul! He leads us in the path of righteousness for *His* name's sake! Yea, though we walk through the valley of the shadow of death, we will fear no evil for He is with us!"

There was a thunderous shout from the people as they broke from their singing to clap and praise, crying tears of gratitude. "We are the children of the Lord," Jeff shouted, laughing through tears. "He is our champion. Evil cannot harm us—not our *souls.* It might take our lives, but we will forever dwell with the Father in glory!"

"Hallelujah!" the people shouted to the heavens, energized with hope. Some resumed singing, while others hugged and even danced under the starless sky.

Above them, the TJ Creature fled into the night, its fearful prey having disappeared.

Jeff breathed a great sigh of exhaustion and climbed down off the truck. Isabella emerged from the rejoicing crowd, took hold of his whiskered face, and kissed him. As they parted, she grinned.

"I love you."

He cocked a smirk. "I know."

CHAPTER TWENTY-TWO

GREENSBORO SLEPT WHILE the Strange Man watched. Atop the roof of The Rave Scene, over the heads of a hundred laughing, reveling youths in the building beneath him, he hovered in silence, gazing indifferently over the twinkling street lights of the town. Johnny Mathis' "Chances Are" drifted lazily from the fixed speakers the Committee had mounted at every intersection, providing a soothing lullaby for the sleeping sheep of Maribel County. It was a nice night.

Too bad it will be their last.

Tomorrow, all his plans for this town—for its people—would finally come to pass and he would bask in the glow of their doom.

It had been three millennia since his fall from heaven, give or take a century or two. It had been over a hundred years since the last Dark Hour, and never had the world seemed *this* prepared. They were ready for the Great Change, but still not half as ready as he was to give it to them.

He knew the Christians were out there in the wilderness, drawing their plans against him, and he knew that, despite tonight's ridiculous debacle of country boys with rifles, those simple folk would inevitably try something else. He had sent his pet monster to shake down their house, but he knew Jeff Weldon—if that insufferable man survived—would fearlessly lead on and they would only be left with a stronger resolve. But it was too late now. The town didn't *want* their help. *They only want me.*

It felt good to be wanted, even if it were only for what vain pleasures he could offer. It was still some shadow of sincerity that could touch his cold, dead insides with a flutter of warmth he hadn't felt since last in the presence of his Lord.

It was on nights like this, when the world slept, secure in their lies, that the Strange Man missed that warmth the most. It'd been a long time since he'd been able to lie to himself. The Truth had stalked him for eons, refusing to budge, refusing to bend. He hadn't felt secure about anything in a thousand generations except the stark, frightening fact that his fate was sealed. Even now, every second he remained on this world was only possible because Jehovah had allowed it.

And soon, His purpose for the Strange Man would be fulfilled and it would be time to go back to his cage. The demon shuddered.

His whole existence was hiding, plotting, dividing, and trying to stave off that horrific moment when eternity's pain would begin. At least tomorrow, he could take a few thousand souls down with him.

He heard Rosalyn approaching before she ever stepped foot on the deserted rooftop. He could always hear her heartbeat, even louder than the music and chatter of The Rave Scene beneath his feet. Her energy was electric and sent waves wherever she went, and he savored them. *She is so much like…*

He pushed the ancient memory aside as she came closer.

"Things are getting exciting, wouldn't you say?" he said over his shoulder.

Rosalyn was silent and he faced her. Her expression was tired and cold; lost was the fire he had come to crave. He could feel her life ebbing away. The Change was taking place in her, turning her into something else. He almost regretted giving her that fruit, its juices filled with the same black ichors that now churned in Greensboro Park Lake. The slime was all part of his plan too, a sort of embryonic fluid, a transforming agent to prepare the children of men to become the children of hell. But this enhanced dose was his gift to her, to make her stronger and more like him. Twisted and changed. Yet a little while now and she would become a beast like TJ Walker, and she would love the Strange Man all the more.

But she was not adjusting to the Change well and the thing that made her fundamentally Rosalyn…the Strange Man saw it eroding away.

He was sad to see it go, yet he knew better than to get attached to mortals. They were expendable.

He cooed, "Tomorrow's the big day. Everything we've worked for, all coming to a head."

There was a screech from on high and the Strange Man looked up to see his faithful Creature circling overhead. Droplets of blood dripped from its wings, sprinkling the Man's chalky white face and hands. In the distance, the Strange Man heard the skittering of his gremlins, seeking out stragglers in the dark. Greensboro teemed with monsters and he had to smile.

"I've waited for this for so long," he breathed delicately, savoring the thought. "You have no idea."

Rosalyn watched the TJ Creature squawk once and fly back to its place in the Committee's cavernous meeting hall beneath The Rave Scene, her eyes saddening. The Strange Man sensed her anxiety and tasted a spot of blood on his fingers. He closed his eyes, elated, then opened them suddenly, flaring his glowing orbs. "The blood isn't from your Other."

Rosalyn winced and clutched her stomach. Miserably, she asked, "Why are you doing this? I mean, really? What's in it for you?"

He thought to lash out at her as he usually did when she asked him about his plans. But now, as his time grew closer, he decided to share with her. To let her in, in order that he might experience some fraction of companionship. Maybe he could lie to himself, for a little while, and not feel so utterly alone.

"Do you really want to know?"

She sagged. "I'm tired of playing games. Can you just tell me the truth, for once?"

The Strange Man loomed toward her, his dead toes dragging across the loose gravel on the rooftop, reminding him once again of the curse that had struck him. Never again would he fly in the heavens, looking out across the nations of the earth. No, he was bound and chained to the Earth, suspended by invisible strings that reached up to the One he hated—and yet loved—so much.

"I do this because I want to see the look on God's face when His creation turns from Him to their own destruction."

There was no boasting in the Strange Man's voice. No dramatic flair. Rosalyn studied him, believing him, surprised by her own measure of trust. "So that's all this is to you? You just want to get back at God? You just want people to worship you instead of Him?"

"Worship *me*?" he chuckled at her accusation, as if the thought never crossed his mind. "Is that what you think this is? I'm afraid you have me confused with Satan. *He* is the only one so bold to think he can replace God. Blasphemous, as well as stupid, that one. I hold no such aspirations."

"How noble," she drawled.

"I could not care what *humans* think of me any more than you care what squirrels think of you. What I do is not about them."

"What's it about then?"

He faced her hard, then looked away suddenly.

Is he afraid? Rosalyn wondered, a twitter of hope in her bosom.

He floated in silence, drifting in the breeze, and when he spoke his voice was oddly moving. "I wasn't always so hideous, my love. There was a time I was wrapped in the rainbow, clothed in splendor."

"What happened?" Rosalyn asked softly.

An uncomfortable quiet. "I gave it all up for a girl." The Strange Man snickered to himself. "Imagine. How juvenile, how…*human*." He spun on her, his tone airy and light as he traced the air with his slender fingers. "She was beautiful and alluring. Long, curly dark hair, chestnut eyes, and the way she danced…Would it surprise you to know that you remind me of her? All that time ago, when I saw you in The Rave Scene for the first time, when I approached you…you reminded me of her."

His brow relaxed as he gazed at Rosalyn's face, his eyes looking past her into another time, another life. With his talons, he cupped her chin, caressing her skin.

Rosalyn fought disgust.

"I gave up heaven for her," he whispered regretfully. Suddenly, his black lips curled into a snarl, and he spat, "Then she betrayed me. Just like you are about to do now."

With a flick of his other hand, he reached behind Rosalyn's back and pulled out a pistol she had concealed in her waistband. He held it out before her, his eyes alight with scandal.

"Oooh, what have we here?"

Rosalyn didn't know if he wanted her to respond or not. He threw the gun to the ground with a clatter and seized her throat, squeezing her fragile neck tight.

"Don't you understand?" he roared at her, tears filling his eyes. "I gave up *everything* for her and she left me for another lover! For a plain, ordinary *man*!"

Rosalyn hacked under the strain, but resisted the urge to pass out.

"I had no choice but to butcher her," he growled, his eyes flickering with hellfire. "The things I did to her…not even man in all his depravity could begin to imagine the depths of desecration I visited upon her body."

Rosalyn struggled to breathe until at last the Strange Man released her and she collapsed on her backside. The demon looked to his hands, as if he had just committed those atrocious acts all over again, and continued in a shaky voice, "But I didn't want to. I loved her…I…at least, I thought I did. I am not made to understand love. Not as you do, not as the Father…"

Rosalyn massaged her throat while sitting up, careful to back away from the raving lunatic above her. The Strange Man flailed to the heavens, shouting so hard spittle flew from his mouth. "I went to God! I threw myself at His feet and begged for mercy, for forgiveness! I had only made a mistake. One, simple mistake, and I had seen the error of my ways!" Twisting back, tears streaming down his face, he glared at Rosalyn as if she could save him. "But He *refused*!" Rearing back, the Strange Man let fly a terrible backhand, knocking Rosalyn across her face. She yelped and rolled backward as he screamed, "You people have it so easy! You sin and you fall and God will *always* take you back. He sent His very Son to pay the ultimate price for your sins and what does He offer His angels? *Nothing*! We are servants, soldiers, but you are sons. You are daughters. He's given you everything and yet you throw it back in His face. You flip-flop back and forth, back and forth. I've watched you! *For ages!* One day you bless Him and vow to serve Him, the next day you deny Him and only serve yourselves! *Hypocrites!*"

As he raised his skeletal claw once more, Rosalyn braced for another blow, but it never came. Instead the Strange Man gripped a tight fist and flew past her, furious.

Quieting, the devil rubbed his weary eyes and stared through Rosalyn. "But the thing I'll never understand is that He'll always believe…He'll wait at the door every single day, looking for that lost child to come back home to Him."

Rosalyn slowly stood, mindful of the gun at her feet, doubting if it ever could have stopped the Strange Man. She hated him for what he'd done to her. What he'd done to Dras. But suddenly, she found that she pitied him, *and* pitied herself for believing in him so. Was *this* the man she gave up her soul mate for? Was *this* the man who led her to betray the trust of her friends and family? *I killed for him*…Where were his charms, now? His magic tricks? They were all lies, a mask to hide the terrible truth.

He was a broken trinket. A wounded beast, snapping to scare away predators.

"I hate you because He *loves* you," the Strange Man confessed, his tears drying. "What I do tomorrow, I do to show Jehovah that, when given the chance, His would-be children will *always* turn from Him to serve their own selfish, blackened hearts. His love in you is misplaced—just as mine was—and I will prove it to Him." He snarled and muttered, "Again."

His body wracked with distress, the Strange Man inhaled deeply and gathered a modicum of his old self back, noticing Rosalyn's gun. "I have brought nations to their knees, rendered kingdoms ruined…and you seriously thought a bullet would be enough to destroy me?"

He shook his head. "I would have suspected something like this from Simms or those other old goats, even Stevenson…" He frowned. "But I expected more from you. I see now that you never really understood me at all."

Rosalyn hung her head.

The bogeyman slithered towards her. "My suggestion is, if you plan to use that thing, you'd be better off using it on yourself." He grinned, lifted up on the wings of her pain. "Just like your father did."

In a breath, he was gone. Rosalyn sat alone.

She stared at the gun lying next to her on the hard concrete. It looked larger than it had earlier, when she'd palmed it and hid it under her coat, intending to murder the Strange Man and end this hell. The gun swallowed up her vision, swelling in her mind.

Her blood pounded as she reckoned how easy it would be to simply pick it up, put it to her temple…and squeeze. Her father had done it, and he had left behind a wife and two daughters. What would she be leaving behind? Who would really miss *her*?

She knew Dras would. She was sure that, no matter how disappointed he would be to find out all the terrible things she'd done, he'd still think there was something in her worth saving. Maybe even worth loving.

But Dras *didn't* know. He didn't understand. She had killed in the name of the Dark Hour, the Ancient One. But she didn't have the Strange Man's passion for vengeance, no scores to settle or principles to prove. She had done it simply out of a desire to be loved.

I'm just a sick joke. She was guilty. It wouldn't be suicide; it would be justice. Maybe, in one last act, she could make the world a better place by removing herself from it.

Palms sweaty, heart ramming against her ribcage, Rosalyn jerked the pistol from the ground and pressed it to her temple. If she were going to do this, she would have to do it fast. *Don't think, just act. That's how you've always lived, isn't it? Never thinking past the consequences? Just living in the moment?* It was what led her to this fate. She had pursued the Strange Man, taken his offer, became his lover and his right hand, all on a whim.

Why not end it all the same way?

Pulling back the hammer, thinking of Annie, suddenly, and hoping her sister would forgive her one day, Rosalyn curled her finger around the trigger. She whispered, "I'm sorry, Mom," and—

Froze. Threw the gun away. Cursed. Bent over. Cried.

"Why won't you let me die!" she screamed at the heavens.

A soft voice from behind answered, "Maybe He's trying to tell you something."

Rosalyn stood, immediately wiping the tears away, recognizing the voice. In a million years, she'd still recognize that voice.

"Dras…" she muttered, trying not to sound upset.

But she understood that he knew, just like he always did. Now, here they were. Finally together.

"Sorry I'm late," he chuckled awkwardly. "I've been looking everywhere for you. Guess I should've checked all the rooftops first, huh?"

Rosalyn grinned through her despair. "Goofball."

There was so much she wanted to say—*no, to do!* She wanted to throw her arms around her friend—her Other, as the Strange Man called him—to kiss him, to tell him how much she'd missed him, thought of him, loved him.

But she couldn't. She didn't have the strength to face him. Not after the mockery she had made of his sacrifice. Still with her back to him, she quickly explained, "I tried to stop him…I tried, I-I don't know what I'm doing."

"I had to come see you," he said flatly, keeping his distance.

"I thought you would be dead by now," she replied, trying to keep from trembling.

"Nope. Still here."

"Dras—"

"I missed you," he said, as though he'd been keeping those words at bay for too long.

Now she could no longer avoid him. She faced Dras with a

smile, breathing in the sight of him, her best friend, back from the dead. "I missed you too," she allowed herself to say, stepping out of the walls she'd constructed for herself over the better part of the last year. *Maybe even longer than that.*

"How've you been?" she said.

He shrugged, rolling his eyes. "Ah, you know. In prison. Not dropping the soap and all that."

She snickered, a million flashes of their childhood together replaying in her mind's eye. All his lame jokes, his lousy quips. She missed that so much. "Yeah."

"You?"

"Evil," she answered playfully, and laughed hard, a cathartic response.

"Right," he joined in. "How's that working out for you?"

"Not so great," she said, her lip quivering just a bit, breaking her smile.

He quieted. "Yeah."

She moved a step closer, still holding back, trying hard not to crawl into his arms and cry until the sun came up. "You—" she began, taking a deep breath, "You don't know how many times I've dreamt of this moment. Seeing you again, I mean."

Dras held out his arms, beckoning her closer. "I'm right here."

"It's not the same," she said, turning from him. She blinked once, her eyes becoming solid black, an effect of the dark change within her. "I'm not the same," she said grimly, then blinked again, returning her irises to normal.

"Who *is*? We're all different. Jeff's actually not such a dork, now, if you can believe it. He's even tolerable to hold a conversation with."

Rosalyn winced at the mention of Jeff. She'd missed him too. "Why did you come back?"

"For you. I thought that'd be obvious. It was always for you."

She snapped at him, guilt-ridden. "Don't say that."

"It's the truth. I came back for *you*, Rosalyn. I love you."

As soon as the words escaped his lips, Rosalyn's heart jumped into her throat. For a brief moment, the two of them stared at each other, reliving the moment when they'd kissed in his kitchen ten months ago. Breaking the tension forcefully, she spat, "I've killed for him, Dras. Did you know that?"

He didn't respond.

"You heard the stories about the Committee, right?" she asked, tears building in her eyes, her voice distorted by rage. "How they found their guts splattered all over the underpass? That was *me*. The gremlins obey me now, just like they do him. I told them to do that. *I* did that."

Dras considered her. "I know."

Rosalyn glared at him. There was softness in his eyes. Why didn't he hate her? Why did he still love her? *He doesn't know*, she thought bitterly. *He doesn't know me.*

"I slept with him, Dras!" she said coldly, hoping to hurt him. Hoping to pierce his heart so he would know how wicked she was, and he'd no longer love her and he'd leave her to die.

Dras staggered and gulped. But he stood his ground. "I…I figured that too. Though," his eyes brightened, humor still his first line of defense, "I didn't think you'd just come right out and *say* it—"

She narrowed her eyes. "Do you love me now—"

"Yes."

"You can't," she accused.

He approached her. "Don't you get it? I love you. It doesn't matter what you do. I *love* you. You're my soul mate. You're…you're everything to me—"

She backed away. "Stop it."

"Rosalyn, God has—"

"No!" she screamed in his face. "Stop it! No more! No more God, no more devil, no more. I just want it all to be over. This is *too much*, Dras!" She wept loudly. "I hate what I've done and what I've done to you! I *knew* what he was. The whole time I knew he was really the one who killed Lindsey and he framed you, but I ignored it."

Dras listened without judgment.

Her screams faded into quiet sobs. "I was so lost…I just needed something…anything…"

"I know what you need." He held out his hand to her.

Rosalyn slapped it away with an obsidian tentacle where her arm had been only an instant before, her eyes suddenly wholly black and evil.

Dras recoiled in alarm. "You're a Shambler?"

"Look at me!" she bellowed, her voice deeper, that sickly spindly arm coiling like a snake on the ground. "Would your God love something like this?"

"What happened to you…?"

"I'm a monster, Dras," she moaned.

He reached for her, overcoming his initial surprise. "I can help you."

"You and I both know it's too late," Rosalyn said, her tentacle twirling until finally receding back into her pores, her arm as ordinary as before. Her eyes faded to their natural chestnut brown, and, for the first time, she realized how close she was to the edge of the building.

"It's only too late if you give up," Dras said, his voice rising.

She jeered through her tears, "Like father, like daughter, right?"

Dras glanced at the edge. Breathless, he focused on her eyes. "Don't."

She placed a foot on the edge, her heel teetering over nothing. "See you around, Dras."

"N-*No!*"

Then she jumped.

CHAPTER TWENTY-THREE

ROSALYN SAILED BACKWARDS over the edge of the building and Dras didn't waste a second in leaping after her. The pavement came up at them fast, the wind whistling, as Dras groped wildly in the air, finally catching purchase. He wrapped his fingers around the calf of Rosalyn's right leg and held on tight. She looked down—or *up*—at him, bewildered to find him taking the plunge with her.

Dras felt his stomach lunge and resisted the urge to vomit. He had no plan, no great idea. He just wanted to be with Rosalyn.

Suddenly, their descent slowed inexplicably. Dras felt pressure on his leg and turned to see that, just as he gripped Rosalyn, someone was gripping him.

Someone who looked a lot like a young Robert Redford.

The angel Christopher braced himself in an open upper story window and held fast to Dras's leg. Dras watched, feeling a strange—though not unpleasant—sense of vertigo wash over him as he, Christopher, and Rosalyn all seemed to freeze in time, while the rest of the world slowed and stretched around them. The sensation was so alien, he could only hold his breath and watch the concentration in Christopher's eyes. When all of reality ceased bending and shifting, the angel let go and ducked back inside the window.

Dras and Rosalyn were safe on the ground.

Rosalyn looked around, no doubt unable to comprehend the fact that they had both jumped off a three-story building and landed without incident.

"I think I'm gonna ralf," Dras coughed, then grinned lopsided.

Rosalyn stuttered, her body tense and shaking, "Wha—How—I—"

Dras smiled. "God's trying to give you a second chance. Why won't you just take it?"

Rosalyn stared at Dras. He seemed so much older now. He'd become the man she always knew he could be…or at least, always hoped he *would* be.

"You…" she began, "You jumped off a *roof* for me."

"Pretty awesome, right? I mean, come on. *I'm* impressed."

"No, I mean, you *jumped off a roof* for me."

"Yeah, I was sort of there."

She wanted to hug him. Kiss him. Slap him. Something. "Dras…"

She moved closer to him, but he was already moving for her. She was ready now to hold him close and cry over him and tell him how much she loved him. How much she'd *always* loved him. A breath away from him—

Police sirens shrieked as the night became a flickering blur of reds and blues. Rosalyn and Dras backed away as a half-dozen squad cars bore down on their location. With the screech of tires, doors flew open and deputies leveled their Glocks on the couple.

"Freeze!"

Sheriff Ryan Stevenson stepped out of the last car to pull up, a haughty smirk stretched across his bearded face.

"Dras Weldon," he began lazily and with great relish. "We're taking you back to Wexler, kid."

Rosalyn pushed herself in front of Dras. "Stevenson, back off!"

He stuck his thumbs in the loops of his pants and tugged, sucking in oxygen. "Sorry, girlie. The Man ain't on your team anymore. We're bringing you in, Weldon. Now, we can do this the easy way or the hard way. Your choice." He sneered. "Personally I hope you pick the *hard* way."

Rosalyn spun to Dras. "Run."

"No." He shook his head. "I didn't run from these goons before, I'm not going to run from them now."

"Stop trying to be a hero, stupid!" Rosalyn snapped. "The others need you, now go!"

"No."

She flooded her eyes with black goo and growled, "I. Said. *Go.*"

That caught his attention. He hesitated. "I'll come back for you."

He raced off, the deputies firing after him. Stevenson hollered jovially, "Won't run far!" The deputies turned to their captain and he snarled. "Well? Go after him!"

They scrambled, some on foot, while others returned to their cars and began pursuit. Stevenson stayed behind, facing down Rosalyn.

"Well, girlie, the Man thought you'd be dead by now."

"I'm full of surprises."

"As far as I'm concerned, you're as good as dead."

The sheriff circled the young woman, sizing her up. Rosalyn stood her ground, unflinching. She could feel the chilly venom curdling in her veins, the thickness altering her heartbeat. It was harder fighting off the Change now.

Soon I'm going to be like TJ.

It was ironic. She had never liked TJ. Thought he was a waste of space. But now, they were the same. But not Stevenson. He might be the Man's go-to muscle, but the Strange Man had made her different. He had introduced the black sludge into her system, to give her strength for the tasks he would ask of her. Stevenson held no allegiance to the Strange Man *or* the Dark Hour. He just wanted power, and he would do anything to get it. And that was precisely why the Strange Man never gave Stevenson the gift.

He's more effective without the power. Give the dog the bone and he'll be content, the Strange Man once told her. *Keep it just out of his reach and he'll stay faithful. And mean.*

Rosalyn knew that Stevenson hated her for having what he would never get. And she hated him for that night he led the deputies to beat Dras nearly to death, then take him away from her. "This has been a long time coming," she said, watching as

Stevenson unclipped his gun belt and laid it on the hood of his car. He rolled up his sleeves and grinned at her, a pointed canine gleaming.

"You ready?" he asked.

"Baby, I came out of the gate ready."

"Come on then, sugar."

The things in the shadows gathered to watch. Breathing heavy, her teeth gritted in a vicious snarl, Rosalyn glared at Stevenson. He paced, hungrily, grinning confidently, flexing his fists again and again. The dark, sticky parasite that dwelt in Rosalyn's heart contracted once and pulsed outward, stronger than ever before. Just underneath her skin, she felt the ooze bonding to her muscles—molecule by molecule—taking over. *Consuming* her. She had fought it before, but now she welcomed it.

Her whole body grew cold and numb, dead to all emotion but rage, all thought but to kill. As the goo expanded within her, her eyes swam in obsidian muck. So filled was she with hate—with wonderful sin—that the tiniest trickle of black oil emerged from the corner of her eye and sluggishly rolled down her cheek.

Stevenson faltered, catching his breath, and Rosalyn grinned, delighting in his fear.

She relaxed, faintly swaying in the cool breeze, as the Change washed over her. Her arms darkened now too, their new oily composure glistening in the pale moonlight. The sludge flailed out and wrapped around her hands, then oozed further, forming tentacles. Rosalyn threw her head back and chuckled, intoxicated.

Her pain was beautiful. Her misery was electrifying. The whole world would suffer.

Stevenson spit once as if to clear his system of disgust, then drew his pistol from his discarded holster and leveled it at the mutating woman. "I gotta say," he relayed to her, "I never liked you."

He pulled the trigger and time froze. Before his stunned eyes, Rosalyn back-flipped and attached herself to the brick building adjacent. The bullet struck the building, spewing red dust, and

Stevenson gasped in shock.

Rosalyn was now human in face alone, the rest of her a writhing, tentacled mass of dark matter, hissing and snapping at him with one of her spindly appendages. Stevenson shrieked and threw himself to the pavement as her slippery arm smashed against the side of his patrol car, caving in the right side, shattering glass and sending the wreckage twisting to the left in a slow slide.

Stevenson gaped at the metal rubble and twirled back to Rosalyn, taking aim once more. This time, the Rosalyn Creature anticipated him and, with the flick of her shoulder, extended a string of oil, ripping the gun out of his trembling hand and zipping it back towards herself like a bungee cord. Kicking out with her feet, Rosalyn arced through the air gracefully, landing on all fours, snake-like tentacles dancing all around her.

Stevenson's face went white as he backed against his ruined car, his bottom lip quivering. Rosalyn collected the shadows around her as she stood, her indescribable shape coalescing into the form of a woman, again, and approached the terrified sheriff. In her hand was his gun. She put it to his forehead, keeping her ebony eyes trained on him. And she grinned.

Just like the Strange Man.

"You've had this coming for a long time, Stevenson," Rosalyn sang.

"No, please—"

"I'm just glad I was the one to give it to you."

BAM!

Rosalyn lowered the smoking gun.

Sheriff Ryan Stevenson slumped backwards, a fresh hole in his head, then slid to the pavement, his days of dirty dealing over and his eternity in hell just beginning.

And I sent him there. Rosalyn sneered, pleased.

Then— *No…I shouldn't have…I…*

She looked at the gun in her hand. Death had come so quickly. So effortlessly.

"What did I do?" The black goo roiling over her body began to recede back under her pink flesh. She watched the retreating muck, felt its pulsing in her heart and mind dulling.

The gun was still hot in her hands and suddenly her wicked deed felt terribly real. Stevenson lay dead on the ground. Rosalyn threw the gun away with an angry shout.

All around her, the gremlins in the dark sang her praises, and for one horrible moment she *understood* their voices. "Our Queen!" they shrieked in tribute. "Our Queen!"

"No!" she screamed back at them, covering her ears to snuff out their noise, but they would not stop their worship. She picked up Stevenson's gun again and fired into their numbers. "I'm not your Queen!" They clicked and clamored, unfazed, while Rosalyn, gun in hand, retreated into the night.

Dras's knees felt like they would splinter at any moment, and the stitch in his side threatened to throw him to the street. Still, he ran.

Five police cars, their sirens echoing through the otherwise quiet streets of Greensboro, bore down on him like a pack of rabid dogs, yet, *miraculously*, they did not overtake him. One daring look behind him told Dras that the lead car had gained twenty feet and was closing faster than ever. Dras broke from the pursuit, left the road, and cut across a side yard. Tires squalled as the car rerouted, and Dras met a wooden privacy fence. With skill he had never possessed before, he leapt onto a trashcan and propelled over the fence. He landed deftly on the other side and picked himself up without missing a beat, running.

That was pretty awesome, he congratulated his skill.

Except he failed to notice the clothesline stretched the length of the yard.

"Ack!" he choked as the line caught him on the throat. He wrestled with it for a second and carried on, reaching the other end of the fence and climbing on the support boards to get himself up and over.

Another yard awaited him and he ran faster still. The sirens were not far away but, luckily, the cars were out of sight for the moment. At this point, he wasn't sure which direction he was facing. Greensboro was a small town, but consisted of many crisscrossing neighborhoods. He needed to get back to the North Woods… which suggested he needed to go *north*, but Dras was never good with natural directions. He had a fleeting thought to look to the sky for the North Star or something cool and resourceful like that, but after his bout with the sinister clothesline, Dras felt it was best to keep his eyes forward. If he could make his way to the railroad tracks, he could follow them back to the woods and he'd be good to go.

If he could *find* the railroad tracks, that is.

Forcing himself to breathe steadily, he slowed, trying to focus on where he was and where he needed to be. He *sort of* recognized this neighborhood.

His heart raced as he looked ahead and saw the fleet of patrol cars skidding around the corner, facing him. He slid to a stop, caught in their flashing lights, and gaped.

"Aw, nuts."

He turned tail, nearly tripping in the process, and ran back the way he'd come, staying on the main road. Logically he knew he should retreat into the interconnecting yards and take a shortcut, but he feared getting lost. He needed to stay on the road until he reached familiar territory. If only he could last that long.

The howl of the police engines filled his ears. His legs felt like concrete and his ears hurt from the pounding blood.

I'm not going to make it.

A cherry-red Mustang cut him off and came to a halt. Rosalyn shouted at him from behind the wheel. "Get in!"

Dras thanked God in his heart and grinned in relief. Rosalyn kept her foot on the brake, but floored the gas, black smoke billowing behind her in a cloud of noxious fumes. Dras slid across the hood of the Mustang, catching the doorframe through the open window and swinging back around to the pavement. Throwing the door open, he climbed in as Rosalyn warned, "Better buckle up."

Before he could slam the door shut, Rosalyn let off the brake and the car screamed into the night, narrowly avoiding a side collision with the lead police car.

The deputy tried to make the sharp turn, but his car buckled and jumped up on the two right side tires before tipping over and spiraling along the East Side streets.

Dras jumped and looked behind them at the destruction. "Schnikes!"

Rosalyn remained focused, both hands gripping the steering wheel.

The surviving four police cars avoided the fate of their fallen brother—who was beginning to climb out of his car, shaken—and righted themselves on the street, pressing onward toward the muscle car.

Dras turned to look at her, to thank her for saving him, but was met by a terrifying sight. Twin headlights, glaring through Rosalyn's side window.

"*Stop!*" he cried, holding out his hand as if he could ward off the oncoming car.

With the sound of bending metal and shattering glass, a police car—late to the chase—rammed the rear left side of the Mustang, sending Rosalyn and Dras spinning in three complete rotations, spraying the backseat with Chiclets of broken glass. The cop succeeded only in disabling his own engine and came to a smoky stop across the street. Rosalyn, despite the shock and damage to her car, shifted gears and took off again. The other police swerved to avoid the smoking hull and zoomed onward.

"Where are we going?" Dras shouted. Rosalyn did not look at him but he thought he could see the black goo gleaming in her eyes.

"Your guess is as good as mine," she responded, distant. "I'm just trying to keep us alive."

He couldn't tell her where Jeff and the others were hiding. He wanted to trust Rosalyn. He *loved* her, no matter what she had become. But for all intents and purposes she was the enemy. With great sadness, he settled for, "I need to get to the railroad tracks."

He hoped that she wouldn't press the matter further. Thankfully, she didn't. "Hold on, then."

She cut a hard right, the vehicle threatening to topple, but all four wheels gripped the hot pavement and they catapulted forward with greater momentum. Behind them, the hounds of the Maribel County Sheriff's Department nipped and bayed at their heels, red and blue eyes glimmering menacingly.

Rosalyn glanced at the rearview mirror, taking into account what she was up against. Right now, getting Dras to safety was her only priority. She hadn't had time to process what *her* life would be like now. She had tried to assassinate the Strange Man and failed, pathetically. So pathetically, in fact, that the Man sent Stevenson—of all the thugs in the world—to do her in. Not that weird TJ Bat-Thing, not the gremlins.

But *Stevenson.*

It made her sick inside. After all she'd done for the Strange Man, she meant nothing to him. She had killed for him. Surely she would have to answer for what she'd done. The Committee was dead. Stevenson was dead. The Strange Man had left her with blood on her hands and, if the wailing police sirens behind her were any indication, a price on her head. She had nowhere to go. Nowhere but the grave. And maybe, after that, hell. *Hold on, Dad, here I come.*

"Grab on to something," she commanded a second before she rounded a sharp curve, yanking hard on the emergency brake, drifting around the corner. Black smoke from the burnt tires swirled in their wake, throwing a veil behind them for the cops to work through.

"Where did you learn to drive like that?" Dras asked, dumbfounded.

She smiled, a bit of the old Rosalyn resurfacing. "Why do you think I failed my driving test the first time?"

Dras chuckled, the tension in the car momentarily alleviated, until he was launched forward, smashing against the dashboard with both palms out. “What—!”

Rosalyn saw the attacking police car behind her and ground her teeth. She braced for another hit as the cruiser slowed and surged again, taking another bite out of the back of the Mustang. This time, the ’Stang’s back bumper tore free and spun away from the car, sliding along the pavement. Dras watched it go, slackjawed. “We lost something.”

Rosalyn divided her attention between the road ahead and the aggressor behind her. The police car fell back a few paces, then revved the engine. “Here it comes again!” she shouted before another bone-crunching ram threw her into the steering wheel. She gripped the wheel tighter, fighting to right herself in the aftermath of the hard hit, struggling to keep the car on the road.

Dras stared around him as the bruiser’s buddies gained speed, flanking the Mustang on all sides. A lifelong couch potato, Dras had always found pleasure in watching *World’s Craziest Police Chases*, but never in his wildest dreams had he thought he’d ever be on the receiving end of such excitement.

He decided it was much better on television.

“We’re surrounded!” he shouted as the broad side of a cruiser grew larger in the passenger window. Without warning there was a shower of sparks as the patroller ground into Dras’s side of the car, the awful sound of metal against metal reminding him of high school shop class, and hurting the back of his teeth. From this distance, Dras could even make out the angry cop’s eye color and he turned to Rosalyn in alarm.

“Um…”

Rosalyn focused ahead, her face a mask of concentration, her eyes solid black again. The car behind shoved once more, this time lifting the Mustang off the ground an inch and leaving it to fall back in place with a loud shriek of the undercarriage slapping asphalt.

“They’re gonna crush us!” Dras yelled as a third car moved in on Rosalyn’s side. With a hard bump it stripped away paint and metal from the driver's side door, hot sparks exploding into the hole where the rear left side window glass used to be. Dras watched as the sparks landed on the interior, burning tiny holes into the seat cushion. "Well, if we don't catch fire first!"

"Glove box!" Rosalyn yelled.

Dras fumbled to open the glove box. A gazillion loose papers spilled out all over the floor, as well as a police-issued handgun. Dras spun to Rosalyn, paling.

She did not look at him. "Use it," she said evenly.

He closed the box. "No."

Rosalyn whipped her head to him, illuminated by the sparks behind her.

"I won't kill them," Dras made plain. "Not even to save myself."

"Dras, they work for the Strange Man—"

"So do you," he interjected.

Her face reddened.

"Do I kill you too?" he asked rhetorically.

She paused, the world afire around them. "You *should*."

Dras shook his head and sat back in the seat, an uncanny calm settling over him, despite the fact that three police cars were boxing them in and grinding through layers of metal to get to them.

Rosalyn wanted to be angry, to argue with him. He was always so stubborn. Restraining herself, she shouted, "Fine! Then we'll have to do this the other way!"

Rosalyn turned to the police car inches away from her face and opened her mouth wide. A slick black tendril exploded from her throat, burst through the glass on both the 'Stang and the patrol car, and wrapped itself around the cop's steering wheel. With a violent twist, the tongue-thing jerked and the cop car swerved away from the muscle car, screeched, and slid along the pavement, until finally jackknifing into the corner of a building.

The tendril retracted and Rosalyn clamped her mouth shut.

Dras's eyes were wide. "That was…gross."

Rosalyn nodded. "Tell me about it."

Another patrol car filled the vacancy to Rosalyn's left, eager to join in the chase. This one proved wiser than the last and kept its distance from the Mustang, while the deputy in the passenger seat rolled down the window and took aim with a shotgun.

WHOOM!

The shotgun blast entered through the glassless side window and exploded the windshield onto the hood of the muscle car. Rosalyn screamed and threw herself on Dras, the car taking a dangerous skid into the patrol car on the right. The deputy with the shotgun grinned and cocked the gun, ejecting the spent cartridge and replacing it with another. Carefully bracing himself on the speeding car, he leveled the gun again, but Rosalyn had regained her composure. She rose, cold darkness in her heart, and turned the wheel hard to the left, ramming the side of the Mustang into the front of the shotgun car. Her car smashed into the steel frame and slid along the side—taking the rest of the cherry red paint job with it—completely crumpling the front end of the car that had been nipping at Rosalyn's behind. Both cars tangled in a mess of steel and glass, twirling through the air together. Only two cars were left, the one that had been grinding on Dras's door before Rosalyn's brave move, and the other, an untarnished vehicle ready to pick up the work of the fallen officers.

Rosalyn floored the pedal, headed in the opposite direction from the patrol cars. Both deputy vehicles braked with an ear-splitting squall and hooked their noses around, facing Rosalyn and roaring after her.

"We're just going around in circles!" Dras moaned.

"I know what I'm doing."

Instead of following the exact path that she had traveled, Rosalyn cut right and ducked down a side alley, trashcans bouncing off the ruined Mustang and hurtling towards the advancing police cars. The mouth of the alley approached fast and Rosalyn made no move to slow down. Dras braced himself.

Rosalyn cannonballed out of the alley and her stomach lurched as they went airborne upon hitting the sloped street, landing hard with a crunch in the alley on the opposite side.

"Where are you going?" Dras asked, looking green in the gills.

"You wanna get to the tracks. I'm getting you to the tracks!"

By now, they had twisted and turned so many times Dras was completely lost, so he had to trust Rosalyn. Meekly, he poked his eyes over the back of his seat to view the two sets of swirling lights behind him. Sighing in anxiety, he slumped back down. Rosalyn looked at him with a Cheshire grin. "What's wrong? Too exciting for you?"

"It's been a long couple of days."

She laughed and focused again on the road ahead. The arc sodium street lamps stretched out overhead in greater intervals as the Mustang passed beneath, leaving the false comforts of the town behind. The two remaining patrol cars never lost step, keeping a steady pace on their prey. Greensboro slowly fell away, the sounds of Bing Crosby fading in the night, and the canopy of lights spread out thin until only the moon was left to light Rosalyn's way.

Dras knew where they were now, and the North Woods were in the *opposite* direction. They were joining onto the lost highway that led to Russellville, but he didn't want to correct Rosalyn. The train tracks were out here too. Yes, he would have quite a walk circumventing the town to find the Haven, but better that than foolishly confiding in Rosalyn on the off-chance that she might still relay the location to the Strange Man.

He felt terrible. He wanted to believe that the girl who played Kenner Star Wars action figures with him was still in there, underneath the hot pink and blue hair and dark, hollow eyes. *She's just lost. That's all. Jesus came to rescue the lost.*

He thought back to his last attempt to tell her about God. It had ended with her screaming at him to leave and, mere hours later, he was arrested for murders he knew nothing about and she ran into the arms of the devil and sold her soul. But they had both grown since then. He had learned more about his faith and he felt that he could share it confidently this time. At least, he hoped he could. Maybe she would be ready to listen. *What if that doesn't work?*

Headlights painted them in blinding white and Dras shielded his eyes momentarily. The growl of a diesel truck barreled toward them, and the tenacious deputies were still on their tail.

Rosalyn smirked. "Hold on. I got a plan."

Dras slowly looked to her, growing worried. "What?"

"Best not tell you."

"Should I close my eyes?"

"If it helps."

Dras closed his eyes as the semi met them on the road. At precisely the right moment, Rosalyn yanked the wheel to the left and cut into the path of the diesel, fishtailing at high speeds directly underneath the trailer. With a "*Woo!*" she slid clear of the semi's rear tires and, under the sound of his angry horn, righted herself on the road alongside the big truck. With another shout of excitement she floored the engine, passed the truck, and raced back towards town.

Behind her, the deputies took a few moments to grasp her crazy maneuver and then struggled to slow down, circle back around, and give chase yet again. Rosalyn watched them fumbling not to crash into each other and laughed devilishly. Spotting a dirt road to her right, hidden by the edges of the forest, Rosalyn turned and drove on. She turned off her headlights, and the Mustang disappeared in darkness.

The deputies passed by the road, oblivious that Rosalyn had turned, and disappeared over the horizon, chasing a car they'd never find now. She and Dras were safe. She turned to find him with his hands still covering his eyes. She cracked a grin. "You can open up now."

"Are we dead?"

"Close. But not quite."

Dras slowly removed his hands and stared at the dark forest around them. With their harrowing adventure finally behind them, he let out a sigh of relief.

They were quiet for a long time afterwards.

The blinking lights of the railroad crossing cast Rosalyn's face in deep red. The guardrail was down and she and Dras sat in the parked Mustang, watching in silence as a train rocketed by. Rosalyn had twisted and turned down enough unmarked gravel roads to get Dras not only to the railroad tracks as he'd asked, but also closer to God's Cliff than he had expected.

So this was it. He was here. *Time to go back to the Haven and find the others.*

But he felt no hurry to move.

Quiet, he watched the train cars pass, using their presence as an excuse to stay in the car with her a little longer. In truth, he didn't want to leave her side ever again. His heart thumped in his chest and ears, a thousand times louder than the screaming decibels of the train. Rosalyn sat beside him, and he wondered if she was feeling the same. They had spent a lifetime holding onto each other, too afraid to let go, to grow apart from one another. Yet, Fate, God, or the devil had forcibly torn them apart and they had been forced to travel life alone. Now they were back. *Do we have any more to say to each other?*

Dras knew he had something to say. He had to tell her about Jesus and the thought terrified him. He had studied the Bible hard while in Wexler, but now every verse fled his mind. He had learned so much from Jeff's notes, leading him to a deeper understanding of Christ and what it truly meant to follow Him. But now…now he couldn't recall a single sentence. He forgot all but perhaps the most important thing.

I love Rosalyn. God loves Rosalyn. Maybe that was all that mattered.

The train finally passed, the crossing rails lifted, and Dras's moment had come. Dark forest awaited him just beyond the car and he knew that his friends were out there, preparing to do the unthinkable tomorrow and make war on the Strange Man.

He wanted to be there with them but, at the same time, he didn't feel it was his war to make. No, his war—his *real* war—was right here in this car. It wasn't about taking up arms and standing against the forces of hell. It was about telling an old friend—his very best friend—about how God loved her.

"So…" Rosalyn spoke and Dras felt a lump form in his throat.

Help me, God, he begged. *Help me not to screw this up again.*

Dras gulped once, wiping his sweaty palms on his dirtied jeans, and said, "I tried to tell you about Jesus once."

"Yeah," she said monotone, looking the other way. "That didn't go over so well, huh?"

Dras felt a flutter of doubt. Was this the right time? Was he just going to drive her further into the Strange Man's arms? "When I talked to you about Him last time…I was scared. It was like, these things that I thought was just a really nice bedtime story…I find out that it's *real*, complete with monsters and everything and I-I freaked. I just wanted you to be a Christian so that you wouldn't go to hell and…" he breathed. "That wasn't right. That's not a good reason to be saved."

Rosalyn turned to him, confused. "*Really?* I thought that's all you church-types wanted to talk about. Hellfire and brimstone. I thought your friends out there would all be happy to have real proof that it all existed and that us sinners would burn for our crimes."

Dras looked at her, hurt and betrayed. "Is that what you really think?"

She blushed and looked to her lap. "I'm just calling it like I see it."

"Then you're not looking close enough," he countered. "Okay, yeah, some people seem to get some kind of perverse pleasure out of thinking everyone's going to hell while they're floating on clouds with angels' wings. But they're not all like that. *God's* not like that. God doesn't want to punish you, Roz. He's not out to get you."

"Could've fooled me."

"You made your own decisions," he said angrily, but quickly cooled. "Bad decisions. We both did. Everybody does. But we can't blame God when we live with the consequences of our mistakes." Dras sighed and gathered his thoughts. "Eventually, our consequences will catch up with us, and if we haven't gotten God's forgiveness, we'll pay the ultimate price."

"Hell, again."

"But that's not why I want you to follow Christ," Dras interjected. "People fight with God. We always have. But, Roz, you gotta know that God's gonna win. The only way we're gonna escape that is by surrendering. God doesn't want to fight with us. It's *us* making the first attack. And fighting is killing us. Look around!" Rosalyn wouldn't look at Dras, and he wondered if he was making a fool of himself. Yes, he was preaching. *But, sometimes you just gotta say it.* So there, laid bare before her, Dras showed Rosalyn his heart. "All these things that you've done…yeah, they're horrible things, but Jesus already paid the price for that. He did it so that you can come to God and be forgiven and—"

"And what?" Rosalyn asked, her eyes haunting. "Live a normal life? No more worries? No more problems?"

"No, there'll be plenty of problems. But being family with God has its benefits. He'll never leave you, Rosalyn. He'll never let you down. But that's not a reason to come to God, either."

Rosalyn chuckled sardonically. "Then what *is*?"

"We don't come to God to get anything, Rosalyn. At least, we shouldn't. We should come to God to *give* Him something. Ourselves. That's all He wants."

"Oh, is that all?" she eyed him, with a smirk.

"He made us to love us. He just wants us to love Him back. Is that so hard to understand?"

"Yeah, well…" Rosalyn trailed off, gazing in the direction where the train disappeared long ago. "I don't know if I'm capable of that anymore."

"What? Of loving?"

She was silent.

"You loved *me*, once," Dras said. "Do you still?"

Rosalyn rolled her eyes. "How can you ask me that?"

"I have to, because you never want to face the truth."

"There is no truth."

"Is *that* the truth?"

A smirk. "Now you're just being a pain."

He snickered and looked in the opposite direction, towards the North Woods. At length he said, "You could come with me."

She responded distantly, as if lost in a fog of fear. "It's dark out there."

"You'd have to step out on faith."

When she didn't say anything, Dras finally looked to her, desperate to have her back. "Don't go back to town."

"It's where I belong."

"You belong with me," he said boldly.

She ignored him. "Tomorrow's the big day, yeah? Apocalypse or Rebirth?"

Dras nodded. The moment had passed. He had told her all that was on his heart. Now he just had to trust God to do the rest.

"Yeah," he said. "I guess I'll see you there. Thanks for the ride."

He shouldered into the car door, but it was jammed tight from their derring-do with Greensboro's Finest. He grinned at Rosalyn sheepishly and crawled out the shattered window. He was halfway out before his foot got hung in the seatbelt and he tripped to the ground. With haste, he jumped up and dusted himself off, grinning sheepishly.

Rosalyn shook her head, a grin at the corner of her lips. "Goofball."

Tittering awkwardly, he offered a small wave and wandered into the night.

CHAPTER TWENTY-FOUR

DRAS STUMBLED THROUGH the North Woods, groping in the darkness. He and Rosalyn had explored these woods when they were younger, yet in those youthful escapades, Rosalyn had always led with her keen sense of direction. Dras couldn't find his way out of a paper bag. Now he was alone, in the middle of the night, in a forest populated by possessed animals and roaming Shambler packs. No doubt about it, he was—

"Lost?"

Dras shrieked like a six-year-old girl and clutched his chest, nearly tripping over a bush. Spinning around, he came face to luminous face with his guardian angel, Christopher. Palpitating profusely, he stammered, "I think a big '*duh*' is in order."

Christopher chuckled as Dras relaxed. "Sorry," the angel said. "I didn't mean to scare you."

Dras found a nearby stump highlighted by moonglow and sat. As he told Rosalyn, it had been an incredibly long couple of days and all he wanted to do was sleep for a week, maybe play some Xbox, eat some ice cream out of the carton, anything but face the Strange Man again.

But if Christopher was here, facing the Strange Man again was probably exactly what he was going to have to do.

"Thanks for the save tonight, by the way," Dras mentioned, suddenly remembering.

"Don't worry about it." Christopher took a seat across from Dras on a downed trunk. "Dras, it's time we had a talk."

"If it's about how girls are different from boys—"

Christopher wasn't smiling.

Dras blushed. "Sorry. Bad joke. Bad time for a joke too, I guess."

"I know you're scared."

"Tomorrow's it, then. The Dark Hour. End of the world and everything."

"Tomorrow is the culmination of everything the Strange Man has been planning for thousands of years."

Dras leaned back, realizing he was really going to have to fight the forces of Hell. "So, who *is* he?"

Without pause, Christopher said plainly, "His real name is Calico."

Not the answer Dras was expecting. "Like the cat?"

"As in 'many colors'. He was clothed in the rainbow, sparkling with color and life."

Dras pictured the grim, pale monster he had encountered in the past and found the connection hard to believe. "What happened?"

"Calico was my bond-mate. In human terms, he was like my brother. I was always thinking about the mission, but Cal…" a ghost of a smile lingered on Christopher's sad face, "He always took time to care about the humans. He saw their frailty and helplessness and he had compassion on them. Soon, though…he found a human that he cared for more than all the others. A Hebrew girl named Rebekah. Her father was a potter and had died in battle against the Amalekites. She was left alone and, in that place and time, widows and orphans were afforded little assistance from society. She had no one to care for her and struggled to provide for herself, begging on the streets for money and scraps of food." Christopher paused, his eyes saddening. "Even selling her body to wealthy men. Cal met this woman and cared for her. But soon, his care turned to physical lust. She was beautiful and he wanted her for himself, as a wife, like the human men have."

Dras remembered an account from Genesis 6 about the sons of God taking human wives.

Monsters were born from the union.

Christopher continued, "He appeared to Rebekah as a mortal to win her affections. He offered to provide for her and, as any girl in her position would have, she accepted. Cal left heaven, thinking that he could live as a human. I was devastated," Christopher sighed. "But not as devastated as Cal would be. As he'd always pointed out to me, humans are fragile. Weak. They make many mistakes and Rebekah was no different."

Dras spoke up. "She broke his heart, didn't she?"

The angel nodded somberly.

"What happened to Rebekah?"

Christopher closed his eyes and shook his head, dismissing an unwelcome memory. "What he did to her was unspeakable."

"He killed her?"

"...Eventually."

Dras looked to the ground. "Oh."

"I remember the day he came before the Lord. He said he'd made a mistake and he wanted to come back. Humans are often blind and so easily deceived, but, as the Host of Heaven, we *know* the truth in full. To rebel against that is apostasy—there's no forgiveness for that. After Cal's fall, his hatred for humanity grew out of control and drove him mad. Wherever there was unity, love, and faith, he sought to destroy it and sow malice. The faith of the early Old Greenesboro settlers *infuriated* Cal. He set out to cause them to fail, to bring them down into misery and despair. Everett Greene, however, stood his ground." A wistful grin crept to the corners of Christopher's lips. "I remember Everett. He was a good man. He led the town to fight against the Strange Man. He tried." Christopher's warmth faded. "He really tried."

"What happened?" Dras asked.

Christopher eyed him. "You know. You've seen it."

"I have?"

"Where do you think the Old Greenesboro ruins came from?"

Dras's heart sank. "Then...the first Dark Hour...they failed. They couldn't stop it."

Christopher nodded. "The men who fought alongside Everett in the First Dark Hour formed a pact. Swearing an oath between themselves and God, they took it upon their shoulders to remain faithful to the Lord and to train the next generation to do likewise.

For a time, it worked. However, as the generations passed, the oath was forgotten. Church has always been a big part of Greensboro life, as you know, but, after a time, people forgot why it was there. Over the years, the hand of God was slowly pried off Greensboro by complacent and apathetic followers. He lost his grip on your hearts and Cal was finally able to return and finish what he'd started."

Dras hung his head, feeling partly responsible, knowing he'd been just as complacent and apathetic as the next guy.

Christopher told him, "When the highway moved, your town lost all faith and became vulnerable. So the Strange Man came back and approached the descendants of the men who originally made the oath: Hayden, Simms, Jacobson, Fergus, Gibson, and Nigel."

"The Committee." Dras moved closer, growing impatient, "I need to know. What is the Strange Man bringing back? Who is his Master? In the van, you said he wanted to bring back the Ancient Ones. Who are they?"

Christopher snorted with great resignation and faced Dras. The angel looked tired, burdened by so many generations of cleaning up after his fallen brother. "You don't get it." Recalling a Scripture, the angel said, "'On that day a fountain will be opened to the house of David and the inhabitants of Jerusalem, to cleanse them from sin and impurity. On that day, I will banish the names of the idols from the land, and they will be remembered no more,' declares the Lord Almighty.' Book of Zechariah. Thirteenth chapter."

"I don't—"

"The fountain was Christ. When He died, as the Scriptures said, the name of Baal was wiped from the people's lips. He was lost to time."

"And the Strange Man wants to bring Baal back, then? Some Lovecraftian super-demon? Something so horrible men go mad at the sight of him, that kind of thing, right?"

Christopher shook his head. "David understood in Psalm 115. 'Why do the nations say "Where is their God?" Our God is in heaven; he does whatever pleases him. But their idols are silver and gold, made by the hands of men. They have mouths, but cannot speak, eyes, but they cannot see; they have ears, but cannot hear, noses, but they cannot smell; they have hands, but cannot feel, feet, but they cannot walk; nor can they utter a sound with their throats. Those who make them will be like them, and so will all who trust in them.'" The angel's voice became firm. "Baal's not *real*, Dras. He never was. That's the joke. That's the ultimate joke. There is only *one* God. Baal is a hoax."

"I don't get it. Why?"

"Why else? To turn people from their Creator. That's all *any* idol is. A distraction."

Dras felt a load lift from his shoulders. "So, that's it? No great Master coming to rule the world? This great god that everyone's afraid of…he's not even *real*?"

"But that doesn't mean the Dark Hour isn't dangerous. Far from it. The people are putting their faith in an empty religion. But, because they believe it so completely, tomorrow they will be giving up their babies as an offering to this false god. Child sacrifice was a common practice among the pagan nations, and God despised it. We've fought hard to stamp it out but Cal is trying to bring it back. When that happens, God will *have* to intervene. God made a promise in Zechariah 13 that Baal worship would not return to this world and He has to do whatever it takes to stop that nightmare from happening again." Pulling his coat tighter, as if trying to protect himself, the angel went on, "You weren't there in the dark times, Dras. You don't understand the gravity of this situation or what it could mean if Baal worship returned. The madness…" Christopher paused, and Dras thought for a moment he heard the screams of the human sacrifices from that bleak period floating in the night. "Destroying Greensboro is not something God wants to do but…it's better than the alternative."

Dras frowned. "Since you put it that way, I feel a lot better."

"So now you understand Cal's plan. He knows that God will have to show Himself tomorrow and He will *have* to deal with His creation. He will have to judge them—totally eradicate

Greensboro—in order to save the world."

Dras ran his fingers through his hair.

"Cal is not motivated by power or profit or even pleasure," Christopher explained. "He does this because he hates mankind for having the one thing he never could: Forgiveness. He has tried to convince God that humans are not worth love or forgiveness or mercy. But God has never listened to him. No matter how many times humanity turns away from Him, the Lord always waits with open arms to accept them into His kingdom, if they will only leave their sin behind to follow Christ. 2 Peter 3:9 is true. 'The Lord is not slow in keeping his promise, as some understand slowness. He is patient with you, not wanting anyone to perish, but everyone to come to repentance.'" Christopher exhaled, his spirit heavy. "If only you heard Him as I do, Dras. He doesn't want to judge you. He wants to *save* you. But tomorrow, if the people commit this terrible act and the Change starts, God will have no choice but to destroy Greensboro for the sake of humanity, and the Strange Man will feel vindicated. It won't really matter in the end because God will never stop loving His creation, but, for one dark hour, the Strange Man will have his revenge and will relish in watching God destroy those He loves so dearly."

Dras considered this. "That's...pretty sick."

"Now you understand the heart of a monster."

"But, you're here now. The angelic Cavalry. You can stop it, right?"

"I..." Christopher shifted, his brow furrowed. "Dras...I thought you would know."

Dras was ready to cut to the chase. "Well, how am I supposed to know if you don't tell me—"

"I'm an Angel of Death, Dras. My mission is the same as it was in Everett Greene's time. In Sodom and Gomorrah."

Dras went pale.

Christopher frowned. "I'm here to destroy Greensboro."

We're all going to die. There's no stopping this thing.

Dras took a deep breath, steadying under the weight of this new revelation. "So…all this time, you've just been scoping the place out, getting ready to blow it all up?"

"No, of course not," Christopher leaned toward him, concerned. "Reid and I, we've been working to inspire Men to fight the Strange Man, but Dras, we're just *angels.* If humanity wants a better world, it's up to humanity to fight for it. Since I came to Greensboro, we've been working with someone—a human believer—we code-named 'The General'."

"Well, that sounds promising. Who is it?"

A wink. "Top secret. But we're coordinating strategies, trying to find people who will stand up for what's right and fight against this."

Dras rubbed his neck. "Any luck?"

Christopher chuckled. "I know it looks grim, but there are others out there—still in town—who believe as you do. They just don't know what to do about it yet. That's what you need to show them."

Dras exploded, "How can I convince them to do anything?"

Christopher shook his head, grim-faced. "I don't know. I wish I did. They've forgotten their Father. I don't know how to make them see again. But I do know this. You have a weapon at your disposal that is greater than anything I have."

"What's that?"

"Love."

Dras blinked back at him. "Right, right, love. Keep forgettin' that. Gotcha. I'll rally the people together and sing 'Kumbaya' and the Strange Man and all the gremlins will flee for their lives."

Christopher smiled candidly. "You've got a good heart, kid."

"Yeah," Dras sighed. "That and a quarter can get me a cup of coffee."

"Come on," Christopher beckoned as he stood. "I'll walk you back to the church."

"Great. We can use your face for a flashlight."

"Angel humor. That's good."

"Well, I try."

CHAPTER TWENTY-FIVE

GUS REYNOLDS DRAPED a blood-spotted cloth over the ashen face of Danny Carpenter. Both Gus and Andrew Simmons had survived the massacre at The Rave Scene and escaped in the Hummer provided by Sheriff Stevenson. Rather than taking the direct route back to the Haven, the two men drove in circles for an hour, hoping to evade or confuse any spies within the city limits.

As it turned out, their efforts were in vain.

When they pulled up to the ruins of the church sanctuary, Gus and Andrew clambered out of the vehicle and walked around in shock. For so long the Christians had managed to maintain anonymity in the North Woods, but finally, on this night of all nights, they had been discovered and attacked. The church was nothing but a smoking husk. Gus came upon the gruesome sight of Danny Carpenter stuck to the earth by a metal pipe and Andrew rushed to the treeline to vomit.

It was horrible.

So far, though, Gus had only found a couple more bodies in the wreckage. He assured Andrew that the others must have escaped deep into the woods and were probably reassembling somewhere, planning a counter-attack. But that was little consolation to the boy who had just lost his father. Since leaving The Rave Scene and the hell inside, the boy had been pale and quiet, barely blinking at all. He held to his rifle, just like Burt taught him, and stood dumbfounded in the midst of the torn-down church. Gus continued to rummage through the rubble, looking for the faces of his dead friends but, thankfully, did not find any more. After covering Danny, he took off his straw hat, and dabbed at the moisture on his wrinkled brow. He sighed heavily, mourning the loss of good people, but maybe more so, the loss of a dream. The Christians had thought they could live in relative peace in the Haven, but Carter told them that wasn't so. They were in a war, and they needn't forget that. Gus was convinced. He had spent a lifetime as a man of peace, always the first to apologize or do an act of kindness to a neighbor that had wronged him. He was a man who believed in forgiveness and mercy.

But Carter had been right. *This is a time for war.*

He'd accepted Carter's charge to raze The Rave Scene. Now Carter was probably dead with the others and young Andrew Simmons was without his father.

A branch snapped in the distance and Andrew leveled his rifle at the trees. Gus's heart jumped. If it were the demons coming to look for stragglers, he knew they'd never survive and their daring escape from The Rave Scene would have been for nothing.

Instead, it was Dras who stepped out of the woods, holding his hands up in fright when he saw the rifle. "Whoa!"

Gus moved closer to Andrew and placed a calming hand on his shoulder. "Easy, son."

The boy lowered the gun and slumped away to sit amidst the destruction. Dras gaped at the sight before him. "What happened?"

Gus clutched his hat, wringing the brim. "We've been hit."

His insides churning, Dras pushed past the older man, scanning the devastation. "Where's my brother? Where's Jeff?"

Dras spotted a sheet-covered body lying on the ground. Panicking, he raced to the grisly display. "Jeff!"

Gus called out for him to stop, but Dras would not. He jerked off the sheet, afraid to look, but needing to see. It wasn't Jeff. He recognized the dead man as Jeff's friend Danny and, even though he hadn't known the guy, he knew he'd meant a lot to his brother.

He felt sad for Jeff, but relieved at the same time, and that only made him feel guilty. Gently, he laid the sheet over Danny's face once more.

"Jeff's not here, as far as we can tell." Shame-faced, Gus added, "We only just got here ourselves."

Dras spun to him, barely interested in the face of the tragedy surrounding him. "Where were you?"

Gus kept his eyes on the ground. "Carter Ross and some of the boys, w-we went to that club tonight. Went to take out the Strange Man. They attacked while we were gone."

"I was just at The Rave Scene," Dras said, growing suspicious.

"Yeah, it didn't…me and the boy made it out."

"The others?"

Gus shook his head. "It was a fool's errand. We should've listened to your brother. We should've waited. I'm sorry."

Dras felt that maybe he should be mad, but he wasn't. He couldn't blame this guy, or any of them. They just wanted to help. "Where would the others have gone if they were attacked?"

Gus looked up, his face still flushed. "We'd talked about having a Site B—a safehouse—but…we just never thought it would come to that so soon."

"They had to have gone somewhere. Any houses close to here that are on our side?"

Gus shrugged. "Hard to tell friend from foe these days."

Dras considered it while Andrew sat with his back to the two of them, his face in his hands, weeping quietly. Finally, Dras turned to Gus. "You guys drove out here?"

Gus nodded and jerked a thumb towards a black Hummer.

"Then let's start looking. Better that than stay out here."

Isabella watched with compassion as Jay Evans sat at his kitchen table trying to stay out of everyone's way and sipping a cold glass of sweet tea. He had always enjoyed his space and quiet, and now he was playing host to the last remnant of the Christians of Greensboro. The sounds of children weeping for lost parents and spouses grieving for lost mates filled his living room, and confusion abounded all around. It somewhat resembled a trauma center,

Isabella reckoned, and Jay looked awkward and affected.

She dropped off a damp washcloth for a beleaguered father to wipe the dirty brow of his infant daughter and came to her own dad's side. Without a word, she wrapped her long arms around his neck and squeezed. He patted at her elbow, uncomfortable with such a public display of affection, even in her growing up years, but she hoped he knew how important this was to her. How much she loved him.

Isabella parted from her father with a kiss to his bald head and headed into the adjoining hallway. Jeff stood by a small coffee table, listening to the other end of a phone conversation.

"Okay," Jeff muttered as she approached. She hung back, searching his eyes, hoping to glean some news from them. Jeff noticed her but carried on with his phone call. "O-okay, Hank. Right. I'll see you when you get back. Be careful."

He hung up the phone and Isabella crossed her arms, tensely. "Well?"

"Franklin's okay. He was hurt pretty bad but Dr. Masters said he'll pull through. They gotta move him, though. Hospital won't hold him past morning."

Isabella frowned. "Better than nothing, I suppose."

"Yeah. They're going to let him sleep for a couple hours then head out here."

"You don't think anyone was listening in, do you? Do you think anyone knows we're out here?"

Jeff shrugged. "I guess we'll just have to trust God."

Isabella tried to smile, but was unable to quell her fear. "I called Father Joe. Told him the pick-up point had changed. Everything's still on schedule, though."

"Good."

Out in the hallway, the muffled voices from the other room were almost tolerable. Once again, Jeff and Isabella found a moment to be alone in the midst of the chaos. He held out his hand to her. "Hey."

She took it and gave it a squeeze. "Hey."

Without another word, he pulled her to him and held her. "We're doing okay," he whispered into her ear and she let loose a long, exhausted breath.

"I hope so. I can't help but think there's more we could be doing."

Jeff kissed her forehead, lingering for a moment. "We've got some new information to talk about. What Sarah and Annie found from the book, what…what Danny saw…Who knows? We might pull out of this yet."

Annie sat underneath the light on the porch, skimming over Ray McCormick's diary. She believed that she and Sarah had already learned all they could from the book. The Strange Man seemed in the final phases of bringing the forgotten pagan god Baal back into the world. Their task seemed insurmountable and Annie had no idea how the Havenites planned to stop him.

Despite that, she did not fear. God was with them, she could feel Him when she was with the others. Many lives had been lost tonight and they were grieving, but Annie still felt the presence of God in their midst. There was still hope.

Closing the book and feeling the wind tousle her locks, Annie breathed in the night. Even if this were her last night on Earth, this was exactly how she wanted to spend it. On a wooden porch out in the familiar country, with nothing but the swaying trees to keep her company.

But her moment of reflection was interrupted by an engine in the distance. The churning of gravel under tires caused her to stand to attention. Was that the sheriff on his way? One of his deputies?

Maybe it's Rosalyn.

A few months ago, Annie had searched desperately for her sister. Rosalyn had simply disappeared off the radar and Annie feared the worst. Discovering that Rosalyn had, in fact, abandoned them to serve at the Strange Man's side…That was even worse than Annie had dreaded.

Maybe she's changed her mind.

Or maybe she's coming to turn us in.

Annie was about to run inside to warn Jeff or Isabella, when a black Humvee crawled past the driveway. It passed on and Annie relaxed, feeling the danger melt away.

Then the vehicle stopped. White lights on the taillight lit up and the black monster slowly moved backwards, angling on the driveway. When it came about, its headlights nearly blinding, Annie braced as if for a collision. A car door opened and a voice from the past called her.

"Annie? Is that you?"

Annie canopied her eyes and peered over the lights. She couldn't believe it.

"*Dras?*"

Within the confusion, Isabella struggled to rally everyone into the living room. She and Jeff—the last of the High Council, as it were—had discussed what they learned from Ray McCormick's diary and, after praying about it, reached the only conclusion that brought their hearts any peace. Now it was time to bring the plan before the others.

Jeff was in the kitchen, urging the displaced Havenites to the meeting when Annie tore through the back screen door. "Hey!"

Jeff tensed, images of Stevenson and his deputies on the front lawn flashing in his mind. "What? What's wrong?"

Annie stood aside as Dras entered with Andrew Simmons and Gus Reynolds behind him. "Dras." Jeff crossed the floor to embrace his brother. "Are you okay? I've been—I had no idea what happened—"

The brothers parted and Dras's face was somber. "Yeah, I'm okay."

Jeff asked quietly, "Did you find her?"

Dras only nodded.

"Come on," he encouraged, "We're meeting in the other room

to talk about tomorrow."

Dras rolled his eyes. "In that case, you and I have *a lot* to talk about first."

Jeff paused. "Oh. Okay. Find Isabella and we'll talk first before we meet with the others."

Dras went on his errand. Absently, Jeff turned to Gus and Andrew. "Thank you guys for finding him. I appreciate you going back to the church to pick up anyone we'd missed." Then something dawned on him. "Wait…No, that's not right. You weren't out in the woods with the others…you—"

Andrew was an unresponsive statue but Gus looked away, ashamed. "We were with Carter. He thought we could save us all a lot of trouble and destroy the Strange Man. Jeff…we failed."

"And the others?"

Gus threw a quick look to Andrew, who faced the opposite direction. "Dead. Burt Simmons and Ed Mathers with them. Last we saw of Milton Wilbanks, he became one of those Shambler things."

Jeff's heart hurt with grief. "And Carter?"

"He told us to run and we did. I don't know whatever became of him but…we didn't stand a chance. I'm sorry, Jeff. I'm truly sorry."

Jeff rubbed the stubble around his mouth, taking the news in. It was a tragedy that could have been avoided. Instantly he thought of Nancy and Michelle Wilbanks in the other room, now without their father. What would he tell them? And what about Carter's daughter, Chelsea, and his wife? The night had been nothing but one defeat after another. Bloodshed upon bloodshed.

He very much wanted to be on that bus with Father Joe in the morning. He wished that they could all leave and forget this terrible place, run away and rediscover that piece of their hearts that this town had ripped from their chests.

No. We have to fight. One last time.

He just hoped Dras had some good news for them.

Patting a strong hand on Gus's shoulder, he brought the two

men back into the fold. "Get yourselves something to eat and drink. I'd stay away from the bologna, though. Jay's particular about his bologna."

Gus grinned, fresh tears of thanks in his eyes.

Jeff listened with Isabella as Dras filled them in on all that Christopher had told him.

Isabella turned to him. "What are you going to do?"

Leaning against the counter, alone in the kitchen with his brother and wife, Jeff folded his arms and took a deep, steadying breath before nodding towards the living room where the surviving Havenites patiently waited. "We can't protect them anymore, Iz. It's like Christopher told Dras. This is their world too. If they want to make a change, they have to fight for it."

"Do you think they're ready?" she asked, doubt in her voice.

"We never know what we're made of until we're tried."

Dras shifted his weight. "So, we ready to do this or what?"

Jeff stood taller. "Not really. But, we're going to do it anyway."

With Jeff leading the way, they entered the living room to the rapt stares of the faces he had grown to care for over the last few months. Jay Evans stood uneasily in the doorway to the hall, a guest in his own home. Gus and Andrew kept to themselves, evading questions pertaining to their whereabouts and the grim fates of those who went with them. Dras took a seat on the floor next to Annie. Millie and Timmy sat front row in Rebecca's lap, and Millie's eyes lit with excitement as Jeff and Isabella took their place before the assembly.

No one spoke.

Jeff saw their expectant faces, the tears of those who had lost people tonight, and at once he knew he couldn't do this anymore. It was the strangest sensation, exactly like the way he felt when God called him to preach.

But now, the sensation was turned upside down.

God was telling him that his preaching days were over.

Jeff didn't argue. He had felt uncomfortable in his role for a long time but held fast to the job, afraid no one else would fill the gap. But now he understood. These people weren't looking to follow the Lord, they were looking to follow *Jeff*, just as they had his father, Jack. Maybe that was part of Greensboro's problem all along.

Right now, as the people waited hungrily for Jeff's words—for his decision—he understood. *They're gonna have to follow God for a change, not the Weldon family.*

A peace washed over him, and he felt the Holy Spirit within was giving him affirmation. *So, this is it. My last sermon.* His life stretched out before him as he thought of all the places God might take him now, if he could only live through tomorrow.

For the sake of the future, Jeff knew that they *must* live through tomorrow.

With Isabella at his side, Jeff prayed for the words to say in his farewell address. Coming up short, he stuck his hands in his pockets and shrugged. "Well, folks, this is it. Greensboro will either be saved or destroyed tomorrow, but…at the very least, we can know that it'll end here."

Faces drooped all across the room.

Jeff continued, "Father Joe's still coming in the morning with the bus to take you guys to Russellville. It's going to be a risk trying to get by the Strange Man's spies, but with Celebration Day and all, we think he'll be too busy to notice. I've already called my Dad and he and Mom are getting the word to all the believers still in town, so don't worry, some of your family and friends will be safe."

"But what about the others?" called a voice from the crowd. "What about everyone else?"

Jeff scratched the back of his neck and finally held up his hands in surrender. "What can I say? We tried. But…it just wasn't enough. Before Danny died, he figured out that a sacrifice will be held at Greensboro Park Lake, where some parents are going to offer up their babies as gifts to the Strange Man's Master." He looked to Dras knowingly. "We've learned that there *is* no master."

Shocked expressions throughout the room. Gasps. Questions. Murmurs.

"The Strange Man's god is, in fact, a trick. It's a ploy to turn Greensboro away from the true God and lead them to do something so horrible that God has no choice but to judge them. *That's* the Dark Hour. If we can't stop them from doing this, God will destroy Greensboro to save it from itself."

The people hung their heads, absorbing the gravity of the situation. One man in the back raised a shaky hand, tears building in his eyes. "How did things get so bad, Reverend Weldon? This was a good town with good people…I just don't understand."

Jeff opened his mouth to answer, but was stunned when Rebecca Walker set the children down and stood to face the man, exhaustion on her face. "Sin."

He looked to Isabella, surprised. Could it be that, after all this time, they had actually *listened* to what he kept telling them? Were they now capable of teaching others?

It was as if God was assuring him that his time as shepherd was truly over. The flock didn't need him anymore. They could cling to a greater Shepherd now.

Rebecca continued, trembling as she realized she was now the center of attention. "I mean, I was like that. I was angry at God because my husband left and life wasn't going the way I thought it ought to. When TJ disappeared and when Millie was sick…That should have been a time for me to come to God for healing. But I didn't want to. I just wanted to be angry. But, thank God, He didn't give up on me. Were it not for meeting you all…you showed me who Christ was and if I hadn't met Him…I would be right there in the middle of town with the rest of the monsters. I was an enemy of God, but He sent His Son to die that I might become His child."

"Amen," a gruff old man muttered.

Another man with thick glasses and a walrus-sized mustache stood. "I'd like to say something, if that's all right, pastor."

Jeff nearly laughed. "Go ahead. Please."

The mustached man turned to his friends. "I'd just like to say that Jesus died for my sins and, because of that, I'm free and forgiven. If He can do that for me, He can still do that for this town." After giving Jeff a quick nod, he sat back down amidst heartier "Amens".

Jeff couldn't believe it. These people had been defeated and hiding for so long but now…*now* they were ready. He had more to say, more plans that needed to be made before morning, but he didn't want this to end. God was doing something here.

"Does anyone else want to say something?"

This time, teenaged Keira Dupree stood, red-faced but determined. "My mom is still in Greensboro and I've been praying every night that she would come to know the Lord. I don't want to give up on her. I don't want to give up on any of them." She sat back down quickly, and Jeff relished in the moment.

After Keira's testimony, more spoke up. Some named loved ones left behind in Greensboro. Some gave personal accounts of how Christ had saved them and given them a hope and a future. Some quoted encouraging Scripture. With every new person, the "Amens" grew louder and soon clapping started. People were getting excited again, reminded of why they claimed this faith in the first place. The Spirit of God filled the house and even Jay Evans looked livelier. He shifted a lot, but there was a curiosity in his eyes, like the words were reaching him. Jeff had been going to church since the first Sunday after he was born, but he had never felt this sweet fellowship before. Now he fully understood the difference between religion and being in the presence of an Almighty God.

"I can't make the decision for you," Jeff began. "I'm not your leader anymore. Isabella and me, we're gonna try one last thing and it may work. It may not. But I can't ask any of you to stay. There's nothing wrong with taking your families and leaving. You've done what you could and God knows that."

"We're with you, Reverend," a voice from the crowd replied before Jeff could go on.

"Gone too far to turn back now," said another.

Agreements were made and Jeff stood back to see that some

brave souls had actually pledged themselves to follow him into battle.

The Last Battle.

He'd known there would be a few who would go with him: Hank, Kurt, and even Franklin, if the man could. But to see *this* many willing to give their lives so that others might be saved…It moved him.

As quiet settled over the people, Jeff surveyed them, feeling that they were finally prepared for what he was about to propose. They were ready to fight. More importantly, they were ready to win. Taking his Bible from the mantle and opening it to a marked passage, he said, "I want to read you something. In Joshua 1:9, Joshua is about to lead the children of Israel to claim their Promised Land and the Lord gives him this charge, 'Have I not commanded you? Be strong and courageous. Do not be terrified; do not be discouraged, for the Lord your God will be with you wherever you go.'

"So this is what we're going to do."

Somebody found Jay's old records and started playing Ben E. King's *Stand By Me* on the player. The planning stage was done. The praying was done. Now there was just the waiting, the expectation of the battle to come. Families huddled together in the living room in silence as the old song played, enjoying the calm. Enjoying each other. Couples held hands. Parents kissed their children. The old timers listened, their eyes closed, as if thinking back on a life well-lived. It was a time of reflection, of savoring the sweetness of life.

Isabella, however, seemed restless. Jeff found her in her old bedroom upstairs, away from the others, sitting in a corner. Weeping. She'd been going through a lot lately, but had yet to tell him what was wrong. He approached her, praying that she would finally confide in him. The chances of one or both of them dying tomorrow were incredible and he wanted to face that fate knowing that he and his wife had been completely honest with each other.

He gently rubbed her arm. "What is it?"

"I hate this town," she sobbed, her face marred by pain. Jeff sat beside her, took her in his arms. "Greensboro has always taken you from me and I've tried to be supportive, but I can't do it anymore."

"Iz…"

"I need you, Jeff," she said, her breathing hitched. "I need you for *me* and I'm sorry if that's selfish, but it's not fair. It's not fair that you should die for them. Not when…"

"I'm sorry," he said. "But you know I have to stay."

Isabella nodded, pressed against him. She raised her head, her tears matching his, and smiled sadly. "I know…and that's why I'm staying with you."

"No," he said, though it killed him to think of facing that last great enemy without her. "Iz, no. Go with Father Joe."

Isabella laughed through her tears. "If you're going to die, then I'm going to die with you. You owe me that much."

Her expression told him that he couldn't change her mind, so he simply touched her face and she kissed his callused hands. She was his warrior. His hero.

"You know," he began, peace settling in his heart, "you're the most stubborn person I know."

She smiled. "I learned from the best," she said, drawing near to kiss him.

When they parted, Isabella pressed Jeff back, still holding his hands. Her eyes sparkled with anticipation. "Now. There's one more thing I have to tell you."

Rosalyn burst through the door to her apartment. Rushed to the closet and flung open the door. She dug around on the top shelf, straining to grab the pistol she had stored up there. Working for the Strange Man had given her an affinity for violence and more than a few enemies. Secretly, she had stockpiled knives and pistols, hidden in various places throughout her apartment. Now, with Stevenson dead, the police would be on full-alert and she could only imagine how enthusiastic they would be to kill the Strange Man's girlfriend who had lorded over them all. In fact, given her betrayal, she figured that anyone who *did* kill her would be the Man's new best friend.

She was Greensboro's Most Wanted, now, and had to prepare. If she was really set against killing herself, she had no other option but to try once more to stop the Strange Man's Dark Hour. Her first instinct was to collect her weapons. The Man was afraid of fire—all demons were, she'd gathered. Maybe the secret to his destruction lay there.

Inside, she felt the beast slithering under her skin. Tomorrow the Change would happen and her plan to defeat the Man would be halted once she became a thing like TJ. Without a will of her own. Only the urge to serve her dark master.

Her fingers brushed against the cold steel of the pistol. She'd fight as long as she could before the Change took hold.

I can't escape, but I'll take as many of those suckers with me as I can.

Taking firm grip of the stashed firearm, she pulled it free and knocked over a dust-covered box in the process. Photographs spilled on the carpet.

Photographs of Dras.

There were all the pictures she had tucked away when he went to Wexler. Lying atop was a folded piece of paper. The note he gave her that night in The Rave Scene almost a year ago, before Stevenson arrested him.

Rosalyn had never bothered to open the note before. She had been too afraid, for reasons she didn't fully understand. But taking the note in her hands now, creased and undisturbed, made her feverishly curious. She *wanted* to know what was in it. Dras almost died that night and this was the legacy he wanted to leave behind.

Am I ready?

The apartment wasn't safe. Every precious breath she exhausted was only putting her closer to the moment when a band of rogue deputies of her own would burst in to beat her and kick her and kill her.

Nevertheless, she opened the note and finally read the words therein:

Jesus loves me, this I know.
For the Bible tells me so.
Little ones to Him belong.
They are weak but He is strong.

Rosalyn sat in stunned silence.

Then she laughed. Threw her head back and guffawed until tears came to her eyes. It was so…so *Dras.* She expected a long drawn-out letter, some final farewell filled with memories and speculation on life and its meaning. But Dras, in all of his wonderfulness, had left her a simple children's song as his last will and testament. She laughed harder, now, crying, feeling fear and dread rolling off her back.

Oh, Dras. You big goofball.

Suddenly, her apartment door banged open. The dark beast under her flesh bristled in alarm as two deputies hurried inside, their weapons drawn. "Hold it!" one of them made out, but Rosalyn was already moving.

A black tentacle coalesced around her arm. With it, she slapped away the pistol in the deputy's hand, encircling his arm, too. Jerking hard, she whirled him across the room, where he landed in her TV set. It exploded in sparks, shorting out the lights in her living room. They flickered and fizzled as the other deputy fired his gun.

Rosalyn bent unnaturally backward, hearing her own back snap painfully—but she was beyond pain now. She felt the blackness cover her eyes, coursing through her, commanding her to move. The cop shot round after round, but Rosalyn dodged, ducked, and twirled out of harm's way, cutting a bee line right for the man. With a firm boot, she kicked him square in the solar plexus, jettisoning him out of the apartment and across the hall where he rebounded against the plaster wall.

She snapped to attention, her tentacles writhing, and turned her focus to the deputy she'd thrown into the TV. He was dazed but standing. Picking up her pace, she marched for him, prepared to rip him limb from limb—and shocking herself at her own brutality.

But the Thing was in control now.

Remarkably, the deputy holstered his weapon and held his hands in surrender. "Wait! Wait! We just want to talk!"

The deputy from the hall staggered in, but made no move to attack. Rosalyn blinked the sludge out of her eyes, willing the goo back into her pores. It raged against her in her mind, wanting to be loose—wanting to murder—but she fought against it. Calmed herself.

Now she recognized the deputy before her as Roy Miller. The other man was Mike Ortiz.

Deputy Miller was bruised, but held his ground, his eyes sharp and alert.

"What do you want?" she asked, the Thing hissing inside her: *"Let us out. Let us consume him."*

"You tried to kill the Man," he said, without accusation.

"I did."

Ortiz rubbed his stomach, sore, and joined his partner. Miller's face was like granite.

"How would you like some help next time?"

Rosalyn narrowed her eyes.

Miller explained, "We can get you to him, then it's up to you. We may not exactly be on the side of right, but we're still *human*."

She paused, gauging if he was serious. Miller, though, remained unfazed. Determined.

Rosalyn sneered to her new ally. "Then let's kill us a demon."

CHAPTER TWENTY-SIX

MORNING CAME TO the Evans farm, finding Jay and Isabella alone in the kitchen. Families quietly shuffled about the house, gathering what few things they took when the TJ Creature made his devastating raid on the church the night before. Jeff was busy discussing things with Hank, who had arrived around four in the morning and gotten very little sleep. In the meantime, Isabella just wanted to spend this time with her father. She'd seen very little of him since all this madness began months ago. After Dras's arrest, she'd been so focused on being there for Jeff, then after the Strange Man took over, her life belonged to the Havenites and their needs.

It'd been a long time since she had a life of her own.

Jay sipped a fresh cup of coffee, the third batch he'd had to make that morning to compensate for his impromptu houseguests. Isabella sat opposite him, drinking her own cup. The old man kept quiet, careful not to look her in the eye.

"Thanks for letting us stay," she said.

He nodded.

She smiled, finding his gruff, manly way a bit boyish and sweet. She had always felt protective of her father. Throughout her youth, her older brothers had told her what their dad was like before their mother left, and the man Isabella knew was a far cry from those tales. Sorrow seemed to physically rest on his shoulders, slumping him forward, and he rarely smiled. Isabella had tried all her life to please him—working hard in school, learning to keep house and cook, helping on the farm—anything to bring back his smile. She had given up so much for him, forgoing most of her youth. But, in the end, it seemed all for naught. Jay Evans only grew sadder over the years.

Isabella wondered if he resented her for marrying Jeff and leaving him all alone in an empty house. "So, where do you go from here?"

He sipped his coffee as if the thought never crossed his mind.

"You know you can't stay," she warned. "Even if Greensboro doesn't get destroyed, they'll find out that you helped us. You're in danger, Dad."

"Ah, I'll be all right," he mumbled.

"Father Joe should be here within the hour. You could go with him to Russellville, at least until this blows over." She sighed. "I worry about you, Dad. I love you and I want to see you taken care of."

He grinned humorlessly, as if ashamed. "I thought the parent was supposed to say that to the child."

Isabella didn't know what to say. She saw regret in her father's eyes, a shadow of wasted years gone forever and a twinkle of hope that things could improve.

"Eh," he grunted and set his coffee cup down. "Maybe you're right."

Isabella's heart skipped a beat.

"Town's not what it used to be. Could be time for a change of scenery."

"Yeah," Isabella grinned. "Change is good."

Finally, Jay looked her in the eye. And he smiled.

In the back of a closet in one of the many bedrooms on the Evans farm, Jeff found a bucket of old toys. They were covered in dirt and had pieces missing, but they served their purpose.

Jeff scribbled his best rendition of Greensboro Park Lake on the underside of one of Jay's old motorcycle posters out in the shop. He spread the map on a table on the screened-in back porch and placed the mismatched toys over key locations, signifying his plan of attack. At the moment, a Troll doll and the better part of a Man-At-Arms *He-Man* action figure stood on the outskirts of the

Greensboro Park Lake schematic.

"All right," he began, pointing to the pink-haired Troll doll. "This is you."

Hank stepped back and crossed his arms. "Why can't I be the other one?"

Jeff groaned. "All right, you're Man-At-Arms, I'll be the Troll."

"What's the plan?"

"They'll be waiting for a signal before they make the sacrifice."

Hank raised a finger. "Before they *try* to make the sacrifice."

"Right," Jeff corrected himself. He had to think positive. They could stop this. They *would* stop this. "We'll wait here with the men that are going with us, and when they come—"

"We'll get 'em."

"What do *we* do?" Gus asked. He stood at Jeff's right, beside a very dark and sullen Andrew.

"You and those with you will cut behind them, making sure they can't escape. Our sole priority here is saving these kids. If the ritual gets interrupted," he locked eyes with Hank, "and it *will*, then they're liable to take the babies and run, possibly completing the ritual at a different time, or…or I don't know what they would do. If it's come to this, we can't put anything past them. We've gotta be ready for anything."

Andrew spoke, his voice a low grumble. "What about everyone back in town? Who goes after them?"

Jeff and Hank shared a look of uncertainty and he eased away from the map. "Andrew, I don't know. We've done everything we can and no one wants to listen. We've gotten word to the believers still living in town, and those who want to leave with Father Joe know where to meet. Those who stay…well, that's their decision."

Dissatisfied, the boy looked away, watching the Havenites mingling outside waiting for Father Joe to arrive with their ticket out of Doomsday.

"Doesn't seem fair," he muttered angrily.

"No one said it was fair," Jeff responded.

"But God doesn't always promise us that things will be fair," interrupted a man stepping onto the porch. "Only that He'll be with us no matter what."

"Carter," Jeff breathed, shocked.

Carter Ross leaned against the porch railing, his clothes torn, dirty, and caked in dried sweat and blood. His cheek was covered in a blood-soaked bandage.

Hank edged to the man's side to support him. "Good Lord, son. What happened?"

"Been running all night, trying to stay ahead of Shamblers," Carter explained tiredly.

Gus asked, "Anyone else make it out?"

Carter shook his head and Andrew swore and stormed away.

"Good to have you back, Carter," Jeff said and found that he really meant it.

The screen door slapped open and little Chelsea Ross came tumbling out, racing for her dad. She squealed, "Daddy!" and gripped him tight. He laughed as if it hurt and lifted her off her bare feet, clutching her to his chest. The little girl giggled as her mother came out in tears. Carter hugged his daughter with one arm and reached for his wife with the other.

"It's all right, girls," he said. "I'm here. I'm okay."

Chelsea kissed Carter's good bearded cheek. Then, she pulled away and looked around. "What about Michelle and Nancy's daddy? Is he here too?"

Carter hesitated. "No, I'm sorry, honey…he…"

The girl buried her face in Carter's neck. Tears brimmed in the man's eyes, and he looked to Jeff, his jaw set. "Whatever you want. Just ask."

Jeff knew that Carter was finally on his side.

"So you see the angels?"

Drac nodded for what felt like the hundredth time as Millie Walker struggled to keep step with him. He was busy placing what little luggage the Havenites had on the front lawn of the Evans farm while the tiny child interrogated him.

"Yep," Dras sighed.

"I do too! When I pray they sometimes talk with me."

"Uh-huh. That's nice, kid."

"Which ones have *you* seen?" she asked, wide-eyed.

He paused. "I thought there were only the two."

Abruptly, Millie switched tracks, and replied glumly, "I'm sorry I lied. I'm sorry you went to jail."

Dras dropped the bags on the ground. "Ah, don't worry about it."

"I was scared."

"I was scared too."

She smiled faintly and plopped down on a suitcase, immersing herself in thought. "Do you think the angels will win?"

Dras shrugged. "I hope so."

"I think they will. The angels *always* win."

"Millie!" Rebecca called from across the yard. Franklin Whitaker was back from the hospital, bandaged and ready to ride the Russellville Express. Rebecca helped Franklin down the steps of the farmhouse's front porch with Timmy hugging his leg, while beckoning her daughter, "Leave Dras alone, honey. Come over here."

"She's fine," Dras shouted, trying to be polite, but secretly hoping Rebecca would insist.

Millie turned back to her hero-of-the-hour, a look of accomplishment on her tiny face. "I got chased by gremlins."

"Me too," Dras stated, feeling a bit overlooked.

"The church was on fire too."

He slumped. "Okay, you got me there." *Why am I comparing war stories with a five-year-old?*

Hearing tires on gravel, Dras glanced down the road and spotted his parents' car approaching. He smiled, glad to see them, when—

"The Strange Man tried to eat me," Millie added matter-of-factly. "Did he try to eat *you*?"

Dras jerked back to the odd child before him. He turned to her with a quizzical frown, raised a finger and said, "Millie…" but he really didn't know how to finish. Shaking his head, with the puzzled frown still on his face, he left the baggage and the girl behind and headed for the car.

"When I grow up, I'm gonna fight monsters, just like the angels!" Millie shouted.

"That's nice, Millie," Dras waved to her and crossed the yard, her chattering trailing behind.

Jack and Louise Weldon parked in the long gravel driveway of the Evans farm. Jeff came out to meet them, and Jack's heart broke. His boys were going into the fight without him and there was nothing he could do to save them. The thought almost overwhelmed him, but he stifled it as Jeff hugged his mother.

"Got everything taken care of?" Jack lifted his chin and asked with authority.

"Yes, sir," Jeff reported. "We're not out of it yet, but at least we have a plan."

"How can you be sure they haven't already started?" Jack asked. Still parenting, still wanting to make sure that his boys were thinking right. *That's all I can do now.*

Father Joe and his parish bus thundered down the road, nearing the house. "Trust me, Dad. The Strange Man has spies, but so do we. Kurt Daughtry and a couple others are keeping tabs on all of the Strange Man's lieutenants. They've been reporting in and, yeah, things are getting closer, but we still have some time."

Jack gave his head a good, hard jerk of approval and winked. Knowing Jeff was in charge made it a bit easier to leave. But not by much.

Father Joe stepped off the bus, a thin older man with an open, honest face and neatly combed graying hair. Trotting at his side was the old sandy-colored basset hound whose tag read "Cougar". The priest had picked up the dog as a stray on one of his many trips to Greensboro. Cougar seemed to have a knack for sniffing out gremlins and his presence made Isabella feel a little safer. They needed all the help they could get.

She collected the relieved Havenites together and families grabbed their bags from the lawn. "Everybody on the bus. This is it."

The people formed a line and began piling into the bus in as orderly a manner as their unbridled fear would allow. Jeff left his parents' side as Dras approached to wish them well, and journeyed to the priest. "Father Joe, thanks for coming. I really appreciate this. I could never tell you how much it means that you've helped us. You've risked so much—"

The priest held up a kindly hand. "Serving our Lord requires no thanks." He extended his hand and Jeff shook it. "I'll get your people to safety one last time."

"I'll call you if—" Jeff faltered, and Isabella felt a little queasy. Her husband corrected himself, "*when* we get out of this."

"Godspeed, Jeff," said Father Joe, making the sign of the cross over him. Jeff humbly received the blessing and put a firm hand on Joe's shoulder.

"You too, Father. You too."

Louise refused to let Dras go. She embraced him, squeezing until he choked. "Mom—Mom, I'm okay. Ease up."

She huffed and released her son, wiping a stray tear from her cheek. "This is so hard."

Dras stuck his hands in his back pockets, looking strong and confident, even though she knew he must be afraid. "You'd better hurry on, Mom. You need to get going if you're going to make it out in time."

Louise trembled with worry, barely able to stand leaving behind her children. She knew they could both die today. She remembered them as sleeping babies in their cribs. So tiny and fragile, cuddling with their stuffed animals. She had kissed their little cheeks while they slept, rubbing their tummies softly, feeling the rise and fall of their breathing.

Now they were grown and facing unspeakable horrors.

Jack patted her gently on the small of her back. "Come on, Louise. Time's wasting and the boys have a lot to do. Why don't you take the bags on up? I'd like a minute here."

Louise's eyes brimmed with tears, as she gave Dras one last kiss on his cheek and hugged his neck. She was crying when she pulled away, but she refused to look back. Instead, she took their bags and headed for Jeff, by the bus.

Her boys were men now. She couldn't cradle them anymore.

Dras watched his mom go, sad for her and scared for himself. His father must have known how he felt. "She'll be all right. She's stronger than she looks. Must be where you get it from."

Dras grinned and turned to his dad. "You think?"

"Well, you sure got your good looks from *me*."

Dras allowed himself a moment of levity and chuckled. It felt good to joke with his dad. The old man had been sick most of his life and he'd never really known the guy. But now, it seemed they had a chance of fixing things or, at least, building something new. *If I don't go and get myself killed.*

"You two take care of yourselves," Dras said.

"You watch out for your brother."

"Yes, sir."

Jack looked to his scuffed boots and sucked in air, not looking at Dras. "You going back for Rosalyn?"

He shifted uncomfortably. "I'm hoping I don't have to. I'm hoping she'll come back for *me*."

"What if she doesn't?"

"What should I do, Dad? How'd you do it? How'd you convince so many people to follow Christ over the years?"

Jack's rough face softened and he focused his cobalt blue eyes on Dras. "Wasn't a big secret, Dras. You just got to love people. Let the Lord shine through you. He's gotta be the one doing the convincing, or you're doing it wrong."

"Yeah," he murmured, not getting the kind of magic words he had hoped for. "I'm hearing that a lot lately. I hope you're right."

Without realizing it, Jack stuck *his* hands in *his* back jean pockets, possibly unaware that he was mirroring his son. "I'm real proud of you, boy. You and your brother, both. Whatever happens today…well, I'll know you tried your best and that's all I could ask for."

Dras felt his throat tighten but played it cool. "Thanks, Dad."

Jack gripped his boy into an embrace, squeezing tight. "Just remember I love you. I always did, even when I forgot to say it."

"I love you too, Dad."

The men parted awkwardly, and without another word, Jack headed for Louise and the bus. Dras watched the old man limp away and smiled to himself.

Rebecca Walker happened by with Millie in tow, and Dras called out to the little girl.

"Hey, Millie, come here a sec."

Millie left her mother's side, her eyebrows raised in curiosity, as Dras knelt before her. "What?"

"Stay safe, okay?" he told her. "And do us a favor. Pray. Contact all your angel friends and tell them we need them now, more than ever, okay?"

Millie nodded, taking the matter very seriously. She returned to her mother and entered the bus. Dras took one last look at the Evans farm. The place was clearing out. He wondered if he'd see any of these people again. Even if they managed to save Greensboro, the Havenites might relocate, starting new lives all over the country, far from this dark and terrible place.

But it was a nice town once. It could be that way again.

Yeah, he had to keep believing that. The situation wasn't hopeless, even if they were up against impossible odds. *With God, all things are possible. Even saving Rosalyn.*

After the last of the Russellville-bound Havenites boarded the bus, Father Joe followed with the hound trailing behind and shut the doors with a hydraulic *hiss.* Dras watched as Isabella snaked her arm around Jeff's waist and the two waved as the bus left the Evans farm. Isabella's father was on that bus too, and the thought comforted Dras. The last of the fighters gathered on the lawn to bid their loved ones farewell. Once the bus's dust dissipated in the bright mid-morning sun, Jeff turned to Dras, Isabella, Hank, Carter, Gus, and all the others who had chosen to go down with the ship. His face was like flint. The good-byes were over. Their families were gone. *Safe.* Now there was the matter of those left in Greensboro and the fate that awaited them if they continued on their course.

"This is it, folks," Jeff addressed the group. "No more talking. The time for fighting is here. Today, we take back Greensboro."

The end had begun.

CHAPTER TWENTY-SEVEN

ON FATHER JOE'S bus, Annie sat directly behind the priest, watching the road ahead and scratching lovable Cougar's neck. Her mother sat beside her, quietly staring out the side window. Annie wondered if she was thinking about Rosalyn.

Meredith and Rosalyn never got along, but Annie knew the two women loved each other. Despite the current state of things, Annie felt hope in the future for both her mother and her sister. God wasn't through with Greensboro yet. Jeff, Isabella, and Dras were still back there and they were ready to fight. More importantly, Annie knew that God didn't *want* to judge Greensboro and He would not unless it was absolutely necessary.

There's still a chance.

Her faith was strengthened by the sight of Millie across the aisle two rows behind her. Her former baby-sittee was sitting with her mother and the Whitakers, her tiny hands clasped together, eyes shut tight, praying.

Annie wasn't too cynical to appreciate the power of a child's prayer. If Millie, who had been visited by the Strange Man's every horror, could find the courage to pray to God for His help, Annie knew there was still some good left in the world.

Annie's optimism was interrupted by a whisper from Father Joe. "Uh oh."

Cougar whined, and Annie looked up, curious. She saw a roadblock ahead, surrounded by deputies.

From the middle of the bus, Jay Evans noticed it too. He leaned across the aisle to Jack and Louise Weldon. "Looks like trouble."

Jack followed the man's gaze and, frowning, carefully made his way to the seat beside Annie.

"What is it, Father?" Jack asked in a soft tone.

Meredith broke from her trance and her whole body went rigid. "What's wrong?" she asked, nearly squealing.

Annie calmly turned to her mother. "Shhh, Mom. Don't upset everyone."

No one else seemed to pick up on the small drama unfolding, or the incredible obstacle ahead of them. Father Joe kept driving, though Annie knew he would have to make a decision soon.

"I've got to stop," he told Jack, his voice worried.

"Maybe it's not for us," she suggested.

Jack shook his head with a sigh. "They've probably got every exit out of the county blocked. They were *waiting* for us to come."

"What do we do?" Meredith asked, no less terrified but, thankfully, quieter.

"We could ram them," Annie said.

Father Joe turned to Jack, amused. "She has a point."

But Jack remained cool. "No. The Good Lord's gotten us this far. He won't let us down now. Stop up ahead and we'll leave the rest to Him."

Annie looked back and saw that Millie was still praying. She decided to join in.

Earl Canton hadn't been expecting company that morning. Most people left him alone these days as he'd stayed pretty determined to keep to himself. Greensboro used to be a place he believed in but now...*People gone crazy*.

Come a few months ago, he'd almost gone crazy right along with them. In a fit of desperation he had almost murdered an innocent man. The experience scared him. Made him rethink a lot of things. Then the town started changing. Everything became nice and pretty and white-washed while no one wanted to talk about the new mayor who took office without benefit of a proper election and the behind-the-scenes erasure of all things Christian. Earl had never been a Christian but he didn't think it was right what the locals were doing. It made him uneasy and he wasn't for sure where or when it would end. Then talks of the Celebration Day came and no one ever really said what it was about.

But everyone knew. No one had the guts to admit what they were doing to each other's faces, but they all knew. It was disgusting. Wicked.

Earl wanted no part of it, no part of Greensboro, and he made sure he was home that day, tucked away from the world in his recliner, trying desperately not to get involved. So, when the knock came at his door late that morning, Earl was quite surprised.

When he opened the door to see Jeff Weldon waiting there, his jaw nearly dropped.

Instantly ashamed, Earl averted his eyes and grumbled, "What are *you* doing here?"

"I came to talk to you," Jeff said firm, but kind.

He hadn't talked to Jeff since the night he nearly hung him from the back of his pickup truck. Despite the violent act, Jeff never pressed charges, and Earl thought maybe that only made him angrier.

Earl grunted and moved away from the open door, revealing a living room covered in empty food containers, newspapers, and beer cans. Jeff looked reluctant to intrude on the man's hermitage.

"Can I come in?" Jeff asked, still standing in the doorway.

Earl flopped down in his worn recliner and waved the young man in. "Come on in, preacher. Say what you gotta say, just know that I probably ain't interested."

Jeff entered and closed the door behind him. "Earl, I don't know how to ask you this. This town…it's not like it used to be."

He chortled and stared at his muted television. "What tipped you off?"

"You know what they're doing today. To the children."

Earl was quiet. Thoughtful. "Yeah."

"What they do today…there's no going back from that."

Shifting uncomfortably, the man settled in his chair. "Why you coming to me, preacher? Huh? What do I got to do with it?"

"You can help me stop it."

At this, Earl outright laughed. "Oh yeah? How do you figure that?"

"The people respect you," Jeff said, without hesitation. "In a way they *never* respected me. I was always just Jack Weldon's kid to them, but *you*...They trust you. I'm not saying it's going to be easy, but, well," he chuckled, "If you could convince them to tie a noose around my neck, I know you can talk them into just about anything. You gotta try and reason with them, Earl."

Earl shook his head, almost immediately. "You're asking me to talk to them about right and wrong? What do *I* know about that? What do any of us know?"

Jeff countered, "You know enough to know that killing babies just so the local Starbucks can stay open is wrong, which is more than can be said for most of those folks down at the Center. You know that we used to care about each other, and used to stand up for what was honorable and true and that's something they've all forgotten. They need to be reminded of how things *used* to be. Used to be God took care of Greensboro and He never asked us to murder children in return. Used to be we all kept our faith, even in the tough times."

"Then the highway moved," Earl said, never finishing.

"Then the highway moved," Jeff agreed. "And everyone went nuts. We lost our way, Earl, that's all. You, me, all of us. But we can find our way back. We *have* to. Before God has to put a stop to our wickedness to spare the rest of the world from the madness going on here."

Earl was quiet for a long time, staring at his TV. "You think it'd come to that?" he asked, hesitantly.

Jeff almost laughed. "I know it will, Earl. It's *already* coming to that. God's already got the backup plan, in case the town goes through with the sacrifice. By tomorrow morning, Greensboro will just be a bad memory. A patch of scorched earth in Maribel County. Is that how you want to go out? I know *I* don't. I'm gonna go back to the lake; try to save those babies. But if the people's hearts aren't changed, it doesn't matter. They'll just try it again, and again until, finally, they succeed and destroy us all. That's why I need you. We *all* need you."

"You're asking me to tell them about faith."

It wasn't a question. Jeff nodded.

"I can't tell them about something I ain't ever had, preacher," he said, then rubbed at the beard that his muttonchops formed on his jawline. "And I ain't gonna be a hypocrite."

Jeff's expression sank.

Earl stood tall, feeling like it was time for a change. Jeff stepped back, uncertain, and Earl reached into the side pouch of his recliner where the remotes to his television, VCR, and stereo lived. He pulled out the folded paper he'd kept there for a while. He opened it, revealing one of Jeff's old Scripture flyers that the rebels had left all over town.

"I thought those were torn down," Jeff said, looking moved with emotion.

"Not all of them." Earl said. "I ain't got a Bible, 'cause them boys at City Hall burned 'em all up. But I've had this and I've been reading the verses you got on it."

Jeff froze, his face lighting up.

Earl finished, "I don't do nothing half-hearted. If I go to Jesus, I go all the way."

A soft grin broke Jeff's stupor. "He's right there waiting for you, Earl."

Earl nodded, gruff and ready to get to work. "Then let's do this right. I haven't prayed in a long time, preacher, so I need you to show me the ropes. Think you can handle that?"

"You got it."

Isabella checked her watch. Carter stood at her side. Behind them were three other men, hunkered down in the treeline surrounding Greensboro Park Lake. Everyone was antsy, their eyes wide and searching. So far, the dark water of the lake remained undisturbed.

There were a few banners up. Some streamers. It looked like it usually did during a community-wide barbecue.

Only today the lake was eating, and children would be the meal.

Isabella wanted to throw up. If it weren't for her responsibility to the men with her, she thought she might break down and cry at the depths to which her old friends and family had sunk. At least her father had come to his senses.

Deciding to do something other than sit and fret, she raised her radio and spoke, "You read me, Donut Boy? Come back, over."

"Roger that, Mama Bear." Hank's tone was light, though she knew her friend was just as on edge as she.

"Any sign?"

"Nothing. And I mean nothing. No birds, no insects, no critters."

"The lake got them all," Isabella interrupted.

"But it ain't getting them babies," Hank said with great certainty. Isabella grinned at how well he could read her mind these days.

"Copy that."

"Any word from Jeff?" he asked.

Carter looked to Isabella, concern on his face. Isabella gave him a thankful smile, but remained strong. "Not yet."

Carter's hand shot up. "Shh," he hissed.

Isabella clipped her radio as she and the men went rigid. Carter waved them down, and crept to sit on his haunches. He carefully peered out through the trees, then gulped. "They're coming."

The Havenites on the Russellville Express noticed they were slowing down. A few curious inquiries sounded from the back but those up front were focused on the roadblock.

Jack recognized Deputy Hollis at the forefront of the outpost, waving an orange flag, signaling the bus to stop. The dog whined and Annie rubbed his coat, her eyes full of fear.

"What do I do?" Father Joe asked.

"Stop, just like they want," Jack said, his cobalt blue eyes narrowing in study.

"We're all going to die," Meredith gasped, in tears.

"Mother, *please*," Annie scolded.

Father Joe brought the bus to a halt, the brakes squealing slightly. Suddenly the bus came alive with nervous conversation and Jack braced himself against the back of his seat to stand, conjuring a bit of the old Jack Weldon magic over the townspeople. "All right, folks, just simmer down. This'll only take a minute." The chatter lessened and the people relaxed a bit.

Wounded Franklin Whitaker tried to stand on shaky legs. "You need help?"

Jack waved him off. *A bus full of women and children, an injured man, three old codgers, and one mutt against a blockade of young armed deputies.* The situation did not bode well, but Jack held faith.

"Sit down now, Franklin. Save your strength."

Franklin sat, but looked ready to rise again at a moment's notice.

Deputy Hollis approached and banged on the door with the palm of his hand.

"Open up," he commanded, his voice muffled through the glass.

"Go ahead," Jack instructed as Louise moved closer to him.

Father Joe pried the door open and offered his best priestly smile. "Afternoon, Deputy. Is there a problem?"

"Road's closed." Deputy Hollis mustered what little bravado he had, one hand resting not-so-casually on his sidearm.

"What's the matter, Andy?" Jack asked, as if he were not on a bus full of wanted refugees. "Road work up ahead?"

Hollis pushed back his hat and boarded the bus. "You know that ain't it, Mr. Weldon. We have orders to take you all in."

A couple of older women began to wail. Cougar growled and Annie looked to have every inclination to let the canine loose on the deputy, but she held him off, patting his sandy mane.

Jack faced the deputy man to man. "Andy, we just want to be left alone. These folks haven't done you any harm. We've got mostly women and children on this bus. What danger could they really be?"

"I'm sorry, Mr. Weldon, I hate to do it. But I got orders from Mayor Graves, himself."

"He's a bad man!" Millie proclaimed, standing in her seat. Rebecca shushed her and gently pulled her down.

"She's right," Annie boldly stated. "We're not afraid of him and we're not afraid of you."

A few folks repeated the sentiment, though decidedly quieter, and Jack stood between Annie and Deputy Hollis, to keep the peace. Hollis, green and eager to prove himself, looked threatened but steadied himself.

"Stay back, Mr. Weldon. I don't want to have to hurt you."

Out of the corner of his eye, Jack saw Franklin gripping the edge of his seat, biding his time. Rebecca placed a restraining hand on his leg.

The protests on the bus grew louder but Jack held his hands out in surrender. "Let's talk about this, Deputy. We just want to go somewhere where our families will be safe."

"Careful, Jack," Louise warned. She was always so worried about him. Always hovering over him.

He ignored her. He kept his steely eyes on the young and frightened deputy, as if trying to charm a snake. "Please, Deputy."

Jack noticed through the windshield that other deputies were inching toward the bus, their hands slowly reaching for their sidearms. *We're sitting on a powder keg.*

"Stay back," Deputy Hollis warned. "I'm not telling you again!"

Jack hesitated, wishing the angry shouts of the Havenites would subside so that he could reason with the young man. "All right. I just want to talk."

Annie saw a sneakier deputy side up to the bus, aiming a rifle at the window.

Aiming at Jack's head.

The deputy leveled his weapon, squinted, and curled his finger around the trigger.

"Watch out!" Annie lunged forward, toppling Jack and knocking him to the seat. The gunshot shattered the glass dangerously close to Father Joe's head and the bullet struck deep in the bus' ceiling. Cougar barked and pounced just as Deputy Hollis went for his gun. Distracted, the deputy wrestled with the dog while trying to retrieve his firearm and Franklin made his move. In an instant, he sprang out of his seat and shoved forward, wresting the gun from the deputy and aiming it at Hollis's head. The deputies outside immediately trained their weapons on the armed man inside. Father Joe raised his hands to show he had no weapons—and to shield Franklin as best he could.

"Put the guns down!" Franklin commanded, pushing the gun to the nose of a sweaty Deputy Hollis. Annie helped Jack stand and the man held a steady hand to Franklin, "Careful, son. We don't want to hurt them."

"They'd hurt *us*," Franklin said through bared teeth.

Father Joe replied softly, "God would have us find another way."

He hesitated, wrath in his eyes, and Annie worried that Franklin would really shoot the man. She realized she was holding her breath. Then he regarded Timmy sitting with Rebecca, looking on his father with fear.

The man relented, lowering the gun before tossing it to the floor. Annie exhaled in relief as the deputy grabbed the firearm and still more deputies stormed the bus, shouting at everyone to stay down and keep their hands up. Franklin was thrown into the seat beside Jack and both men were assigned two guards who instantly trained shotguns at their heads. Louise slid down across from Rebecca, her eyes brimming with frightened tears, and Annie sat protectively in front of her mother. The situation was quickly diffused and Father Joe surrendered. "What would you have us do now, Deputy?"

Deputy Hollis turned to the older man, still trembling from his ordeal. At last he said, "Turn this bus around. Drive us back to

Greensboro."

Back into the lions' den, Annie thought.

CHAPTER TWENTY-EIGHT

THOSE CITIZENS OF Greensboro who were not fearfully hiding in their homes, gathered at the Center. Outside, the merely curious accumulated around the giant plasma screen monitors fixed to the building's face, waiting to see what the much-talked about Celebration Day would bring. Inside, the mood was somber but hopeful as the devout greeted each other while finding their seats.

Will Baxter stepped into the sanctuary, trying to regain his composure in front of his congregation.

"Good afternoon, Reverend," a flock of church ladies cheerily greeted him, led by Miss Jenkins in a gaudy, flowery hat.

He'd been strong before, lying through his teeth as the Strange Man instructed him, keeping a brave face to hide his deceit. But today, the most important of all days, he found himself barely able to stand without passing out. Smiling nervously, he muttered, "Good afternoon, sisters. Glad you could make it today."

"We wouldn't miss this for the world," Miss Jenkins sang delightfully, not realizing the terror to come.

You're all cattle, he thought bitterly, but grinned nonetheless. "If you'll excuse me, Miss Jenkins, I need to get ready."

Without giving her a chance to bid him farewell, Will pushed past, frantically searching for the exit. There were so many people here. He suddenly felt ill as he realized they were all going to be turned into mindless, raving monsters because of his lies. The Strange Man promised that he'd be repaid for his aid—that he'd be able to serve over the creatures as a prince. That had sounded so tempting at first, but now... He was so disappointed in himself and wondered if this was how Judas felt after he betrayed Christ. Right before he hung himself.

Will contemplated suicide as well, wondering if he would find release and forgiveness in death. Right now he just wanted to run far away, to disappear forever. But before he could carry his gloomy reflections out into the sparkling sun, the Strange Man oh-so-casually bumped into him. Will nearly shrieked.

"There you are, Will," the Strange Man—in his John Graves suit—chuckled as if he didn't know Will's second thoughts.

He shrank back. "I-I—"

The Man placed a strong, icy hand on Will's shoulder, somehow sapping the young man's strength, and purred, "Time to start, Reverend."

"I—"

He couldn't finish the protest. He felt cold inside, numb to his guilt and fear, filled only with the thought that he must do his part. Slumping, Will agreed. "Yes, Master."

The Man patted the false prophet on the back and guided him to the stage. Like a good puppet, Will obliged and carried himself the rest of the way to the podium. "Make me proud," the Strange Man called after him.

Will faced the multitudes and tapped the microphone twice. "May I have everyone's attention? We're about to begin."

The crowd simmered as, behind the Strange Man, the door to the backstage ready rooms opened and Rosalyn Myers entered without restraints, escorted by Roy Miller—promoted to acting sheriff following Stevenson's murder last night—and a small troupe of frazzled deputies including Deputy Ortiz. Alarm lighted the Strange Man's sculpted face. "My, my. Isn't this a surprise?"

Rosalyn sneered. "Miss me, baby?"

Sheriff Miller spoke up, "We caught her trying to get away. We thought you'd want to handle her personally."

Will watched the Man size the girl up. He wondered if the demon would kill her now, in front of all his followers. That would certainly put a damper on the Dark Hour—might even be enough to ruin everything.

Secretly he hoped the devil would make his move.

"Leaving town, were we?" the Strange Man said, low enough that the mumbling crowd couldn't hear, but Will could.

Rosalyn smiled. "Thought I might. Town ain't big enough for the both of us, and all that. We'd just bump into each other and it would be this whole awkward thing."

He chuckled, sardonically. "You think you can leave me so easily?"

"Well, I thought, being that you sent Stevenson to kill me, the relationship was pretty much over, yeah."

"Was that a bit over the top?" he cooed.

"Just a little, but I'm used to it. Face it, Big Daddy, you *are* a bit of a drama queen."

He nodded his head from side to side. "It was a carnal reaction, I admit." With a quick nod to Miller, the Strange Man ordered, "Sit her up front. After all, she's worked so hard for this day. I want to make sure she doesn't miss a thing."

Miller nudged Rosalyn and did as he was told. Rosalyn blew a kiss to the Man, spiteful.

"Enjoy the show," the Strange Man snarled, then redirected his attention to Will onstage.

I'm really going to have to do this. Why couldn't Jeff stop this madness?

The congregation finally settled, eagerly awaiting an encouraging word from their pastor. As the Center was a melting pot of all forms of religion, there were many holy men brought in by the Man to see to the spiritual needs of the community. But Will Baxter was homegrown, and most people still thought of him as "their pastor".

They trusted me…

Will straightened his tie and did his best Jeff Weldon impersonation, "Folks, I'm glad you all made it. This is an important day, isn't it? Some might even say, the most important day in Greensboro's history."

Nods from the crowd. Some looks of sadness.

In the back, Doris Berkley entered, her hair and makeup plastered in place, with Becky in tow. *When did they get back?* Will wondered absently. Both women looked a bit out of place but, judging by their clean appearances, Will thought they must be enjoying their return to civilization. They took seats in the back, and Doris in particular focused on the stage.

"It's been a hard road for all of us," Will continued. "This town has seen a lot of heartache. But that's all changed over the last year. Things have finally started to turn around and it's all thanks to this man. So, please, I want you to give a round of applause for the man responsible for this change."

Will stood aside and donned his premiere college boy smile, gesturing for the Strange Man to take the stage. "Our mayor, John Graves!"

Men and women rose to their feet, clapping and cheering, tears of gratitude and worship already running down their faces. The Strange Man took Will's position behind the pulpit and waved to the assembly, looking as humbled as he could.

From the front row, Will spotted Rosalyn rolling her eyes.

"Please, please," the Man said softly. "Sit."

The clapping continued and the Strange Man sighed in mock appreciation. "Please, sit. Sit."

Slowly they did, adoration lingering on their faces.

"Really, I don't deserve this," he said. "The Change has come to Greensboro only because you *wanted* it to come. When I arrived here, I was touched by your warmth and compassion for one another, but I was also troubled by those who worked so hard to tear apart that sense of community."

Some rumblings of agreement from the crowd.

"These *Christians…*" the Strange Man snorted, "The term Christian means 'little Christ'. Ha. Christ-like?" He shook his head. "Hardly. Would the Christ they claim to follow hate and persecute others for their individual beliefs?"

Defiant "no"s echoed across the room.

"No. Christ was a man of peace. Of love. He loved and accepted the whole world, for all of its differences, and He encouraged those who thought of Him as a messiah to treat others the same. But these delusional people have twisted His words and

His meanings and used them as a platform for their campaigns of hate and terror."

The air in the room shifted and the people grew more agitated, clapping and shouting. Rosalyn squirmed uncomfortably in her seat, and saw Miller similarly reacting where he stood.

"But at last we made them see that their narrow-minded, self-righteous behavior was not welcome here," the Strange Man roared and the crowd hailed him with praise. "They have retreated and now you and your children are finally safe to worship *however* you see fit. Or not at all!"

More booming applause. Rosalyn felt sick. Couldn't they see his lies? Why wasn't someone challenging him? These people had believed in God and Jesus and the Bible for generations until one man swooped into town, and a mere two years later, they'd burned the Bibles and the churches and stood behind the killing of innocent babies? It was insane! Rosalyn wanted to believe that it was the Strange Man's supernatural influence. She had experienced firsthand how that numbing darkness could thrall a person and cause her to think and do things that she never thought she would.

But Rosalyn didn't feel that darkness now. The Strange Man wasn't casting his spell. This was just what the people wanted. Or *thought* they wanted.

She pitied them. *You stupid fools. You deserve everything you get.*

The Strange Man spread his arms, his pose full of power and authority. "But today isn't about them. It's about you! You who remain are ready for the Change to come. To finally shed the ancient dogmatic practices of generations past and find the truth! I've come to give you that truth! But…" The Man trailed off, and the crowd grew quiet, seeing him dismayed. "Learning the truth comes with a price, doesn't it?"

Now there were a few sobs in the crowd. The people nodded and couples drew closer. The Strange Man gave them a moment to mourn. "You've given up a lot today. But the sacrifice that you have given only shows how much you want to know the truth."

Please, Jeff. Please stop him.

"Right now, your children are being given as a sacrifice to the god that *I* serve. It was a hard choice to make, but you made it and I know he is pleased with you. My god rewards those who sacrifice. He sees the desires of your heart, and he wants to give them to you. Everything you want—power, money, fame, happiness—he desires that you would have these things. The god that I serve, he is not so jealous that he demands your total obedience to him like a pet or a slave. No, he only asks that you remember him when he calls. And, in return, he allows you to live however you want. To worship however—or whoever—you want. He offers you freedom. Peace. Not division, like the Christians' God. Unlike the Christians' God, my god doesn't expect you to follow on blind faith. He will show you signs and miracles and you will know that what you have done today was good and right. Today…my god will reveal himself to you and you will believe."

A peal of thunder rolled overhead and the light in the room dimmed. As one, the congregation looked to the expansive skylight above—built just for this one moment, Rosalyn knew—and saw the darkening skies. She muttered, "Here we go."

"Look," the Strange Man proclaimed, then softened, relishing the moment. "The Hour is come."

CHAPTER TWENTY-NINE

A SMALL TROUPE of cloaked figures gathered by the withered edge of Greensboro Park Lake. Despite the streamers and decorations dressing the place up, the pavilions looked dead and decrepit. Haunted.

Isabella, Carter, and the men with them held their ground, waiting for that one perfect moment to spring into action. She waited on Jeff. The two of them had planned this moment, dreamed together of the time when they would make their last stand for the fate of Greensboro. She had no intention of starting this battle without her husband by her side.

Yet, as the hooded shapes drew nearer, Isabella saw the rolling carts full of babies and knew that she might not be able to wait. Even from here, the babies' cries could be heard and Carter muffled a gag.

"Good Lord." He choked back tears.

Isabella shook her head, furious at what she was seeing.

The radio in her hand crackled and Hank's voice whispered over static, "What's happening? We can't see."

"They're here," she responded. "Stand by. Wait for the signal."

"What's the signal?"

Isabella turned to Carter, but the rugged man only shrugged.

She lifted the radio to her lips. "We'll get back to you on that. Over."

Carter turned a stern eye on the men. "Be ready."

They nodded, fear on their faces.

Lakeside, the lead figure removed his cowl, revealing a scarred face that Isabella did not recognize, with a long, dark, braided beard. The middle-aged man extended arms toward the lake—his flesh covered in disturbingly intricate tribal tattoos, made all the more unsettling as Isabella could swear the symbols were writhing like snakes on his muscles. He stared at the clear heavens above, a look of delirious bliss on his face.

"I've waited for this moment for so long," he bellowed to the heavens.

The figures behind him waited, clutching the handles of the carriers.

"Come to me, O lord! Hear the cry of your servant! Do your will in this Dark Hour!"

Carter turned to Isabella in the bushes. "Hey, I think that's that shrink, Dr. Altman. He used to come by the station to counsel sometimes. What's he going on about?"

Isabella didn't answer. Only watched and waited.

Overhead, thunder shook the skies and dark clouds pulled together. Isabella instinctively looked up, watching as the moon eclipsed the sun, blotting out its light. Everyone at the lake, both the righteous and the wicked, stared into the black dawning, but it was Hank who broke the silence over the radio.

"Um…is *that* the signal?"

Could be, Isabella thought. *But a signal for what?*

The Bearded Man fell to his knees, weeping in exaltation. "Yes! The Change is upon us! The Great God Baal has come to deliver us!"

Carter fidgeted, bouncing on his haunches, ready to strike. "We have to move," he growled through bared teeth.

"Prepare the offering!" the Bearded Man ordered.

Isabella's breathing quickened as the hooded figures reached for the babies. She wanted to move. To fight. But she froze in revulsion. Carter jerked toward her, expectation on his face, when the extraordinary happened.

Light was returned.

The lake and its worshippers were soaked in the hi-power wattage of Day Lights. There was a creak, the sound of an old rusty door opening, then slamming shut. Everyone watched as a dark silhouette stepped into the light and faced the lake. The hooded men stopped in their work and the Bearded Man stood, guarding his eyes to get a better look at the stranger.

The cultist sneered. "Who are *you* supposed to be?"

Jeff Weldon answered, loudly. "Haven't you heard? We're the Devil Smashers."

This one's for you, Danny. She beamed.

Carter grinned, as well. "That's my boy."

Isabella barked into the radio, "There's your signal, Hank!"

"NOW!" Carter roared, and the bushes exploded with men rushing towards the lake. The Bearded Man shrieked in surprise and terror as Jeff Weldon's army descended on the hooded figures.

Jeff screamed, "*For Greensboro!*" and ran full force into the melee.

Darkness settled over Greensboro, and the gathered flock inside the Center stood to attention, gaping at the ominous eclipse visible in the skylight. The Strange Man watched their expressions of awe, wonder, and fright in rapt silence. Rosalyn ignored the instant midnight, instead focusing on the Strange Man. Even though he wore his beautiful face, she could see the demon within, and she wondered how she could have ever fallen for his deception.

The demon was distracted by his imminent victory. Rosalyn and Miller shared a look that said *Now or never.* Her "captors" stood back, freeing her to do what she'd come to do.

Utilizing the dark gift within, Rosalyn raced for the stage and bounded unnaturally to the Strange Man's side. Her muscles flexed and she commanded the obsidian sludge in her veins to ready for an attack. Then—

He turned to her, his eyes sparkling with something she had never seen in him before.

Pure and utter joy.

It terrified her, pinning her in place.

"I've won," he whispered to her, as if he himself hardly believed it. "He's coming. Jehovah is coming…He'll see what's been done here…He'll see and He'll destroy them all for what they've become…"

Rosalyn felt tears welling in her eyes. He was right. Retribution—*judgment*—was about to fall on their land and there was nothing she could do about it. *It's too late. I can't fix this.*

The Strange Man did not raise a hand to her, his deadly protégé, and Rosalyn realized she had no attack left in her. Dropping her arms to her side, she stood there helplessly while the Strange Man cackled and the crowd grew unsettled and expectant. The auditorium was in an uproar as everyone talked and speculated on what wonders this new god would show them.

"*What are you waiting for?*" Miller hollered at the foot of the altar, but she tuned him out, captivated by the sight before her. Rosalyn stared at the wild congregation. Their hungry eyes lifted to the unnaturally dark skies and some were singing, shouting, or crying. They praised the abyss and called out to the false god they thought was coming for them, loudly praying their petitions, begging to be blessed and rewarded for killing their children. They looked like ravenous animals, crowing for raw meat. Arguments broke out as people began to fight over who deserved the greater blessing when the Strange Man's god arrived. Punches were thrown. Women tore at each other's clothing, each demanding that her child was the greater sacrifice. Their shouting and arguing quickly became growling and snapping and barking, and the black shape slithering under Rosalyn's skin writhed in desperation to join their satanic communion.

"Do you feel it?" the Strange Man whispered, watching the sea of decadence before him as if it were a beautiful sunset. "*This* is the Great Change, Rosalyn. And it's nothing I've done. It's what you've done to yourselves."

Rosalyn wept. Hopeless tears trickled down her cheeks and she bit her lip to keep from crying aloud. "No…"

"You wanted to know what The Coming Evil was? Look around you, my love. It's you. It's always been you."

War had come to Greensboro Park Lake and, with it, a day of retribution.

Isabella and the last vestiges of the Devil Smashers held their ground as the tides of darkness crashed against them. Their profane ceremony halted, the cloaked lake worshippers abandoned their young sacrifices to battle the interlopers. Only the mysterious Bearded Man, crazed with dementia, remained by the dark lake's side, fallen on his knees, arms splayed wide in exaltation.

"Hear me, Dark God!" he shouted over the rush and roar of the two armies around him. "Rise and claim your servant! Change me into your image! I beseech thee!"

Isabella heard the madman's gibberish, but only as if through a fog. Gripped tightly in the arms of a hooded cult member, she struggled as another fanatic—this one a woman—approached, yanking a blackened blade from inside her tunic. The features of her face were concealed by her cowl as the shadowed woman approached. Isabella thought to call out for help, knowing Jeff was nearby, but she decided she could handle the thugs herself.

She *did* have four brothers, after all.

Heaving a grunt, she raised her legs and shot forward, slamming the shadow woman's throat and sending her sliding backward into the dead grass, her knife flying away. Still bound by strong arms, Isabella let go a furious growl and tossed her head back, busting the nose of the man who held her. He yelped in surprise and released his hold, groaning as he held his bleeding face. Isabella wasted no time spinning on the man and sent a deft kick to his doubled-over frame.

Both her attackers defeated, Isabella allowed herself a savage grin and brushed aside a few loose strands of hair before rejoining the fray.

Jeff and Carter held their own, side by side, as three hooded assailants flanked them. Jeff absently wondered at the identities of the men hidden beneath the cowls, realizing he probably knew them. They were fighting their neighbors out here, and any loss of life would be tragic.

Carter shouted, exhaling as he threw a punch that crumpled the face of the nearest cultie. The man stumbled and fell to the ground, and was immediately replaced by another of his dangerous kin.

"We can't keep this up forever!" Carter yelled as the ex-reverend dodged the blade of his current combatant. With a firm bump from his shoulder, Jeff dispatched the blade-wielding maniac. He straightened, taking a chance in the midst of the storm to catch his breath.

"Head for the babies," he ordered.

Carter hesitated at the sight of more hooded men approaching. "You sure you can handle them all by yourself?"

Isabella stepped in, fists balled, eyes leveled at her enemy. "He won't have to."

Carter grinned at the new and battle-improved Jeff and Isabella Weldon, and rushed off to the shore of the murky lake where small babies awaited their fate.

Isabella glanced at her husband, bracing herself for the fight. "You're always late."

He shrugged, his muscles tense. "But I always make an entrance."

"I love you, by the way," Isabella said as the first cultie to reach them threw a wild punch in her direction. She caught it, hooking her arm in the wiry man's and twirling him off balance. Jeff caught him behind the shoulders and jerked him to the ground.

He smiled at his wife. "I love you too."

Howls of madness carried across the chilling air. Inside the Center, the Strange Man peered over his congregation devolving into chaos. At his side, Rosalyn shrank in despair. *We're all going to die.* As if admiring the ocean on a tropical beach, the Strange Man softly said,

"Look at them. They rejected His decrees and the covenant He had made with their fathers and the warnings He had given them. They followed worthless idols and themselves became..." he grinned, "*worthless*."

Biting and snarling, the people degenerated into their primal nature. The Strange Man turned to face Rosalyn, the sight of Greensboro literally losing its mind behind him, evidence of his dark handiwork. "You become what you worship, my dear. Mankind...your arrogance is astounding. Your cruelty towards one another is unparalleled." The demon closed his eyes in sweet ecstasy, "The greatest evil is not the devil or his angels but the darkness that resides in the human heart."

Rosalyn's lip quavered. "What have you done?"

"I'm only offering the people what they have always wanted since the Garden of Eden. Freedom without responsibility. Choice without consequence."

Rosalyn shook her head, hurt and angry. "But, you...you did all of this because of...*a girl*?"

The Strange Man gazed at the growing blackness. "Love is the cruelest of all God's creations."

"You're crazy."

He spread his lips, showing his pointy green-stained teeth. "Duh."

A single loud *crack* sounded without warning, a gunshot blasting the Strange Man square in the forehead, twisting him backwards in surprise. Rosalyn ducked, fearing the mob below had turned homicidal. The crowd's antics died down and everyone turned to the doorway to face the Center's new visitor:

Earl Canton.

He stood at the entrance, a worn cowboy hat on his head, dusty boots on his feet, and his denim jacket and jeans loaded with enough ammunition to take on a small army. He held a smoking Winchester rifle.

The deputies returned to their senses, aiming their pistols on the gunman, but Miller raised an authoritative hand. "Hold your fire."

In the quiet, Rosalyn rushed to the Strange Man's fallen form, dropping to her knees. For one breathless moment, she hoped for the miraculous. That one bullet from a lone gunman had felled the devil. The Strange Man looked dead enough, the back of his head blown out and blackish blood oozing on the altar.

But just as Rosalyn began to celebrate in her heart that Greensboro's nightmare was finally over, the Strange Man's eyes blinked open—

And they were on fire.

In a flash, he shed his ruined handsome face, donning once more the terrible visage of the beast that had damned so many. Rosalyn fell back on her hands as the Strange Man rose to a stand in one fluid motion.

Earl held his resolve as he watched the monster and announced, "I see I've got your attention."

CHAPTER THIRTY

THE CENTER ERUPTED in shrieks at the sight of the floating demon in their presence. Minds bent and hearts melted and Miss Jenkins passed right out, gasping for Jesus. People moaned and wept and fell to their faces, realizing they had sold their souls to hell's ambassador.

"Look at him!" Earl boomed, shouting over the weeping. "You've known it all along but didn't want to admit it to yourselves. *Look at him!* That's who you gave your children to! The same devil who already took so much from us!"

The Strange Man, eyes glowing with unbound rage, leveled his glare on the hunter. Earl met the Strange Man's eyes, his own face stone cold. "You killed my boy, demon. Thought I'd let you know how I feel about that."

The Strange Man bared his fangs, his jaw extending with a sickening *pop*, and hissed. A ripple of invisible supernatural force shot out from the devil like a freight train, cutting a swath through the crowd, throwing people backwards. Pure, unleashed detestation contacted with Earl with the devastating force of a hurricane, folding him over and catapulting him through the sanctuary, the lobby, and finally the glass front doors.

Earl landed hard on the pavement outside, rolling four times before stopping, his leg broken in the violent outburst. Panicked screams followed him as the congregation emptied out of the Center, clawing their way through any available exit, desperate to be away. Through the entrance, Earl saw the Strange Man floating amidst his congregation, discarding people from side to side with nothing but the power of his uncontainable contempt. Bodies flew, toppling over those escaping, creating a quagmire of human shuffling and struggle.

The Strange Man pushed his way outside, exiting the Center into the day-night, stalking his prey. Earl scrambled for his gun with great effort, determined not to die lying down. The Strange Man flicked one arthritic finger and pushed the gun away with the power of his will.

"Did you really think a *gun* was going to stop me?" the monster crooned, slithering closer to the fallen man.

Earl braced himself to a kneeling position, but smiled through the pain. "Nah," he said matter-of-factly. "That was just to goad you out of hiding behind that purty face. Got the *real* stuff right here."

The battered and bleeding man reached behind his back and pulled out a Bible Jeff had given him earlier. With a snarl, Earl held the Bible out like a ward, but much to his shock, the demon chuckled. "Sorry. Have to try harder than that."

Earl looked to the holy book, then back to the devil, confused and terrified. "But, I thought…"

"I'm beyond that, now," the Strange Man exhaled slowly, as though freshly awakened from a restful sleep. "Do you know why demons cringe at the Word of God? It's because they fear the truth of their own powerlessness—they hate to be reminded of their inevitable end. But I welcome it, you see. I *welcome* His fire and retribution."

"You'll die too…"

The Strange Man bent low, slowly pressing his face to the man. "But not before you. That's all that matters to me now. You don't understand. I *want* God to come. I want Him to destroy everything He sees."

"You—"

"Yes. I hate you that much. I hate you enough to destroy myself just to see your filthy, *whoring* kind burn."

Behind the Strange Man, the chaos inside the Center infected the streets. Earl saw the spectators gathered in the road reacting to the image of the Strange Man's startling transformation. Seeing the collapse of society at hand, many had already taken to throwing trashcans or large rocks into storefronts, looting. Even cell phones and laptop computers seemed essential in a world gone mad.

While greed prompted many, others it seemed, like Dave from the video store, hefted their beer cans high as they climbed lampposts or sat atop cars, cheering that the end of all things had come in such a fantastic fashion. The Doom of Greensboro was quickly becoming the party to end all parties as black-clad teenagers built bonfires and danced around the pyres, singing and shouting. Beer-guzzling alpha males pooled their strength and tipped over cars, howling at the eclipsed sun, shedding all inhibitions. The dethroned upper class broke free of the Center, colliding with the streetside revelers like the tide, screaming for family members lost in the crash.

"Look at them," the Strange Man whispered into Earl's bleeding ear. "Here they stand, teetering over the mouth of hell, and yet they still refuse to bend their knees to God. Absolutely exquisite."

As the pandemonium invaded Main Street Greensboro, Sheriff Miller and those who chose to hide in the Center collected themselves. The shouts of the vacating townspeople could still be heard as a few loose stragglers pooled around him and his small band of deputies. Faces expectant, they waited for his command.

Two deputies, both armed with shotguns, hurried to his side from the back door. Both were covered in sweat and terror. "It's hell out there, Roy. Whole town's gone nuts."

Miller wasn't surprised. He expected that, now that the girl—and Earl, for that 'matter—had failed to kill the monster. "How many of our men out there?"

Mike Ortiz replied, "Can't tell. We think—" he hesitated, taking a breath, then rushed to finish, ashamed, "We think maybe they've *joined* them, sir."

Miller expected *that* too.

"What do we do?" his small following asked. He glanced around, spotting the esteemed reverend cowering behind a chair, mumbling to himself and twitching his head, as if shaking off invisible flies. *He's snapped*, Miller knew. Searching, he found Rosalyn still standing at the altar, staring up into the glass ceiling at the eclipsed sun beyond.

"What's happening?" Miller asked her in an even tone.

Rosalyn did not face him. "It's the end."

"Of what?" newly recovered Miss Jenkins asked, fanning her flushed face.

Rosalyn turned around, half of her face now slick black and drooping with tentacles. In her remaining human eye, tears welled.

"Of everything."

The violence that erupted at Greensboro Park Lake shocked Isabella in its matter-of-factness. Three quick stabs to the gut from a lake worshipper's blade left Gus Reynolds dead. Carter lost a finger on his left hand in the melée and Kurt Daughtry was wrapping strips of his shirt around the wound to serve as a tourniquet. Because of their reluctance to kill their enemy, the Havenites' war proved all the harder. Some were dead, many were wounded, but on they fought. The handful of casualties among the Strange Man's followers were mostly accidental; the result of enemies wrestling on the ground over a knife.

The Church was losing and the babies were still in danger.

The dark skies crackled with lighting and a deep, bass pulse rippled from the clouds, rumbling past the lake, stirring the trees. The Bearded Man, tears of bliss cascading down his aged cheeks, remained on his knees in quiet adoration of the haunted lake as two cult members broke from the attack and commenced with rolling the baby carriers to the edge of the shore.

"Yessss," the Bearded Man hissed. "Receive our offerings…"

Isabella took a hard right hook to the cheek that drew blood from her nose, and snarled in defiance as she let fly a side kick to the offending attacker. The cultie bent over, holding his stomach, and she kicked again, jabbing the toe of her boot into his groin. He rolled onto the ground with a groan and she spotted Jeff handling another robed villain. Taking her brief reprieve to survey the battlefield, she watched her friends fighting for their lives. They were outnumbered and she didn't know how they could win.

Then she heard the tiny cries anew.

Her heart fainted within her and she screamed, seeing the carriers inches away from the obsidian waters of the tainted lake. "Jeff! The babies!"

Without waiting for anyone else to act, she raced for them, crying. She could not see the faces of the men who were mere seconds away from feeding the babies to their doom and she was grateful. For, if they *did* survive this, she didn't think she would be able to stop hating those men.

I'm not going to make it. The terrifying recognition nearly buckled her otherwise strong legs and she felt numb down to her fingertips. A snake-like black tongue slithered out of the lake and greedily coiled around the nearest carrier's leg.

"Please, no…" she whimpered, leaping over the body of one of her friends and pushing on, dodging the clashes raging around the lake's edge.

Carter Ross bit down hard on a stick to master his pain as Kurt finished bandaging him. "That oughta hold for now," he said and Carter nodded, his face hot with torment. Before he could mutter his thanks, he saw Isabella speeding towards him, screaming in a way that broke his heart.

"Carter!" she wailed, madly pointing. "The babies!"

He spun and saw that the sacrifice was beginning.

"Don't let them get the babies!" Isabella screamed, balling.

In an instant, Carter was running for the lake's shore, his own pain forgotten.

The Bearded Man screeched, his shrill, deranged laughter filling the night. "Come, lord! Come and feast!"

The two hooded men beside him continued their mission, rock-faced and single-minded, submerging the front wheels of the first cart into the hungry lake. Carter was on them in a flash, pushing one of the men to the ground and seizing the bar of the carrier, pulling it back to shore. Isabella was close behind, gripping the remaining carrier by the side and jerking, steering against the strength of its driver.

"No!" she sobbed as she struggled. "Let them go! *Stop!*"

Carter had pulled his carrier a safe distance away when the cultist he pushed to the ground charged him, swinging fists. The bigger of the two, Carter easily dodged the limp attack and caught the man square in the side with a hard fist. The cultie coughed and fell over, in the process of pulling a knife from within his robes. Animal instinct on fire, Carter straddled the combatant, clasped his hands together, raised them high, and brought them down hard on the man's face. There was a sick *crack* but the man continued to struggle. Adrenaline surged through Carter's veins, warming his body and pushing him onward. He attacked the man again, terrified that if he let him back up, it would be the last mistake he ever made.

After four more strikes, the cultist grew quiet and still. Carter pulled back, his hands bloodied and shaking. His stomach lurched in revulsion at what he'd done. *I didn't have a choice*, he tried to tell himself. Even though it was true, he didn't feel any better.

With the cultist dead, Carter lifted the cowl and recognized the knife-wielding man as Metsy Buchanon, the guy who used to change his oil downtown. Carter hadn't known the guy very well, but they'd always made casual chit-chat and exchanged smiles. *He's dead. I killed him.*

Carter's body sagged with exhaustion and shame and he rolled off Metsy's remains. So much blood on his hands. Ed Mathers, Jake Tucker, Milton Wilbanks, Burt Simmons, and now Metsy Buchanon.

The sounds of the nearby struggle banished the painful memories of his mistakes and he realized that the last carrier was still in possession of the Strange Man's followers. Seeing that the babies he'd rescued were all right, he called out to Kurt Daughtry, who dodged private scuffles to join Carter on the edge of the lake.

"Take these kids! Go on!"

Kurt nodded wordlessly, gripped the bar on the carrier tight, and wheeled the babies away.

Carter breathed deep, feeling in some small way redeemed.

He wiped the blood from his hands onto his shirt and hurried to Isabella's aid. She was crying and shouting, an odd mix of terror and rage, and Carter stood by her side, taking firm hold of the remaining cart.

"I'm here!" he hollered, wanting to comfort her. "I've got it!"

Then he realized that the cult member that had previously hindered Isabella's rescue attempt was currently screaming and flailing on the ground as he was dragged by his feet into the dark waters of the lake and violently drowned. Isabella wasn't pulling the cart away from a man—

Isabella is fighting against the lake itself!

Black tentacles of uncompromising malice tugged at the carrier legs and Isabella screamed, "It's the lake! It's alive!"

Carter gasped at the sight of the sentient beast—that his own daughter had swum in on many a summer day—and nearly lost hold of the carrier. Isabella's panic and desperation commanded him to act, to help, and he tugged as hard as he could. Still, the lake held, and held tight.

To their left, the Bearded Man giggled, long lines of drool dangling from his mouth like a rabid dog. His wide eyes were wild and his body convulsed with elation.

"Yes! Feast, O lord! Feast on your sacrifice!"

Isabella screwed up her face, blinking past her tears of horror. "It's no use!" she yelled, but Carter had already reached that conclusion and was switching to his secondary plan.

Quickly, yet as gently as he could, he began scooping the wailing babes out of their blankets, taking a big armful of them, as many as he could carry without dropping one. Swearing in frustration, he spun to the waging battle behind him, eager to find a friendly face in the midst of the carnage. Finally he spotted Hank Berkley, using a downed branch from one of the many withered trees on the lake's edge to club a cultist, and shouted, "Hank! We need help!"

Hank gave a good *whap* to the side of his opponent's face and dropped the stick as he raced to Carter's aid.

"Take them!" he yelled.

Hank did the best he could and shouted at two other young Havenites who were responding to Carter's cry for help. Together, the four of them formed a sort of bucket brigade, emptying the carrier of its tiny passengers and scurrying them off into the night. At last, the babies were lifted from the death trap and Hank was left holding the last little one. With two babies in his arms, Carter lit off into the forest as the lake began to gurgle and moan, pulling itself up on gooey haunches and writhing in the shadow of the eclipse.

Isabella released the empty carrier and the lake's angry arm immediately smashed it against a tree. The lake roared, seeking its denied prey. Now fully congealed, it splayed out long, thick tentacles and latched onto the yellowed shore, pulling itself to dry land.

The mysterious Bearded Man fell into a reverent hush, watching in disbelief, then excitement, as his god took life. "Yes! Command me, my lord!"

The lake answered by raising an arm the width of a tree trunk high into the air, and unfurling it on top of the deranged cult leader, turning him to red pulp and forever silencing his exaltations. Isabella recoiled as the pagan priest's blood splattered her clothes. She tugged Hank's arm as she ran by. "Come on!"

Hank started after her, but stumbled, twisting his ankle. He let out a yelp and Isabella stopped to help him. "You okay?"

"I've had worse," he grumbled, standing. "Take the little one." He handed the baby to her.

As Hank extended his arms, though, a black tentacle shot through his chest with a wet *splurch*, reaching for the child. Isabella cradled the infant close to her bosom and turned to shield him.

When she turned back, Hank was pale, his body dragging against the ground, the viscous spike supporting his weight entirely.

"*Hank!*" Isabella screamed.

But Hank was already dead.

Isabella sank to her knees. "Oh, Hank…Hank…no…"

Then, in a cruel twist, the tentacle twitched and flung Hank's lifeless body far from the scene, unceremoniously re-depositing it somewhere in the North Woods beyond. Isabella jumped to her feet and with bitter rage roared at the lake, "Why won't you die!"

The possessed waters hurled a volley of sticky arms after her. Isabella ran for the forest, the hysterical baby in her arms. Crying almost as loudly herself, Isabella forged on, calling into the war around her, "Jeff…Jeff…" Fearing that her husband had died as unfairly as Hank had, she at last convinced herself not to look for him. The baby was what mattered now.

Carter emerged from the woods, drenched in sweat with a small light of hope in his eyes. "The babies are off. It's okay."

She handed him the infant from her arms and collapsed in despair. Carter took the child and looked up. "Where's Hank?"

Isabella only hid her face in the dirt, sobbing uncontrollably.

CHAPTER THIRTY-ONE

"WHAT DID YOU hope to accomplish here, hunter?" the Strange Man's black tongue hissed. Earl remained on his knees, the Bible in his hand, spellbound by the landscape of humanity at its worst. "What was Jeff Weldon's grand plan? For you to keep me busy while he and his followers stopped the sacrifice at the lake?"

Earl blinked back tears, finally realizing the futility of their entire rebellion. *He knew what they were up to all along…He just didn't care.*

"The sacrifice at the lake doesn't mean anything," the Strange Man scowled. "Just a test to see how far into degradation your town was willing to go. Let the Reverend stop the sacrifice. The damage has already been done. In their *hearts*, the town murdered their children. Sin begins in the heart and Greensboro is rotten to its core. The babies are inconsequential now. The town made its choice and must reap the consequences."

Earl hung his head. The Strange Man loomed over him, leering as if he savored the man's broken spirit. "I love seeing you Christians fail," the demon sang, trance-like. "The look on your faces when you realize all your faith is useless…simply priceless."

Earl squeezed his eyes shut, the sounds of screams and malicious laughter filling his mind. Defiant, he growled, "It's not all useless." Trembling, bracing for his death at any moment, Earl reached into his back pocket and retrieved a creased picture. He held it before the demon: an old photo of a younger Earl holding his baby son. "This is my boy. Charlie."

The Strange Man blinked in confusion.

Earl continued, his lip quaking, but his voice holding strong. "The day he was born was the best day of my life. The day you took him from me was the worst. But in between, I loved him with every bit of my heart, which is more than you'll ever be able to say. You're nuthin' but spite and rage and hate, and I was like you once, but then I realized God loves me more than I even loved my boy. So I guess, no matter what you do to me today, that puts me ahead of you." Earl grinned through happy, vindicated tears, "How's that for faith?"

The Strange Man reared back and raised a hand, his slick, glistening talons outstretched. His face a twisted mask of disgust and defeat, the monster growled, "When you see Him, tell Jehovah I'm sending home His saints today."

Earl held firm, ready to meet his Maker with no regrets, when the killing blow was suddenly averted by the sound of an approaching motor. When no claws rendered his skin, Earl glanced up to see the Strange Man's attention fixed on a church bus bumbling its way through the bedlam-ridden streets.

A sick smile split the monster's face. "Aaaaahhhh…this day gets better and better."

Deputy Hollis stood at the forefront of the bus, braced against the seats at either side of him, gently lurching to and fro. Father Joe did his best to carefully steer through the teeming mobs occupying Greensboro's Main Street, but only with great difficulty.

"Wow…" Hollis breathed, taking in the scene of people tearing the town apart.

Hollis turned and saw the occupants inside the bus lean into their windows, faces pressed to cold glass to get a look at the anarchy firsthand. Even the other deputies relaxed their guard on their prisoners, transfixed by the chaos all around them.

"What's going on?" Meredith Myers asked, breathless.

Jay Evans barked from the back, "Looks like the people got what they wanted."

Annie shot up, her eyes wide and urgent. "We have to help! This is it! This is the Dark Hour! We have to stop it!"

Rebecca Walker balanced Millie and Timmy on her knees,

holding them close to her chest. "*How?* If it's gotten this bad, then that means Jeff failed and it's too late anyway."

Annie snapped, in defense, "I don't believe that! There has to be a way to fix this!" She spun to Jack. "Do something, Mr. Weldon! I know you can!"

Jack Weldon was still seated next to Franklin under armed guard. He hung his head and said nothing. Hollis called back to Annie, "Sit down, girl. Everyone remain calm. We'll figure out what's going on."

"Father protect us," Father Joe gasped.

A scream tore through the bus behind the priest and everyone, including Hollis, huddled against the front windshield, paling in fright.

The Strange Man hovered before them, an island amidst the sea of raving people. Earl Canton lay at the demon's feet in a crumpled heap, alive but looking the worse for wear.

"It's him," Millie declared. "The bogeyman."

The Wilbanks girls whimpered, calling out for their father—whom Hollis understood was now one of those black-oil monsters—and Tessa tried to comfort them. Franklin cut hard eyes to young Hollis. "Well, Deputy, there's your Boss. What do you think of him now?"

Deputy Hollis stammered, perspiration beading on his forehead, his eyes darting from side to side. Eager gazes remained on him, waiting for him to answer.

Unable to bear the burden of their accusing stares any longer, Hollis stuttered, "I-I'll go check. I'll f-f-figure this out."

The few deputies standing beside him shared worried glances, hesitant to join him. "Come on," he commanded them with all the authority of an impotent child. "I ain't goin' out there by myself."

"I'd better stay with the prisoners, right?" one deputy towards the back volunteered, drawing burning eyes from his compatriots. Hollis flustered, pulled his belt a little higher, then stepped off the bus, his charges behind him. As one, the Havenites swarmed even closer to the front glass, eager to see what would happen next.

Hollis and his quivering group inched closer to the Strange Man, the deputies keeping considerable distance from their fearless leader.

"Why, Deputy," the Strange Man smiled, inclining his head ever so slightly to the left, "You've brought me presents."

Hollis swiveled to the bus full of frightened people. "Uh, y-yes, sir. I c-caught them trying to leave town, sir. B-Brought them back, just like you w-wanted."

"Excellent," the demon opened his arms, as if beckoning Hollis for a fatherly embrace. "What's the point of putting on such a grand show without a proper audience?"

From his place on the ground, bruised and bloodied Earl Canton shouted at the young deputy, "Get them outta here, ya dope!"

The Strange Man flicked a talon and violently backhanded the downed man, scattering him to the pavement. "Pay him no mind."

Hollis' wide and watery eyes glued themselves to Earl.

"Well, let's bring them out, shall we?" The Strange Man chuckled. "I want them to have the best seats for the grand finale."

Weak and blood-soaked, Earl watched Hollis with pleading eyes. The young deputy's heart boomed in his chest, but he finally turned his horrified attention to the Strange Man. "B-but, sir. There's a bunch of little kids in there. It's not…it's not safe out here," he said, his voice nearly drowned by the screams and laughter of the damned. "Shouldn't we…?" Hollis trailed off, throwing helpless glances at his fellow lawmen, praying one of them would back him up. No one spoke. All eyes remained on the ground. Hollis gulped, facing the Strange Man once more to catch the demon in a hateful snarl.

"Shouldn't you *what*, Deputy? Leave?"

"They're just kids, sir."

The Strange Man's yellow eyes burned bright, dark shadows spilling down his gaunt face. His snarl opened and sharp teeth extended. From deep in his throat, the sound of a tornado barreled for the surface. Hollis shrank back in fear, the deputies at his rear scattering like frightened sheep, lost to the chaos of Greensboro. The young deputy stood alone, shivering in place, as the Strange Man stood over him like a cold and growing shadow.

At just the time Hollis thought his meager defiance would cost him his life, a fresh wave of terrified shrieks sounded from the Center's entrance. The Strange Man paused, jerking towards the sight of Sheriff Miller and three deputies retreating backwards down the steps, firing their sidearms at…*something coming out of the church*, Hollis marveled in revolt and fascination.

The Thing was as tall as a house and crawling on glittering black-green tentacles. Even more tentacles whipped out, catching Deputy Ortiz full force in the torso and jettisoning him across the street as he screamed. The slippery, coiling Thing was made even more hideous by the fact that Rosalyn Myers was somehow—*impossibly*—attached to its "head". In fact, the Thing seemed to *grow* out of Rosalyn's left temple. Her body hung in the air, limp and flailing with each step the Abomination took. And the Thing had eyes. Teeth.

As soon as Hollis took in the full sight, he turned away and retched.

The Strange Man called out lovingly to the Thing, "Ah, there's my princess! You are looking lovely, my dear."

From her place in the bus, Annie quickly turned away, only able to look at the Thing out of the corner of her eyes, fearful to stare directly into its many eyes and swirling limbs. "Rosalyn," she breathed, her stomach twisting in knots. "What did you do…?"

CHAPTER THIRTY-TWO

HANK WAS DEAD. Carter could tell just by the hopeless look on Isabella's face.

Hank...

He'd served with Hank as a deputy. They'd been friends. They'd fought and joked and caught bad guys together.

Isabella was doubled over on the ground, weeping uncontrollably—broken.

Kurt came up behind Carter and tapped him on the shoulder, palpitating. "We're going. Is that the last of them?"

Carter nodded, his nose stinging and his eyes moistening. He gave Kurt the child and nodded towards the forest. "Go on. Just go."

Kurt didn't ask questions. He took the little one—the last baby to be rescued from the lake beast—and rushed to safety. Isabella cried so hard that she seemed to almost stop breathing.

"It's madness," she barely gasped. "So much..."

Carter dipped to his knees and gripped her arms tight. "Stop it! Do you hear me? Stop crying!"

"Hank's dead..."

"But *we're* not! These people need us, so *stop it!*"

Still she would not look up. As long as Carter had been at the Haven, Isabella had been the quiet strength of the group, the fierce lioness unshakable in her faith. They'd butted heads, but he respected her incredibly.

But it seemed that, at the end, Isabella had had enough. She had been strong long enough. Had fought as hard as she could for as long as she could, but it was all gone now. Her strength, her courage. Her defeat pained him to a depth he'd not expected.

He stood to his feet, surveying the apocalypse by the light of

Jeff's Day-Lights. The dark monster that had once been the lake was now fully ashore and trampled cultist and Havenite alike, its tentacles lashing out in a blitzkrieg of death, snatching up victims. Some were pulled apart, some were flung haphazardly, and some were merely used as blunt weapons to pummel others. Wails from the dying and peals of terrified howls from the pursued echoed across the darkness at Greensboro Park.

The world had spiraled into hell and he was helpless to save it. Only a miracle would rescue them now.

Then, over the commotion of the lake's rampage, Carter heard the amazing. A loud, throaty holler, shouting over the din of the others. "*Fortify!*"

Caught by the sound, Carter looked across the distance and could just make out the silhouettes of survivors rushing like an avalanche towards the two-story wood and stone pavilion that housed the Greensboro Park Lake banquet area.

A smile fought through his tears and turmoil, and Carter grinned.

"It's Jeff," he breathed, his heart burning anew. "He's still fighting."

"Then what are we waiting for?"

Carter turned and saw Isabella standing, wiping the grime from her face, her breath hitching, but her sobs gone. "Let's go help him."

He marveled at her newfound determination. "Welcome back."

Deputy Hollis used his sleeve to wipe the vomit from the corners of his mouth. The Strange Man continued to face the Thing on the steps to the Center, lavishing in its obscenity, and Hollis—newly possessed of a sobered mind—hurried to Earl's aid. With a heave, the young deputy helped Earl to his feet.

"Come on," Hollis said, his voice cracking with fear. "We have to go."

"That thing…" Earl's voice trailed off in awe as his sight fell upon the coiled mass of tentacles—

"Don't look at it!" Hollis commanded, sounding braver than he felt. "Just head for the bus!"

"So glad to see that you've decided to change into something more comfortable," the Strange Man spoke to Rosalyn, he at the foot of the steps and she twisting and writhing at the top. Like Romeo beneath Juliet's balcony, the Strange Man held his hand to her in adulation. "Come, my love. Let's raise some hell."

Hollis and Earl slipped behind the hellborn Lothario, and the deputy thought for a moment that they might actually make it to the bus and drive away from this madhouse.

But then he heard the Shamblers.

More than a hundred Shamblers galloped for the Center, bellowing and snorting and snapping with their faceless black maws. Hollis fumbled for his gun and took jittery aim against the beastly mob. "N-No! Stay back!"

As they neared, the creatures flopped to the concrete, throwing themselves before Hollis. It seemed as though his courage had brought them to their knees, until Earl tugged on his coat.

"Look…"

Hollis turned and saw that the Shamblers were bowing before the Rosalyn-Thing. The Strange Man, having completely lost interest in Hollis and Earl, presented the black monsters to Rosalyn. "Look at them. They fear and loathe you. Worship and adore you. They are your children and your slaves and you, my sweet, are their Queen."

The Shamblers rose as one unified body and howled pitifully in terrified praise.

Hollis could not speak, their dreadful moaning reducing him to tears.

Now it was Earl's turn to pull on the deputy. "Come on, boy! The bus!"

Hollis allowed himself to be half-dragged towards the church bus, as the Shambler herd crowed under the starless night. Jack Weldon and Franklin Whitaker waited at the steps of the bus to receive Hollis and Earl. Once the two were safely inside, Annie screamed to Jack, "What are we going to do?"

To Hollis's dismay, the old preacher remained silent.

Christopher stood atop God's Cliff, hands thrust into his trenchcoat pockets. Even from this considerable distance, he heard the screams of the rioting masses and saw their bonfires lighting up the night.

"Let there be another way," he mumbled under his breath, saddened by the debauchery playing out below.

The van pulled to a stop behind him, spewing loose gravel. The driver's side door opened and slammed shut and Reid joined Christopher overlooking Greensboro.

"It's time," Reid said quietly.

"We gave it a good run, didn't we?"

"Some people just don't want to be saved, Chrysti. We've seen this all before."

Christopher sighed, his shoulders drooping. "What happens now? We destroy the town and they rebuild? Then what? We show up in another hundred years when Cal decides to pull this stunt again?" The somber angel darkened. "I'm tired of this. I…I really thought this time would be different."

"I know you did. I guess that's what we get for placing our faith in humans." Reid extended his hand, palm up. "Ready?"

Christopher regarded his partner, frowning. He grasped Reid's hand.

A tumultuous thunderclap rippled through the air as the dark clouds parted. A lone pillar of twirling flame descended from the sky.

Will Baxter knelt alone in the Center sanctuary, his face moist with tears as he faced the ground. He wept for himself and wondered what he might do to one day make up for all that he had committed in the name of his dark master.

From high above, Will heard a high-pitched whine, growing closer like a cyclone. Tears streaking his face, he looked up and beheld the fireball plummeting towards the Center skylight.

Aimed right at him.

Jeff Weldon marched along the battle line that had been drawn at the pavilion's stone foundation, shouting to the last of his troops. His brow was cut and blood ran down his temple, obscuring his vision. A hard throbbing pounded in his foot and he felt sure there was a break down there somewhere, but he pushed the pain out of his mind. The lake beast—the collection of his town's secret sins given shape—slithered towards them like a gelatinous fog bank. Its leathery tentacles shattered trees and tore deep grooves in the soft earth as it pulled its slimy bulk onshore, thirsty for revenge against those who had taken away its offering.

Jeff could see and hear the people giving in to blind terror as the gorging monster approached. Trying to salvage their morale, Jeff barked, "Christ gave Himself as an offering for our sin! We're free from its power! Don't be afraid! Hold your ground!"

They did, trembling where they stood, and prayed.

Some of the surviving cultists fell prostrate before Jeff as if he could save them. "Forgive us, Reverend Weldon! Ask God to forgive us!"

Jeff considered them briefly. "Get behind the line with the others. Go!" They cowered behind the army of praying believers as Jeff roared, "That's it! Pray! Everyone pray!"

The Havenites took hands and bowed, praying against the beast. Jeff literally felt the wave of hope and life returning as the sounds of weeping subsided, replaced by reverent murmuring of earnest prayers. Even the remaining cultists, huddled in the nooks of the pavilion, were audibly praying for forgiveness, returning to God's mercy.

Tendrils snapped around the Havenites, but the line held. Not a man was plucked from the fold. It seemed that the lake beast had found its boundary and could go no further, reduced to high-pitched screeching and wild, impotent flailing. The thing was stuck, pinned to the earth by the power of God.

"Jeff!"

He spun and saw Carter and Isabella hurrying towards him. His heart melted at the sight of his wife, and he rushed to her. She met him halfway. Their arms found each other, and they held close. "Are you okay?" he asked, his resolve weakening.

Isabella pulled from him, held the side of his face, and whispered through tears, "Hank's dead."

Jeff faltered and felt bile rise in his throat. He couldn't breathe. Couldn't think.

"I'm sorry," she sobbed.

"No, no, no," he whimpered, pulling her to him, "It's not your fault…"

"I don't understand," Carter cut in, angry. "The babies are safe. We stopped the sacrifice! Why isn't this going away?"

Jeff shook his head, despair struggling to take hold in his heart. "I don't know…there must be something we missed. The Strange Man must have a backup plan or something—"

"Look!" a cultist yelled, pointing to the skies.

That's when he heard the first explosion from Greensboro. Everyone turned their eyes south to town where, to their grief and astonishment, fire rained from heaven.

"We're too late…" one of the Havenites said.

"It didn't work," mourned another.

One by one, fireballs fell from the sky, accompanied by fantastic eruptions. Their reverent silence was shattered by the shrill, ground-quaking cries of the lake-creature. It reared back and gave a terrified squeal before oozing back towards the lakebed where it hid.

Jeff watched as another ball of fire splashed against the horizon, sending up a conflagration that lit the dark sky. *Dras…Rosalyn…*

His chest hurt and his head swooned. Were they gone? Had Dras found Rosalyn? Were they together when the end came?

Isabella touched his arm. "I'm sure he made it out in time."

He hesitated, torn between seeing his wife to safety and watching out for his brother. He'd spent a lifetime watching out for his brother and, now, when Dras needed him the most, he couldn't be there for him.

"Yeah…" he finally agreed, on the verge of tears.

Then Jeff heard the bat-like squeals. The bleating of muscular wings. The *fhroo-fhroo* of cold air.

Barely visible in the stray beams of the Day-Lights, he glimpsed the TJ Creature.

"We're not out of this yet!"

CHAPTER THIRTY-THREE

THE FAMILY WORSHIP Center detonated in a shower of mortar and splinters. The Strange Man stood before the exquisite devastation, his eyes closed and his arms welcoming, as shrapnel ricocheted off his invincible form. The Havenites on board the bus dropped to the floor as the windows shattered in explosive array.

Annie was the first to her feet amidst the dazed and weeping Havenites. She staggered to the door, her ears still ringing from the blast, and searched the blazing remains of the Center.

"Rosalyn!" she screamed, then choked on black smoke. "*Rosalyn!*"

Her eyes stung and she blinked back tears, batting away at the smoke. "Where are you?"

There, in the charcoal plumes that emanated from the smoking foundation into the darkened sky, Annie spotted the tentacled shape of her sister, grappling to a nearby building and swinging out of sight.

"Roz!" she shouted, stumbling off the bus. "Wait! Come back!"

Another roaring wind sounded overhead seconds before the next fireball leveled a building across the street. The bang rocked the pavement, sending frightened rioters fleeing in all directions. Annie toppled over, her world turned upside down, and hacked against the smoke and dust invading her lungs.

"Annie!" she heard Franklin call from the bus.

She squinted in the swirling haze, realizing she'd wandered from the safety of the bus and became suddenly desperate to find her way back. Back to her mother. "Mom!" she screamed hoarsely.

Without warning, slick black spindly appendages wrapped around her arm with a sickening *schlap*. In an instant, creatures within the dark fog violently jerked her into the abyss.

The TJ Creature dove for the earth, its milky eyes scouring the land, looking for prey. "It's okay!" Jeff shouted, parting from his wife. "He hunts by fear! If you aren't afraid he can't see you! Keep praying!"

The faithful gathered by the pavilion did just that, but Jeff knew it was not easy. Their faith masked them from the Creature's sight, but the field was littered with the fearful and dying. After landing, the Creature swooped through the landscape like the Grim Reaper, using its sickle-like elbow blades to cut down the wounded. Jeff shut his eyes against the sight, determined not to see the Creature's merciless butchery, but could not drown out the death warbles of the slain. Carter turned on him, mortified. "Can't we do something?"

His stomach lurched, but Jeff took a deep, resolved breath, knowing his fear could bring the Creature their way. The men lined against the pavilion's walls covered their ears and continued praying, miserable tears rolling down their hardened faces.

"I can't watch this anymore," Carter balled up his hands and made to march out and fight the Creature. Jeff held him back, pointing to the towering, tentacled lake monster on the sidelines.

"No! If you get to close to that thing, you'll be dead in a second!"

Carter watched on in helpless agony as the Creature slew the last of the injured troops, curling his fists until his knuckles turned white.

The man who had alerted the others to the rain of fire confronted Jeff. "We're going to die if we just sit here, you idiot! Run!"

Without waiting for an argument, the man took off.

"Wait!" Jeff held his hand to stop him, but the man broke through the ranks, tearing from the pavilion. He was immediately caught up in a quick lash of the lake-thing's membranous tentacle.

Screeching as he was yanked into the sky, the man was pulverized in the anaconda-like arm before the others had a chance to understand what happened. But the damage was already done. As they realized that the lake was still in the fight, fear entered the camp.

And the TJ Creature's eyes were opened.

Its black lips pulled back to reveal long, bone slivers for teeth and it scanned the area, desperate to pick up the scent again. Some of the men stopped praying and looked ready to run if the beast caught sight of them.

"Hold your ground!" Carter waved them back. "Don't be afraid!"

The TJ Creature leaned forward with a menacing sneer, flapping once and landing in the midst of the small crowd. Its arms outstretched, elbow-blades dangerously close, it reached at empty air, trying to find its invisible adversaries. Jeff put Isabella behind him and whispered to the others, even though he knew the Creature was as deaf as he was blind. "Everybody calm down. Wait for him to pass."

The beast snarled and jerked to the right, slashing out with its pincers, blindly striving to make contact. Its bone blades were so close that one woman had to jump back to keep herself from being split open. On tiptoes, the people backed away, circling the beast as it moved throughout their camp, gnashing and snapping, striking at nothing. The remaining Havenites and cultists held their collective breaths as they shied away from the predator in a life-or-death game of Marco Polo, but as the monster neared a younger Havenite, the man cracked.

"It sees me!"

With a throaty, "Haaah!" the TJ Creature caught the young Havenite, lifting him by the throat. With a vicious squeeze, it broke the man's neck and tossed his body to the lake-monster, which caught it and smashed it into the dirt. Many panicked, and the towering bat-man found itself in the midst of a hysterical crowd, a smile pulling on its face.

"Wait!" Jeff yelled. "Calm down! Everyone calm down!"

Some of them ran into the open, preferring to take a chance at outrunning the lake's arms. They failed and paid with their lives.

Others tried to climb the side of the pavilion, looking to escape over the roof, but the Creature simply seized their legs and pulled down, slaughtering them as they struggled to get to their feet.

Isabella panicked, herself, seeing the tide of battle turning so suddenly. She clutched her stomach, eyes wide and tear-filled. Jeff's met them, dark understanding dawning.

"The baby!" she whispered.

Carter looked between the two of them. "*What?*"

Jeff's heart broke, seeing Isabella shaking with fear. "She's pregnant," he said, revealing what Isabella had only told him the night before.

His wife wept. "I'm scared, Jeff. I can't help it. Don't let it take our baby!"

Jeff felt a tickle of fear inside him, but found that his most prevalent emotion was anger. Anger at his people for not listening to him. Anger at the monsters that had made his home into their own private hunting grounds. His hands became fists and he steeled himself. He had had enough. Live or die, it was time to end this.

But Carter beat him to the punch.

"AAH!" Carter roared, tackling the TJ Creature to the ground. "Run! Get her out of here!" He raised both hands together and brought them down like a hammer on the Creature's face. "Die!" he screamed. "DIE!"

Once the surprise faded, the Creature caught both of Carter's arms in one firm grip and, with its other hand pushed the Havenite clear. Carter bellowed as he flew through the air, landing somewhere on the other side of the pavilion. With a flap of its wings, the Creature righted itself and resumed its hunt.

Its eyes narrowed, focusing on Isabella.

She screamed as it licked its lips, marching for her. Jeff grabbed her arm and pulled. "Hurry to the truck!"

The Creature gnashed violently and, in an instant, flapped its wings and headed straight for Isabella. Jeff threw himself in front of her as she cried out, but the Creature twisted in the air, circumventing him and landing squarely on top of Isabella. Wrapping its long, slender fingers around her throat, the beast strangled. She gasped and coughed through tears, but the killing machine easily overpowered her.

"Get off!" Jeff cried, beating at the monster's back with his fists and feet.

Not her! I can't lose her!

But the Creature squeezed, its wild, unblinking eyes focused on Isabella's, watching the life flutter out of her. Jeff wept tears of rage, regret, and loss, struggling uselessly against the monster. Isabella's fingers dug in the dirt, grasping for life, as death encircled its icy talons around her throat.

"*No!*"

Finally, her fingers stopped.

Her eyelids fluttered and, after one horrifying gasp, she breathed no more.

Jeff stood there, his whole body shaking, his vision blurry with tears. *God, please no…*

Meredith wasted no time in running out of the Havenite bus, wailing into the murky night. "Annie! Annie!"

"Back on the bus!" Franklin urged as Greensboro was destroyed around her.

"Not without my daughter!" she sank to her knees, grief consuming her.

Franklin limped down the steps, cold determination etched in his heart. "I'll get her," he said, ready to storm off into the smoke, when another fireball ignited the block three streets down. Meredith tumbled backwards, but Rebecca was there, helping her up. Franklin lifted Annie's mother to her feet and the duo half-carried the woman back onto the bus to an available seat.

"Are you all right?" Franklin asked as Meredith reeled from the concussive force.

"Please," she whimpered. "Please get my daughter. I can't lose her too."

"I will," he promised as Rebecca stood, alert, searching the dirtied faces on board.

"Franklin?" she asked, her voice rising with panic. "Where's Millie?"

"There!" Father Joe pointed through the front windshield into the smoke enshrouded streets. Rebecca screamed.

Little Millie Walker ran full force towards the Shamblers.

"*Millie!*"

Its work finished and its thirst satisfied, the TJ Creature slowly stood to its full stature, stepping over Isabella's body and turning back to her grieving husband, heaven's fiery retribution lighting the sky like distant fireworks.

Jeff looked at the beast, shocked beyond hate. Beyond thought.

Isabella—their unborn child—had been murdered right before his eyes…His whole world was dead.

He felt no fear—felt nothing at all—and simply vanished from the Creature's radar. The brute lumbered away, distracted by other would-be victims like a dog nosing around for a bone.

But Jeff was not done with the monster. His teeth gritted together, the skin on his knuckles tightening, he stalked for the Creature, determined now. They'd failed. The Dark Hour was upon them. His friends were dead. His wife…*Our baby*…

He faltered in his thought, tears burning.

Dras was probably dead, too. Greensboro would be gone within the hour. None of his hard work mattered anymore.

Crazed with desperation, he blocked the Creature's path. Even now it didn't see Jeff, just stared dumbly at space, sniffing the air for fearful stragglers. Jeff reared back, cocking his fist and ready to unload. Ready to beat at this thing, to tear it down, until it was dead.

Yet, as he glared at it, he couldn't strike.

The big dumb thing looked lost and ignorant. Its face—

gruesome as it was—appeared almost childlike and oblivious to the misery it was creating.

TJ's under there, a warm spirit reminded Jeff. TJ Walker, whose mother and sister loved him very much, despite his sins. *Rebecca loves him…He's her son…*

Jeff thought of the baby in Isabella's womb who would die soon now that Iz was…The child that they'd prayed for for years…

Could he take another's child just as ruthlessly?

He lowered his fist, biting his lip, his hate giving way to pity. Then, oddly enough, to compassion.

"I forgive you," he uttered through bitter, angry tears. The Creature looked left and right, deaf to Jeff's words, just a stupid animal now. Not a killer. Not a demon. Just a man—no, a *boy*—corrupted by hate, victimizing others out of his own hurt.

"You killed Danny," he sobbed, "…but I forgive you."

The beast snorted, as if catching a foul stench.

"You killed Isabella," Jeff wiped at his wet face, voice cracking. "…but I forgive you."

TJ snapped now, letting out a low, confused growl.

"You killed…" Jeff thought of his baby he'd never see now. His beautiful child he'd never be able to hold. So many things he wanted to do as a father. "You killed my baby…but I…"

I can't God. I can't forgive him for that. I can't—

But in his heart he heard *"You have to, Jeff. Let him have it all."*

"I…" he blubbered, his chest heaving, but felt strength renewed. Felt God soothing his heart, working through Him. "I forgive you…"

Jeff took TJ's face in his hands and forced their eyes to meet. The beast snarled and jerked, but Jeff held him in place. "I forgive you," he said again, stronger now, his voice strange and calm, even to his own ears.

To his astonishment, the pinkish hue of TJ's face returned and spread. The black goo hissed like steam and slowly seeped back into the boy's pores. When Jeff had punched that Shambler a couple days ago, the sin goo had clung to him like paste—bonding to his anger. But, love—mercy—seemed to have the opposite effect, *repelling* it. For how long, Jeff didn't know. He couldn't absolve another man of his sins, but perhaps he could take the sting out of it, if only for a time.

TJ fought against the change, growling and shouting, but Jeff would not let go. "I forgive you, TJ." The wings bent and folded, shriveling to charcoal and breaking off TJ's back. His bone blades rattled and sheathed in his arms. The sludge retreated into his body and Jeff was staring at TJ Walker again, still in the jersey and shorts he'd worn ten months ago when his master, the Strange Man, had come to set him on the path that would transform him into the Creature.

At last Jeff released him, and the boy looked at his pink flesh as if for the first time in years. TJ blinked back his bewilderment and looked to Jeff, quiet. "What—what did you do?"

Seeing that the Creature was "dead", the Havenites shouted for joy, returning to the safety of the pavilion, away from the lake's reach.

TJ looked at his hands. His voice was soft and uncertain. "What…" He grew increasingly heated. "What did you *do*?"

Jeff leveled at the boy. "It's over, TJ."

TJ stormed for him, powerless now. "*What did you do?* I had *everything!* I was strong again! You took that away from me!"

"We're not afraid of you anymore, TJ. You can't hurt us now."

The boy looked about to cry, miserable. "You ruined everything!"

TJ pulled his fist back as if to attack, but Jeff stood his ground. The boy faltered, staggered back, then ran into the woods, cursing and shouting in hopeless failure, lost in the shadows.

Jeff hung his head, the battle over. For him, at any rate. There was nothing left to do but return to Isabella's side and wait for the Dark Hour to destroy them all…

But as he faced her body, he saw Carter, returned from the fight, bent over her, breathing into her mouth. Jeff scrambled for him. "What are you—?"

"Help me!" Carter shouted back, then reached over Isabella again, cradling her neck in his hand, touching his lips to hers, and breathing.

CPR. Jeff rushed to Isabella's chest, pressing his palms together on her breastbone. "What do I do?" he stammered.

Carter finished breathing and sat up. "Seven quick pushes. Count 'em off."

Jeff did, trying to remember what little he'd seen from the movies and hoping that God would provide the rest. "One. Two. Three. Four. Five. Six. Seven."

Carter leaned forward and breathed again. Sitting up, he nodded. "Again."

"One. Two. Three. Four. Five. Six. Seven."

Another breath. "Do it again!"

Jeff and Carter repeated the procedure focused only on their task. Helpless, the others circled the woman and prayed. What seemed like hours rolled by, the only sound in the air Jeff's counting as he fought to bring the love of his life back from the dead.

Carter jerked upright. "Iz…?"

Her eyes fluttered opened. She coughed for air.

Jeff laughed hysterically, bursting into uncontrollable tears, and threw himself over her, holding her, kissing her. Isabella put one arm around her husband and held him close.

Carter wiped the sweat from his face and stood, taking a breath.

Clutching his wife, Jeff looked to his friend. "Thank you."

Carter nodded and sat on the ground, utterly exhausted. "No problem."

Franklin bounded down the steps after Millie. Rebecca was frozen on the bus, begging him to save her little girl. The bus broke out in tearful murmurs. Finally, Jack Weldon pushed through the crowd, preparing to leave the bus to aid Franklin. He'd stood by long enough. He had to pitch in. Louise reached for him, her nails digging into his arm. "Jack," she breathed, her eyes fearful. Always so scared to lose him. "No…please stay."

Jack thought of his sons. They were out there somewhere, fighting. Maybe even dying. All so Greensboro might have a chance to live. *It should be me out there*, he told himself. *I'm as good as dead anyway.*

"No, Louise," he told her, his mind made up. "It's time to let me go."

Louise's grip on his arm slowly loosened and she stepped back, weeping as Jack slipped from her fingers, turned his back on the life they had made together, and ventured outside into the black beyond.

This old dog ain't dead yet.

Shrieking helplessly, Annie clawed at the pavement as the Shamblers dragged her into their numbers.

"Yes," the Strange Man cooed, floating around the twitching dark shapes, watching them toy with the young girl. "She is your Queen's *sister*. Destroy her and your Queen will reward you with unspeakable tortures in retribution." Annie watched in shock as the slavering, writhing beasts wailed and slapped themselves with long obsidian arms, beating against their backs and chests as the world turned to blinding fire around them. "That's what you desire, isn't it?" The Strange Man circled them, stroking their glossy, bald heads delicately. "You crave your own destruction. You welcome it, for you are most wretched. Not even your God wants you now." The beasts moaned, low pitiful groans, and Annie wept for these terrible things.

Millie emerged from the thick gray clouds, the sky behind her dazzling with another heaven-sent ball of flame. Panicked townsfolk took shelter as the bank down the street erupted in blazing shards. Millie remained unfazed by the impact, pushing onward. She aimed a chubby finger at the Strange Man, bold as a lioness protecting her cub. "You get away from her!"

The Shamblers snapped and hissed at the toddler, reeling Annie in to enclose her in a defensive circle. "Millie!" she screamed. "Go! Run away!"

"No," Millie declared defiantly. The Strange Man hovered to her, dragging his toes along the ground.

"Well, if it isn't the tiny titan." The demon clacked his skeletal hands together.

"I'm not afraid of you," she said.

The bogeyman halted. "Yes. But you cannot save your friend, little one. You can't save *anyone.*"

"Millie," Franklin huffed, limping to the girl and scooping her up in his arms. He held her close, turning away from the Strange Man to shield the youngster. A moment later, Jack stepped into view at Franklin's side. His cobalt blue eyes leveled solidly on the demon and Annie saw the Strange Man's sneer falter.

Annie couldn't help but grin. Through her frightened tears, she glared at the Strange Man. "Now it's *your* turn to be afraid."

CHAPTER THIRTY-FOUR

DRAS WELDON RODE into town on his bike just as a fireball the size of a Buick spectacularly ripped apart the Courthouse where he was convicted and dubbed "The Greensboro Ripper". The clock tower on the Courthouse dislodged from the flaming debris and hurtled headlong into Dras's path. With a surprised yelp, he yanked the handlebars and narrowly avoided the clock face as it collided with the pavement and rolled into Don the barber's storefront window.

Another comet lit up the sky, zeroing in somewhere over the horizon. In the moment he sacrificed to gaze up at the beautiful—yet terrifying—image, he caught a strange shape against the flickering light. His eyes narrowed against the wind and he made out what seemed to be Rosalyn. It looked like a black octopus was carrying her in spindly arms.

"Rosalyn!" he shouted, equal parts thrilled and fearful, and steered the bike towards the retreating beast. "Hold on!"

Christopher's eyes shot open, breaking his concentration. "Wait!"

Reid opened his eyes too, turning to his partner, startled. "What?"

"It's Dras," the angel said, breathless. "He's down there."

"What's he *doing*?" Reid growled, stepping closer to the edge of God's Cliff, peering down as though he might spot Dras in the fiery bedlam below.

"He's come back for the girl." Christopher grinned. "He won't give up. Maybe there's hope for the town, after all."

Reid leveled a disapproving stare over the rim of his glasses.

"Chrysti…we have orders."

"We have orders to *save* this town. If it's by fire, then so be it. But if there's another way…"

The other angel shook his long, unwashed locks. "You never quit on them, do you? They're humans. You can't trust them."

Christopher pursed his lips. "God does." The angel turned back to the van, his trenchcoat billowing in the hard winds of the Dark Hour. "Ease off the bombardment for now. Give the kid a fighting chance."

"Where are you going?" Reid called after him.

Christopher slid open the side hatch on the van and reached for the radio. He regarded his partner with a mischievous grin. "Time to check in with the General."

"So, you're the one who's been hurting my family," Jack spoke conversationally to the demon, mindful of Annie still held in the clutches of the Shamblers. Presently the Shamblers looked utterly confused, recoiling in terror with every distant explosion.

"I'm afraid we haven't been properly introduced," the Strange Man said, his tone almost reverent.

"Jack Weldon," Jack replied gruffly. "You've been giving my boys a hard time."

The Strange Man laughed, as though speaking to an old friend. "I should say so. They're quite the handful. You should be proud."

Jack responded without hesitation. "I am." Turning to Franklin, he jerked his chin back towards the bus. "Take the child. I'll handle this."

"You sure?" Franklin asked. Across town, something else ignited.

Jack nodded. Franklin hurried off, but Millie called to Jack over his shoulder. "The shiny monsters! They need a daddy! They just forgot!"

Jack weighed the girl's words, then faced the Strange Man. "Let Annie go."

"What does it matter? You'll all soon perish." The Strange Man gestured theatrically to the devastation occurring around him. "I'd give this place another five minutes. Tops."

"I'm not impressed."

The monster chuckled, inaudible against the explosions. He shouted to be heard over the escalating noise. "You fought a good fight, Reverend Weldon. I had plans to bring all of this upon you much, *much* sooner, but the faith of this town kept me at bay for far too long. A faith that *you* did much to encourage. Were it not for you, this town would have shriveled up and died long ago."

Jack steeled himself, despite the guilt he felt. For leaving the pulpit. For getting sick.

For getting old.

Suddenly, a wave of depression crashed against his soul, threatening to carry him out to the sea of despair. He thought of his children—of the world he was leaving behind for them. He was going to die, going to be with the Lord, but what would become of his boys? *Just war against monsters like this?*

I'm not going out without a fight.

Jack clenched his fists, feeling vigorous youth returning to his long-lived bones, *pushing* out the cancer—if only for this one moment in time. The pain simply melted away, fleeing from his body, and he felt a man half his age, ready to right the wrongs of the world. Ready to start a revolution. And he saw his opportunity right in front of him. Not the crooked demon hovering before him, nearly salivating in the midst of all the ruin, but the no-faced black-oil beasts cowering in fear at the raining heavens.

The Shamblers.

Millie's words came back to him, a hard slap to his senses. *"They need a daddy! They just forgot!"*

An old Scripture awakened in his preacher's heart. 2 Chronicles 7:13 and 14. He recalled the Lord's familiar words to Solomon at the dedication of the Temple. In the shadow of this eclipse, while God brought divine judgment against a town corrupted by hellish evil, the words took on new, powerful meaning.

He stepped forward, boldly approaching the snapping maws of the Shamblers. They hissed at him, their tri-tails rising up like rattlesnakes, and poised to strike, but Jack did not fear. Faith emanated off him in waves and the Strange Man inched back, unable to intervene. "What are you doing, old man?"

Jack ignored him. He held out his hands, as if in surrender, edging closer to the Shambler nest. "Listen to me!" he proclaimed with authority, the old lion within shaking the dust and age from his mane, ready to roar once more. "I know you feel lost. You feel shame. But it doesn't matter what you did that brought you to this place. It doesn't even matter what you've done since. I know that somewhere in there, there are still people who hurt and want that hurt to go away. God can forgive you. You can be the people you once were."

The Shamblers' hissing subsided, replaced by low growls. The hunkered things regarded one another, as if in suspicion of these words, but their writhing and twitching had all but faded. Becoming calm, they regarded the aged man, once more.

"What are you doing?" Annie shrieked at him.

Jack recalled the scripture from memory, having preached on this passage many times in his life, as he carefully touched one of the Shamblers. "In 2 Chronicles 7:13 and 14, God told the Israelites, 'When I shut up the heavens so that there is no rain, or command locusts to devour the land or send a plague among my people, if *my people who are called by my name*, will humble themselves and pray and seek my face and turn from their wicked ways, then will I hear from heaven and will forgive their sin and will heal their land.

"We don't need the whole town to repent to save us," Jack told Annie. "We just need God's people to return to Him." He smiled warmly at the Shambler before him. "*These* are God's people too."

The Strange Man hurried to the Shambler pack, frantic. "Don't listen to him! You are damned! You are lost!"

"God still loves you," Jack said louder, focusing on the monsters, caressing the smooth surface of the nearest Shambler, not repulsed, but caring. "You were part of His flock once. Just call out to Him. Let Him forgive you, folks. Forgive *yourselves.*"

Jack removed his hand, and the demon and preacher both held their breath in the silence that followed. Even Annie remained still, her unblinking eyes on the beasts around her. Suddenly, one by one, the Shamblers fell to their knees, raised their featureless faces to the heavens, and released a mourning cry.

"No!" the Strange Man bellowed.

"Annie!" Jack shouted. She snapped to, slipped through the Shambler horde, and clung to his arms. The two of them looked skyward, watching as the eclipse slowly passed. They shielded their eyes as the first blasts of bright sunlight broke through the gloom and the fires from heaven ceased falling.

Shamblers continued to cry, their inhuman wailing becoming more human. The black goo that had enclosed them in pain and misery began to melt, driven back by the bright light of the sun. Sludge dripped away and human faces met beautiful blue sky once again.

The remaining slime coalesced into a single thick, snake-like entity. It shrieked against the light and tried to slither away, but was immediately cooked by the sun, shriveling to a hard black crust before collapsing into fine black ash that drifted away in the breeze.

Across town, the Leviathan of Greensboro Park Lake trembled and roared against the invading day. Jeff and the others watched as, caught in the eye of God and unable to hide, it burst into a brilliant pillar of bright blue flame, swaying in the air, then finally collapsed to the banks, dead.

In one final, dramatic *poof*, it flash-burned to ash.

The lake's waters sparkled clear again, as if in thanksgiving to the Creator who had not forgotten His creation.

The Havenites cheered, danced, hugged, and sang. From his place on the ground at Isabella's side, Jeff looked to Greensboro, to see that the fiery onslaught had ended.

"Is it over?" Isabella breathed, her voice raw.

Jeff smiled down at her, brushing sweaty strands of hair from her face, lost in her eyes. "Yeah. I think it is."

Suddenly she grabbed his arm. "The baby..." she gasped. "Is our baby okay? Is—?"

He shot eyes at Carter. "We have to get her to a hospital."

"We'll have to go to Russellville," Carter said. "Greensboro will be a warzone by now."

In a moment of terror, Jeff remembered his brother, lost somewhere out there searching for Rosalyn. What had happened to them? Were they safe?

Forcing his doubts aside, he fumbled for his keys and tossed them to Carter, who caught them in midair. "Get the truck."

Jeff took Isabella's hands and led her to her feet. "You okay?"

She nodded, her face pensive.

Carter honked the horn as he brought the truck around. Jeff helped Isabella to the passenger side and she slid in. Turning to the men, Jeff shouted, "Bring the wounded and put them in the back. We'll take as many as we can to Russellville and come back for the rest."

He prayed silently for Dras and Rosalyn as wounded Havenites were loaded into the truck bed. Then he banged on the roof. "Time to move."

Carter pulled out and away and Jeff took one final look at Greensboro in flames.

God, watch out for Dras. The little freak needs all the help he can get.

The sun shone once more.

Dras felt a surge of relief and excitement. They were winning! The eclipse was gone, the town wasn't destroyed, and they were *winning*. But there was one more fight to face. He always knew he would have to come back here to finish what he started almost a year ago. He failed the first time, but he had no intention of proving himself a fool twice.

Dras pulled up to The Rave Scene, and felt a shudder.

He'd followed Rosalyn here, seen the Thing carrying her jump into one of the top story windows. Dras pulled the bike to a curt halt and hopped off. Every particle of his essence wanted to race in there, kill whatever dragon held his soul mate in its wicked grasp, and charge back out into the sunlight the victor. But, his mind buckled under the memory of the beating he took here last time. His muscles involuntarily flinched as the ghosts of the rogue deputies repeated their cruelties on him. Pulling out his hair. Breaking his arm. Shattering his jaw.

His body ached and he shivered uncontrollably, knowing that he might face the same fate again. Only, now, he might not make it out alive. This place might really be the death of him, after all.

"Okay, God," he breathed fast, his teeth chattering. "This is what we came to do."

Dras faced the building, realizing how quiet the streets had become now that the Dark Hour was over. He took one last, affirming breath, set his sights on his target and marched forward.

"Help me not screw this up."

CHAPTER THIRTY-FIVE

INSIDE, THE RAVE Scene was black as pitch and deserted. Dras pushed open the double doors and entered the cavernous dance club. Taking careful steps, he moved further into the dark, empty room. The reassuring light from the newly freed sun snuck a single beam of white light in through the open door. Dras stayed in the light, knowing that if any Shamblers were lurking about, they'd be held at bay by the brightness.

"Rosalyn?" he spoke into the shadows. "Are you here? Are you okay?"

He moved about the club, dust swirling in the sunbeam, and squinted against the dark, trying to find his friend. "Rosalyn?"

"Go away," the dark answered back.

Dras hiccupped in fright. "Roz? Roz, where are you?"

A crash somewhere in the invisible gloom. A burly shape leapt past his view, crossing the light with a pained sizzle and landing in the shadows on the other side.

"What has you? Is it a Shambler? Are you okay?"

"Dras," Rosalyn's voice groaned, sounding…different. Garbled. Changed. "Can't you just leave?"

"No," he stated firmly. "You know I can't. I've come back for you. I-I think we *won*. The Strange Man lost. You're free now."

A sad laugh from the darkness. "Sorry. Don't think so."

"Don't say that." Dras stumbled around, careful to keep in the light, but wanting desperately to charge into the shadow for her. "I've got these angels on my side, see. And they're pretty hardcore. So, whatever you're afraid of, you don't have to be. The Strange Man can't hurt you anymore."

"He doesn't have to," Rosalyn glumly replied. "I've already done that to myself."

Dras fidgeted with impatience. He had no idea what was going on out there in town. No idea what battles were being fought, where the monsters were. He wanted to be out of this place. Far away from here with her. Only with her.

"*Please* come out," he pleaded. "I just want to see you. Let me help you."

Finally, Rosalyn's small voice broke the stillness. "Remember that time when I dared you to rub your face on that tree in my grampa's backyard?"

Dras frowned. "I got poison oak, right? All over my face? Man…you were a jerk."

"Sorry about that," Rosalyn's voice echoed from the rafters, and Dras thought he heard a bit of a laugh. The old Rosalyn returning.

"It was gross," Dras grinned. "I looked like a…" Suddenly, he thought he might know where this was going. He thought of TJ. Of the beast his unrepentant sin had turned him into.

Oh, Rosalyn…

"A freak?" Rosalyn finished for him.

"What's wrong? What happened?"

"This is so much worse than poison oak," she whimpered. "So, *so* much worse."

"It doesn't matter to me." His heart broke and his nose burned like he'd inhaled pool water. "I'm still here for you."

"Promise you won't run." Rosalyn cried now, full of shame. Her sobbing filled the halls and Dras's knees nearly folded beneath him.

"I just want to help you," he said. "Please, Rosalyn, I just want to help."

Slowly, the Thing in the black shuffled and Dras backed away as, inch by inch, a towering creature like a walking squid filled his petrified vision, stepping out into the light. And, fixed to the head of the squid-thing…

Rosalyn.

She wept openly, hanging impotently as the beast hissed and fizzled, slowly burning in the daylight. It was in pain. *She* was in pain.

Unable to bear it any longer, Rosalyn crept back into the darkness, just out of sight of the blinding beacon. Dras stepped towards her and reached his hand into the dark, touching her shoe—the only part of her he could reach.

"Are you mad at me?" she asked, her voice breaking.

"No," he said, shaking his head. "You made a mistake. I made mistakes too. I've got a God who's good at forgiving those."

"He won't want me."

"You don't know Him like I do." His brow furrowed in concern. "I'd like you to meet Him." He relaxed a little, listening as Rosalyn's sobs ebbed. "It's either that or join the circus, right? And you hate clowns."

Rosalyn snorted a laugh, instantly at ease, and cried all the harder. "Dras, I'm so sorry." The tentacles bent and lowered her towards the ground. She held out weak, shaky arms and Dras was there in a heartbeat, holding her, pulling her to him. Rosalyn buried the side of her face that didn't belong to her hellish conjoined twin into Dras's shoulder, wailing now, soaking his shirt.

He cried too, stroking what hair she had left, loving her unconditionally.

"Don't leave me," she begged. "Please don't leave."

"I won't."

He cupped her chin in his hand and stared into her one remaining dark puppy dog eye. In that moment, seeing her at her most hideous, Dras finally realized she was so much more than a friend to him. She was everything. Dras thought of the kiss they shared in his kitchen that normal Sunday afternoon not so long ago, and wanted to share it again. He wanted to spend his life kissing her, holding her, cherishing her.

Rosalyn searched his face, her tears drying. "Dras, I—"

His heart stopped, praying she would tell him she loved him. He wanted to tell her too. Wanted to shout it from the rooftops. Wedding bells, china patterns, the whole she-bang. *Bring it on.*

But doubt flickered in her eye. Or maybe just fear that Dras couldn't possibly love her when she was like this. She looked away, breaking the bond between them. "How-how do we fix this?"

He swallowed his anxiety. She was right. He had to focus on the problem at hand. Time for love later. *Hopefully.*

"God can fix this."

"You don't know that."

"What else, then?" he snapped, sounding harsher than he meant to. Now wasn't the time for doubt. Doubt had led Rosalyn to this place. "Look, you tried dealing with all of this your way and this is what happened. You've got to let go, Roz. Let God fix this for you."

Rosalyn studied his face, as if waiting for the smile to crack. But Dras was completely serious when it came to his faith now. "But what do *I* do?" she demanded.

Dras's eyes darted to the monstrosity attached to Rosalyn's head, but quickly turned away, the very sight of it making him nauseous. "I…don't know." Then he met her eye again, curiously. "You've gotta figure out what's keeping you from God. This thing is tied to you because you won't cut it loose. What got you here in the first place?" At last his most personal question finally dared to be known. "Why—why did you choose *him*?"

Rosalyn looked to the floor, her tentacles bristling. "The Strange Man, you mean…"

Dras felt sick inside, his newfound attraction for Rosalyn sabotaged by the horrible knowledge that she had already given herself to the Strange Man—both emotionally…and physically.

Still, he loved her. He wanted her to be okay.

As though sensing all of these things, Rosalyn cleared her throat, suddenly seeming embarrassed to mention the demon that had shattered both their lives. "I felt alone…after you left."

Dras gulped, guilt perching atop his shoulders and taking finger-jabs at his conscience. "Go on."

"I guess that," Rosalyn rubbed her arm uncomfortably, and the beast attached to her let out a low rumble. A purr, sharing her turmoil. "I guess I felt like I did when my dad died. Like the person that mattered most to me had…abandoned me."

Dras kept a respectful distance, knowing how hard it was for her to talk about her feelings. Especially with him, seeing as how he had caused her some of this hurt. "Do you hate your Dad?"

Rosalyn looked to him sharply. "*No.*" A pause. "Yes…it's complicated."

"Do you hate *me*? For leaving you too?"

"That's different," she said. "You didn't choose to leave. My dad *did*."

"Right," Dras declared, picking up on something. "Your dad *chose*. He made that decision. Not God."

Rosalyn bit her lip, thinking.

"God didn't kill your dad, Roz—"

"He could've stopped him," she interrupted hotly, revealing her anger. "He could've stopped me from turning into…this."

"Didn't He try?" Dras braved. "Didn't *I* try? God gave you every chance to choose a different path, but you picked this one." Shaking his head, he said, "You get mad when you feel God is butting in your life, wanting something of you. I get that. I did too, once. You feel like your free will or individuality or whatever is being threatened. But when we screw up, we put all the blame on God for not stepping in and taking over for us."

"That's not fair," Rosalyn coldly replied.

"Isn't it?" he asked. "Can't have it both ways, Roz."

Seething now, Rosalyn pulled away and the tentacles raised her with an air of arrogance. "What are you trying to prove?"

Dras inched back, feeling the hint of a threat in the way the roiling limbs curled around him, only held off by the light at his feet. "I just want you to see that *you* did this."

"I know that, all right? Don't you think I know that?"

"*No*," Dras stepped forward once more, determined. "I *don't*. I think that's the problem. Don't you see? You're your own worst enemy. It's *pride*, Rosalyn. I understand, all right? I know that what your dad did hurt you in a way that may never be fixed. And I'm sorry for that. I'm sorry that I added to that. But I think that, deep down inside, you thought that the only person you could count on was yourself. But you can't even count on that, Rosalyn. Look at you! Look at what was inside you, all this time. But it's afraid of light—afraid of truth. You have to face the *truth.*"

Rosalyn flinched, as if hit. Her lip snarled in contempt, her eye growing blacker.

Dras did not back down. "What the Strange Man gave you was just a larger dose of the blackness that was already inside. He just brought it out. But this thing, it was always there. It's in *all* of us! Haven't you figured that out yet?"

Rosalyn cooled. "He said that The Coming Evil was already here. He said it was people."

"Exactly! That's my point! We've all got sin. We've all got that crap festering inside us wanting to get out. Wanting to hurt people and to take things that we want, no matter the consequences. We're selfish, and lustful, and liars, and thieves. That's humanity! But God is trying to offer you something better than that. He can do that—He can break that monster's hold on you and you can be made different. It's not easy, trust me. But it's the only way you're ever going to have hope of being something *better.*"

Rosalyn lowered herself closer to the ground. Not touching the floor. Not yet. But she was coming around. "But…what do I *do*?"

"There's nothing you *can* do. You're only standing in the way. Just…let it go, Roz. All this pain you feel, all the hurt you have inside, all of your trust issues and your anger…just give it all over to God and trust Him to heal you. Just trust Him."

Dras's heart rammed against his chest and he felt his entire soul afire, like electricity surged through his veins. In a split second, he thought back over the long, strange journey that had consumed the last year of his life. The battles, the horror…but the joy too. The peace. It was monsters and war all around him, but Dras Weldon knew where he stood with God, and everything else seemed insignificant in light of that truth.

Now, if Rosalyn could just find that too. Then, Dras knew, everything would be okay.

"Well, well," a third voice echoed in the hall, sounding rather pleased with itself.

Rosalyn's body went rigid with fright and she immediately ascended to the shadowed rafters.

Dras clenched his jaw, still feeling that blue lightning flickering inside, and turned around.

Where the Strange Man hovered, waiting.

Chapter Thirty-Six

"Daddy!"

The Wilbanks girls crashed into their father's trembling arms, Tessa close behind, and he kissed the tops of their heads and snuggled their long, red hair. All around, similar reunions took place as former Shamblers held their husbands and wives, their children, their parents, their friends, joyfully weeping and whispering repentance underneath the warm, protective sun. Even those revelers who celebrated their coming destruction during the eclipse found themselves moved by the return of so many lost friends and family and came out of their hiding places to join in the touching restoration with the Havenites.

Greensboro was united again.

Jack Weldon stood away from the gathering, smiling, his bones aching, exhausted. Louise tentatively approached. "You did it," she breathed.

"Wasn't me," Jack huffed, then grinned, patting the small of her back.

"I…I was holding you back. If you had listened to me, none of these people would have…We'd all be…" she broke off, stifling a whimper.

"It's okay, Louise."

"I guess I've been holding you back a lot, Jack." She hung her head. "I've been so afraid of losing you that…"

She began to cry, and he held her, powerful and fast, remembering the strong man he used to be. The strong man he felt inside him today. "No more fear," he said. "I don't have many more days left on this ole Earth. Let's stop wasting them. Let's live them together."

Louise nodded against his chest, crying freely and hugging her husband close. Jack looked to the heavens, then back to the reunited families before him, and felt hope rekindled.

Hope for all of them.

Rebecca Walker stepped off the bus, where Franklin was waiting for her, Millie in his arms. She barreled at them both and Millie leapt from Franklin's arms to her mother's like a monkey. Rebecca laughed and cried and clutched her precious child close. It was a bittersweet moment for her. Having Millie made her world shine, and yet reminded her of the other child she'd lost.

She would never get over losing TJ. Never forget the cute and precious things he did as a small boy, as he got older, before he started hating her for divorcing his dad. She wanted to remember the good times with him, now. Those would be the things she told Millie as the girl grew up. The good things about her brother.

Timmy raced for her and Franklin, running full force into his father's leg, squeezing him, relieved. Franklin tousled his son's hair, his smile like the morning sun. "Hey, Tim."

"I'm glad you're okay, Dad," the boy said, fighting not to show how worried he had really been.

Franklin hoisted his son into his arms and held tight. With Timmy to his shoulder, Franklin moved closer to Rebecca, who still held Millie.

"Hi," he said casually, as though they hadn't just survived hell come to Greensboro.

She returned coyly. "Hi, there, yourself."

"I was thinking," he continued, "Maybe after they rebuild the coffee shop—"

Rebecca laughed, cutting him off.

Stone-faced, but failing to completely stifle the grin perking at the corner of his lips, Franklin finished, "—I thought you might wanna go out. Get a cup of Joe. Talk about some things."

"Whatever would we talk about?" she raised an eyebrow.

Franklin now let his grin loose. His face softened, belying the smudged ash there, and he leaned in and kissed her tenderly. Rebecca did not resist, but nearly melted beneath him.

Millie and Tim, squashed between their respective parents, wrinkled their noses. "Ewww," they whined in perfect unison.

Franklin and Rebecca pulled apart, their eyes still embraced in a kiss.

"I'm sure we can think of something," Franklin said.

Rebecca moved in, thirsty for more, but their moment of romance was short-lived. The sounds of screeching iron and squealing pigs shattered the newfound peace and everyone looked to the northern sky where, to their shock and dismay, they beheld a hurricane of gremlins.

Dras hurtled through the air, landing hard on a table and splintering it under his wiry frame. The Strange Man instantly hovered before him, his chains rattling in the otherwise quiet Rave Scene. Dras struggled to regain his senses, his body trembling, and pulled himself to wobbly knees and cut hands.

"Leave him alone!" Rosalyn shouted, her tendrils bristling.

The Strange Man calmly turned to her, where the Thing kept its distance in the shadow, and waved his finger as if at a disobedient child. Instantly, Rosalyn's extra appendages went slack, obedient to the demon's every whim.

"Uh-uh," he sang. "You sit this one out, my dear."

Rosalyn gritted her teeth, but kept her place, unable to resist the Man's supernatural control.

Dras stood to his feet in the interim. The Strange Man regarded him once more, coolly. "Well, boy. We meet again."

Dras hung his head, worn, and chuckled lowly. "You lost already. Don't you realize that? The Dark Hour is kaput, Chuckles."

A sudden wave of sadness washed over the Strange Man's gleeful mask, and his bright eyes flickered and dimmed. Then, in a flash, bestial features once more consumed him and the creature snarled. "It's only a matter of time before you fall again. No matter how many times God forgives you, you will always stray from Him…and I'll be waiting. I'll *always* be waiting."

The Strange Man's eyes flared like the sunrise and he flinched forward. With dark, invisible power he hefted Dras into the air and tossed him to the other end of The Rave Scene. Dras let loose a helpless holler before crashing into the bar and landing behind the counter. Bottles and broken pieces of mirror rained down on him.

"Get up!" the demon roared, slithering closer, his shoes scraping the hard wood floor. "Stand up! Is this what God sends against me? Are you *it*?"

"Dras!" Rosalyn shouted, imprisoned by her own monstrous flesh.

"What do you say, boy?" the Strange Man spat hatefully, waiting for Dras to emerge. "Is God with you today? Will He spare your life again or call you home? I hope for the latter, personally. But be sure to tell all the saints that I was the one who sent you there! That I beat that smug smile off your face! Tell them I had my way with the love of your life and I crushed all your dreams!" Green spittle flew from the demon's mouth as he raved, tears building in his eyes and staining his face. "Get up and face me!"

One bloodied hand reached up from behind the bar and groped the counter. Slowly, Dras rose, crawled over the counter like a little kid floundering in his sleep, and collapsed to the floor across the threshold.

He grunted and winced. "Wow…not my day…"

"Dras, are you okay?" Rosalyn called.

"Been better," he groaned and stood, cracking his back into place.

"Such a brave face." The Strange Man scowled. "But I know the *real* you, boy. All your fears, your insecurities. I've studied you for years. I've studied *all* of you. Every last simpering child in this cursed town."

Dras bent over, coughing oxygen back into lungs, shaking the glass out of his hair. The Strange Man zoomed closer, flexing his talons, and raged, "They're not worth saving!" With ferocious inflection, the Strange Man jabbed a crooked finger into the darkness where Rosalyn watched. "*She's* not worth saving! She betrayed you, don't you see that? She turned her back on you! That's what love does! It's blind and stupid and will only lead to your end! I've tried to *save* you from that—"

"Hey," Dras cut in. "Give it a rest, will ya?"

The Strange Man seethed.

"I love her, get it?" Dras declared. "*God* loves her. No matter what you've done, you didn't change that. You're done."

The demon swelled with fury, gathering the darkness to him like a tidal wave.

Dras faced the collecting shadows and growled, "And stop calling me *boy*."

With a throaty roar, the Strange Man lifted his arms and launched a wave of unrelenting hate. The very shadows came alive, pummeling Dras like a whirlwind. The dark storm cackled across The Rave Scene with energy, flinging chairs and tables to either side, propelling itself towards Dras. Dras steadied himself with clenched fist, feeling the electricity rippling in his soul, lighting his heart on fire.

Defiantly, he raised one lone hand and held it against the onslaught—

And kept the hate at bay, freezing the hungry shadows in place.

The Strange Man flinched in stunned reaction. Dras remained standing, grinding his teeth as he felt his face turn red with exertion. Sweat rolled down his brow, but still the Dark did not overcome him.

"Dras!" Rosalyn shouted excitedly. "You're doing it!"

Dras shut his eyes, concentrating, feeling the Divine channeling through him, until he was finally able to close his fist and, as he did so, the Evil dispersed to either side like water split by a wedge, exploding its deadly potential into the nearby furniture. The bar to Dras's right and left instantly disintegrated and the boards in the floor curled from the supernatural impact. Despite the damage, Dras remained unharmed. Nearly collapsing, he staggered, relief coursing through him.

Thanks, God.

Looking up, feeling humorless, Dras said, "You through? Because I'm pretty tired now."

The Strange Man thrust his hands out, clawing at the air, and another baleful surge rippled through the air, barreling like a locomotive. The shadows whistled as they closed in. Dras's eyes widened in surprise, but he held his hands out as well, silently crying out to God. The same holy fire erupted from every pore in his body as God fended off the storm. But the Strange Man would not quit. He leaned forward, nearly horizontal with the ground, pouring all of himself into the blast, his glowing eyes narrow slits.

Likewise, Dras stepped into the pulsating mass of flickering shadows, the air rippling between him and the demon like heat waves on desert sands. The walls quaked and the overhead light bulbs *popped*, spitting sparks on the two combatants locked in a contest of wills. Drywall cracked and the floor buckled under the preternatural pressure, as the front glass of the club plumed out in a glass mist. Chunks of the ceiling broke loose and collapsed to the ground in magnificent collisions, but Dras and the Strange Man did not move. Their eyes remained fixed on each other as The Rave Scene broke apart around them.

Screams split the afternoon as renewed panic seized the collective heart of Greensboro. Newly reunited families clung to each other, scurrying to any building left standing in the Town Square as the snickering, clicking monstrosities slashed and tore *everything.* Cars were reduced to metal ribbons, street lamps were uprooted and flung to the blue skies above, and tiny, vicious claws ensnared fleeing men and women, pulling them deeper into the blitzkrieg of death.

Rebecca clung to Franklin, who carried their two children, limping as fast as his injuries would allow. Rebecca led the way, tugging on his sleeve. Whipping her head to the right and to the left, her terrified eyes finally settled upon a hope for salvation.

"Smokey's! Come on!"

Remarkably, Smokey's Bar & Grill was left standing in the wake of God's judgment, and others had spotted the oasis in the carnage as well. Clancy, the hefty woman who ran the diner, had the door open as Father Joe waved people inside.

"In here!" Clancy shouted over the devastation. "Hurry!"

Rebecca suddenly wondered where Clancy had been during the eclipse. *Was she hiding in there this whole time?* A current of anger spilled over her like a waterfall, but she quickly stifled it. It didn't matter anymore. It just mattered that they *lived.*

Rebecca reached Smokey's, narrowly avoiding a discarded taxi cab flipping end over end her way. She instinctively ducked, pulling Franklin and her family along with her, as the useless hunk of metal careened into the face of a nearby building, bringing the whole structure down.

Father Joe immediately rushed into the street, abandoning his post at the door to usher Franklin and the children inside. His faithful dog, Cougar, was at his side fearlessly barking at the devils in the distance. Clancy opened her arms, prepared to receive Millie, but before she could, the woman was immediately carried off by a small, shrilling band of gremlins. The creatures hauled her into the air and tore her to pieces before the plump woman could scream. Millie covered her eyes without a whimper, as Franklin bore her and Timmy into the diner alongside a herd of other petrified cattle. Rebecca pushed away the thought of Clancy's grisly fate, waving her arms with Father Joe, desperate to save any who would look their way. "Come on! Hurry!" Deputy Hollis with Earl Canton, and still more raced inside and Rebecca worried they'd run out of room. But they had to *try*.

"It's retribution!" Father Joe yelled, watching the devils separating families that had just been restored, saturating the town in fresh pain and misery. "We've beaten them, and now they're lashing out in one final strike!"

Rebecca could clearly see that, but understood that it helped to say it aloud. It helped to categorize the senseless horror they were both seeing. She wondered if Greensboro's nightmare would *ever* be over.

Please, God, don't forget us. Please help.

"Mommy?"

The little voice was intent. A small hand slipped into hers. Rebecca gazed down into the innocent face of her daughter. Kneeling before her, she urged, "Millie, you have to go back inside, now. It's not safe out here."

Jack and Louise Weldon hobbled across the street, their heads low, dodging gremlins as the beasts zoomed by. Louise cried and Jack winced in pain. Rebecca held Millie close to her chest as Father Joe raced out into the warzone, making the sign of the cross in the air and repeating some Latin that she did not understand. Whatever it was, it seemed to do the trick, as the priest cleared large gaps in the dense fog of evil, scattering gremlins. Jack and Louise hurried inside Smokey's with the others, and Father Joe trailed behind, continuing his simple attack that served as a powerful barrier.

When he returned to his place by her side, Rebecca saw the exhaustion on the priest's face. "I can't hold them forever," he gasped, reaching into his pocket and pulling out a silver flask. Without explanation, he flung the contents of the vial against the door and window of Smokey's, uttering more Latin as he did so.

"What is that?" Rebecca shouted over the noise as the gremlins edged closer.

"Holy water!"

"But, Mommy…"

"Not now, Millie! Inside!"

"But, Mommy," Millie repeated louder, but still calm. "My friends are here now."

Rebecca turned away from Father Joe as he worked in a frenzy to anoint the building against demonic attacks, and faced her daughter, consumed by confusion. "What friends?"

Millie pointed over Rebecca's shoulder and the woman turned. Squinting against the sun, she spotted a strange sight down the block. A row of men stood atop a nearby building, backed by near-blinding light. They stood there, most unusually, and Rebecca frowned, slipping into a calm eye of the swirling storm around her. "Who…?"

As one, the men roared, and, instantly, the gremlins froze in place, their laughter finally silenced. Would-be victims easily slipped out of their pincers and raced away, their quiet sobs the only sound on the street. The gremlins surrendered their pursuits and gleeful demolition and turned, trembling, to the line of men. Rebecca blocked the sun from her eyes and saw a man in front—blonde hair and a long, dark trenchcoat gently flapping in the soft breeze—raise his hand. Suddenly, his palm ignited in cool blue-white fire, but he seemed not to notice or be afflicted. Instead, he leveled that flaming hand at the monsters below. Without a word on his part, the men surrounding him shouted like thunder and leapt off the building.

Rebecca gasped. The men were no longer men. Instead, their entire bodies erupted into masses of tightly coiled fire—not the marvelous blue flame of the leader, but orange fire. These fire-men reached the street and flew forward, and Rebecca's heart melted, overjoyed, as the gremlins shrieked and turned to escape.

But there would be no escape for their hordes.

The living fire overtook the gremlins, washing clean the streets, purging them of the devils' wickedness. The tiny beasts screamed and squirmed in the expanding flame, but the blazing ocean overtook them. Soon, the shrill cries ebbed away as the gremlins were plunged into the inferno and finally vanquished.

By now, everyone inside Smokey's had stumbled out in awe, watching the beautiful fire purifying their town. Millie held her mother's hand, a pleased smile stretched across her face as the tide of fire broke into separate flickering pillars of flame once more. The gremlins were gone, their laughter vanished. One by one, the fire-men looked to each other, their forms relaxing, the battle won.

One of the pillars in particular stalked over to Smokey's, eliciting a frightened hush from the hiding townspeople. Immediately they raced back inside, closing the door and watching through the glass, murmuring between themselves.

But Millie and Rebecca remained standing with Father Joe, spellbound. The pillar approached Millie and, in a *whoosh* of air, the fire extinguished and revealed what looked like a wiry man, about mid-40s, with long unwashed blonde hair, thick-rimmed glasses, and dressed in a ratty t-shirt that read "God Is Nifty". He knelt before the girl, smiling a thin line. Rebecca held her breath, clutching her daughter's hand tight, but Millie calmly gazed into the angel's eyes.

"We brought your reinforcements…*General.*"

Millie beamed and Rebecca and the priest regarded the girl in amazement. Behind the geeky angel, two more pillars of fire approached and extinguished, to be replaced by large Vikings of men. Millie looked at all of them, her angels, and giggled.

"Thanks, Reid."

The unkempt angel stood with a wink and turned to Rebecca. "She's a special kid. The Lord's got great things in store for her. Train her well."

Rebecca's eyes were frozen open, and she nodded dumbly. "O-okay…"

The long-haired man turned to his compatriots, then all three looked to the heavens and shot into the sky in a burst of light. The remainder of the army, likewise, disappeared in beams of light, headed heavenward. Headed home.

Only one angel remained. The leader with the blue-white flamed hand who stood atop the building down the street. Without a word, he too, sped away. Not upward but rather across town.

Pushing aside the incredible events, Rebecca looked down to her daughter. Millie's eyes twinkled back at her in response. "They were my friends," she said. "They're nice."

Rebecca burst into laughter and squeezed her daughter tight.

"Yes, they were."

CHAPTER THIRTY-SEVEN

ROSALYN'S WORLD FELL apart around her.

Dras's legs gave way and he slumped to the floor on bruised knees, his fingers splayed out in front of him, as the blue electricity combated the Strange Man's power. Even the Strange Man appeared fatigued, his jaws clenched and a tiny trickle of black blood oozing from his nose into his mouth.

But the devil was winning, and Rosalyn was helpless to intervene.

She tried to move, to reach out to her friend, but the dark Thing attached to her bound her in place with its awful devotion to the Strange Man's will. Rosalyn was a prisoner of her own weaknesses, she knew, and it angered her.

Dras isn't going to last much longer. He's going to die! Where are you, God? Why won't you save him?

Suddenly, a quiet, still voice, alien to Rosalyn's own, asked her in return:

"Why don't you*?"*

Rosalyn flinched, stunned by the words. By their truth.

"I-I can't," she whispered aloud.

"Why not?" The Voice again, plain and direct.

"Be-because..." Rosalyn hung her head, ashamed. *Because I'm only human. I'm...I'm weak...*

"But I'm not," the Voice interrupted, full of might and certainty.

"Oh, God..." she whimpered, talking to Him now. Tired of running. Tired of being angry. Sometimes it seemed easier to blame God than to blame her dad for what happened. *I loved him so much...*She wept, her hands pinned to her side, unable to come to her face even to wipe away the tears. Helplessly stuck, she cried. The Strange Man told her once that her father had killed himself in response to her mother's adultery. Did it matter anymore?

She wanted to forgive her dad. Forgive her mom.

Will you forgive me, *God? Is it too late?*

The Voice did not answer her, though. Rosalyn waited, hoping, *praying*, but it did not return. Was He still there? Was He still listening? Fixed to the beast bleeding out of her head, Rosalyn shut her eyes and reached out with the only thing that she could will to move—her heart.

Please, God, don't leave me. I need you, God. Please forgive me! I'm done…

I quit…

Broken now, fearing that God had forever left her, Rosalyn's hopes dwindled…until she felt a tiny flicker, a swelling in her soul. Her eyes shot open, and she felt instantly lighter.

You're there! I feel you! You didn't leave!

The Voice answered, *"I will* never *leave you."*

The Thing gurgled and with a disgusting wet *snap* detached from Rosalyn. Suddenly free, she plummeted to the floor into a pile. Feeling exuberant and renewed, she arose quickly and gawked at the screeching beast swaying in the darkness. A brilliant shaft of daylight punched through a section of crumbling ceiling and lit up the Thing. It jerked and writhed in pain, its black flesh charring and breaking into ash. Rosalyn stepped back, watching in stunned amazement as her beast shriveled, died, and crumbled to charcoal dust.

I'm free, Rosalyn's soul breathed anew. *I'm free.*

But the battle was not won yet. Her blissful peace hardened into grim determination. Praying that God would give her the power to do what must be done, she marched out of the shadows and felt electricity surging up, out of the depths of her spirit, hungry to be let loose.

Dras caved under the Strange Man's relentless odium, his muscles aching and crying for relief, his spirit quaking within him. Still he held, his heart beseeching God's continual empowerment. The whipping shadows buffeted him. Boards curled by his side under the waves of smoky energy, and he avoided the deadly projectiles. Huge chunks of ceiling continued to rain down and Dras realized The Rave Scene would crush him at any moment.

I'm going to die here, he thought without sadness. Sure, he wasn't happy about it, but he wouldn't stop fighting, even if that meant his death. *But what about Rosalyn?*

He was dimly aware of a loud crash somewhere in the club—vaguely cognizant of an otherworldly scream. *Is that Rosalyn? Is she okay?* He wanted to leave the Strange Man behind and search for her, to check on her, but he could not let go. Could not leave. *Not until it's finished.*

Please, God, help me.

On his knees, with the skin of his face stretched back as though he were piloting a fighter jet with the top down, Dras felt himself sliding backward, being scooted across the floor despite his efforts. *No*, he grimaced, his teeth shaking loose. The Strange Man was winning, seizing upon Dras's human frailties. Dras held on with the last reserves of his strength.

I'm sorry, God. I tried. I really did.

At just the moment that he felt his body would simply quit, his eye caught the shapely form of the most beautiful woman in the world. Squinting, tears rolling out of his eyes and falling sideways behind him, he looked up into the face of the one who had come to his rescue.

Rosalyn Myers.

The beast was gone. Now it was just Rosalyn, profiled in the light spilling in through the doorway. She held out her hand and offered a smile. Straining with all his might, he moved his hand until it clasped hers. With very little effort, she pulled him back from the brink of the Abyss and helped him stand. Time seemed to stop, his body was rejuvenated, and Dras no longer heard the crashing structure around him. No longer felt the Strange Man's oppressive will. Now, he only felt peace. Perfect and utter peace.

This was right where he belonged. With her. It had always been with her.

Somehow he could tell she felt the same. Their eyes met, their souls bonded, and they rested their heads against each other, weary soldiers in a battle whose end had finally come.

The two turned and looked as one at the Strange Man. Blue electricity flared up at their ankles, encircling them, whipping their hair in a whorl of winds. The couple directed their hands towards the demon, as the flickering lightning coiled about their arms, charging in a high-pitched whine. At once, they released their collective energy and it crackled as it split the air in the club, punching the monster dead in the chest. The powerful current knocked the Strange Man off his feet and threw him back across the hall, where he crumpled in a ball. Finally broken.

Excess power danced harmlessly about them, discharging in a dazzling show of cerulean and white light. Dras stared up at the ceiling, warmed. At his side, Rosalyn's arm brushed against his, exciting his heart. He glanced to her and saw that she, too, watched the lights zipping and flowering in sizzling pops, tears in her dark doe eyes. A smile was on her lips and it caused Dras to smile. He gently took her hand. She looked at him, sharp, surprised, then grinned.

The lights soon dimmed and The Rave Scene finally ceased its shuddering. Dras and Rosalyn approached the Strange Man as the creature rolled from side to side, struggling to get his bearings. With violent eyes he lashed out at them, showing his fangs. "You think this is over? It's never over! I'll never stop!"

"You will, Cal," a voice called from the threshold's light. "This time, you will."

Dras and Rosalyn beheld Christopher strolling in, his coat billowing behind him like flapping wings. The Strange Man gnashed, but his attacks were impeded by the chains that hung loose from his body. Now those chains constricted, binding him in place as they glowed hot iron red.

"No!" he screamed, sounding legitimately afraid.

Christopher regarded his old friend, his bright eyes dulled and sad. "I'm sorry, Cal. You know it can't end any other way."

The ground beneath the demon split like a burst seam and the sounds of the damned filled The Rave Scene. Dras and Rosalyn stepped back as bright fire escaped from the crevice, wrapping blazing tongues around the Strange Man. Christopher watched, his handsome face pained beyond measure, but eventually had to shut his eyes.

Inch by inch the demon was pulled back into the Pit as his chains multiplied, circling him like hot metal vines. Only his glowering hellish eyes remained uncovered and he leveled them at Dras and Rosalyn, as if swearing his vengeance.

Rosalyn slipped into Dras's arms and watched the devil until, finally, he was swallowed up and the ground reformed, only the wisps of glowing embers swirling in the aftermath.

Dras wanted to believe it, but felt—given the way his day had gone *so* far—it was better to ask. "Is it over?"

Christopher nodded, able once more to open his eyes. "Yeah."

Rosalyn stared at the spot in the ground where the Strange Man had vanished into hell. "Good."

"Let this be a lesson to you," Christopher began, his voice lightening. "God has set before you life and death, blessing and cursing. Choose life, that both you and your children may live."

Dras nodded, his heart pumping with excitement. *We did it. We finally made it.*

"You've got a second chance, "Christopher further admonished, heavily. "Make the most of it. And keep the light burning. When the flame dies out, there is only darkness."

"We will," Rosalyn said quietly, and Dras knew she meant it.

"So…what's next for you?" Dras asked the angel.

Christopher's smile widened and happy tears threatened to emerge. "Now? Now I get to go home." He looked to the cracked ceiling above. "It's been a long time."

"Thank you," Dras said, realizing those two words would never be enough.

Meeting his eyes once more, the angel's grin softened. "No. Thank *you*." He paused and tapped a nearly hidden ear piece. Reid's voice came back, "Clean up's all done, Chrysti. You ready to jet? I hear they're preparing a huge banquet in our honor and I'm starving." The other angel's mirth could be heard all the way through the receiver.

Christopher chuckled. "You go ahead. I'll be right there."

"Got it, Chief. Oh, and tell the kid he did good. For a human."

"Will do." After taking the device out of his ear—finally off-duty—Christopher tucked it into his coat pocket and looked to the couple. "Take care, you two. I'll see you both at home…one day."

Christopher's clothes and skin shredded off his body, making way for the glowing blue-white creature beneath. He gave a small wave and beamed up into the sky, gone from sight.

Dras and Rosalyn held each other, looking to where he disappeared, smiles on both their faces. Then, Dras stiffened. "Home. He meant like when we die, right? Like heaven? But he said '*one* day'. Like one day far, *far* in the future, right? Not right now? 'Cause, I'm kinda done with this death stuff for awhile."

Rosalyn laughed, soft and true, and gave the seat of his pants a good sideways kick. "Come on, skeeve. Let's get out of here."

Arms wrapped tight, the duo left The Rave Scene behind, their voices trailing out into the sun.

"I got your note," she said. "Finally."

"Yeah?"

"*Jesus loves me*? That was it? Your famous last words to me?"

A shrug. "Nothing else seemed to matter."

"You're such a goofball."

He stretched with pleased exertion. "I know. It's a gift."

EPILOGUE

Five years later

ISABELLA WELDON BUSIED herself in the kitchen of their newly re-purchased country house on Grover's Pond, removing a pot of steaming potatoes from the stove. Roars and giggling emitted from the front room, and she really hoped Dras wasn't playing too rough, but she was too busy to check just yet. Carrying the load of Thanksgiving dinner was weighing her down at the moment, and everything else would have to wait. Hurriedly she moved across the kitchen, careful to dodge fifteen-month-old Danny toddling behind her with Dras' overpriced Snake Eyes action figure and a transforming robot in hand, set the pot of potatoes on a trivet and dropped some butter into it.

"Jeff!" she hollered over the soft purr of the electric mixer, grinding out the lumps in the mashed potatoes. "Honey, can you grab the bowl for the potatoes?"

Jeff entered the kitchen, a streak of gray accenting his brown hair, a parting gift from prolonged exposure to the long-dead Lake Monster of Greensboro Park. Baby Danny warred with his toys around the kitchen, but paused long enough to grin big at his dad, and Jeff patted his fair head with a smile. "What'd you need?" he asked Isabella.

"Bowl. I'm *really* behind," she said, flustered. "The house is a mess. We still have boxes to unpack and your mom's gonna think—"

"Don't worry about it," he laughed. "It's not that big a deal." He crossed the room, grabbed the bowl out of the top cabinet, and handed it to her, nearly slipping on a discarded green monster doll on the floor in the process. "Hawp!" Catching his balance, he huffed and picked up the odd doll. Passing Danny, Jeff re-entered the front room amidst shouts and laughter, grumbling to himself.

Dras tickled his five-year-old niece in the living room. Tall and skinny for her age, the girl had green eyes like her father, and long, thick dark hair like her mother. She flailed on the couch in fits of hilarity as Dras poked at her ribs and armpits.

"*Faith*," Jeff said loudly, holding up the monster doll. "I told you to pick up your toys before everybody got here."

Dras and Faith halted their merry-making, giving Jeff their best deer-in-headlights look. "Um…" Dras winced. "That one's actually mine. Sorry."

Jeff rolled his eyes and ducked back into the kitchen as Dras pounced on Faith once more, tickling her, her screams of delight filling the house with noise.

He's still got a little watchdog in him. Dras smiled to himself and playfully sacked Faith with a couch cushion.

Since his final encounter with the Strange Man, time with family had seemed so much sweeter, almost sacred. Sheriff Miller had been instrumental in getting the Greensboro Ripper verdict overturned, thanks to a certain security video taken underneath The Rave Scene where John Graves unwittingly confessed to Jeff the part he'd played in Dras's arrest. Dras had been so incredibly thankful to see the case appealed and dropped so he could enjoy his niece from her very beginning. Still, the constant glint of mischief in Faith's eyes never ceased to remind him of the one person who hadn't seemed to let go of the Dark Hour completely yet, the person he'd missed so much during those five years.

The doorbell rang and Jeff shouted from the adjoining kitchen, "Dras, get that!"

He released his niece and headed for the door, but Faith was up in an instant, giggling and running past him. "I got it! I got it!"

With both hands and all her weight, she turned the knob and

pulled, revealing Louise Weldon, dressed for chilly weather, standing on the other side of the screen door, holding a pie-shaped object wrapped in aluminum foil.

Faith brightened. "Gramma!"

Dras pushed open the screen door and the gray-haired woman entered. Faith reached for the foil, trying to take a peek at what hid beneath. "What's that, Gramma?"

Louise smiled, but kept the dessert out of Faith's reach. "It's a pumpkin pie."

"My favorite!" she squealed.

"After supper, little one," Louise reminded, then carefully handed the pie to the girl. "Will you take this to your mother?"

Faith happily obliged.

"Careful!" Dras and Louise both shouted after the child precariously balancing the dessert, bare feet padding to the kitchen.

"I got it, I got it," she groaned, disappearing around the corner.

Just inside the kitchen, the sounds of Faith dutifully reporting, "Look what Gramma brought! It's pumpkin pie!" carried into the front room. Dras turned to his mother and helped her out of her coat.

"Thank you," she replied, her smile fading.

"You okay?"

She nodded, visibly calling on her strength. "It's my first Thanksgiving without your Dad. But…I'm coping." Dras warmed, sticking his hands in his back pockets. His father had died in January. He'd been sitting in his recliner, watching some old western that he used to love. He'd closed his eyes, and never opened them again. Dras had spoken at his funeral.

Louise stepped in and patted his chest. "He was so proud of you boys."

"I know, Mom."

The woman fought off a tear and moved to the kitchen, calling out, "Where's my Danny? I want to see my baby boy."

Faith, however, cut the woman off, flapping her skinny arms. "Gramma, Gramma! Come see my new room!"

"Oh, my!" Louise chuckled at her enthusiasm. "Well, lead the way."

Faith yanked on Louise's arm and pulled her toward the stairs. Dras smiled after them, closing the door behind him, when—

"*Hello?* Standing right here."

Dras whirled on the door in surprise to see Rosalyn at the doorstep, holding a suitcase and a duffel bag slung over her shoulder, brandishing a bemused expression. Long gone were her multi-colored locks and emaciated rock star image. Now she was a full-figured college girl, her hair bright and bouncy, her face glowing with a healthy shine. She looked good.

No, Dras corrected, his heart picking up. *She looks fantastic.*

"Hey!" he laughed.

"Hey, stranger," she said, dropping her bags and meeting him halfway for a hug.

"It's good to see you," he growled, lifting her off the ground. She laughed hard, holding on until he set her back on her feet. "When did you get in?"

Rosalyn unraveled her scarf and slipped out of her coat. "Just now, actually. I'm staying at Mom's, but I thought I should head here first. I know how snippy the old man gets when we're late for dinner."

"I heard that!" Jeff shouted from the kitchen.

Jeff entered the room, holding little Danny in his arms, and gave Rosalyn a hug.

"Hey, big brother," she smiled up at him.

He gave her a one-armed squeeze. "Glad you're back. *Finally.*"

"Me too." Rosalyn turned her sights to Danny. "Wow! Look at him! He's so much bigger than when I saw him last."

"Wanna hold him?" Jeff asked, and Rosalyn froze, wide-eyed.

"Oooh—"

"You'll be fine," he chuckled.

"I don't know—"

"Here," he said, handing her the baby. "Don't drop him."

Rosalyn tittered. "Thaaaanks." Gesturing to her bags, she said,

"Oh, I've got something in there for Faith."

Jeff groaned. "Great. *Another* toy."

"And this one wets its diapers."

Turning to the staircase, Jeff hollered upstairs, "Faith! Rosalyn's here!"

From upstairs, another holler in return. "What'd she get me?"

Dras and Rosalyn stood in the open doorway, awkwardly shuffling about. Not going anywhere, careful not to look at each other. Just…standing.

What do I say to her? Dras wondered absently.

The last five years saw Rosalyn finally moving to Vermont to go to college. The separation had been hard, but Dras and Rosalyn both believed it was vital that they take some time to find themselves. They e-mailed everyday—nothing big: just little notes, shared links, and funny pictures—and called once a week. Usually their calls reverted to their old pattern of finding the same program on TV and providing a running commentary. They'd laughed a lot, talked about a lot of things.

Seeing her in person, though, being so close he could touch her…

Dras certainly knew what he wanted to say. He'd *wanted* to say it for the last five years, but he wasn't quite certain where to begin.

"So—" he initiated.

"So!" Rosalyn echoed, quickly jumping on, clumsily.

"How's it feel to be a college graduate now?"

She nodded, a casual smile. "Really good." She sighed, and rolled her eyes. "School was getting old."

"How's Vermont?"

"Still there," she stammered, nervously. "Still pretty. Especially this time of year."

He grinned, staring at the floor. Nodding. Lots of nodding. "Yep, yep."

Suddenly, as if just remembering, Rosalyn slapped him on the shoulder. "How's work?"

"Busy. We're one of the few construction outfits in Greensboro.

After half a town gets blown up, your phone never stops ringing." He trailed off, then, "Oh, have you seen the new church?"

"Um, yeah, I think that was finished last time I came."

"Right, right," he mumbled.

Rosalyn scrunched her nose and hefted up Danny. "You wanna take him? I'm feeling kind of weird here."

"Oh!" Dras replied cheerily, reaching out as Rosalyn handed him the baby. "Sure. No problem."

Rosalyn instantly looked relieved, and about that time Faith came bounding down the stairs and raced for her. "What'd you bring me? What'd you bring me?"

"It's in my bag." Rosalyn smiled.

Immediately, Faith took to the bag in question, unzipped it and began rummaging around for her treasure, revealing a rather silky pair of panties in the process. Dras blushed. "Oh. Oh, Faith, you probably shouldn't—"

"Where's it at?" she whined.

"Uh—" Rosalyn began, awkwardly trying to help the girl and shield her privacy in the process.

Isabella popped her head out of the kitchen, toweling off her hands and looking stern. "After supper, Faith." Then, looking back to the kitchen, she called out, "Jeff, you're about to drop it."

"No, I'm not," he drawled, out of sight, then Dras heard a *thunk*. A heavy sigh and, "I'll get a towel."

Jeff passed the uncomfortable scene at the front door en route to the linen closet. He leaned in to Dras while Rosalyn was busy with Faith. "*Well?*" he whispered.

Dras bit his lip and growled. "I'm working up to it, all right?"

"Why can't you just drop and propose, like a normal person?"

Dras fumed and Jeff headed to get the towel.

"Jeff!" Isabella shouted from the kitchen. "Hurry! It's dripping!"

"Coming, dear," he groaned from the hallway.

Dras was about to turn to Rosalyn, to try and steer the strange conversation somewhere…well, more strange…until his mom broke through, moving for the apparent mess in the kitchen. "Oh, my. Let me help you clean that up."

She disappeared, followed by Faith, who went to investigate. "That looked good too," the little girl said, joining the other women in the kitchen.

Dras sighed. *Finally alone.* He turned to Rosalyn, trying to steel himself for the big moment.

"You thinking about closing that any time soon?" she asked.

He realized that he'd been holding the door open with his foot the entire time. Startled, he faltered. "Oh! Sorry." She stepped aside with a nervous giggle as he switched Danny to his other hip and closed the door. "Anyway…" he took a deep breath. "Rosalyn, there's something I was wanting to talk to you about."

"What?" she asked, combing her hair behind her ear, her dark, doe eyes sparkling with expectation.

"Star Wars!" Danny exclaimed suddenly.

Rosalyn smirked. "I see you've trained him well, Master Jedi."

Dras felt weak in the knees, but braced himself. *Dude, you faced the Strange Man in mortal combat. Suck it up, will ya?*

"Well, I—"

"Jeff!" Isabella bellowed, hurrying out of the kitchen and cutting in between Dras and Rosalyn.

"I'm *coming*!" Jeff roared from down the hall, agitated.

Isabella huffed in frustration, then smiled wide at the sight of their new visitor. "Oh, hey, Roz!"

"Hey, Isabella."

The two women gave each other a friendly hug, then Isabella turned to Dras, her arms outstretched. "Here, I'll take him." Dras happily passed on the child, who let loose a string of laughter as if he were on some amusement park ride. Isabella wiped at her damp forehead, facing Rosalyn. "Dinner's about ready. I apologize ahead of time for the potatoes."

Dras frowned, flustered. "Yeah, yeah, potatoes are ruined. Now, can you—?" He made a shooing motion but Isabella proved too preoccupied to notice.

"Dras, will you set the table?" she asked, as Jeff finally returned with a towel. The husband and wife team set off for the kitchen, Rosalyn following close behind.

"I'll help," she said.

"The good china's over there," Isabella pointed to a cabinet and Rosalyn went to work.

Dras stood alone at the doorstep, his chance to proclaim his undying love slipping through his fingers. He grimaced, set his shoulders, and slumped to his chore.

"There," Isabella declared with a breath of relieved finality, setting the Thanksgiving turkey in the center of the dining room table. "It was not easy, but I present to you: Dinner." Crowded around the dinner table, the guests applauded her efforts as Isabella took a mock curtsey before sitting down.

Jeff stood now, taking his father's place at the head of the table for the yearly toast—a new tradition following the Dark Hour. It was a strange feeling, not having his father in the house this year, sharing in their meal. Jeff looked around at warm faces smiling back. He had his brother with him. Dras sat across from Rosalyn, both careful not to look at each other, save for a blushing glance.

Goofball, Jeff grumbled inside.

Rosalyn looked vibrant and more alive than he'd seen her since maybe before her dad died. She had turned into every bit the woman he knew she could be. On top of that, she sat beside a very sober Meredith Myers, along with grown-up Annie and her new college boyfriend, Curtis. Even Jay Evans was present and accounted for, seeing fit to leave his cave a lot these days. To his left sat his lady friend, Beatrice, and the man looked happier than Jeff had seen *him* in…well, ever. Isabella had extended dinner invitations to Franklin and Rebecca Whitaker—along with Millie and Tim—but they were out of town for the holidays, visiting relatives.

And, of course, there was Isabella with their two children. Faith had barely survived the womb and her birth had been an unimaginable blessing. Now, God had given them Danny. "We have a lot to be thankful for," he began, feeling in full how blessed they really were.

Isabella raised a glass. "Hear, hear."

Jeff took a deep breath, careful to look into each face, a bit of the old preacher returning. "Five years ago, we almost didn't make it. A lot of things could have been different." He smiled. "But God is good."

"God is good," the guests murmured, appreciatively.

"I think it's important this time of year that we remember what we had to go through to get here. The friends we lost." Jeff trailed off, allowing for a moment's silence. He always thought of Danny Carpenter when they had the big Thanksgiving Day meal. He thought of the man's funeral when, upon a request that he'd made to Jeff early in their devil-smashing days, Jeff played AC/DC's "You Shook Me All Night Long" at the gravesite. Even now, in his mind's eye, Jeff could still see the shocked expressions on the gathered faces at the funeral—the blush in the older ladies' cheeks, as well as those of Jeff's own mother—and he knew Danny would have approved.

Jeff also thought of Hank and the family he left behind. Becky left for college and never returned to Greensboro for visits. A year later, Doris left town too, to parts unknown. Jeff could never obtain a forwarding address or phone number.

Jeff's heart hurt, missing his friends, but when he saw Rosalyn, he warmed. "The friends we got back," he said finally, looking her way. Annie reached over and squeezed her sister's hand lovingly. Meredith wrapped an arm around Rosalyn's shoulder.

"Things aren't perfect," he reminded, trying to remain light. Despite the fact that the heavens had opened and spit out a destroying rain of fire, there were still those in Greensboro who missed the good economy that John Graves brought. There were also those who believed that the Dark Hour was greatly exaggerated by "religious and superstitious people". "A natural phenomenon" some said. "Some freak accident of nature." Even now, after all their town had seen, some of them still would not believe. "But—" Jeff quickly turned hopeful, "I'm happy to say that the Good Church of the Faithful is doing well in the new building and has been growing." He paused, then grinned. "If you want a more detailed report, you'll have to ask the pastor."

Rosalyn interjected with a laugh. "How's that working out for you? Tell the truth, Jeff. Do you ever sit in church and just want to stand up and start preaching again?"

Isabella laughed, and Jeff chuckled too, turning a bit red. "Ah, *no*. I think the Reverend Earl Canton is doing just fine."

Jeff never returned to the pulpit following the Dark Hour. Instead, he and Isabella re-opened Smokey's. Now it was a family diner, with a large picture of Clancy hanging just inside the door, still welcoming patrons years after her death. "I'll take breakfast rush over deacon meetings *any* day."

More laughter. Jeff quieted first, watching them all laugh and trade ribbing comments. *We came so close to losing all of this.*

Faith rolled her eyes and chimed in over the ruckus, "Can we eat now?"

Those gathered laughed at her candor and Jeff smirked down at a child he'd thought he'd never see. "Okay, okay. I guess the old man's said enough. Dras?" he turned to his little screw-up brother who had somehow grown into a man while he wasn't looking. "Would you do the honors?"

Dras nodded as the others bowed their heads, and said grace.

After dinner, while the rest of the family lingered around the house, swapping stories or playing with the kids, Rosalyn found herself alone on the front porch, leaning against the railing and watching the quiet starry night. Greensboro was so much different than Vermont. She'd spent a lifetime trying to leave this once-dead town behind, but she found herself thinking of it a lot lately.

Or, rather, one particular resident.

She didn't deserve to be here. She knew that. After the things she'd done during the Dark Hour…

But a lot of people did crazy things during that dark time. A general pardon had been granted by Sheriff Miller and Rosalyn had been included in that. The actions of those under the Strange Man's thrall—and those who simply went mad during the Hour—were pardoned on account of "temporary insanity due to extreme external influences". It all sounded good on paper but really just amounted to everyone in town wanting to drop the whole subject and move on with their lives.

Rosalyn, though, was not as easily forgiven. She'd felt the eyes watching her, fearful that she'd try and resurrect the demon. *I had to leave.*

Maybe now I can come back?

"It's pretty," she said over her shoulder, still watching the stars.

Dras stepped closer to her, leaving behind the laughter and busy conversation of the house. With his hands in his back pockets, he joined her by the railing and looked into the night sky. "Yeah. A lot prettier when it's not shooting fireballs at us."

They shared a brief chuckle, relieving tension.

"I really missed you," he said, softly and sincerely.

"I know," she replied, grinning uncontrollably. "I've missed you too. I guess I don't realize how much I miss you until I see you again."

Did I really just say that? Suddenly, images of that strange, yet powerful kiss in the kitchen years ago came rushing back, as well as all the mixed feelings of excitement and anxiety that one kissed had caused. *Just say it.* Biting her lip, gathering every last reserve of strength she thought she had, Rosalyn turned to Dras and—

"I'm in love with you," they both declared at precisely the same moment.

Then, a surprised expression. Leaning in, they both asked, "Wait. You *are*?"

Liberated, Rosalyn faced him, rushing through her words, "I'm tired of Vermont, Dras. I got to leave Greensboro and travel and go back to school and it's been really great. It's been good to be on my own and to just spend that time working on getting things right between me and God, but now…I want to come home."

Dras's face lit up like Christmas morning and he stepped closer to her, inches from her lips, and Rosalyn silently begged he'd kiss her again. "I've wanted nothing but to be with you since that night that I was nearly beaten to death by rogue deputies—" He broke off, and they laughed at the absurdity their life had become, then Dras continued, "—but I was willing to wait. I didn't want you to choose to follow God for me. I wanted you to do it—"

"On my own," she interrupted, moving even closer to him. "I know. I get that. And I did. And I wasn't ready before. But—"

He froze, staring at her with hopeful eyes. "Now?"

Centimeters from touching, Rosalyn hesitated, until finally—

"Just kiss her already!"

Rosalyn and Dras turned to see little Faith propped up on the back of the couch, watching them through the living room window. Beside her, Isabella with Danny in tow, Jeff, Meredith, Annie, Jay, and the others eagerly watched, guilty grins on their faces. At his daughter's interruption, Jeff sheepishly blushed and clamped a hand over her big mouth.

Rosalyn laughed until she felt Dras's eyes on her. She turned to see him and he looked so wonderful in that moment. Without thinking about it anymore, she closed her eyes and leaned in.

And kissed him.

Rosalyn melted into the kiss, Dras tenderly taking her face in his hands. She held onto him, now determined to never let him go. Jeff hooted as the rest of the family closed the curtains, and resumed the festivities, leaving the two to begin their life together.

"Well," Rosalyn heard him saying as the curtain fell, "it's about time."

THE END

Do not be overcome by evil, but overcome evil with good.
—Romans 12:21

RIFT JUMP
Multiverse Romance with Monsters!
The day Michael Morrison died was the day his life began.
A sinister threat is growing in the void between realities, and Michael has been recruited to stop it. Ripped from his own violent life, he is sent rift jumping to other worlds seeking out the agents of the Dark. The love of his life, Sara, joins him as he battles Civil War spaceships, sea serpents, and superpowered humans.
RIFT JUMP
GREG MITCHELL
GREG MITCHELL
Splashdown Darkwater
MASON
Out Now! ISBN 978-0-9876531-4-7

SplashdownBooks.com
FAITH AWAKENED
GRACE BRIDGES
Fred Warren
The Muse
the duke's handmaid
caprice hokstad
ALPHA REDEMPTION
P.A. BAINES
nor iron bars a cage
caprice hokstad
TALES OF THE DIM KNIGHT
ADAM & ANDREA GRAHAM
Reality's Dawn
R. L. COPPLE
THE CRYSTAL PORTAL
TRAVIS PERRY & MIKE LYNCH
Reality's Ascent
Winter
KEVEN NEWSOME
Odd Little Miracles
Fred Warren
aquasynthesis
kat heckenbach
FINDING ANGEL
Fred Warren
The Seer
CAFFEINE
Diane M. Graham
I Am Ocilla
blood & brine
caprice hokstad
ROBYNN TOLBERT
Star of Justice
R. L. COPPLE
RIFT JUMP
kat heckenbach
SEEKING UNSEEN
DEVIL'S HIT LIST
FRANK CREED
AVENIR ECLECTIA
Prophetess
KEVEN NEWSOME

AVENIR
ECLECTIA
VOLUME 1
Come with us on a journey
to a planet the universe forgot.
Space stations...moon miners...
undersea angels...
an unstable home.
Multi-Author
Mosaic Microfiction
from the online
shared-world project.
GRACE BRIDGES
JEFF CARTER
JEFF CHAPMAN
FRANK CREED
PAULINE CREEDEN
KARINA FABIAN
JOSEPH H. FICOR
KAT HECKENBACH
HOLLY HEISEY
GREG MITCHELL
KEVEN NEWSOME
TRAVIS PERRY
MARY RUTH PURSSELLEY
J. L. ROWAN
WALT STAPLES
H. A. TITUS
FRED WARREN
EDITED BY
GRACE BRIDGES
AND TRAVIS PERRY
Splashdown Books 2012

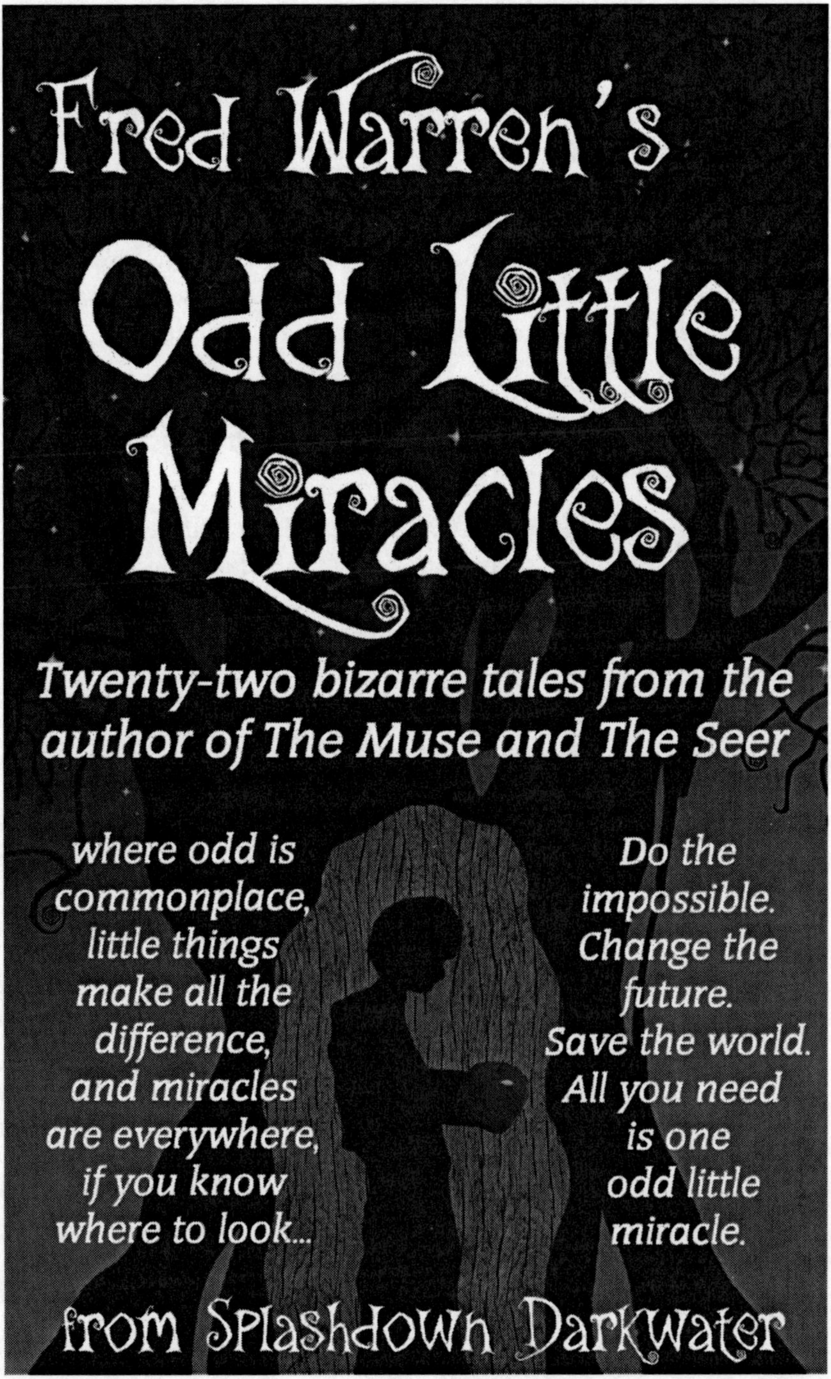
Fred Warren's
Odd Little Miracles
Twenty-two bizarre tales from the author of The Muse and The Seer
where odd is commonplace, little things make all the difference, and miracles are everywhere, if you know where to look...
Do the impossible. Change the future. Save the world. All you need is one odd little miracle.
from Splashdown Darkwater

FRANK CREED'S UNDERGROUND

BOOK 1 ~ Persecution in Chicago has reached the Flashpoint.
In the year 2036, all nations are run by a one-world government.
The One State has only one threat: "Fundamentalist Terrorists"
—Bible-believing Christians!

But they have not yet encountered Calamity Kid and e-girl…

BOOK 2 ~ 2037. At half their usual might, Calamity Kid and his cell are targeted by the One State's Federal Bureau of Terrorism and encounter traps and snares set by a faceless opponent—questioning the suspicious arrival of a bio-engineered One State traitor as the media blames them for the very violence they're trying to contain.

BOOK 3 ~ The hottest new thing on the street is a highly addictive virtual reality experience. There is, however, one side-effect: it's lethal.

When the One State contracts the Ash Corporation to manufacture Virtual-e, intended to reduce global population levels, Calamity Kid and his crew are tasked to stop its production in North America.

Goths aren't all
the same, you know.
Some are Christians . . .
to whom God sends visions.
Violent crime plagues
Winter's university, and
it's more than flesh
and blood at work.
She's the only one who can
stop it. But at what price?
Winter
Keven Newsome
Prophetess
Keven Newsome
www.KevenNewsome.com
Out now from Splashdown Darkwater

CPSIA information can be obtained at www.ICGtesting.com
Printed in the USA
LVOW131117200213

320933LV00001B/14/P

9 780987 653185